FALL: A YEAR OF CHANGE

A SILVER LEAF UNIVERSITY NOVEL

LISETTE BLYTHE

FALL: A YEAR OF CHANGE

A SILVER LEAF UNIVERSITY NOVEL

CONTENTS

Book Cover Design by Emily's World of Design

Edited by Elizabeth Anne Lance

First Edition

First Edition: February 2023

ASIN: B0B69LGDVJ

ISBN: 978-1-957791-02-9

Published by
Three Fortnights Press
New Orleans, LA

*For Evelyn M.
Do what you want to do,
be who you want to be,
and live your life to the fullest.
Dream big little one.*

*For Al Johnson.
You told me I could be a writer,
long after the dream died.
I did it.
Rest well.*

CHAPTER 1

Seonghun was convinced that their new roommate was a little unhinged.

He and his friend Minjun had been inseparable since they were children. While Seong was considered quiet and introspective, Min tended to be the life of the party. Seong forced Minjun to look at things seriously once in a while, while Minjun made Seonghun see the funnier side of life. With Minjun's persuasion, they both had applied for a study abroad course in the states and were accepted to Silver Leaf University in West Lafayette, Indiana.

The program they were a part of encouraged branching out to meet new people, which was how the two of them had met Yongjoon. As a result, the three of them had stayed together in the same dorms all four years. Min and Seong shared a room while Yong consistently had a single. Since meeting in their freshmen year, the three men stuck together, always studying or just hanging out. Minjun and Yongjoon frequently liked to attend parties on campus. Seonghun would tag along from time to time, but was mostly left to his own devices those nights. Instead of going to the never-ending parties, he liked to frequent the agriculture lab when his friends were out.

Their final year had a welcome surprise.

As seniors, they got priority housing choice; the dorm they were placed in was one of the nicest. Instead of a singular room, the three men shared a suite. It housed a common area, a kitchenette, and a bathroom. They each had their own individual rooms. The biggest surprise, however, wasn't that it was a four-bedroom suite; it was that a young woman named Maliah had been placed with them.

Yes, it was a co-ed dorm, but most people were under the impression that it was one floor men, one floor women. No, everyone was mixed up. At the beginning of the year there were some scuffles in other groups with people being moved around, but their little cohort remained.

Despite their efforts to get Maliah to join them, she never really spoke to them other than a hello or a goodbye. They tried to do something as a group, such as instituting a game night; on those nights she never came back to the dorm until late when everyone else was sleeping. She never had friends stop over; when she was in the suite, her door was closed.

Confusing Seonghun even further was the fact that she left little to no trace of herself behind. They knew she cooked in the tiny communal kitchen; they smelled it, but if you went in after her, it was as if no one had ever been in there. There wasn't an odor or anything coming from her room, but she never left anything in the bathroom to indicate she showered. Not even her toothbrush decorated the cramped bathroom like everyone else's.

"Is it actually just the three of us, and a roommate ghost only we can see?" Seong asked Minjun.

They were sitting in the common area studying while Yongjoon played video games. While none of them shared a major, studying together worked out fairly well. Someone would toss out a question, while the others would answer it from the standpoint of not knowing the answer. It forced the other person to be able to explain their thought process with their own answer.

"Why would it just be us three to see the ghost?" Min stared at him weirdly over his psychology textbook.

Seong wondered if he'd happened upon the one statement that would make his friend think he was losing his mind.

"Also, she isn't really haunting, she's just hardly ever here."

Yong looked at them. "She's here all the time, guys, she's just sneaky." He paused the game he was playing. "You both realize that our schedules are similar in time, right? Monday, Wednesday, and Friday, we're out of the dorm from about seven in the morning until four in the evening. None of us come back here for lunch because we're nowhere near the dorm."

It was true. Seonghun was an agriculture major, so he spent the majority of his time in the labs. Minjun's major was political science while Yongjoon's was pre-law.

"What does that have to do with anything?" asked Seonghun.

Yongjoon smiled, both of his dimples winking. "Skip your second class tomorrow, come back here to the dorm. Don't mention out loud that you're going to do it, just come back. She's here, and she's… well, you'll see."

Min tried pestering Yong into elaborating further, but he wouldn't relent.

"You want to see; you're going to have to show up. I give her space because I think I embarrassed her, but maybe if she understands we aren't judging her, she'd be a little friendlier."

"Do you guys even know her major?" Seonghun asked.

As his friends shook their heads, the door to the dorm opened. Seong watched as Maliah stepped in. She was short; Seong wasn't entirely sure how short she was as she seemed to slouch to make herself smaller. Her big brown eyes were sitting behind oversized glasses that covered her face from her cheeks to nearly her eyebrows. Their lady roommate was always in a baggy sweatshirt, even baggier jeans, with a hat over long dark twisted hair that stretched down her back. The only bit of her dark brown skin you could ever see was her face and hands, but what drew his attention was a sprinkling of tiny moles across her nose that looked like freckles. They were cute, giving her a youthful look. Seong couldn't really tell if she was eighteen or twenty-five.

"Oh, hi." She gave a small wave before heading directly to her room, shutting the door with a soft click that echoed around the common room. There was complete silence from her room after.

Seonghun didn't know why he was so curious about her, but he assumed it was normal. *They shared a small space, right? Why not get to know each other? Was she scared of them? Did she not like them? Did they smell?* He surreptitiously sniffed his armpits when he saw Min giving him a weird look, so he stopped.

Yongjoon glanced at his watch. "Do you guys want to go get dinner, maybe some ice cream at Avery Hall? There's always tons of girls milling around."

Minjun snorted. "It's an all-girls dorm. Of course, there are girls milling around. I'm game though."

As they closed their books, Seong took a chance, walking the short five feet of distance from the couch to knock on her door.

"Um, we're going to dinner and wanted to know if you cared to join us?" he called out tentatively.

"N-no thank you, I already ate," was the muffled reply that came from behind the door.

He shrugged, leaving with everyone else to go eat. He tried to put thoughts of Maliah out of his mind as he lightly shoved Min in the hallway before running away laughing. At the dining hall, no matter how much he tried to focus on his meal, his thoughts seemed to return to the quiet girl in the corner room, though he couldn't quite figure out why.

CHAPTER 2

When they arrived back at the dorm, full of ice cream, it was quiet. Seonghun smelled something in the air, sweet, almost floral. He looked over at Maliah's door; it was cracked, but the light was out. She was gone.

"Mario Kart?" Yongjoon held out controllers for both of them.

They accepted, hunkering down on the two small love seats in the common area for a few matches. After a while, Seonghun retired to his room to read a few more chapters of his textbook before succumbing to sleep.

He awoke in the middle of night, disoriented and thirsty. Slipping his glasses on, Seong went into the kitchenette to find a drink. As he turned on the light, he saw a foot going into Maliah's room. The foot had on the highest shoe with the thinnest heel he'd ever seen. The door quickly clicked shut. Staring at her door, he registered that sweet scent again. It was almost perfume-like but was fainter than a perfume would be.

"What is that?" he whispered aloud. Shrugging, he grabbed a glass of water from the sink, quickly returning to his room.

The next day the friends vacated the dorm for a day of classes. As he sat in his class. Seonghun watched the clock steadily, something he hadn't done since his bout of homesickness in the first semester of his college career. When he was finally released, he booked it back to the dorm. To his surprise, Min stood at the entrance, speaking with another student. Seong caught his eye. Saying goodbye to his classmate, Min walked over to greet him.

"Shouldn't you be on the other side of campus?" Seong asked.

"Yongjoon had me curious. What on earth could she be doing?"

"Let's go find out."

Both men walked into the dorm, up the three flights of stairs to their suite. As they got closer to their door, they heard noises. Standing in front of the door it sounded like singing. It was loud, but it was in tune. Seonghun put his key in the lock, turning it while opening the door.

In the middle of the common area was Maliah. Her jeans and sweatshirt were gone, replaced by the tiniest shorts Seonghun had ever seen. Sparkly headphones adorned her head as she danced around with her back facing them. The smell was back.

"Do you smell something sweet?" Seong asked Min.

"Shh, listen." They closed the door quietly as she sang while dancing around the common areas.

Let it go
Can't let this thing called love get away from you
Feel free right now, going do what you want to do
Can't let nobody take it away, from you, from me, from we

As she did a spin, her eyes widened at the sight of the two men. Minjun was struggling not to laugh. Seonghun was gawking, quickly noticing she didn't have on a bra under a thin white tank.

Slowly sliding the headphones off her head she looked at them for a beat. The music was so loud, they could hear it blaring from the head-phones. Seong saw the panic in her eyes as she stared at him.

Finally, she spoke, "Um, hi. Bye," while making a beeline to her room.

"Wait a minute, WAIT!" Min made a move to get in front of her, but she was too fast.

Seonghun blocked her door quickly as she got to it, causing her to bump into him. He felt her chest brush up against his, immediately real-izing that the sweet scent he kept smelling was coming from her.

Clearing his mind, he spoke, "We were just curious about you; we came back to the room to ask you to lunch. We're sorry to have scared you." He came up with this by the seat of his pants, but Minjun was nodding, corroborating his story.

"I-it's okay, if you could just... move please." She tried to edge around Seonghun.

He wanted to hold firm, but looking at Minjun's expression, he realized that he was blocking a woman from accessing what she felt was safe. She was small; he was not. His six-foot-four inch height tended to unnerve people. Quickly, he moved aside, allowing Maliah to rush into her room, shutting and locking her door.

Minjun looked at him. "It was worth a shot. I'm gonna head to lunch before my next class. Are you coming?"

"N-no. I think I'm going to just study for the day. Here, in the dorm." It was like he couldn't stop his nervous babbling.

Minjun stared at him strangely, but nodded and soon left.

Seong sighed, sliding down the wall to sit on the floor. Thinking for a moment, he opened his mouth. "We really didn't mean to scare you, you know. We just thought it would be nice to get to know you." Silence greeted him. He cleared his throat, trying to continue. "My name is Seonghun, but you know that already, I think. Minjun and I are from South Korea. We went to the same school, applying to come here together. We have been friends for a really long time. We wanted to see America; this was our opportunity to do so. We're here on scholarship. What about you?"

Silence behind the door. Then…"I'm on s-s-scholarship too." Her voice was quiet.

Seonghun wanted to jump for joy, but he got the feeling that if he made any sudden loud movements, she would stop talking. "I'm here for agricul-tural science," he continued. "I want to be a farmer back home. I mean, I was a farmer before this, but now I get to bring back more information on how to be a better one. I like living in the country. It's peaceful. There is a lot to do in the city, but there is nothing like seeing the stars while hearing nothing but nature around you." He went quiet for a while, waiting, but she didn't say anything. Standing up, he brushed himself off. "I have to go now; I have my lab this afternoon. Sorry again if we startled you."

He walked out the dorm, taking the shuttle to his lab building. Arriving at class, he sat next to his biology lab partner, Casey. She had always been kind to him, offering her notes, asking to eat lunch together, or just hang out after class. She was quite pretty with green eyes, freckles, and straight brown hair. But something about her didn't feel quite right to Seonghun. Still, he tried to maintain pleasantness in class, working well with her during the labs.

As he sat, she smiled at him, tossing her long hair over her shoulder. "My sorority is having a party this evening. You should come."

"Yeah, I don't go out much. It is not my thing." He opened his textbook, trying to focus.

"Well, I know you have roommates. We could all hang out with my friends, that's much quieter." She batted her lashes at him.

He smiled back weakly, not responding. It felt like every week he was pushed to see her outside of class. The teacher finally called everyone to order, so they could get to work. Despite his misgivings of her as a person, Casey was a good lab partner. She was focused, taking on a decent share of the work. However, she tried to find excuses to touch or brush up against him. Touches that he didn't initiate, or indicate he wanted, made him incredibly uncomfortable; he made it a point to not acknowledge them in the hopes that she would stop. It hadn't worked yet. When class ended, he nearly ran out of the room before she could ask for his phone number again.

CHAPTER 3

When he got back to the dorm, his friends were watching TV, chatting quietly. Seong glanced over at Maliah's door, seeing that it was closed. Yong looked up, grinning as he saw the direction Seong was staring.

"Min told me you two saw her."

"Yeah, how did you know what she would be doing?" Seonghun asked.

"Because I walked in on the same thing accidentally." He took a bite of an apple. "She was dancing around, singing, turned around, saw me, quickly hightailing it into her room. I think she does it while we're gone, as her classes are on Tuesday and Thursday mostly."

Seonghun changed the subject to his lab experiments. For the past year he'd been hybridizing a strain of lavender that was hearty enough to grow throughout the winter. He wasn't particularly interested in lavender, but it was a difficult plant to grow; the knowledge he was gaining from it would help him out immensely at home.

After a few questions, Yongjoon stood up, stretching. "I'm going to the gym to work out. Do you two want to come?"

Minjun sighed before nodding, trudging to his room to change.

Seonghun shook his head. "I want to study some more."

"Do you want us to bring you back dinner? We'll probably head to the diner."

"Yes. Can you bring me back two bacon cheeseburger meals? Both with fries please." Seonghun requested.

"That is a lot of food," noted Yongjoon.

The cheeseburger meals in the dining hall were known all over. You could barely close the container they gave you as it was stuffed with fries, while the burger patty was only slightly smaller than a hubcap. Seong's friends fussed at him when he chose it more than three times a week.

Seonghun shrugged. "I know."

Minjun reappeared, saying goodbye before they left. As Seong walked to the door of his room, he was surprised to see a note taped to his door. The paper was thicker than notebook paper, creamy in color. Touching the sheet, it was rough in texture. Unfolding the note, he saw, well, him. Seong wasn't an arrogant man, but he knew women found him attractive, especially when he took off his glasses. He didn't really understand the hype. Yes he was tall, he thought he had a nice smile, but so did many other people.

It looked like the drawing was done in pencil. The sketch showed him with angular cheekbones, curious eyes fringed by dark lashes, glasses perched upon a strong nose above full lips. In the drawing he looked as if it were observing someone.

Is this how he looked at her? He waited for a beat before settling next to Maliah's door. "I'm not sure how much you can hear in your room, but I just wanted to apologize again for catching you off guard. We were just curious." He paused, waiting for her to say anything. When nothing was spoken he continued, "I wanted to thank you for the drawing. You have amazing talent. I don't really see myself the way you drew me though." As he spoke, a thought struck him. He wondered if it wasn't that she didn't want to speak, maybe she couldn't. He decided to take a chance.

"I'm not sure if it is hard for you to speak, or if you don't want to speak. But if you would like me to go away you could knock twice. If you want me to continue talking, you could knock once. It wouldn't hurt my feelings if you wanted me to go away. I understand people need space sometimes." He paused, waiting until he heard a singular soft knock.

Smiling, he did as she asked. "I'm really glad we got selected for this campus. There are lots of green areas for me to explore. When I first got here, I was severely homesick for the wide open spaces I ran in Korea. In the agriculture area there is actually a field that has lots of flowers and plants. In a couple weeks, we'll be allowed to harvest seeds in the field. The only rule is we have to give up half of what we harvest so that they are able to replant again in the spring. There are some I would love to send home, but I don't know the rules about sending seeds out of the country. It's something I will have to look into." He stood up, walking to the kitchen to get a soda. Coming back, he sat down on the floor again. "One of my favorite flowers out there is actually a bush. A big, blue, peony bush. I think the flowers on it are very pretty. I'm going to try to get the seeds from it, so I can study it some more. Maybe one day you could tell me what your favorite flower is." He looked down at his soda can. He'd basically talked her ear off; he didn't want to scare her away. "I need to make some phone calls while I do a little homework. Maybe I will talk to you later."

Seonghun got up to walk into his room, being sure to close the door to give her space. He wondered if she was just nervous to talk to them or if it was everyone. She never brought any friends back to the dorm. But they didn't really either. He was happiest hanging with his roommates. Sure, there were friends in his class, but no one he'd really wanted to spend time with outside of class. Calling his parents, he spoke to them briefly before starting homework. He'd been digging into his notes for an hour when there was a light tap at his door. Opening it, he saw Yongjoon with a couple of Styrofoam boxes.

"We're going to head over to Frat Row. There are apparently parties tonight. Want to come?"

Seonghun shook his head. Yongjoon knew he would say no, but he always asked. Seong felt awkward in groups, not really speaking unless he knew people. There were some exceptions to that rule, but for the most part, he kept to himself and his close friends.

After saying goodbye, he waited for Yong to walk out of the suite before crossing the ten feet of the common area to tap on Maliah's door lightly. "When I had them get me dinner, I asked them to get me an extra sandwich for you. If you want it, you're welcome to it." He paused for a minute, struggling not to ramble at her silence. Instead Seong set the container beside her door before continuing.

"I'll set it outside your door. I'm going to watch tv while I eat. You're welcome to join me. We don't have to talk, but it's sometimes nice to share a meal with someone. You're also welcome to eat in your room, of course. I'm just trying to say there are no strings attached to the food." As soon as he walked away, Seonghun sat on the couch, turning on the TV to Jeopardy, just loud enough so she could hear that he was no longer in front of her door. Holding his breath, he waited.

It wasn't long before he heard the door open quietly, allowing him to exhale. He looked up as slow footsteps were heading toward him. Her twists were piled on top of her head in a bun, allowing him to see her face clearly. She had on different glasses that didn't cover her face completely. They were tortoiseshell on top, rimless on bottom with gold accents. Her eyes, not quite meeting his, were large and dark brown, almost black. She had on a simple baggy black t-shirt and jeans that flared out at the leg. Her feet, which could barely be seen under the pant legs, were covered in striped mismatched socks. He quickly looked away just in case he made himself nervous, thus possibly spooking her.

"Feel free to sit wherever you feel comfortable." He ate a fry, trying to pay attention to the game show. He smelled the sweet floral scent again; Seong wanted badly to ask her what she was wearing that smelled like that, but hesitated. Out of the corner of his eye he saw her relax slightly, open her box, while looking down. Slowly she sat on the small couch opposite. Much like all the furniture of the dorm, it was a light colored solid wood, with smooth dark blue waterproof cushions. When they initially moved in, Yong touched the scratchy cushions, wrinkling his nose at the feel. "The static these are going to generate in the winter is going to be insane," Seonghun remembered him saying. The couch was firm to the point of being uncomfortable; Seong could only manage sitting an hour or two before his back started aching.

"Thank you." It came out soft but he heard it clearly.

"You're welcome."

They both ate quietly while watching the game show. Seonghun loved game shows with random trivia facts. He got the greatest jolt of glee when he got an answer correct. He noticed Maliah hiding a smile when he wiggled as he got answers correct.

"I know it may seem silly, but I learned a lot of my English from shows like this."

"If it means a lot to you, it's never silly," she said, eating a fry. Suddenly she got up.

He was scared she was going to leave, but instead watched as she walked into the kitchen, grabbing two bottles of water. Maliah walked back to her seat, slowly sliding one of the bottles toward him.

"Thank you."

She nodded, returning her attention back to her fries. He didn't want to scare her away with the hundred questions he had, so he thought it best to start out small, something easy that wouldn't be too difficult to answer.

"Can I ask what your major is?" Seonghun prodded gently.

"Uh, Psychology. W-w-w-with an emphasis on art and music therapy." She swallowed her food before trying to speak, but failing. She took a breath before trying again. "Art helps me. I-I-I believe it can help other people."

Seong tried not to react visually to her stutter. He'd never spoken to anyone with one before; it was a bit jarring. There was so much more he wanted to ask about her major. Instead, he nodded before focusing on the show. Once Jeopardy ended, he flipped through the channels, finding a rerun of a sitcom he'd seen before. The two of them sat quietly, watching the show as questions piled up in Seong's head. After about an hour there was a commotion in the hall as they clearly heard the jingling of keys. She looked at the door before looking at him helplessly.

"I understand. Go on. I'll talk to your door later." He smiled at her.

She ran to her room without a backwards glance, shutting the door as his two roommates opened the main door, talking loudly. They weren't alone. On Minjun's arm was a girl with white-blonde hair. Her tummy was bared in a red crop-top as she clung possessively to him. They went directly to his room, shutting the door behind them. Yong joined Seonghun as he cleaned up the trash on the coffee table.

"Looks like you two had fun," said Seong.

"That girl latched onto him as soon as he came through the door. I think they are in a couple of classes together." He looked closer at the mess. "Did you have company? I thought you were going to eat both meals, but there are also two half-drank bottles of water here."

Seonghun's ears burned red. "Yes, just a classmate. They came over so we ate while we talked a little about some trouble they are having in one of our classes."

Yongjoon was confused at his embarrassment. "You know you're welcome to have people over at any time, right? We all do. Well, most of us." He glanced at Maliah's door. "That reminds me. Some girl was asking about you. She mentioned your name to her friend," Yongjoon pointed at Minjun's door, "said something about how she was hoping you would come. I asked her to clarify; she said she was in your lab."

Seonghun rolled his eyes. "You remember I told you about the girl in my lab that is always asking me to do stuff? It has to be her." He sighed. "I don't want to think about her right now."

After they finished cleaning, Seong bid Yong goodnight, retreating to his room. As he got dressed for bed, the image of Maliah in her tank top, braless, came unbidden to him. Climbing into bed, he felt himself get hard as he allowed himself to remember how her long delicate neck looked. Grabbing himself, he began to slowly stroke, building up to his orgasm.

"Oh god," he moaned. Instantly he felt guilty. It felt acutely uncomfortable to use people he was familiar with in fantasies. While one could argue he barely knew her, it still didn't feel right, even if— Seong shook his head, not completing the thought. She wasn't his girlfriend, or even anyone he was seeing. She was his roommate, one that was obviously quite skittish around people. He grabbed tissues to clean up before going to sleep, vowing not to use her in that way again, no matter how pretty her eyes were.

CHAPTER 4

As Seong walked out of his room the next morning, he saw an envelope attached to his door. Peeling it off carefully, he lifted the unsealed flap. Inside was a drawing of a daisy with a sprig of lavender in an X pattern. Both flowers were incredibly detailed; they had been delicately painted with what looked like watercolor paints.

Seonghun walked back into his room, pulling out the other sheet of paper that she had left him. Opening the armoire in his room, he slid out a small box. Seong froze for a moment, trying to remember where he set the key. Suddenly he popped up, opening his desk drawer, poking around until he found a singular key on a ring. It had a rounded metal head, delicately designed with a scrolling pattern. The body of the key was long; at the end, it looked like two teeth with a small gap in between, much bigger than the slight gap in his own two front teeth. Using the elaborate key, he quickly unlocked the box. Carefully, Seong touched the plane ticket that brought him to Silver Leaf's campus, along with the ticket from the first bus ride he took here. Other momentos, along with pictures of his family, lived in the box. He set her notes on top of all his memorabilia. Locking the box, Seong gently placed it back on the shelf where it lived. Satisfied, he left his room, but abruptly stopped his walk to the bathroom. The blonde girl from last night was seated on their couch with Minjun's shirt on.

"Hello," she purred, staring at him.

Seonghun only had on his sleep shorts. His frame was broad; though he hadn't been on his family's farm in a while, he worked out constantly. He typically wasn't around people without a shirt on unless he was swimming at the gym, due to his stature. He nodded politely at her before crossing quickly to the bathroom, trying to get away from her roving eyes.

Glancing over at Maliah's room, he saw there was no light on, but the door was cracked, indicating she was gone already. Shutting the bathroom door, he started to get ready for his classes.

When Seong stepped out of the bathroom, he saw that Minjun had joined the woman on the couch, with his tongue down her throat. Seonghun cleared his throat. "Min, could you ah, take that anywhere else but here?"

Minjun looked up, smiling lazily. "Sorry." Grabbing her hand, he yanked her back to his room.

Seong rolled his eyes as he left the suite. His course load was light today; he didn't have class until the late afternoon, but he was leaving early because he wanted to go to the mall. Because of transfers it took a bit of time to get anywhere off campus using the bus. He caught one right outside of the dorm. Two transfers later, he arrived at the mall. Once inside, he immediately searched out the giant blocky directory that stood near every entrance. After a quick search, he finally navigated to the stationary store.

He'd never been in this store before, as he had no use for fancy papers. He sent his parents emails if he wanted to write; if he sent them packages, Seong scrawled a quick note on notebook paper. The drawings that Maliah gave him were beautiful. He couldn't reciprocate; his drawing skills were nil. There was no reason he couldn't put his words to nice paper, however. While the mall was busy, with the sounds of people shopping echoing off the walls, the stationary store was nearly silent. Seong could even hear a fan blowing quietly. Slowly, he began perusing shelves that were full of greeting cards, notecards, and thick journals. He went to walk away when he paused for a moment, gently trailing his long finger down the spine of a bright orange book.

"Can I help you sir?" An older woman appeared.

"Do you carry journals that have plain paper that you can draw on?"

The woman thought for a minute before walking further down the aisle. Seong trailed behind her as she walked toward a stack of brown books.

"This is one of my favorite journals, it's simple but pretty." She handed him a brown leather book. The leather was soft, wrapped around the paper that was then stitched within it and tied closed with leather strips. Opening it, he touched the paper. It was the same texture as the paper he'd received from her, albeit a bit thinner. If she couldn't paint on it, maybe she could draw. He smiled gratefully at the woman.

"This is exactly what I was looking for, thank you."

"These types of journals are nice in the fact that when you're finished with the pages, you snip the stitching here," she pointed to the spine, "pull out the paper, then you can find someone to stitch new paper into it. If you need anything else, my name is Barb, I'll be around unpacking stock." Barb walked off, leaving Seong to his own devices.

Tucking the journal under his arm, he kept walking until he got to the letter writing materials. Looking around, he felt a little overwhelmed until he saw it. Over in the corner of the stand was cream colored paper with a cluster of daisies printed on the top. He also saw some printed with sprigs of lavender. Selecting both boxes, he marched his purchases to the front. After paying, Seong grabbed a soft pretzel to snack on while he waited for the bus to get back to campus. Realizing all he had today was that simple pretzel, he exited the bus shortly before the stop before his dorm to pick up food. When he opened the door to the dorm, Min was thankfully by himself. A quick glance over told him Maliah was still gone.

"Min, um, the girl you brought home last night," Seonghun began. Minjun paused his game, waiting patiently. "She has a sorority sister named Casey, who is my lab partner."

"Yeah, I saw her at the party last night. She asked why you weren't with us."

"About that. She's been trying to get me to see her outside of class; I'm just not interested. I think she may feel that you..." Seonghun hesitated.

"Sleeping with," Minjun supplied.

"Sleeping with her friend," he continued, "provides a reason for us to get together outside of class. I have turned her down numerous times but she is not getting the hint. Please don't put me in a position to hang out with her."

"I won't, but Seonghun, you've barely done anything but go to classes the entire time we've been here. I've never seen you chat up a girl except that one time, even then, I didn't witness it, Yong did. You don't go out, you don't really live your life. You study, you watch TV, you go play in the greenhouses."

"I go out with you guys sometimes, I just don't like parties. I like when we bowl, or go eat, or any other activity that doesn't involve large quantities of alcohol, half-drunk people, or loud music." He walked over to his room to dump his bag. "I just don't feel the need to party hard. I'd rather read, play a game, or even study."

"That reminds me, Yongjoon said you had company over the other day? How did that go? What did you do?"

"It was nothing, just a classmate helping with some concepts I didn't understand."

Minjun looked at him. Yongjoon wouldn't have caught it, because they hadn't been friends as long, but Seonghun and Minjun had been friends since they were children; he knew when Seonghun was telling a lie. He became restless, avoiding eye contact while blushing.

"You know," Minjun stared at his best friend, "I could warm myself from the heat coming from your ears."

Seonghun's face began to heat as well.

"If you need me to keep a secret, you know I can," he waited.

"Maliah came out to watch Jeopardy with me while we ate dinner," Seonghun said quietly. "I don't want to make her feel weird or awkward."

"Did you guys talk? What did she say? Are you two friends?" His best friend fired questions at him back to back.

"We watched a show together. That's all." Minjun didn't need to know about the talking outside her door.

Just then the door to the suite opened; Maliah walked through, cutting off Min's inquisition. Seonghun felt his eyes pop out of his face. She was dressed in a simple black dress that went right above her knees with her twists in a bun. High heels make her short legs longer. To him it looked as if she'd put something on her eyes, making them look even bigger. His heart lurched slightly as she looked over to where they were, slowing her walk.

"H-hi," she said quietly.

"Hi," they responded.

She continued to her room, shutting the door.

Glancing at Seonghun who was staring at her door, Minjun muttered to himself, "I don't really think that was all."

Seonghun made excuses to study, retiring to his own room. Pulling out the journal along with some of the paper he purchased, he sat at his desk, scribbling a note.

Maliah,

Your artwork is beautiful. The daisy and the lavender seemed to leap off the page. Did you draw the lavender because you heard me talking about it, or are both your favorite?

I didn't think I would learn all I have about flowers in my courses. I thought it would mostly be agriculture-based crops like corn, wheat, rice, and hay. I do enjoy learning about them; when I do start my farm, I hope to have a little side garden full of flowers.

I was at the mall and saw this journal. I thought you may find some use for it with your drawings. Things that are beautiful should always.have a nice place to be stored.

I hope this isn't overstepping a boundary, if it is, please let me know. The day we heard you singing, you seemed so scared. Is there something we have done to make you nervous? All of us are nice people. At least, we try to be.

This has gotten to be longer than I wanted. Please enjoy the journal.

I hope to talk to you soon.

-S

He sealed the note in the envelope before tucking it into the ties of the journal. Peeking out, Seong saw that Minjun had left the common area, Maliah's door was shut, and Yongjoon was nowhere to be seen. Seonghun crossed over to the closed door, set his present down, knocked lightly on the door before scurrying back to his room, shutting the door quietly. Sitting on his bed, he began focusing on his lab report. After a while he heard the front door shut. He was tempted to open his door, but he really needed to get his report done.

Two hours later, there was a knock at his door. Pulling his glasses off of his face, Seong wiped his eyes before opening the door to his friends. "Have you eaten recently?" Yongjoon asked.

"No, I've been working on this report." It was never a good thing for him to go an extended period of time without food, his friends both knew this.

"Do you want to come with us? Have you done enough?" Minjun asked.

"Yeah, I think so." Turning his light off, he left his door cracked. Looking over, he saw Maliah's door was shut. He glanced over at Minjun, who was staring at him guiltily.

"What's wrong?" Seonghun asked.

"Ashley is joining us for dinner."

"Who's Ashley?" he asked, confused.

"The girl that was here the other night."

Seonghun froze. "Is Casey with her?"

"I asked her not to bring anyone," Minjun said.

"That's fine, Min, I have no problems eating with other people, it's just that Casey, well, she's nice in class, but there is something about her that doesn't feel quite right." However, when they arrived at Ashley's dorm, Casey was waiting with her. Seong eyeballed Min.

"It's fine, she promised," Minjun said.

Before any of them could say a word Ashley began speaking. "Hi, Minny! I know I said it would just be me, but Casey was working on a lab report forever! She just needed a break. I thought she could join us for dinner."

Yongjoon and Seonghun looked at each other, mouthing, "Minny!?"

Minjun looked at her for a moment before responding. "That's fine, Seonghun isn't staying. He just walked with me to pick up food. He is busy as well, and just wanted to get out to clear his head. Yongjoon will be staying though."

Yong smirked, one of his dimples showing.

Casey started grasping at straws. "Are you working on the lab report? Maybe we can work on it together?"

Seonghun looked at her. She was smart, pretty; by all accounts, a nice person. But something wasn't sitting right in his soul with her. "Ah no, this is some work for my other classes, excuse me." With no other words, he walked into the dining hall alone.

CHAPTER 5

Back in their suite, he noticed Maliah's door was cracked with the light out. Sighing, he put the extra box he bought in the fridge before heading to his room. His countenance brightened slightly as he noticed a note on his door. Pulling it off, it felt heavy. When he unfolded it, a packet of seeds fell out. Seong's heart lurched as he gazed at the packet of blue peony seeds. Opening the sheet fully he gasped. She had painted a beautiful blue peony, with the bloom so heavy the stem was bending, petals scattered on the ground. It looked so real, he thought, as he gently stroked it with his fingertips. Below it, written in a beautiful calligraphic script was a small poem.

I am— yet what I am none cares or knows;
My friends forsake me like a memory lost:
I am the self-consumer of my woes—

Seong slowly read the lines of the poem, trying hard to take in the meaning. He was a bright man; his grades got him this scholarship, but his brain was working double time to understand the words as well as the meaning. Once he powered through, he continued reading the note.

Thank you for the journal. I will make use of it. I like both daisies and lavender; daisies for their beauty in simplicity, lavender for its scent. I hope you have your garden one day, Seonghun. You make the country sound like the most beautiful place on earth. I didn't draw you more attractive than you are. I drew you as you are.
-M

Seonghun walked into his room quickly, scrawling a note on the lavender printed paper, letting her know he picked up extra food that she was welcome to in the fridge. As he raised his hand to tape it to the door, he stopped. Staring at the note for a long time, he impulsively scrawled one more line.

Are you free on Saturday? I would like to show you a place special to me.
-S

He held his breath as he placed it in the usual spot before walking back to his room to puzzle out the poem. He understood the words, but not exactly what it was saying. Opening his laptop, he set an appointment for the writing lab tomorrow. Locking the sheets in his box, Seong decided to sit in the common area to enjoy a movie with his dinner. Midway through, Minjun sent him a text apologizing about what happened, explaining that he probably won't be seeing Ashley anymore. He also asked Seonghun to stay up because there was something they wanted to talk to him about. There was no way he could sleep with a request like that. When he realized he wasn't really watching tv, just daydreaming, he walked into his room, trying to decipher the poem.

'I am— yet what I am no one cares or knows' was the first line of the poem. Did this mean she didn't have anyone to care about her? Did she not have a family that cared for her? He'd never been in her room, nor had he looked in, so he didn't know if she had pictures of her family up. He kept small, framed photos of his family as well as his friends. He loved his little family dearly; they were close. Everyone in his life he was loyal to without thought. Was anyone loyal to her?

He heard the main dorm door open followed by lots of noise. Minjun knocked, opening his door before he could say 'come in'. The two friends plopped on his bed, looking at one another before focusing twin gazes on Seong. "What's wrong?" Their faces looked beyond serious.

"Casey is—" Yongjoon paused. "Casey is in love with you."

Seonghun blinked. "What?"

Minjun started to talk. "She kept going on about how she realizes you're shy, that you just need someone to lead you. Also how you two belong together."

"That isn't love!" Seonghun sputtered. "That's an obsession, I'm not equipped to deal with that! We barely talk in class. I avoid all her advances while trying to focus on the work!" A quick way to freak him out was to start professing feelings that made no sense.

"Yeah, Ashley hadn't heard her go on like that before. After Casey left, she apologized profusely, but I specifically told her that Casey made you uncomfortable. She didn't listen, so I won't be seeing her anymore. Even though she did this thing with her tongue, it—"

"Min!" Seonghun turned scarlet.

Yongjoon glanced at him. "He talks about this all the time. Why are you so bashful about it? I know you've—"

"Yes, but, it's personal to me."

"You may want to talk to your lab teacher about switching partners," Yong said seriously. "She's fairly convinced you two are going to end up in a relationship. That isn't all: She got really weird when you left. Like she was furious, but trying to hide it."

Seonghun nodded. It's what made him uneasy about her, he realized. You never truly knew where you stood with her; she was constantly hiding her reactions to make her seem like a different person. He'd seen something flash in her eyes when he'd turned her down before. Seong knew it wasn't his imagination.

"Do you guys want to watch a movie?" Minjun asked.

"Yes, just give me a few moments. I'll be out shortly," Seonghun said.

The two men left, arguing over what to watch. Opening his laptop he sent a message to his lab professor. Explaining the situation as best as he could, Seong sent the message, immediately ready to join the other two. Walking into the shared space, he noticed Maliah's door was closed; the note was gone. As he settled into movie night with his friends, he hoped he hadn't been too forward with her.

As the credits rolled, Seong's roommates went into their rooms. He cut the television before walking over to Maliah's door. Taking his usual place on the floor, he knocked softly. "Maliah, are you there?"

It was silent, but soon he heard a soft knock in return.

"You're a very talented artist." He laughed softly. "I say that as if I know what art truly is. But I know that what you draw is beautiful. The peony should be framed if I'm honest." He looked out toward the common area. "I hope I didn't overstep my bounds, buying you the journal. I just thought your art would enhance it."

She spoke, muffled through the door. "It is beautiful, thank you. Also, I'm free on Saturday. May I ask where you want to take me?"

"There is this park. It's small, but there are a lot of daisies there along with a little pond. I think you'd like it. It's quiet, you could bring a sketchbook if you'd like."

There was silence for a long time, Seonghun thought she was refusing. The door suddenly opened, startling him. Scrambling to stand up, he ended up startling her, causing her to immediately back up.

"Sorry!" he whispered.

"It's okay, I know I'm a little jumpy," she said quietly. "This isn't a trick is it? You take me to some strange place to leave me or hurt me?"

"N-no. It is just a nice space; I thought I would share it with you." He was baffled. Why would he take her to a place just to abandon or hurt her?

She looked down at her feet. He looked down as well. Maliah wore plain pink pajama pants with a blue sweatshirt that had the Silver Leaf logo on the front. Her feet were bare; Seong smiled as he saw her nails were painted sparkly pink. He smelled that sweet smell around her again.

"Okay," she said.

"Okay?"

"Yes. What time do you want to go? S-s-s-should I bring anything?" She looked up at him;

Seong noticed her glasses were crooked. He wanted to straighten them but thought against it.

"If we catch the bus at ten, it will put us there at eleven-thirty. I thought I would make sandwiches for lunch if that is okay?" he offered.

"W-well, we don't have to take the bus first of all, I have a c-c-car. Secondly, you've fed me t-t-twice now. I'll take care of lunch, I have an idea," she said softly. "Do you have anything you don't like, or are al-l-lergic to?"

Seonghun shook his head. "Do you want to leave here at eleven?" he asked.

"Yes, that's fine." She started slowly backing into her room.

"Goodnight, Maliah."

"Y-you can just call me Liah, goodnight." She closed the door softly.

He listened closely for a moment; the silence in her room was broken by soft music that he heard filtered through the door. Smiling to himself, he retreated to his room, getting undressed for bed. Seong's laptop was still open; there was an email back from his lab professor. Thankfully, the man approved the move. Seong would be assigned to another table with another student. Sighing in relief, Seonghun laid down for the night. He reminded himself to ask what that smell was during their date. Date? Was it a date? No, it was two roommates getting to know each other. Satisfied with that, he closed his eyes.

CHAPTER 6

Luckily for Seonghun, he didn't have lab on Fridays. He just had two of his normal classes. After the last one, he walked to the writing lab. After sitting for about fifteen minutes, his name was called by a tall man with long curly hair.

"What can I help you with Seonghun?" the man asked pleasantly.

"English isn't my first language; while I understand it, there are sometimes nuances in writing I sometimes don't get."

The gentleman nodded, encouraging him to continue.

Seonghun pulled out a sheet of notebook paper, having meticulously copied the poem. He didn't want anyone else touching the sheet she had given him for an inexplicable reason. "I don't understand this poem basically and was wondering if you could help me decipher its meaning." He handed the paper over.

"Well, let's start at the beginning," the man said after he read the poem. He keyed in some information in the computer in front of him before speaking again. "The name of the poem is called 'I Am'; It's by a man named John Clare." The man turned the computer monitor around to face Seonghun. "He wrote this when he was sick. He was in an asylum, writing about his loneliness. The first stanza talks about his love of the beauty of the world; how he will find peace in it when he dies."

Seonghun looked at the man, alarmed.

The man continued. "The second stanza talks about how he felt alienated from his friends and family when he was in the asylum. The final stanza talks about how he hopes there is an afterlife." He looked at Seonghun. "It's a profound poem. Sad, but uplifting in its hope, I think."

Seonghun looked at the screen for a minute before looking at the man. "If-if someone were to give you this poem as a way of knowing them, what would you think they were trying to tell you?"

The gentleman sighed. Leaning back in his chair, Seong saw him think hard on the matter. "You'll have to make your own thoughts on this, but what I get is this person was hurt. They are lonely; they hope that one day the loneliness ceases, through life or death."

It was quiet while Seonghun took that in. "Do you think the person could be suicidal?" he ventured.

"I can't comment on anyone's mental situation, Seonghun. They may be sad, but the rest of the answers to your questions are probably going to have to come from them."

He nodded, thanking the man for his time. Heading back to the dorms, his heart was heavy. What happened to make this woman so sad? He stopped at the little convenience store on campus to pick up a pint of chocolate ice cream. Staring at the different flavors, he grabbed a pint of strawberry ice cream as well. Walking out of the store he ran into someone. "I'm sorry." He looked down to see Casey beaming up at him. "Oh, hi." He went to walk around her, but she stepped in front of him again to his annoyance.

"Hey! I'm so glad to have run into you." She smiled at him. "We're having a party tonight, I wondered if you wanted to come?"

Seonghun looked up to the sky for help from a deity he wasn't even sure he believed in. "Casey I—"

"I'm also sorry you had to leave so quickly the other day. I was hoping to maybe have a meal with you." She bounced on her toes in front of him.

"Casey, look. You seem like a nice person, but I'm not interested in dating or hanging out outside of class. I'm solely focused on my studies. I apologize if I ever led you to believe otherwise." It was brief; she hid it well, but Seonghun saw that flash of rage in her eye. This had to be what Yong saw as well. At that moment, Seong knew he was making the right decision.

"I understand. No hard feelings?" Her smile was brittle.

Seonghun nodded before speeding back to his dorm. Opening the door, Minjun was on the couch with Ashley again, trying to swallow her tonsils. With a quick glance at Maliah's door, Seong spoke up, "Min, can you help me in my room?" Minjun detached his face from Ashley's, following him into his room. "I thought you weren't seeing her anymore?"

Minjun looked sheepish. "I wasn't... then she did the thing with her tongue again."

Seonghun rolled his eyes. "Look, I'm not telling you who to date, that isn't fair to you, but please be careful with her. I ran into Casey at the store. I told her I wasn't interested. She wasn't very satisfied with what I had to say. I don't want trouble, Min."

"The second there's a problem, I will stop with her, but to be honest, I think she was embarrassed at her friend's actions. I could also be mistaking her embarrassment into something I want to see just because I don't want her to stop doing that thing with her tongue." Minjun turned red.

Seonghun snorted. "Can you take that into your room? It looks like you were one step from having your hand down her pants. We do have additional people that live here."

Minjun nodded as he left. When Seong heard his door shut, he walked into the common area again to tap on Maliah's door. "Liah? It is me, Seonghun. You don't have to open the door, but I was at the store. I picked you up an ice cream when I grabbed one. I hope you like strawberry. I'll be in my room reading if you need anything." Setting the ice cream by her door, he walked back in his room, leaving the door open. Sifting around his desk, he found the pulpy science fiction novel he'd been reading. Soon he was immersed in the world of the book while eating his ice cream. He laid there reading until Yongjoon tapped lightly on his door frame before walking in. Yong glanced at the empty ice cream container on the nightstand before flicking his eyes toward Seong.

"Come workout with me," Yong said.

Seonghun nodded, shooing his friend out so he could change. Seong shed his clothes, quickly donning the compression leggings he typically wore with a t-shirt to the gym. As a final touch he placed a ball cap backwards on his head. As they were getting ready to leave, Maliah's door opened. Her hair was down today, pulled back from her face with a hair tie. She had on another black dress that went to her knees, covering her completely at the top. There was no cleavage to be seen. Seong noticed the sleeves went halfway down her arms as well. This time she had on hot pink heels. After she turned around from locking her door she jumped at seeing the two men. Everyone froze.

Yongjoon spoke up, "You look nice."

Maliah nodded her head, looking down. "They're my work clothes," she whispered. Maliah walked out of the door, but glanced back at Seonghun. His ears turned bright red.

Yong didn't say anything. He managed to keep silent on the walk to the gym, but pounced as soon as Seonghun started lifting weights. "So, you want to tell me what that look back from Maliah was?"

Seonghun nearly dropped the weight. Nothing was really going on with them, but he felt like he was on the verge of making a friend. He couldn't understand why he was so hesitant to talk about it. Maybe it was because she seemed so leery of everything; he didn't want to break her trust.

"She watched Jeopardy with me briefly. We didn't really say anything. When it was done she went back to her room. That's all."

"That's more interaction than any of us have had."

Seong quickly changed the subject to Minjun and Ashley. "How long do you think that is going to last?"

Yongjoon started laughing, nearly sliding off the bench. "As long as she does that thing with her tongue, Min might marry her." They both cackled loudly. "I don't think it's truly serious. Ashley is fun, but you know he doesn't date long term."

Seonghun then told him about the interaction he had with Casey.

Yongjoon frowned. "Before she started acting weird like this, did you have any attraction to her at all?"

Seong shook his head. "No. I turned her down every single time she asked me to go somewhere or do something. She's been perfectly nice, but it felt like the niceness was just a mask. I know it sounds weird, but I can't explain it any other way."

Yongjoon shook his head. "You don't have to explain any further. Sometimes you get feelings about people that are either off putting or you feel drawn to them."

As Seonghun stepped on the treadmill, he thought about what Yongjoon said. He was realizing that he was drawn to Maliah, very much so. After going to the writing center to get her poem analyzed, he was even more curious. Was she hurting? Was she thinking of hurting herself? He tried to get his mind off of it.

"How are your classes going?"

Yongjoon smiled happily and began to speak on his courses. Listening to him talk about torts, whatever they were, gave Seong a quiet joy that his friend loved what he was doing.

When they finished, Yong showered there. Seonghun decided to wait until they got back to the dorm. He texted Min to see if he wanted them to bring food. In response, Min indicated that he'd ordered Chinese, enough for all of them, so the two friends hurried home.

When they got there, Seonghun was relieved to see Ashley was gone. "Yeah she said something about comforting Casey," Min said, digging through a box of cashew chicken.

Yong glanced at Seong, not saying anything before he just shrugged.

"I'll be out in a bit, I'm going to shower," Seonghun said. Walking to his door he saw a note attached. A red ripe glossy strawberry greeted him from the page. At the bottom in her beautiful script she left a small note.

Strawberry is one of my favorite flavors. How did you know? What is your favorite animal?
-M

Seonghun smiled before locking the note into his box. Grabbing his shower caddy, he went to clean the sweat from his body. As the weak water pressure tried its hardest to beat on his shoulders, his stomach rumbled. Seong sped up to get to the food quicker. As he continued showering, the image of Liah's legs in those heels popped into his head out of nowhere. He hadn't realized he was looking that hard.

Instant erection.

Cursing himself, he turned the water on cold, bringing his senses back. He'd been around women that were friends before, though they were few and far in between. He'd never had this issue before. It felt disrespectful; he needed to get a grip. As he cut the water, he realized he forgot to bring in clothes. Seong secured his towel around his waist. As he opened the door, he heard Minjun's voice.

"We ordered plenty, you're welcome to join us."

"N-no thank you," he heard Maliah say.

Her head was down, so she ended up walking right into Seong's lower stomach. She nearly fell, but he steadied her with his hands on her arms. The sweet smell was permeating his senses along with the feel of her soft skin. He felt the problem he thought he took care of in the shower, rising again.

He quickly removed his hands. "I'm sorry!"

It was as if Maliah's brain short circuited. "I-it-it i-i-i-i-is o-o-o-ok," she stuttered. He saw her begin to shake.

"Are you okay?" he whispered.

"I-I-I-I n-nuh-need t-t-to go." She ran into her room. All of them heard the lock click.

All three men stared at her closed door in astonishment. "Is she-okay?" Yongjoon said slowly.

"I don't know," Seonghun whispered. He walked into his room, feeling awful. He hurriedly got dressed before walking into the common area to see his friends gathering their food. When they saw Seonghun, Yongjoon spoke up. "We're going to give her some space, so she can calm down. Do you want to come? We're going to play Scrabble."

He shook his head. "I'll go in my room if I'm bothering her."

They nodded, leaving him containers of fried rice along with beef and broccoli before exiting their suite. Grabbing the food, a set of chopsticks and a fork, he sat outside her door.

"You may not want to talk, that's okay, but I was a little worried for you. Is it okay if I sit beside your door?"

Almost immediately there was a soft knock.

He opened his carton of rice, quickly devouring the savory meal. "I'm sorry if I scared you. I didn't mean to. We try to be courteous to the fact that a girl is living with us; we carry our clothes into the bathroom when we go to shower. It completely slipped my mind when I saw food." He shoveled more rice in his mouth, trying to figure out how to bridge the silence. "Are you hungry?" he asked.

Another single soft knock sounded.

"I have food out here. I know you feel comfortable in your room, if you reach a hand out, we can trade boxes."

It was quiet for a bit so he went back to eating his rice. He heard the click of the lock, and the door cracked open. He picked up the container of beef and broccoli along with the fork, quickly sticking it through the opening. He felt her grip the box so he let go, pulling his hand back. She shut the door.

"There is a girl in my bio lab class. She's... pushy. I tried every way to tell her I wasn't interested in hanging out with her, but she wouldn't take no for an answer." He put down his food. "When I went to get ice cream earlier, she saw me in the store and tried again. I finally told her that I wasn't interested. It made me think of you. I just want to make sure that I'm not forcing my company on you."

A note slid under the door on the thick paper. Seonghun unfolded it.

You have always given me a choice on whether I communicate or not. It may not show, but I do like spending time with you. It's just hard sometimes for me to communicate like everyone else.

"I'll be right back." He stood up, running to his room to grab a pen and a book to write on. Sitting back down, he began to write.

Do you still want to go to the park tomorrow? I understand if you don't want to.

He slipped the paper back under the door before standing up again.

Going to the fridge he pulled out two sodas. Knocking lightly on her door again he called out "Drink?"

She cracked her door; again he stuck his hand in with the soda. She lightly brushed her hand against his as she grabbed it. Seong felt something inside him tug at her slight touch. Something very different than when Casey tried to stroke his arm. She quickly closed the door. It was silent for a while as they ate. She slid the paper under the door.

You promise this isn't a trick?

He read the words and felt sad she had to ask. Something happened, but he didn't know how to broach it.

I promise that it is not a trick. Also, my favorite animal is a cat. We have a cat on the farm at home that keeps the mice out of the barn.

Slipping the paper back under, he polished off half the rice. "Do you want to switch cartons? I've eaten half the rice, so you could have the rest."

She opened the door, holding out the container of beef and broccoli. "I ate most of the broccoli out of it. I'm sorry," she whispered.

"It's not a problem at all. I like the meat just fine. Are you a vegetarian? Should I have not bought you a burger?" he asked.

"N-no, I e-e-eat meat. I really l-l-like veggies too," she stuttered.

He quietly traded her boxes so she could shut herself inside again. Seong desperately thought of what to say while eating the tender strips of beef. She slid the paper back to him.

I'll go. I'll still bring lunch.

Seong finished eating before writing his note.

I'm glad. I'm going to go to bed now to give you some peace. Thank you for hanging out with me. I can tell it was difficult.

He slid the note under the door before throwing his carton away. When he came back, the note was waiting for him.

It's hard, but you don't push. Thank you. Have a nice night. I will see you in the morning.

He smiled as he took the paper, storing it with the rest, before lying down.

CHAPTER 7

When Seonghun woke, he was aware of two things. First off, he fell asleep with his glasses on. The screw had popped out of his glasses, rendering them useless until he could get them fixed. Unfortunately, his glasses were not a fashion accessory. He couldn't see without them. Secondly, his dreams last night consisted of Maliah. He wondered how she sounded when she laughed. Groaning into his pillow, Seong sat up, blindly searching for his toiletry bag. Finally finding it, he unearthed a few pairs of contacts. He thanked his past self for using a marker on each bottle letting him know which ones were right eyes or left eyes. Seong quickly got dressed before going to the shared bathroom to put his contacts in.

It was early; there wasn't a sound in the suite. He rushed through his morning routine. As he finished, Seong nearly ran into Maliah again. He stopped short so as to not have a fiasco like last night. "Hi," he said quietly. She was still in her flannel pajamas. He made sure to focus on her face.

"Hi."

He was quiet for a moment when he had an idea. "Do you have anywhere to be this morning?"

"I-I w-w-was going t-t-t—" She stopped talking, closed her eyes while taking a deep breath, before trying again. "I was going to pick up lunch, but that's it."

"Would you like to get breakfast with me? You won't hurt my feelings if you say no." He wanted to offer her every opportunity to be comfortable.

She twirled a twist around her finger as she considered. "Did you want to stay on campus to e-e-eat or l-l-l-leave?"

"I don't know many breakfast places off campus."

"How about I take you somewhere for breakfast instead?" she offered. She didn't stutter.

Seonghun smiled at her, nodding.

"Can you meet me out here? I-I-I have a thing about o-o-th-th—"

He noticed her hitting her leg as she tried to get the words out. Not thinking, he grabbed her hand. She snatched it back quickly.

"I'm sorry, I didn't mean to grab you. You were hurting yourself," he said quietly.

"I know. You're fine. I'll just meet y-you out here." With that, she shut herself in the bathroom.

Seonghun shook his head, walking back into his room. Pulling down a duffle bag he began to load it with a small blanket, two books, earbuds, a splitter, a small notebook, and pen. Zipping up the bag, he pulled a sweatshirt from his closet before walking into the common area. Seong turned on the tv, setting the volume on low to wait for her. Maliah walked out of the bathroom, dressed similarly to him. She had on the dark colored jeans that he'd seen before. They were tight in her waist and thigh, flaring out into a large leg. She had on black Doc Martens with a red long sleeved t-shirt.

"Are you ready?" she asked. She fiddled with her keys. He followed after her silently. As they climbed down the stairs she looked at him. "We have to take the bus to the football stadium. It's where my car is." She said it clearly with no stuttering.

Seong nodded while he opened the door, letting her walk out first. Standing near the street where the buses picked up, they waited quietly. When they arrived at the stadium, they got into her tiny hatchback car. Seong's knees felt as if they were to his ears.

Maliah turned on the car; all of a sudden music blasted out of the speakers.

I'm not here for your entertainment
You don't really wanna mess with me tonight

She quickly turned down the music before glancing over at him. He must have looked a little shell-shocked because Liah burst into giggles. It was one of the nicest sounds he'd ever heard.

"I'm sorry, I listen to music a lot. Typically I can't really blast it in the dorm room without disturbing everyone," she explained. Liah navigated the car across the bridge to Lafyette. It was a short car ride that ended in a parking garage.

Away from campus, Seonghun noticed she relaxed more. Getting out of the car, he scrambled to walk beside her. It was quiet, but it didn't feel awkward. There was no need for idle chatter from either of them. Maliah led him across the street to a little diner.

"Welcome, sit anywhere you like, we'll be with you in a moment," a waitress with a sunny yellow shirt called out to them.

Maliah looked at Seong. He gestured to the seating. "Please pick."

She slid into a booth next to a large window. Seonghun took the opposite side. "This is near my job, so I come here from time to time for lunch. The food is always good," Maliah explained.

Opening the menu, Seonghun saw something outlined in bright yellow, called The Challenge. It was two biscuits, sausages, eggs, large hashbrowns with cheese, all covered with sausage gravy. He was sold.

"Would you consider splitting The Challenge with me?" he asked her. She scanned down the menu to read what it was, laughing instantly. Liah's laughter made warmth fill his chest. It was bright, cheery.

"If we eat all of that, we aren't going to have room for lunch," she said.

"I'm a growing boy. I always have room for lunch." He gave her puppy dog eyes. "If we split it, it won't be as much food."

She tried to hold back the laughter. "Did you not wear your glasses to specifically give me those eyes?"

Seonghun's ears burned red. "I fell asleep in my glasses by accident last night. I'll have to get them repaired."

Just then a waitress walked up with a coffee pot. They both turned their mugs over on the table, allowing her to pour in the fragrant brew. She asked for their order. Seonghun looked over at Maliah smiling.

"W-we'll have The Challenge please, eggs scrambled." She closed her menu, handing it to the waitress.

"Thank you."

"You're welcome," she said.

It was silent for a beat before he spoke again. "You said your job is near here. What is it that you do?"

"I ac-actually have t-t-two jobs." Liah took a deep breath before she started again. "I'm an assistant curator for an art gallery around the corner. I also give basic guitar lessons in a therapist's office for music therapy."

"Which job do you like best?"

"Music therapy," she said without hesitation. "It's closer to what I want to do with my life. Also, I don't have to dress up. I keep the art job because it allows me to absorb art, learning more about it."

Seonghun hesitated briefly before plowing forward. "Can I ask about your stutter?"

She looked startled. "It-I just get nervous sometimes. If I can keep calm, it's fine."

"Is there something I can do to make you less nervous around me? Or our roommates?"

She went silent for a moment, stirring cream into her coffee. "Have you ever looked in our dorm at the rooms that have co-ed suites?"

Seonghun shook his head.

"Out of all of the rooms, there are only seven that are co-ed like ours. Each of us, be it the men or the women, were put in the co-ed situation for a reason. We all had severe problems with our roommates that required us to move out immediately." She wouldn't look him in the eye.

"Liah I—"

"I'm not ready to talk about it. I don't know if I ever will be. But I have a severe distrust of living with someone now. The main instigator of the events should have been expelled, kicked off campus. Instead I have a restraining order; they have to stay fifty feet away from me." At this she looked at him. "I feel like I'm taking a risk even talking to you, that's why I tend to stutter more around you three. I'm terrified."

Just then a massive plate covered in gravy was set in between them.

Maliah's eyes widened.

"This is a mess."

Seonghun snickered. As they unwrapped their silverware he spoke up. "You don't have to talk about what happened if you don't want to. That's your right. But we wouldn't judge. How about I tell you about us while we eat?"

Maliah nodded.

In between bites of the delicious mess, Seonghun talked about growing up with Min and the scrapes they got into as children. He spoke of them both learning English from tv shows as well as studying. Seong told her how he was the first in his family to go to college. He talked about meeting Yongjoon; how he took them under his wing, allowing them to go home with him from time to time.

"Are you from Indiana?" he asked, scooping a mouthful of sausage, egg, and gravy into his mouth.

"Yes. I'm from Indianapolis." She took a sip of coffee but didn't say anything else.

"It's a big city, is there a chance you went to high school with Yong?" he probed gently.

Maliah pulled out her phone, bringing a map up of the city. "Do you know where he lives by chance?"

Seonghun stared at the map, manipulating it to make it bigger. "There, Springmill Road, by that park."

She snorted. "No, we didn't go to the same school. I lived in the city proper. I went to the IPS school district half my freshman year of high school, before getting a scholarship for the rest of my years of high school to a private school."

"You must be really smart to get a scholarship for high school and college."

She stared at him for a minute. Though it was unnerving, he met her gaze. It felt like a test of some sort. "Not as smart as you think. I'm just determined."

"Determined to do what?" He pushed the plate away, full finally.

She was quiet as she scraped the gravy from the food to unearth the hashbrowns. "To succeed, to not be poor, to help people."

He seized on the last part. "Who is it you want to help?"

She smiled. "Everyone, but let's start with underprivileged children of color. I want to expose them to art and music, showing them different things they may not get to see in their lives. Using that, I want them to be able to create their own joy in the world."

"That's an admirable goal."

"It's a long way off. After undergrad I still have a couple years of schooling." She looked up as the waitress dropped off their bill.

Seonghun was quicker than her grabbing it.

"I'm able to pay you know, the whole two jobs thing," she pointed out.

"So am I," he said simply. Seonghun's scholarship provided for his every need, including a hefty monthly stipend. Because his friends split food costs evenly, he often ended up with most of his stipend in the bank. He rarely bought clothes and had no need for a ton of material things. Seong's secret weakness was books.

"Well, thank you." Liah drained her coffee cup with Seonghun following suit. Both of them slid from the booth before heading to the front to pay. The owner was manning the cashier.

"I've never seen you here for breakfast before, just lunch. Did you enjoy it?"

"It was very good. If I didn't have to work after eating, I would order The Challenge for lunch." She laughed as Seonghun handed over his card. After leaving a tip they were getting ready to leave, when the owner presented them with a bag.

"I know you're probably full now, but these will taste good later, freshly baked."

They both thanked the man before leaving the restaurant. Seonghun spoke up as they walked back to the car. "You must be a really good customer."

"I eat here every time I work. The BLT has a ton of bacon on it and the tomatoes are always really good, even in the winter. It makes me wonder if he has a greenhouse or something." They climbed into the car. As Seonghun fastened his seatbelt, she spoke again. "I need to pick up lunch, then you can direct me to the park." Pulling out of the garage, she went about three blocks before parallel parking in front of a plain building. There were no words on the front; it had a red and white striped awning over the door. "You're welcome to come in, but I will only be a moment."

"I'll stay here, thank you."

She nodded before getting out. Opening the back seat, he watched Liah pull the basket out before strolling into the building.

His phone had been vibrating constantly since they ate. Pulling it out, he saw he had twelve texts from Minjun alone. Yongjoon had sent him five. Sighing, he called Minjun.

"Where are you? I've been texting," Minjun demanded.

"I'm out running errands. What do you want?"

"We're going to breakfast; you're never up this early."

"I'll be home after a while. Is that what Yong wanted?"

The back door of the car opened; Seong watched Liah put the basket on the seat.

"We thought you were ignoring my texts."

As she got back into the car, he got a whiff of her sweet scent again. "Min, I've never ignored your texts, why would I do that now? I'll talk to you when I get back." He disconnected the call before he got more questions.

Maliah was staring at him.

"I don't go out much by myself, except to maybe do laundry or the store. I also sleep late a lot, so my friends are baffled at the schedule change," he explained.

She nodded. "So you weren't ignoring his texts?"

"I kind of was, because I was talking with you, but he'll be fine. He's not insecure in our friendship, he's just curious about what is going on with me." He pulled up navigation on his phone to show her where the park was.

It was quiet in the car as Maliah drove. She still had the music on, but it was a low hum.

"Can I ask you something?" Seonghun ventured.

"S-s-sure."

"Please don't be nervous. It's not personal. I don't think so, but what perfume are you wearing?"

"Oh. It's called, um, Nectarine Blossom and Honey. That's it."

"You smell good," he blurted. "I mean it smells good, I mean it's nice." Seong's ears were blazing.

She glanced at him quickly before looking forward. "Thank you. It's kind of expensive, so I bought this pen that was the cheapest thing I saw at the time. It's running low though. I'll need to pick up another one soon."

She pulled into the parking lot of their destination, cutting the engine. Seonghun stepped out of the car, taking his duffle. Maliah opened the trunk, pulling a backpack out. Slinging it on, she grabbed the lunch basket before looking at Seong. "Where to?"

"Follow me please." With that he started walking. He walked through the park for about five minutes until he came to the edge of a wooded forest. Seonghun knelt down, pulling out the blanket he packed. Spreading it out, he sat down before digging out his book and earbuds. Maliah sat down, pulling out a sketchpad, the journal he gave her, and her own headphones.

"I'm here if you want to talk, but otherwise, just pretend I'm not here," he said gently. He plugged in an earbud, leaving one out so he could hear her. Seeing that she was settled, Seong started reading. Liah faced the little pond as she drew. He enjoyed the quiet of the day; it seemed as if she did as well. They were there so early that there were hardly any people out. The sun was out, but there was still a slight fall chill in the air.

Seonghun kept an eye on Maliah, making sure she wasn't uncomfortable. She seemed focused on the pond as she drew, so he went back to being fully immersed in his book. He didn't know when it happened, but the food, combined with him feeling relaxed made him drowsy. His eyes slowly closed.

CHAPTER 8

He didn't know how long he was asleep before he heard his name. "Seonghun. Seonghun, wake up."

He felt someone gently shake his shoulder. He grabbed the hand, thinking it was Minjun's. It was too small to be his friend's. His eyes popped open when he remembered his morning. Breakfast, the park, Liah. Blinking rapidly to focus his contacts he looked at her realizing he was still holding her hand. "You aren't shaking," he said.

Liah shook her head. "I don't think you'd hurt me."

"I wouldn't. How long have I been asleep?" He casually let go of her so it didn't seem like a big deal.

"Three hours. You looked peaceful, so I didn't bother you, but I thought you might be getting hungry."

"Wow, three hours? I take you to a place and immediately crash. I'm so sorry." Seong flushed red instantly. What kind of outing was this?

"Don't worry about it. It's nice you felt comfortable enough to sleep. I had plenty to see," she said as she began unpacking the basket. The top of the basket had plates, cups, and utensils strapped to it. The food was stacked snugly inside.

Seonghun stretched before peering over at her. She handed him a plate with a massive sandwich on it, some type of potato salad with a bag of chips. She pulled out a glass bottle with a fancy label. Pouring them a glass of bright orange liquid, she gave it to him before she began to serve herself.

As Seonghun poked at the potato salad suspiciously with a fork, she glanced over. "It's German potato salad. It isn't mayo based, it's more vinegary than American potato salad. It can be served warm or cold." She sat beside him, biting into her sandwich.

He followed her example, trying the sandwich first. It was delicious. Stacks of cold cuts, a vinegar based dressing, shredded lettuce, onions, and tomatoes on a french baguette. It was massive. Setting it down, he took a sip of the fizzy liquid.

"Tangerine soda, one of my favorites," Maliah said as she continued nibbling at her food.

After a while, he slowed down eating before looking at her. Her hair was pulled back in a ponytail, he could see small gold hoops in her ears. They suited her. "I went to the writing lab the other day."

She looked at him. "Are you having problems in a writing class?"

"No, I write just fine, but sometimes when it comes to poetry, I get lost. I don't understand what is being said. The poem you gave me, one of the tutors in the lab helped me with it."

"Ah. You have questions?"

He nodded.

"The poem is how I feel a lot of the time. You speak of your friends. They are your support system. If something goes wrong, you have someone to talk to." She opened the bag the owner of the diner had given them, passing him a gooey strawberry cinnamon roll. "I don't. I have no one. You talk about how proud your parents were that you got this opportunity. My parents see me as nothing but a burden, an annoyance." She said this as if she was talking about the weather.

"Liah that can't be true." He licked the icing from his fingers as he watched her plate her own cinnamon roll. Neatly she cut it in half before she took a bite.

"It's very much true. I thought I found a friend group, but I ended up being tricked in the worst way possible. I had to spend a little time in a hospital to recover. Part of the reason the person didn't get expelled was that her parents paid for my treatment, continuing to pay for my medication as 'restitution'." Maliah used finger quotes.

"Hospital?" Seonghun asked.

"I had a mental breakdown," she said quietly. "I've always been an anxious person, but this spun it out of control."

He didn't know what to say. Seong wanted to hug her, but didn't want to lose the ground they had gained that day, so he grabbed her hand, squeezing it tightly.

She looked at him, smiling sadly. "I'm better, but remnants of everything still remain. I'm hopeful that by processing everything while working toward my goals, I will be a little less... jittery? Anxiety ridden? Less than how I am now." Liah pulled a piece of the sticky dessert apart, popping it in her mouth.

"I think you're just fine the way you are," Seonghun said quietly.

"I had a meltdown because you touched me. I go through periods where I just cannot interact with people. You have been nothing but nice but sometimes I have to just pass you notes because the words won't come. Thank you for the sentiment, Seonghun, but I'm not fine the way I am." She had started hitting herself on the leg with the hand he wasn't holding. "I'm twenty years old, I've never kissed anyone, to say nothing of intimacy because the idea of being that close to someone throws me into a severe tailspin."

Seonghun didn't know what to do, so he did what he felt. Putting his plate down, he scooted so he was in front of her, grabbing both of her hands so she would stop.

She tugged away from him. "I'm kind of a mess, Seonghun."

"You're a nice mess. A nice mess that draws really pretty flowers. Who agreed to come out to share the day with me. We're all varying degrees of mess, Liah. You're just a little more severe than most."

She gave him another half-smile before focusing on picking at her dessert.

"You said you give guitar lessons. Do you play any other instruments?"

"Yeah. I uh, play the violin, but no one ever wants to learn to play the violin. Everyone wants the guitar because it's cool."

"Can I hear you play sometime?"

"I haven't played for just a single person in a long time."

"Well if you decide to, I'm here." Seonghun noticed that she was starting to shake. "Are you okay?" he asked.

"Yeah, I'm fine. I'm just cold. This shirt isn't doing it."

Seong dug in his bag, handing her the sweatshirt he brought with him.

"Thank you." She slid it on her shoulders, quickly zipping it up. Seonghun was very tall; the sleeves came over her hands.

"You're welcome." He liked seeing her in his sweatshirt. He liked... her. He liked hanging with her, even if much wasn't said. "Can I ask you for a favor?"

She turned her eyes to him.

"Will you have dinner with my friends tonight? You don't have to say anything, I promise to keep Minjun calm, but I think you'll like them."

She tapped her lip with her sweatshirt covered hand. "A favor indicates that I will be owed a favor at a later date, correct?"

"I guess so, yes. What favor do you need?"

"Nothing right now, but I'm sure I'll come back to something." Liah searched the basket for napkins, handing him one. "Do you want to go get a hot chocolate?"

He nodded so they began to pack up.

"Thank you for bringing me here. You were right, it is peaceful." As they walked to the car together, her hands trailed the daisy blooms.

"Wait a minute." Seonghun stopped. He broke off a stem of a daisy. Facing her, he reached out, touching her face, tucking her hair behind her ear. She flinched slightly but didn't back away. He tucked the blossom in her hair.

"There." He smiled, pleased with his handiwork. He looked at her face and saw those big brown eyes focused on him. "Your eyes are really pretty," he whispered.

Liah's eyes were inquisitive; she couldn't hide how intelligent she was if she looked at you. She looked as if she were contemplating every single thing around her. They were round, fringed with thick lashes. He knew some girls put stuff on their eyelashes or even had fake ones to make them that way. He wondered if she did that.

"Thank you," she whispered back. It was silent for a moment. "Hot chocolate?" she asked again.

Seong nodded, following Maliah to her car.

They sat in the little coffee shop continuing to talk, drinking their cocoa when Seonghun's phone started ringing.

"It's Min, can you give me a minute?"

Maliah nodded as she poked at the marshmallows in her drink.

"Yes, Min?"

"WHERE ARE YOU?! I AM SO BORRRREEEDDD!"

Minjun was loud enough that Maliah heard him. Seong smiled at her as she tried to stifle her giggles.

"Is that a girl!? Are you with a girl!? Who are you with!?"

At this point Maliah was doubled over with the struggle of not laughing out loud. He wished she wouldn't hide it, he loved hearing her laugh.

"Min, I'll be back in like thirty minutes or so. Will you order pizza tonight? We have a guest. Use my card if it's my turn."

"Who is the guest? Who is coming? Is it that girl that I heard? Does she like pineapple on her pizza? HEY GIRL, DO YOU LIKE PINEAPPLE ON YOUR PIZZA?!" By this point Min was shrieking.

"Min, why are you yelling about pineapple?" Seonghun heard Yongjoon in the background.

"Seong is with a girl, he won't tell me who she is, but he said there is a guest coming for dinner. So is it the girl?" Minjun was babbling to both men at the same time.

Seong rolled his eyes.

When Seonghun glanced back at Maliah, she was dashing away tears from her eyes. "Uh, yes, I do like pineapple on my pizza," she whispered.

"Min! She likes pineapple on her pizza."

"Got it! Come home soon!" Without another word Minjun hung up the phone.

"Min is kind of exuberant. I'm going to text him to let him know it's you, so he doesn't jump on you like a puppy." He quickly sent the text. Less than a second later Seong's phone went ballistic with messages from Min. "I-uh…" Seonghun looked down helplessly at his phone.

Maliah hesitantly put her hand on his arm. "I-I-I'll be f-f-f-fine."

"You've barely stuttered all day; it's back in full force. We don't have to do this. I can make them meet in the open area of the dorm while you head to your room. I just thought it would be nice," he said quietly.

"You have been nothing but accommodating to m-m-me. Let me reciprocate." Liah looked at her watch. "W-w-we need t-t-t-to get going though. The stadium bus stops soon." She stood up, tossing her cup as he followed her.

Driving back to campus, Seonghun was a bundle of nerves. Minjun was kind, but he was so bouncy sometimes. He hoped that Maliah wasn't overwhelmed. On the bus Seonghun noticed her rubbing her hands obsessively over her thighs. He gently tugged her hand, gripping it tightly. Looking at her, he spoke in what he hoped was a reassuring way. "This is your home. You have the right to go to your room if you're overwhelmed. If it's too much you can walk away with no excuse."

She nodded, but he didn't let go of her hand. At their stop they walked hand in hand back to the dorm. As they arrived at their door, Maliah took a deep breath, opened the door, and gawked at what she saw.

Their two roommates were rolling around on the floor wrestling, with Yongjoon screaming. "YOU NEED TO CALM DOWN, MIN!"

"HE NEVER BRINGS ANYBODY HOME!"

"HE'S NOT BRINGING ANYONE HOME! HE'S COMING HOME WITH OUR ROOMMATE!"

They continued tussling while Seonghun smacked his forehead with his free hand, rolling his eyes. "Good grief," he muttered. "Guys?" Seong tried to speak loud enough so they could hear, but the rolling around continued. He glanced over at Maliah who was trying really hard not to laugh at the scene in front of them. "I'm going to yell. I don't want you to be startled."

"Okay," she said.

"WILL YOU TWO GET UP!?" he shrieked.

The two roommates glanced at them. "Sorry. Minjun got a little....Minjun-ish," Yongjoon said.

Minjun said nothing, staring at their clasped hands. Seonghun squeezed her hand slightly before letting go. Playing it as casually as possible, Seonghun spoke to them both. "Is dinner here yet?"

"We ordered after we talked to you, so it should be here any minute,"

Minjun said. He looked at Maliah. "I got ham and pineapple. No one ever likes it but me so I rarely get it."

"I like the salty and the sweet together. Kind of t-t-t-the s-s-s-s-" She took a deep breath before trying again. "L-l-l-ike with kettle corn."

"Me too." Minjun smiled gently.

"I'm g-g-g-gonna put my s-s-st-st-stuff away. I'll be b-b-back." She went into her room, shutting the door behind her.

Minjun looked at Seonghun, pouncing instantly. Seong towered over his best friend, but Minjun was determined to drag Seonghun into his room. Once there, he shifted uncomfortably.

"Well!?" Minjun finally said.

"She needed some quiet. I took her to a quiet place," Seonghun said.

"Where are your glasses?" Minjun asked.

Seonghun reached over to his nightstand table picking up the pieces of his frames. "I fell asleep in them again."

"So you weren't trying to, I don't know, be cute without them?"

Seonghun looked confused. "She sees me every day in glasses, why would I try to be cute without them?"

"Never mind. There is more to this, I want to know everything. I'll find out later though." With that Minjun left him in his room, closing the door. Seonghun sighed, took off his shoes, unbuttoning his jeans. He really wanted to take out the contacts, but he couldn't see without them. Seong dug out his sweatpants as he heard the door open. Pizza was here. He hurriedly slipped on his sweatpants before rushing out to the common area as Yong was setting down the pizza. Seeing that Liah's door was still closed, he walked over, tapping on it lightly.

"Y-y-yes?" she whispered.

"It's me," Seonghun said.

There was a beat of silence before she opened her door. He walked in, shutting the door for privacy. Taking a moment, he glanced around. She had no pictures of friends or family up, there was some art he assumed she'd drawn. The lights were all out except for twinkling star string lights. "Are you okay?" he asked seriously. Seong just wanted her to be comfortable.

"They seem very nice, Seonghun. I just can't trust it." She sat on her bed, wrapping her hands around her knees.

"Maybe if you talk about it, it would help?" he asked.

She shook her head rapidly. "That's a fast way to end the evening with me hyperventilating."

He looked at her. "You still have the daisy in your hair."

"It's the first flower anyone has ever given me. I'll be keeping it."

Seonghun's ears turned red. "Like I said before, I won't force you to do anything. But come out, maybe have a slice of pizza. If it gets to be too much, you walk back in your room with no questions asked." He looked at her. Liah had changed into sweatpants too but still had his sweatshirt on. She looked pretty. He wanted to let her know.

He wanted to kiss her.

Both of those things were a bad idea.

Instead, he held out his hand. Maliah slowly reached out, grabbing hold tightly. Pulling her to her feet, she stumbled a bit but Seonghun caught her. "I-uh. I'm sorry." Seonghun had his hands on her hips as he tried to steady her.

"It's fine, you aren't going to hurt me." When she said it, it sounded like she was trying to reassure herself.

"Liah..."

"Maybe someday, Seonghun. But not today, please."

Saying nothing, he removed his hands from her waist, opening the door.

As they walked out, their roommates were pretending not to have been watching the door. Everyone sat on the couches surrounding the TV. Yongjoon had put on an old movie called *Mystery Men*.

Before serving himself, Seonghun put two slices of pineapple and ham pizza on a plate, handing it to Maliah without thinking. It was quiet as everyone ate. To Seonghun the movie was ridiculous in the best way.

Finally Minjun piped up. "If you could have a pretty much useless super power, what would it be?"

Yongjoon responded instantly, "The ability to pull the exact card out of my wallet no matter what."

"If I fall I always land on my feet," Minjun said.

"W-w-whenever I d-d-d-d-" She started hitting herself on the leg; Seonghun quickly grabbed her hand. She took a deep breath, "Whenever I drop something, I-I-I still manage to catch it before it hits the floor," she whispered.

"Teeth are protected from getting stuff lodged in between them," Seonghun offered. He was eating pizza with one hand, refusing to let go of Liah's. They all continued watching the movie when Seonghun felt Liah's grip loosen from his. He glanced over to see she had fallen asleep.

"Liah. Liah, why don't you go to bed? You had kind of a long day." He shook her gently. She opened her eyes, staring directly at him through crooked glasses.

"I'm sorry, I'm not usually around people much, except at work. It's kind of exhausting." She stretched as she stood. "Thank you for dinner. Do I owe you anything?"

Minjun shook his head. "We take turns. It's always nice to find someone who will eat the same thing as me." She smiled shyly before shuffling to the bathroom.

Yongjoon looked at Seong. He was staring at the bathroom door. "You like her," he whispered.

Seonghun looked at him startled. "She's very nice, I like spending time with her, yes."

"You know good and well what I mean, Seong."

"Oh. Um. Well." Seonghun immediately turned red.

"There's nothing wrong with that, you two seemed to have clicked. But I think you've chosen a difficult path."

Minjun stared as Seonghun continued to get redder. "I could probably fry an egg with the heat from your cheeks."

Just then, the bathroom door opened. Maliah appeared. She looked back one last time, waving before going into her room.

Min stood up. "Can I talk to you for a bit?" he asked Seong.

Yongjoon pulled out the game controller before queuing up Mario Kart.

Seonghun walked into his room with Minjun.

After his best friend made himself comfortable, Min said one word: "Spill."

So Seonghun told him everything. About sitting outside her door talking, passing notes, The Challenge, and daisies.

"Do you know why she's so skittish?"

Seonghun waggled his hand. "Something bad happened to her. Her last roommate had something to do with it. Bad enough that the person should be expelled but only got a restraining order. She won't go into it though."

"Is that why she's terrified of us?"

Seonghun nodded.

"So, we show her we aren't the same. How do we do that?" Minjun asked.

"I don't honestly know," Seong admitted.

"Whatever it is that you're doing, I think it is working. She trusts you to an extent." Minjun looked at the door. "I know you like her, I see the way you look at her; how you grab her hand when she stutters. For both of your sakes, I would take it slow."

Seonghun arched his brow. "When have you ever known me to move quickly with anything?"

Minjun laughed. "This is true. Maybe you'll be good for each other." He patted Seonghun's leg as he got up.

"Min." His dearest friend turned to look at him. "I don't know where to go from here," Seonghun admitted.

Minjun stared at him as he thought. "You two came together because you took a step; you found a level to reason with her. Don't change it up because you're starting to have different feelings. Let her take steps toward you. Just keep being yourself."

"Thank you."

Minjun gave him an encouraging smile before walking out of the room. He silently shut the door behind him, giving Seong some much needed privacy. He sighed, pulling a sheet of writing paper from his desk.

Liah,

I hope today wasn't too taxing on you. I had fun getting to know you. I know we don't know each other very well, and it's hard to trust people, but know that I always try to be honest no matter what. I'm going to ask the same from you as well.

Did you enjoy hanging out with us? Sometimes my friends go to parties, but I rarely attend. A bunch of drunk obnoxious people aren't really my thing. We do go out bowling, or we may go to a bar. All three of us are twenty-one. You're always welcome to join us. Except for the bar I guess since you're only twenty. When do you turn twenty-one?

Seonghun chewed on his pen for a bit as he hesitated to put his next words down.

You made mention of never being intimate with someone before. I don't mean to pry, but does that mean, you've never had friends? When I think of intimacy, I don't just think of sex.

His ears burned as he wrote the word sex.

It could be an arm slung around a friend or horsing around. Little things, I guess. Some days I just need a hug. I get overwhelmed. I know that Min would hug me, no questions asked. Same for him. He's exuberant, but he's also super sensitive. I guess that's why all three of us get along. We don't really have boundaries between us.
I think I'll end this here. I spend most of my Sundays studying. Sometimes I go out to the greenhouse. Not this week though, so I'll be in my room most of the day. You're welcome to stop in. I also forgot to thank you for the peony seeds. Thank you very much. I'm not sure if I can take them back with me, but I will surely try to figure out a way. Have a good night.
S

He sealed it in an envelope, returning to the common area. Yongjoon was still playing video games. He watched curiously as Seonghun taped the note to her door. Seong sat by him, grabbing a controller. "Where's Min?" Seonghun asked, as he selected his driver.

"Ashley sent him a picture; he took off as if the hounds of hell were at his heels." Yongjoon snickered.

"Did you see what it was?"

"No, and I didn't really want to," Yongjoon admitted.

Seonghun nodded his agreement.

"So, she seems really nice."

"She is."

"What are you going to do?"

"I'm going to keep going as we are. She needs a friend more than she needs anything else really." He threw a shell at Yongjoon's car, tripping him up, making it easier for Seonghun to take the lead. Winning two games back to back, Seonghun tossed his controller on the table. "It's too soon to say anything of what I want. But I like spending time with her. I like the way her mind works, how she processes things. We're friendly. It's good."

Yongjoon nodded. "Sounds decent." He patted Seonghun on the back as he stood up. "I'm headed to bed. Are you planning on working out tomorrow?"

"Yes, but I need to get some studying done. Want to go in the evening before dinner?" After an agreed upon plan they both retired to their rooms for the night. Despite what he said to Yong, as Seonghun closed his eyes, he wondered what her mouth would feel like under his

CHAPTER 9

"Seonghun?"

He moaned, rolling over while covering his head with his blanket.

"Seonghun, p-p-p-please, c-c-c-c-can you w-wu-wake up?"

Seonghun turned back over, opening one eye partially. He saw a very blurry outline of a short person. "Yeah?"

"I-I-I-I'm s-s-s-s-s-" There was a pause. "I a-a-a-a-a-am s-s-s-s-s-s-"

Seonghun blindly grabbed for her hand. "What's wrong, Liah?" His voice was raspy from sleep.

"Nightmare," she said simply.

"Mmm." Scooting over as far as the tiny twin bed would let him, he pulled back the cover. "Get in."

She hesitated.

"I won't hurt you, but I typically sleep late. I'm not getting up any time soon. Get in."

She slowly climbed in the bed with him. He threw the blanket over both of them before dozing off again almost instantly.

THE SCENT that Seonghun now knew as nectarine and honey blossom invaded his senses, even in his sleep. "Oh god," he moaned out loud, trying to shift. He felt his arms around something.

Someone.

Opening one eye, he remembered. Early in the morning, Liah. Looking down, she was pressed into his chest. His bare chest. All the blood in his head was slowly draining to his, well, other head. They were about to have a serious problem. "Liah," he whispered.

Her eyes opened instantly and she gasped when she realized how they were situated. Quickly scooting away, she would have fallen off the bed had he not grabbed her arm, yanking her back from the edge of the bed.

"S-s-s-"

"You're okay, Liah. Remember? You had a nightmare; I told you to get in. No apologies needed at all."

"Yeah, okay. Okay." He sensed she was calming down. He let go of her so she could leave the bed.

"Thank you for letting me stay."

"You're welcome. Do you want to talk about it?"

She shook her head no.

"Sometimes it helps."

"I know, but I-I-I have a therapist for that. No offense or any-t-thing."

"I'm here if you want to talk."

She nodded as she walked out of his room.

He flopped back into his pillow, sighing. She felt so tiny wrapped around him. It had been a long time since anyone was wrapped around him. Come to think of it, he wasn't really ever wrapped around his last girl-friend. The moments they had were stolen. Shaking off the cobwebs of the past, Seonghun walked to the common area. He saw Liah's door shut. He hoped she was feeling okay. Once he got into the bathroom, he turned on the shower immediately before he squinted in the mirror. He wondered if Yong would take him to get his glasses fixed. His contacts were so uncom-fortable. Seong sent him a text before brushing his teeth. He rushed through his shower as he'd lost track of time. As Seong dressed, his phone beeped. Yongjoon would take him before they worked out, so he could get his glasses fixed. Stepping out of the bathroom, he wondered if Minjun had even come home at all. Seonghun sent him a text asking as he dropped his caddy back into his room. Smiling brightly at the note that was taped to his door, Seong grabbed it before walking into the kitchen. He pulled a bowl out of the cabinet while searching for the box of instant oatmeal packets he bought a while ago. Starting the electric kettle, he dumped four packets of the oatmeal into his bowl. Waiting for the kettle to cut off, he opened the note.

Seonghun,

You're quite welcome for the seeds. When you talked about the peony bush, I had to search to see what it was. It is a beautiful plant. The article I read says that the blooms get so heavy that they can droop, making the petals scatter to the ground. They are fragile.

You and your friends are really nice. I can see how things can get silly between the three of you very easily. You all seem very balanced with no one being left out. You mentioned that you guys go bowling. Have you ever gone roller skating? Sometimes I go to do a few laps when I have time.

I wanted to thank you for your words on intimacy. I don't frequently have nightmares, but when I do, they are truly bad. Normally I tough them out while sitting in my room. I just don't sleep, instead I cry, or draw, but your note gave me the courage to ask for help. My therapist will be pleased when I tell her.

I'm sure as a baby I was hugged, or held, or loved on, but all I remember from childhood to my 18th birthday is pain. I'll leave that there. I was the only black girl in a private school. It was very obvious I was on scholarship. I didn't vacation anywhere while working an insane number of hours. If I wasn't at school or studying, I was working, sometimes under the table so that I was able to earn more. I scraped together every single dime I had to buy my car. The kids at my school didn't know how to interact with me, so they didn't. A few of their parents tried to make me a charity case, but that didn't go over well with me. College was supposed to be a new start. It was supposed to be a fresh chance to be my own person, to make friends. That didn't turn out so great.

Seonghun stopped reading to pour water in his oatmeal and add a small pat of butter. Picking up his bowl, he tucked the note under his arm as he walked into his room. Getting comfortable in his desk chair, he continued reading.

So now, I'm back to where I was in high school. Only it's worse. I have a medication regimen because I couldn't deal with my reality anymore. I have a stutter that my therapist says is trauma based; it may go away if I process everything. But how do I process anything that happened? How do I deal with the fact that my life is nothing but a shitty hand of cards? I don't know. Maybe I wasn't meant to deal.

So, that was heavy. To lighten it up a bit, I turn twenty one in a couple of months. December 6th. I won't be celebrating by drinking. It's advised I don't drink on the medications I'm taking. I don't actually celebrate my birthday. No one usually acknowledges it. I'll probably work, depending on what day it is, maybe treat myself to some takeout Mexican food.

Thank you again for being there. Sorry to have interrupted your sleep.

-I,

This was a lot of knowledge about her. Seonghun ate his oatmeal as he thought. He couldn't imagine not being able to go to his father if he was having a problem, or his mom if he just wanted to talk. Who did Liah talk to? How did she vent? What did someone do when they didn't have anyone to talk to? He picked up his phone, calling Minjun.

"You know, going slow with someone isn't sleeping with them after your first date," Minjun said in lieu of hello.

"I didn't— we didn't. It wasn't a date," Seonghun stammered.

Minjun laughed. "I know nothing happened. What do you need?"

"If you didn't have me or Yongjoon to talk to, who would you talk to?"

"I'm a pretty friendly guy. I have friends, they just aren't close friends like you two. I'd be forced to make close friends I think. Why?"

"Who does someone talk to if they don't have friends?" Seonghun ignored his question.

"Maybe themselves?" Minjun suggested.

Seonghun was quiet for a bit. "Where are you at?"

"Yongjoon and I are kicking around a soccer ball, then we're headed to The Den to get snacks. We wanted to get out of the house in case something did happen with you two."

Seonghun laughed. "Yeah, that's not likely."

"A week ago, you thought our roommate was a ghost. Never say never."

Seonghun pulled the phone from his ear as Minjun yelled something at Yongjoon.

"Do you want us to bring you lunch?"

"Yes. Use my card, bring something for her as well please."

"Got it, talk to you soon." Minjun hung up.

Seonghun rinsed his bowl before returning to his room. Laying on his bed with his textbook for bio, he started taking notes. After about thirty minutes, he turned on the little speaker he kept by his bed, playing Bruno Mars softly. He wasn't sure how much time had passed before he heard the door to the suite open. A second later, Minjun burst through Seonghun's room holding styrofoam containers, with Yong following behind. "I figured she'd be in here."

Seonghun shrugged. "I think she's a little embarrassed she came in in the middle of the night." He held out his hand to Minjun for the food.

Min gave him one. "I can give it to her."

"Min." Seonghun had a warning in his voice. "Knock on her door, let her know you have food. If she doesn't respond, set it by her door, letting her know that you did and walk away. Come back in here if you want to."

Minjun walked off. Seonghun heard the knock, listening in. "Maliah? It's Min. I brought you food. Well I mean, Seonghun paid for it, but I got it because I have one of his cards. We each have each other's cards just in case we're out grabbing food. Anyway, he asked me to pick up food for you. I got you both fried chicken salads, because they are really good, plus I don't think he'd eat his vegetables properly if I didn't get him a salad from time to time."

Yongjoon, sitting on Seonghun's bed, started laughing at their long winded friend.

"Hi! Here is your salad. Do you want to come eat on the couch with us?"

"I-uh. W-where's Seonghun?"

"I'm in my room, Liah. I'll be out in a second," he called out.

"O-o-o-o-Alright."

He closed his book, sat up, and stretched. Turning off the music, he grabbed his container of food, walking to the living room with Yongjoon.

"I honestly think this is the most I've eaten in a long time," Liah admitted as she picked through the salad. "I usually only eat one meal a day."

"Why?" Yongjoon asked as he opened his container that contained a burger. Seonghun looked longingly at it.

"When was the last time you ate something green?" Minjun stared at him.

Seong turned red.

"That's what I thought, eat the salad." He turned to Maliah. "Sorry."

"It's okay," she said quietly. "Art, schoolwork, work, it all takes up a lot of my time. When I'm working at the gallery I'll grab a sandwich from the diner. By the time I get back here, I'm tired; all I want to do is crash."

"You two are the worst," Minjun pointed at both of them. "If it isn't fried, he doesn't want it."

"Hey! I ate a bowl of oatmeal today," Seonghun protested.

"That's because you didn't want to leave; it was readily available."

"It still counts." Seonghun pouted.

"I just have a l-l-lot on my p-p-p-plate. I have a f-f-f-f-" She sighed. "I have a big course load, two p-p-p-p-part time jobs, and my o-o-o-" She closed her mouth for a moment. "I have a lot. E-e-e-eating is the last thing on m-m-mu-my mind."

Seonghun wanted to grab her hand desperately, but he didn't know if she wanted to even be touched.

"So is your major art?" Yongjoon prodded gently.

She looked at Seonghun strangely. He understood. "Your life is your own. I wouldn't talk about anything we've spoken about unless you told me I could." He did tell Min she had roommate issues, but didn't really say much about it.

She nodded gratefully. "No, psychology. I plan to use art t-t-therapy in my practice."

"What is that?" Minjun asked.

Maliah put her fork down. "S-s-s-somet-t-t-times it's hard for people to talk. Some people find it e-e-e-e-"

As Seonghun saw her ball up her fist, he knew what was coming. Putting his fork down, he casually slid his hand into hers.

She took a breath, trying again, "Some people find it e-e-e-easier to do an activity t-t-t-to talk about their p-p-pain. Maybe showing it on canvas or through pottery rather than speaking aloud." She sighed. "It's the same with music. Losing yourself in music helps."

"Is that why you dance in the common area?" Minjun questioned.

"Ah… yes? It helps. A lot."

She seemed calm, so he let go of her hand before going back to his salad. He didn't notice the glance she gave when he pulled away. Minjun changed the subject to a tv show, allowing Maliah to eat quietly. Seong kept his ear to the conversation while keeping an eye on Maliah. She was still wearing his sweatshirt.

Liah glanced over at him. "Thank you for lunch."

"You're welcome."

"I have to go study now."

"Thank you for sitting with us for a bit."

Nodding, she stood up. She gave a slight wave to the two other men, threw her trash away, before retreating into her room.

He looked over at Minjun. "How are things with you and Ashley?"

Minjun shrugged. "It's not serious. I'm kind of bored."

Yongjoon smirked. "Even with the thing with her tongue?"

"Kind of. I mean, she kind of leans on that while not doing much else." Minjun started gathering trash. "I don't mind putting in work, but it felt like I was chasing both of our orgasms. You have to help a little."

Seonghun turned red.

Yongjoon noticed. "Why are you so red?"

"In all the time we've been friends, haven't you ever noticed that he doesn't talk about sex? Even when he was having it, he was pretty tight lipped. Only reason I found out he was actually doing it was that I happened to be in the same store as him when he was trying to buy condoms," Minjun said as he threw away his garbage.

Seong was progressively going toward a purple shade on his ears. "I'm going to go study."

Yongjoon stared at him in amazement. "Why are you so embarrassed?"

He stood up. "It's personal to me. If I make that connection with someone it's—" He bit his lip as he tried to put into words how he felt. "I didn't love her. But I felt something for her that was intense. I don't like sharing. It also feels like a smear to her memory to talk about her that way."

"Didn't she try to get you to propose by lying to your parents?" Minjun pointed out.

"I just want to honor the positive memories. If it happens again, I'll probably be the same way," Seong said quietly.

"What about the others?" Yongjoon asked.

"What others?"

"The other people you've slept with," Yongjoon said slowly.

Seonghun shook his head. "I've been here for four years; you've literally seen me with one person briefly. There haven't been any others. I don't take sex lightly."

Minjun nodded. "They were together for years before they even broached the topic." He started laughing. "She basically had to beat him over the head for him to realize she was interested in him."

"How did you not realize that she was attracted to you?" Yongjoon asked.

Seonghun shrugged.

"He doesn't realize how attractive he is," Minjun said. "He has girls staring at him constantly, even his lab partner. He doesn't see it or understand when they approach him."

"I'm a nerd who talks about plants all the time."

"You're a tall nerd with broad shoulders, muscles, and a nice smile," he pointed out.

"What do my shoulders have to do with anything?" Seonghun asked, confused.

"What he is saying is girls find you attractive, they want to get to know you, but you tend to push everyone away."

"Eh." Seonghun shrugged. "I don't feel anything. I like being by myself.

I like being with you guys. I like..." He paused for a minute, red creeping back into his ears.

"I think she likes being with you as well," Yongjoon stated quietly at the unspoken words. "She looked a little put out when you took your hand away."

Seonghun quickly changed the subject. "I'm going to study for a couple more hours. Would you be ready to go then?"

Yongjoon nodded while looking at Minjun. "We're going to go get his glasses repaired before going to the gym. Did you want to come?"

"Nah. Don't get anything to eat though, I'll cook." With that Minjun went into his room.

Seonghun looked at Yong. "If it's bad, I have oatmeal."

Yongjoon laughed as he turned on the tv.

CHAPTER 10

Liah,

Your note was heavy, but informative. Thank you for sharing a bit of your life. I think human touch is important. Maybe not to everyone, but to me it is. I've always been able to go to my mom or my dad for a hug or kind words or even a head scratch when I've had a bad day. I'm sorry that you don't have that.

It was pointed out to me earlier that I tend to grab your hand. I'm sorry if it makes you feel uncomfortable. If you want I can stop. You start to hit yourself. I don't know if you know it or not. But I don't want you to hurt yourself, so I grab your hand I guess. If it bothers you please let me know, I'll stop. I don't want to make you feel bad.

You mentioned a therapist. How often do you see them? Does it help? I was thinking about how you don't really have anyone to talk to, but you do in your therapist. I hope it isn't presumptuous, but you're always welcome to talk to me as well. My door is always open.

I have never roller skated. It sounds fun. Would you like to go with us sometime? Actually, there was something else I wanted to ask you. This past summer we discovered a drive-in theater in a town about 40 minutes away. Next weekend is the last show for the year until spring. Do you want to go with us?

S eonghun held his breath as he wrote the question. He was sure she would say no, but it didn't hurt to try.

We always celebrate our birthdays with cake at home. While we're on campus, sometimes it's cupcakes, but always some sort of treat. Last birthday, Minjun wanted to light candles for some reason, so he made us sit in the bathroom with the shower on while Yong blew them out, to make sure we didn't set off any smoke alarms. Do you like cake?
I actually have to get some studying done before I go to get my glasses repaired. I will talk to you soon.
-S

Sealing the note, he wished he had something to put in the envelope. She always drew him such pretty pictures. He had no artistic talent whatsoever. Sighing, he set the note aside as he worked on his assignments.

Two hours later, Yong knocked on his door, indicating he was ready to go. Seong hurried to get dressed. Throwing his requisite hat on, he grabbed everything, the note included, before walking out of his room. He was surprised to see a note already on her door. He turned to look at Minjun who was watching tv.

"What are you doing?"

"You said she responds better to notes, so I left one," Minjun said, looking at him.

"Yeah but I—" Seonghun paused. He didn't know why this bugged him so much. He quietly taped his note to her door before walking out with Yongjoon.

"You know he's curious about her right?" Yongjoon said as they walked to his car. He made a deal with some people who lived in an apartment close to campus. They didn't have a car, so they let him park his in their space. In exchange he took them to the grocery store once a week.

"I know. But you know how exuberant he gets."

"He'll calm it down for her." Yongjoon unlocked the car doors. Driving off campus, they went to the little glasses shop near the mall. Seonghun handed over his glasses to the salesperson. He then proceeded to try on silly frames with Yong until his name was called thirty minutes later.

"Mr. Yu, I was able to fix your glasses, but I need to show you something." The salesperson flipped them over, pointing at the screw. "I've added a bolt, but it's a temporary measure. The rings that the screw fits through are stripped. You're going to need new glasses."

He took the silver frames Yong had given him off his face, handing them to the clerk. "I'd like these please." They were more sophisticated than his typical round frames. The glasses came to a sharpish point on each side.

It took a bit longer than they had anticipated because the optometrist had to take facial measurements, making sure Seong got the right lenses. His prescription was big enough that he had to get the thinnest lens possible so his eyes didn't look weird. Finally finished, they made their way to the gym. While running on the treadmill, Seonghun told Yongjoon he invited Maliah to go to the drive-in with them next weekend.

"What did she say?"

"I don't know yet. I hope there'll be an answer when I get back." He upped his speed on the treadmill before he asked the next question. "Do you know what Minjun wrote to her?"

"Yes."

He wasn't expecting that; he nearly stumbled on the treadmill. He caught himself, continuing his run. "Well, are you going to tell me?"

"He asked her to help him cook dinner. Min's trying to get to know her. He said that she's important to you."

"We're just friends, sort of."

Yong shrugged. "I'm just repeating what I was told." It was silent for a while as they both were running at a high speed. "Are you ready to face Casey in class tomorrow?"

Seong moaned. "No. But my professor is switching us around. He promised to be discreet about the reason."

"Are you prepared when she ambushes you?"

"I was thinking of just running when class ends."

Yong roared with laughter, startling the people around them. "We're going to see you running across campus."

Seonghun blushed as he set the treadmill to cooldown. "I don't understand. I told her I wasn't interested in anything beyond being lab partners. She has to know this isn't okay."

"Man, she sounded kind of unhinged during the dinner. Like you were hers and you just didn't know it yet."

"Well, I'm not, I won't be." Turning off the treadmill he began stretching; Almost immediately, he felt something pull hard. "Shit!"

His friend looked over at him, concerned.

"My back." Seong twisted his torso slightly. The pain caused him to nearly buckle at the knees.

Yongjoon hopped off the treadmill. "It's okay. Let's get you back to the dorm." Walking next to him, they slowly left the gym. Yong got him safely seated into the car. Driving back to the dorm was agony. He felt every single bump in the road. When the car stopped, he nearly teared up because he knew the most painful part was yet to come.

"I'm going to drop you off here while I park the car. As slow as you're moving, I'll be back before you hit the door." Yongjoon put on his emergency blinkers, getting out of the car to help him stand upright.

Seong bit back a scream at the pain as Yong helped him. He had pulled muscles at the gym before, but this was bad. He couldn't afford to miss classes tomorrow, but he didn't know what to do. Hunched over, he started the slow shuffle toward the dorm.

Yong got back in the car, speeding off. After parking he ran back to the dorm to see that he'd had made it to the doorway.

"Alright, you got this. Come on." His friend grabbed him by his waist to support him. They bypassed the stairs, immediately taking the elevator. Arriving on their floor they opened the door to an odd scene. The suite smelled of pasta sauce. Their two roommates were on the couch. Maliah was holding Minjun's hand, very focused on painting his nails.

"Are you painting his nails?" Yong stared at their roommates, confused.

"Look! She did the other one!" Min started waving around a hand with bright orange fingernails before taking a good look at his two friends. "Did you hurt your back again?"

Seonghun looked at Minjun. He knew his friend saw he was struggling not to crumble. "Okay, Let's get you laid down."

"Min, I need a shower. I've been running for an hour."

"We can do this. Yong, get him to the bathroom. He can mostly take it from there. I'll help him in a second. I need to get him some clothes."

Maliah looked at Seong. "I don't know what to do."

Min looked at her. "Can you give us about twenty minutes, then start to make him a plate?" He looked at the two men proudly. "She taught me how to make spaghetti!"

Yong shuffled Seonghun off to the bathroom. As he gently seated him on the toilet, Yongjoon looked at him. "You got it from here?"

"Yeah. Min will help me get into the shower." He gently started toeing off his shoes. He tried to lift his arms to take his shirt off and immediately put his hands down. "Shit! How did I seize this quickly?"

His roommate stripped him of his shirt carefully, "You know you have to stretch really well."

"I do farm work all the time. I have never had this issue until I stopped."

"You aren't in Korea anymore," he said. "You haven't worked a farm in a few years. You're using different muscles. Farm work doesn't give you that stomach." He tapped the ridges of Seong's six pack.

"You're right."

"I'm going to go eat. If you or Min need me, call."

"Thank you."

Yongjoon nodded before going off in search of food. Seong shifted uncomfortably on the toilet. Minjun came in with clothes.

"You ready?"

Seonghun nodded. Together they got him up. He was able to get his own pants down. The two of them had been naked countless times as little boys, so there was no embarrassment. Slowly getting him in the shower, Minjun closed the curtain, sitting on the closed toilet.

Seong washed his body for a minute before he asked the question he knew Min was waiting on, "Why was Liah painting your nails?"

"Well, after I convinced her to go grocery shopping with me for dinner, I noticed she kept hitting her thighs or scrubbing her hands on her legs, so I was trying to find something to keep her hands busy. I didn't think you'd be pleased at the way I normally keep girls' hands busy, nor do I think she would go for that."

Seong's bar of soap went skittering out of the shower.

"Min did you…"

"I didn't do anything to her, Seonghun. It was a joke, calm down." He stuck his hand in the shower curtain to give back the soap. "I noticed her toes were painted. I asked if she went to a shop to get them done. She said she does them herself, so I asked her to paint my fingers."

"That was nice of you." Seonghun turned the shower off. Minjun handed him a towel to dry off.

"She's a nice girl. Skittish, but very nice. Also she cooks really well."

"Min, I need help with my pants, I can't bend well."

Minjun opened the shower curtain, bending over to help Seonghun with his boxer briefs and sweatpants.

"Where's my shirt?"

"You don't need one. You're going to lay down, come on."

Minjun grabbed his bathroom toiletries while keeping an arm around him, leading him to his room. Looking around, Seonghun saw that Liah's door was shut; she was nowhere to be found. He cheered up a bit at the note he saw on his door. He reached out to grab it as he passed through the doorway. Slowly getting situated on his stomach, he laid down while looking up at Minjun.

"Thank you."

"You're welcome. I'll be back with a plate and some meds in a bit." When the door shut behind Min, Seong went to open the note when a soft knock sounded. "Come in, Liah." He shoved the note under his pillow.

"H-h-h-h-"

"You're the only one who would knock," he answered for her.

"Minjun s-s-s-said you h-h-h-hurt your back."

"Yeah, I pulled a muscle. It's the third time this has happened. Why are you so nervous to talk to me?" He couldn't see her because she was by the door.

"I b-b-brought you something." She finally walked up so he could see her. Liah pressed a large sticker into his hands.

"What is it?"

"It's a hot pad. You stick it on your parts that a-a-a-are h-h-h-h-hurting; it warms up."

"Thank you. Can you put it on?"

"Oh. I-uh. Let me get Minjun." She moved to walk to the door.

"If you're getting him because you aren't comfortable touching me, that's fine. If you're concerned about my feelings about you touching me, it's okay," he said quietly.

They were both silent for a beat. Then Maliah spoke up. "Where does it hurt?"

"Touch the middle of my lower back with your finger," he said.

She did as he asked.

"Slide your finger to the right just a little bit."

She did as he asked. Seong felt her gently press a slight bulge that wasn't present earlier.

"Right there." His entire back was broken out into goosebumps; he felt faint from her scent.

Maliah, removed her hand to grab the patch. Peeling the backing away, she smoothed it on the area, waiting patiently.

"Oh...ohhhhhhhhhhhh!" Seonghun moaned out loud. "What is this magic!?"

"I keep them for my cycle. They have different shapes for different parts of your body."

"OH MY GODDDDDDDDDDD!" Seonghun shifted slightly as he cried out. Minjun opened the door to see what the commotion was.

"Are you two okay?" Minjun entered cautiously with a plate.

"Min! It's hot. It feels so good!" He began to wriggle in the bed.

"Um. Okay. Well, I brought food, a drink, along with some medication. I'm just going to sit this on your desk."

"Min, wait, how am I supposed to eat?"

Minjun glanced at Maliah. "Can you feed him? He can't really move from his stomach until the meds kick in."

Maliah nodded.

"Make sure he eats his vegetables before that cinnamon roll." With that, Minjun walked out of the door.

"You made cinnamon rolls?" Seonghun asked.

"They aren't homemade, they are from a can, but I always eat them with sp-p-paghetti." She grabbed the pills and the soda which Minjun had thoughtfully put a straw in. "Open your mouth please."

He did as she requested. Seong felt the corners of his mouth turn up as he watched her focus on dropping two ibuprofen in his mouth before giving him a swallow of soda. Setting the can down, she pulled his desk chair closer to the bed in order to feed him.

"Wait," Seonghun said. "You see the little speaker over there? Can you turn it on? There is a switch on top." Slipping his phone out of his pocket he turned a playlist on. When his phone connected to the speaker, 90's R&B played on low.

"You're sick, so we're not going to listen to Minjun right now. But you do have to eat your vegetables." She held up a cinnamon roll; he took the offered bite, savoring the sweetness.

Slowly she fed him. He devoured the spaghetti, even eating all of the green beans. Polishing off the last of the cinnamon roll, he felt comfortable. "Thank you, Liah. I know this is a lot. Especially for someone you just started talking to."

"You let me sleep in your bed after a nightmare, even though you barely know me. This was nothing." She stood up to take the dishes to the kitchen.

"I don't want you to leave," he whispered.

She stopped, staring at him for a long while. Slowly, he met her eyes, hoping she saw that he truly wanted her to stay.

"I'll be right back," she finally said. Walking out of the room, she shut the door softly. As soon as the door closed, he pulled her note from the pillow, opening it. Chuckling, he smiled at the cartoon drawing of Minjun, Yongjoon, and him on the couch, talking.

Seonghun,
The thought of hugging someone is thrilling and scary. Thrilling in the fact
that I think affection sounds nice. Scary in the fact that my family is not affec-
tionate at all. The earliest memory of me trying to hug my mother was her
stiffening and pushing me away. The relationship you have with Minjun and
Yongjoon sounds lovely. The comfort that you get from one another is nice.
It doesn't bother me that you grab my hand. It makes me realize that I'm

becoming rigid. The more rigid I become, the harder it's for me to speak. It reminds me to take a breath and get out of my head. That no one is going to hurt me at that moment.

I see my therapist mostly through video chats, around two times a week. More if it is a really bad week. I told her how you guys caught me dancing and releasing energy. She encouraged me to try and get to know you saying that I can't shut everyone out forever. She would actually like to "meet" you sometime.

Seonghun's door opened; Maliah came back in. He shoved the note back under his pillow as she walked in with her textbooks and a box. "This is not what I actually had in mind," he admitted.

She looked confused. "What did you want?"

"I was hoping you would lay with me and talk."

She opened her mouth, closing it quickly. "I can't lay with you. You're starfished on your bed."

"Starfished?"

"Spread out."

"I can move over." He scooted toward the other end of the bed as far as he could. It left room for her.

"I w-w-w-will make y-y-y-you a d-d-d-deal." She took a breath while flexing her hands. "I need to read a chapter. I will sit by you while I read my book. If I'm okay afterwards, I'll lay with you."

"It sounds good. Would you mind terribly if I read your note while you're here? I haven't had a chance yet."

"It's fine. I'm not embarrassed by anything I wrote. I do like communicating in that way though, it's nice." She grabbed her sociology book before climbing onto the bed next to him. He dug her note out from the pillow, continuing to read.

All of you are welcome to come skating with me at any time. I have my own skates, but they have rentals there. It's one of the things I've done since childhood. I told myself when I was a kid that as soon as I earned my own money, I'd have white skates with pink glitter laces and pom poms. And I do.
The drive-in. It makes me sort of anxious. I haven't really analyzed why. I've

spent time with you before alone. Maybe it is because it is all three of you. I don't know. Can I let you know later in the week?

I'm about to use an expletive. I fucking LOVE cake. LOVE IT. Lemon cake with lemon icing is my favorite. Yellow cake with chocolate icing and rainbow sprinkles is second place. I know the rainbow sprinkles don't really add anything to the flavor, but they make the cake (or cupcake) look cheerful.

There is a knock at my door but you aren't here. I should probably go see who that is.

CHAPTER 11

He chuckled softly as he closed the letter. She looked up from her book questioningly, her glasses crooked as usual. He reached out a hand to straighten them but she flinched away. He dropped his hand immediately.

"Liah, what happened?"

She began to shake her head no.

"You flinch when I go to touch you, you constantly ask if I'm going to hurt you; I suspect the reason you're anxious about the drive in is that you're worried about being in a car defenseless with three people. Something bad happened, I can tell. But for me to not startle you, I have to know what happened so I know how not to scare you."

He didn't think it was possible for her eyes to get bigger, but she kept widening them while looking toward the sky trying to keep tears at bay as she scooted off the bed.

"Liah, please don't leave," he begged. He was terrified that he'd finally run her off.

"I don't know how to do this!" She started crying. "I like talking with you. I like exchanging notes. But talking about everything that happened last year makes it come back like it's still happening. Bringing it up causes nightmares." She was sobbing hysterically at this point. "I know I need to talk about it. My therapist says the more I do the less power it has, but I don't even know where to begin."

"Okay." Seonghun wished he could sit up, but he was basically incapacitated. "Okay, We can sort this out."

Liah was crying so hard she was shaking while slowly backing up toward the door.

"Please don't run away," he pleaded.

She stopped moving backwards and her crying was a little less hysterical; however she was still shaking while looking like she wanted to bolt.

"Come sit back down, please?"

Maliah shook her head before sitting in the desk chair.

It was quiet, with the exception of sniffles. "Let's try this. How long ago was the last incident?" Seonghun asked.

Maliah stared into space for a minute. "Two weeks before the spring semester last year ended. They moved me into this dorm early because I stay on campus taking classes year round anyway."

Seonghun thought about it. Her stuff was here when they arrived. They spent the past three summers at Yong's house. He thought of something else.

"You live in Indianapolis and have a car, why would you stay on campus year round?"

Maliah shook her head again. "I lived in Indianapolis," she corrected. "When I turned eighteen, my parents told me to get out. I live here, in West Lafayette now. I don't really go to Indy."

He was astonished. "Your parents cut you off?"

She shrugged. "I knew it was coming. It was one of those things they always said to me growing up. How they couldn't wait until I was eighteen; I would see that they were actually being gracious to me. How they couldn't wait to see me fall on my fat ass."

"Why did they have kids if they didn't want to care for you?"

"Kid. One. Me. I was an accident. They had a shotgun wedding."

"Grandparents?"

"Both sides are dead," she said matter of factly.

"How is this easier to talk about than what happened last year?" Seong asked.

"I grew up knowing cruelty. I was fucking stupid when I got here. Thought everything was going to be much better so I didn't leave my guard up. What happened was partially my fault for that."

Seonghun shook his head. "You shouldn't have to think people are going to hurt you."

"I didn't and look what happened. I'm kind of falling into the same trap with you three. Quite frankly, I can't afford to. I don't have the mental capacity to block off another attack. I graduate soon, then I'm off for my masters. Hopefully, some place far away from Indiana."

"Where do you want to go?" He had to keep her talking. The more she talked, the less she would be inclined to leave.

"I've applied all over. Hawaii, California, South Carolina, England, even Amsterdam. It all depends on the financial aid package I get. I'm in line to be first in my class in the entire psych program. I just have to see the money portion of it."

Talking about her studies had relaxed her slightly. She'd stopped clenching her hands; she hadn't stuttered at all. "Tell me about your plans after school. I know what you're majoring in and that you want to do art and music therapy. Do you want to open your own practice?"

"I have two dreams. The main one is to open my own practice to focus on children and teens with mental illness." She paused for a minute, focusing on his face. "Have you ever been to camp?"

"No, I can't say that I have." He wondered where she was going with this.

"When I was a little girl, I used to watch all these movies about kids who went to camp and found their forever friends, nice people to hang around, adults who encouraged their hijinks. I always wanted that. I thought I would find a friend. My dream would be to open a camp for kids with psychological disorders. Hiking, swimming, boating, art, and music, tons of therapy. I'd want them to see that they aren't alone."

"That sounds admirable."

"It's a long way off, if it does happen."

They were silent for a while when Maliah stood up. "I brought you my box of heating pads. They wear out in about two hours. You'll probably need someone to put on a new one. I'm sure Minjun can do that for you if you text him."

"You could stay," he said quietly. "Stay and put it on."

"I don't think that is a good idea. Good night, Seonghun." She gathered up her books. As she left the room, she closed his door softly behind her.

Seonghun buried his face down into his pillow, screaming his frustration. Grabbing his phone, he sent Minjun a text.

CHAPTER 12

"So you upset her, made her cry, calmed her down, then she left?" Minjun sat on the bed next to Seonghun.

"Yeah. I keep pushing. Maybe I should stop pushing?" Minjun shrugged.

"I like hanging out with her, Min. She's driven, focused, smart." He put his face down in his pillow.

"She knows how to cook. She doesn't measure anything, just throws whatever she needs into a pot," Minjun added. There was a tap at the door. Min yelled for whoever to come in.

Maliah cracked the door. "I was making sure you called Minjun to change the patch on your back. It's handled, so I'm going to bed." She went to close the door.

"Wait," Seonghun called out. "I want to apologize. You've told me twice now that you don't feel comfortable talking about it. I'm sorry for trying to force the issue. I won't bring it up anymore."

Liah nodded. Without any other word, she walked out of the door.

Seonghun and Minjun looked at each other.

"I think you're back at square one," Min said.

Seonghun sighed, burying his face in the pillow again.

Minjun patted his shoulder as he stood up, slowly taking the patch off his back. "How does your back feel?"

Seonghun shifted around. "I kind of feel like I could walk around."

"I don't recommend it. Get some sleep and see how you feel in the morning." He applied the new patch; within moments Seonghun felt the heat blossom on his back.

"OH GOD YES!" he cried out.

Minjun snickered. "If you're that loud during sex, it's a wonder you never got caught."

"I don't think sex ever felt this good." Seonghun moaned as he took up the majority of his bed again.

"That's the true pity. I'm headed to bed, text me if you need me." He threw a blanket over Seonghun before leaving.

Seonghun buried himself in his blanket, trying to get some sleep. His dreams consisted of people running in different directions, a really weird tug of war, and a slice of lemon cake chasing him. When his alarm went off in the morning, he didn't feel rested at all. Gingerly he slid out of bed, slowly standing to his full height. Though he still felt the twinges of a pulled muscle, it was nowhere near the pain he would normally be in. Quickly getting dressed, he threw his books in his backpack, along with some of the stationery.

Walking out of his room, he saw Liah had two notes on her door, but the door was still shut. Seong left the suite, hoping to catch breakfast before his first class. As he sat in the dining hall, he realized he didn't know what to write to Maliah. He pulled up a search on friendship poetry. Reading while eating his breakfast burrito, he happened upon something that made him smile. He saved it because he needed to get going.

Seonghun's classes passed easily until his lab. Trudging into the lab Casey was sitting there, eyes on the door. When she saw him, she smiled brightly. Gently sitting on the stool, minding his back, he nodded, taking out his books to avoid eye contact.

"Did you have a good weekend?" Casey asked.

"Yep."

"That's good." She saw that he didn't seem keen on speaking, thankfully going silent. The teacher called the class to attention by announcing that they would be getting new lab partners.

"I think changing up partners fosters an environment where you learn to work with different personalities."

Casey snapped her pencil.

Seonghun glanced at her. "Are you okay?"

Ignoring him, she raised her hand. "What if we're okay with the lab partners we have now?"

"That is great you have learned to communicate with one person. We want to foster that growth with other people." The professor caught Seonghun's eye. He nodded slightly as he kept talking.

"Why did he nod at you?" Casey demanded.

"Excuse me?"

"Did you ask to switch? What did I do to you!?" Her voice was getting hysterical.

"Uh…"

"Miss, if you could calm down so we can hand out new assignments."

"WE WORK SO GOOD TOGETHER! IF YOU WOULD JUST OPEN YOUR EYES!" Casey grabbed his wrist with an iron grip.

"What in the— get off of me!" He tried prying her hand from his wrist, but she had the strength of someone who had just snapped. Her fingernails were digging into his flesh. Seong felt the sting of a minor cut.

The professor tried to separate them as she was shrieking. He finally yanked away from her, tweaking his back again. "Oh god!" He nearly went down but caught himself on the table. A tall slender man with dark long hair walked up.

"Are you okay?"

"My back. I hurt my back before I came in, it was fine, but when I yanked out of her grip I twisted it again. I need my phone." While all this was going on Casey was screaming, making a scene while the professor was trying to calm her down.

"Do you live on campus? I have a car, I can drop you where you need to go," the young man said quietly.

"Please. It will save me from having to call my friend. He's on the other side of campus."

"Come on. Let's get you out of here." Gently he grabbed Seonghun's arm. Together they shuffled out of the building.

"I'm Seonghun by the way."

"Shiwon. What happened back there?"

"She has been showing interest in me outside of the lab. I let her know on Friday that I wasn't interested. My roommate has been ah, hanging out with her friend. She went to dinner with them one evening and espoused some ideas about the relationship we're meant to have. I don't think she is alright."

"No, she doesn't seem alright at all," Shiwon snorted. Slowly they made their way to his car.

Seonghun directed him to his dorm; they arrived shortly at the back parking lot. "Do you need help getting upstairs?" Shiwon glanced at him.

"No, I got it." Seonghun got out of the car, shuffling toward the door.

"Nah, you don't." Turning off the car, Shiwon hopped out to lend a hand.

"You're going to get a ticket." Seonghun said through clenched teeth.

"Let me worry about that." Steadying Seonghun on his arm, they made the slow journey to his room. Once they got to his door, they both heard music playing.

"I need to knock. One of my roommates, she's a little skittish, I don't want to scare her."

Shiwon knocked loudly. The music cut off; a minute later Maliah answered the door wearing Seonghun's sweatshirt.

She glanced at Shiwon first who was just staring at her before looking at Seonghun. It was then Seong realized, for one of the first times in his life, someone was taller than him. Shiwon had about two centimeters on him. Holy shit. He looked down at Liah who seemed like she wanted to run for the hills.

No one said anything until Shiwon spoke up. "You said your roommate was a girl, you didn't say she was hot."

"Um," Maliah gave Seong a once over. "You went to class with your back like that?"

"I was feeling better. I walked out of here. Then, well..."

"He was attacked by some girl in our lab," Shiwon said. "Where is your room?"

Seonghun began shuffling toward his room. "Thank you for all of your help, Shiwon. I appreciate it."

"No problem, that was hard to watch. Do you have it from here?"

Seonghun nodded. Shiwon let him go. He pivoted toward Maliah who was heading to her room. "Hey, what's your name?"

Maliah turned to see him addressing her. "Maliah," she said quietly.

"You want to go get a coffee?"

Seonghun stopped in his tracks.

"No thank you," she walked into her room, closing the door quickly.

"She's really shy," Seonghun explained.

"She's cute," was all Shiwon would say. He looked over at Seonghun. "Oh. I didn't realize you had a thing for her."

"I don't. She's my friend. Sort of? I've pissed her off." Seonghun shuffled toward his bedroom.

"The next time someone flirts with her or asks her out, have them take a picture of your face. That is not a 'she's just my friend' look." Shiwon walked toward the front door. "Take care of yourself, I'll see you on Wednesday."

"Thanks again, Shiwon. Maybe you'll end up as my lab partner."

Shiwon smiled, walking out of the suite. Shuffling the rest of the way to his room, Seonghun dropped his backpack before using his leg to close his door. Easing gently down on his bed he sighed as he prepared to lay down. Before he could get fully comfortable, there was a tap at his door.

"Come in."

Maliah opened the door. "Do you need a patch put on your back?"

He nodded. "Can you help me get my shirt off?"

"I could just lift it and apply the patch."

"I don't really like anything touching me when I'm like this. I want my pants off too, but I'll wait until Minjun gets home to help with those."

Maliah was silent for a minute. "Do you have on underwear?"

Seonghun looked startled. "What?"

"As long as you have on underwear, I'll get you undressed," she said quietly.

"O-okay."

Stepping in front of him she looked at him as if he were a puzzle. "Lift your arms as high as you can without it hurting."

Seonghun lifted his arms so that his elbows were at chest level. She lifted his shirt and pulled his arms through without him having to do anything. Deftly folding it, she put it on his desk.

"How did you learn how to fold that fast?"

"My first job was at a clothing store. You fold a lot at the end of the night." Her eyes were focused on his nightstand.

"Are you okay?" he asked her, concerned that she wouldn't even look at him.

"I'm a virgin. I'm not dead," was her reply. Shaking her head, she focused on his face. "Is it easier for you to stand up, or for you to lift your hips off the bed?"

Seonghun was still puzzled over her phrase so it took him a moment to respond. "Um, hip lift."

Stepping forward Liah stood in between his legs. "Unbutton your pants please."

Seonghun was a mess. He didn't know whether to look at her, the wall, or the ceiling. He should probably wait for Minjun, but he wouldn't be home for hours and he wanted out of these pants. Looking at his lap, he unbuttoned the four buttons.

"Ready?" Maliah looked at him.

He nodded.

"Lift."

Bracing his weight on his arms, he lifted his lower body. "Please hurry, it really hurts." Seong panted with the effort. She slipped her hands to the waist of his pants and began tugging them down. He felt himself getting hard. "Fuck," he uttered the word, exasperated.

"Are you hurting wors-oh." She saw what the problem was. Taking a deep breath she continued pulling them down. "It's a natural reaction, you know? You have a girl pulling down your pants. It's fine. You aren't going to do anything stupid, right?" He was silent as she pulled his pants off his legs. Folding them she sat them on top of the shirt. "Right Seonghun?"

"너와 키스하고 싶어" He did want to kiss her; however, it probably

wasn't the brightest thing to say at the moment. Luckily, he said it in his own language.

"Pardon?"

"Sorry, nothing. I'm not going to do anything stupid." He counted to ten, forcing himself to calm down.

Maliah pulled the blanket from under him and set it to the side. Seonghun laid on his stomach waiting patiently as he heard the crumple of the patch packaging. She pressed it gently on his back; his eyes nearly crossed at the welcome warmth. Throwing the blanket on him, Liah turned to leave.

"Please stay," he said it quietly.

"Not a good idea."

"I promise I won't push anymore."

"It's not just that. I don't know how to be around you guys. I don't know how to be around anyone. You weren't wrong with your guess about the drive-in. I shouldn't live my life this way, but I do. I'm constantly waiting for the other shoe to drop, waiting for the kill shot." Maliah squatted in front of him so she could look him in the face. "You seem like a nice enough guy. All of you do. But I'm not fit to be friends or whatever else you were thinking of."

He must have looked startled.

"Like I said, I'm a virgin, that doesn't make me stupid about sex or relationships. I see how you look at me sometimes."

His ears burned red.

"If I can't process friendships, I definitely can't do anything with that." She walked out of the room but came back shortly with a glass of water with a straw, and two pain pills.

"I can't take those, I just took some a couple of hours ago," he explained.

She nodded, setting everything on the nightstand, along with his phone, before walking out.

"Liah. Please. I'm not asking for a relationship or sex. I'm asking you to let me in. Let me be your friend. Everyone could use a friend. You said you don't know how to be around us. You cooked dinner with Min and painted his nails for some weird reason. You ate with me. We talk through notes constantly. You're doing just fine." He was speaking so rapidly because he felt that this was his last chance.

"Can you just give me some time? I need to process this."

"Take all the time you need."

"Bye, Seonghun."

"Bye, Liah."

She walked out of his room, leaving the door open.

With nothing really to do, He reached for his phone, turned on a playlist, before closing his eyes.

CHAPTER 13

"Seonghun, wake up."

He turned sleepy eyes to a blurry Liah.

"I need to change your patch, but I don't want to tug at your body while you're asleep."

"Okay."

After gently prying off the old patch she added a new one, tossing the wrapper in the trash before leaving again.

"Thank you," he said, staring at her.

"You're welcome." She paused at the doorway. "Are you hungry?"

"I'm literally always hungry."

Suppressing a laugh she walked out of the room before coming back with a bowl of spaghetti heated up.

"Cinnamon roll?" he asked hopefully.

She shook her head. "There were none in the fridge. Everyone else demolished them. To be fair I only made one can, there's only six in a can."

Liah sat on the desk chair, slowly feeding him. It was mostly quiet except for the soft music and the scraping of the fork on the bowl. After she finished feeding him, Liah carefully held up the glass of water, letting him take long gulps with the aid of the straw. Once he had his fill, he watched her gather the dishes to take to the sink.

"I'm going to ask you again to stay."

"I can't. I told you I need time, plus I have to get dressed for work."

"I'm sorry."

"Don't be sorry, be mindful. You can't keep asking me the same thing in the hopes of getting a different answer. That's a manipulation tactic."

He flushed as she walked out of the room without a backwards glance. Seonghun was basically lost. He took the pain pills on his nightstand as he fretted. After a while she walked back in, wearing a black sheath dress and black heels.

"Do you need help with anything before I leave?"

He shook his head. "I have to go to the bathroom, but Minjun will be back in a little while; I can hold it." He didn't want to ask the poor girl to help him with that. Maliah turned to leave. "Liah?"

She turned back.

"You're capable of being an amazing friend. You didn't have to help me today. But you did."

"Someone hurt you. You didn't deserve that." With that she walked out of his room. He heard the main door close.

He laid there and stewed in his own mind until he heard the door open again. "Who's there?" he called out.

"Min."

"Can you come in real quick?"

Min walked in to see him lying on his bed. "What happened? You left before I did today. I thought you were feeling better."

Seonghun told him the story, including Shiwon asking Maliah out for coffee.

"Wow," was all he would say.

"Have you seen Ashley today? Did she say anything?"

Minjun shook his head. "We've cooled off, I haven't seen her in a couple of days. How about you try to sit up so we can see where you are with your back?"

Seonghun slowly sat up, wincing.

"Wait a minute. How did you get your clothes off?" Minjun asked.

Seonghun turned a brilliant shade of red.

"Oh, well then." Minjun snickered.

"It wasn't anything. She was very matter of fact about it."

"Then why are you about ten shades of red?"

"Just help me get to the bathroom please." Standing up, Seong realized that he was feeling not at the point of being a hundred percent but was able to move. Those patches were amazing. He was usually down for a couple of days at least. With Min trailing him, he went into the bathroom. When he came out, he saw Min on the couch. "Is Yongjoon still in class?" he asked.

Minjun nodded.

Walking slowly back into his bedroom, Seong searched around for a pair of sweatpants. Grabbing his phone, he sent a text, asking Yong for a favor. While he waited for an answer, he checked his email before sending notes to the professors in his other classes, explaining what happened. He had an email from his lab teacher, apologizing for what happened. Casey had been removed from the class; his new partner would indeed be Shiwon. He also asked Seong to send the information of the classes he missed today, so that he could corroborate what happened, just in case he missed points or assignments. As he was sending off the information his phone rang with a text from Yongjoon.

"Consider it done."

Reaching in his desk, he pulled out a couple of sheets of writing paper.

Liah,
It feels like everything changed in the blink of an eye. We were becoming
friends, but now there is a strain. I know you said you need time to process. I
plan on giving you that, so don't feel you have to respond to this note. Getting
to know you has been one of the brightest things in my life in a long time.
You're driven and smart, I like listening to you talk about your plans.
What happened to you is a shame, but it hasn't been all bad. It made you this
person that is so empathetic to children, you want to teach them how to cope
with their emotions in a way no one helped you. I hope you achieve everything
you want and more.

Seonghun then copied the poem he found earlier by Henry David Thoreau.

Thank you for the heating pads. I'll replace your box of them ASAP. Enjoy the treats. I put them in the fridge.
-S

He folded the papers before sticking them into the envelope. Seong turned his music to something a little livelier while pulling out the same book he was reading with Liah the past weekend. It had literally been two days, then everything went to shit. Seong sighed, diving deep into some science fiction. It wasn't two minutes before he remembered something. "Min!"

"What?"

"Come here please?"

Minjun walked into his room. "Yes?"

"If someone were to say to you 'I'm a virgin, I'm not dead' what would that mean to you?"

Minjun seemed lost in thought for a moment. "Was anything sexual happening?"

"No."

"It honestly sounds like someone saying I've never had sex, but that doesn't mean I don't get urges. Why?"

"Liah said it to me, when she helped me take off my shirt but wouldn't look at me."

"Yeah, that's what she meant. She finds you attractive."

Seonghun didn't know what he was supposed to do with that knowledge. At this point there wasn't anything he could really do. Just then he heard the door open again. Yongjoon walked into his room carrying a paper bag.

"As requested,." Yongjoon set the bag on his desk, before sitting beside Seong on the bed. "What are we gossiping about today?"

"Seonghun pissed off Maliah, but she thinks he's cute. Also, he was attacked by Casey," Minjun supplied.

"I wasn't attacked, I was grabbed. I tried yanking out of her reach and twisted my back again. A nice guy who's going to be my new lab partner brought me back home, asking Maliah out in the process," Seong corrected.

"You have had an eventful day. No wonder you asked for cupcakes."

"They aren't for me," Seonghun turned red.

"Ah, that also explains why you didn't ask for chocolate," Yongjoon noted.

Seonghun slowly stood up, grabbing a pen from his desk. His room-mates both watched as he scrawled her name on the bag, hobbling out of the room to put them in the fridge before attaching the note to her door.

Yongjoon glanced at Minjun. "Did Maliah respond to your note?"

Minjun nodded. "She said she's not really in a mood to socialize with anyone, but realizes she left me with three blank nails. So, she gave me the polish."

"Nothing else?"

"Nah. She'll come around. In the meantime, I'll leave notes on her door about shows I like, things I've seen. She can choose to answer if she wants. If she tells me to stop, I'll stop."

Yongjoon nodded as Seonghun came back in.

"Before you lay back down, do you want to get comfortable on the couch and we can watch a movie?" Yongjoon suggested.

Seonghun agreed, shutting off his music, they all moved to the couches in the living room. The trio spent the evening eating leftover spaghetti, while chatting about the movie. Eventually everyone went to their corners, but Minjun followed Seonghun to change his patch.

"You only have this one left," Minjun noted as he went to apply the last one.

"I have to replace her patches tomorrow. I'll probably buy every box they have at the store. Thank you," Seonghun said as Minjun smoothed the patch on.

His friend patted his shoulder before leaving, shutting his door once again. When the door closed, Seong started another note.

Liah,

I got word from my professor that the girl who grabbed me has been removed from class. The guy that brought me back to the dorm, his name is Shiwon, he's going to be my new lab partner. He seems very kind as he decided to take a stranger who was in pain home. I was going to call Minjun. I was glad I didn't have to do that. He seems very... unbothered about everything around him. He even took your rejection in stride. Hopefully, that doesn't translate into his work. I have to keep my GPA up, but I really don't like carrying people on assignments.

I understand you're mad at me, but please don't take out any feelings you have about me on Minjun. He really likes getting to know you; he would be the best friend you'd ever have. I would know. He's been mine since before we were born. Our families are neighbors, our moms were pregnant at the same time. They did things together all the time during pregnancy. There is a picture of them standing belly to belly that we both have a copy of. My mom said whenever they did that, we'd both start kicking, as if we were eager to meet each other. He's always been there; it's going to be weird when we get back and we're not going to be side by side all the time. He'll want to live in the city. I'll miss Yongjoon too. He's promised to bring his mother to visit when we get back. I've gotten lucky with his friendship. I don't have many friends, but the ones I have are invaluable.

Though they were slightly at odds right now, he included her in that statement. Seong hoped she understood that. His pen hovered over the paper as he debated what he was about to write next. She'd shared so much with him; he couldn't see a reason why to not share with her.

You spoke of intimacy in the form of being physical with someone, sexually. I'm a bit more old fashioned than Minjun is. There is nothing wrong with the way he lives his life. He has consensual sex. He makes sure that the other person understands that he's not looking for forever, at this moment. As long as there are no hurt feelings, I don't see any problem you know? But being that close with someone I barely know; I can't imagine it. I had a girlfriend before I left Korea. We broke up shortly before I got accepted to this program. I have a lot of guilt because we should have broken up a lot sooner. I didn't feel as strongly for her as she did for me. I tried to tell her, but anytime I would try to initiate the discussion, something would happen. The final straw was her telling my mom I had proposed. It sort of broke my mom's heart, though the girl didn't realize. My mom figured I would have told her first before asking anyone (she wasn't wrong). It was the push I needed. I finally broke it off, and nothing she would say or do would change my mind. She was being manipulative, hoping I wouldn't say anything and go along with it. I couldn't imagine spending my life with someone who would do that.

There was also the fact that she didn't understand that sometimes I feel...odd. Like I don't belong in my skin. When I get like that, the last thing I want is to be touched. I understand that I'm fairly physical in my affections, but there are times when I'm just... not, and she never understood.

Seong ended the note there for now, in the hopes she would write back to him. He began a small drawing on the bottom. Picasso he was not, so he drew a stick figure reading a book. Sticking the note in his desk, Seong opened his door to peek out. The note on Liah's door was gone, so that meant she was home. As he closed his door for the night, he hoped she ate a cupcake.

IN THE MIDDLE of the night Seonghun woke up, needing to use the restroom as well as take a pain pill. Gently shuffling off his bed, he walked to the bathroom and heard soft crying coming from Liah's room. Seong took care of his business before lightly tapping on her door.

"You don't have to respond, as I know how you feel, but I wanted to let you know I heard you; you don't have to be alone. If you want me to go away, knock twice. If you want me to stay, knock once." He waited.

One quiet knock sounded on the door.

"I'm not going away, but I can't sit on the floor right now, I need to go get a chair. I'll be right back." Walking to his room as fast as he could, he piled his blanket on his chair before dragging it to her door. Wrapping up, he sat back, clearing his throat as he thought how to begin.

"Rough day? One for yes, two for no."

She knocked once.

"I'm sorry. Did the cupcakes cheer you up at least?"

Another knock.

"That's good. Was it work that was hard?"

Two knocks.

"Does your job as a curator make you happy?"

There was a knock, a long pause then another knock.

"So it's tolerable is what I think you're saying. Not something you would want to do in the long term."

A single knock.

"I couldn't imagine having to dress up every day for work. Dressing up is okay sometimes, but not for a long time. I get so uncomfortable."

Another knock.

He was quiet for a while, not really knowing what to say. Maliah opened her door. Standing there in sweatpants and his sweatshirt she looked at her feet for a while. When she looked at him, her eyes were swollen from crying, her glasses crooked as usual on her face.

"I f-f-f-f-feel guilty," she said quietly.

"Why?"

"T-t-t-t-t-" She sighed.

"Take your time, I'm not going anywhere," he said softly.

"I need to tell you some things," she said slowly, "but I'm tired. I feel defenseless. The best night of sleep I've had in a long time is sleeping with you. I feel g-g-g-guilty for even asking because I know I haven't been the best person. But the nightmares are overwhelming." Tears started falling. "I don't know what to do anymore."

There were a million things he could say. He just held out his hand to her. "We can talk in the morning after your classes. Would you be more comfortable in my room or yours?"

"Yours please. I can't be in here right now."

Wrapping his blanket around him, he grabbed the chair with the hand not holding hers, leading her into his bedroom, shutting the door.

"I'll get in first then move as far as I can toward the wall, to give you some space. You can get in after. Do you want music?"

She nodded. He put his nighttime playlist on softly. Sliding in bed he moved as much as he could to the other end, waiting for her. Slowly she took off his sweatshirt. Under it she had on a plain white t-shirt. He rolled to his side, so she wasn't undressing while he was staring at her. She slid into his bed, facing the opposite direction.

"Turn off the light. I'll talk to you in the morning when you're ready. Goodnight, Liah."

"Goodnight, thank you."

"It's what friends do." He closed his eyes, dozing off almost immediately.

CHAPTER 14

Seonghun woke up engulfed in Maliah's scent. He was beginning to believe it wasn't just her perfume, but actually just her. Looking down, she was still asleep, laying on his chest. Gently, he pushed her hair out of her face. That little motion was enough to wake her.

"You're safe, I'm not going to hurt you. You're in my bed, you couldn't sleep, you asked to sleep with me. Nothing sexual happened. We just slept." He said everything slowly so she could process it.

"I know, I remember. Thank you for affirming though." She wasn't as fast to move from his arms as she was the first night.

"It's late. Are you missing classes?" he asked hesitantly.

"Yes, but I have paperwork on file for days like this. I actually have something to ask you. If you aren't busy today, do you want to meet my therapist?" She blinked, rubbing the sleep from her eyes. "I figured I'd meet with her, then I could talk to you about everything."

"That's fine. I need to go to the store today as well as try to get to the garden area to grab seeds if I can."

She looked at him for a minute. "Do you have a driver's license that's legal here?"

"I do, but I don't feel comfortable driving. Yongjoon doesn't have class today, he'll take me or I'll catch the bus."

She focused on his mouth for a moment before dragging her eyes back up to his. "Does the garden area have a place to sit?"

"Yes."

"Okay. Let's do this. I'll get ready. You can do the same after me. I'll take you to the store, from there I can have my therapy session in the garden area." Maliah slowly left the bed. "Seonghun, thank you. I know I don't deserve, well, anything with how I act."

"Kindness isn't something you dole out based on a metric. It's just how people should be. You can't sleep, I can make it better. Simple as that."

Maliah nodded. Walking out of the room she shut the door behind her. Seonghun sighed, lying in bed a little longer. He wished she was still here. Seong wanted to touch her. What's more, he wanted to see actual pleasure on her face. Burying his face in his pillow, he screamed his frustration. After his minor tantrum, he sat up, testing his back by stretching. He was stiff but felt better. Once he got some pain reliever in him, he would feel mostly back to normal. As he started pulling his clothes to wear for the day, he noticed Liah grabbed the sweatshirt before she left. He wondered if she ever planned on giving it back.

Walking into the common area, he noticed that Minjun's door was open, but Yongjoon's was closed. Yong loved to sleep as much as Seonghun did, so it wasn't surprising. Texting Min, while walking over to the bathroom, he noticed Maliah's door was shut; he assumed she was already finished in there, so he entered. As he began to shave, he received a message from Minjun begging him to go out this evening, just them. He needed to talk. After he finished, he sent Min a text, confirming dinner tonight, before climbing into the shower. Once finished, Seong stepped out of the bathroom with steam billowing behind him, knocking on Liah's door.

He'd only ever seen her in her work dresses, oversized denim, or sweatpants. Her work dresses were simple. They were black, sometimes paired with a bright shoe, but most of the time even her shoes were black. Today Maliah wore a purple sweater dress that went a little past her knees. Tights and black boots completed her outfit. She still had on the sweatshirt he loaned her. A black leather shoulder bag was slung across her body.

"Are you ready?" she asked.

He nodded.

"You don't have any gardening equipment?"

"It all stays in the greenhouse, you'll see," he explained.

She nodded and together they left the dorm.

DRIVING TO THE STORE, it was mostly silent between them. Seonghun honestly didn't know what to say to her. The silence wasn't uncomfortable though. It was never uncomfortable as the two of them lived in their heads a lot anyway. As they arrived at the store, he broke first. "Did you want to talk?"

She sighed. "I'm going to ask that you wait until after my therapy appointment. I'm not in the greatest of headspaces. I feel gross, and guilty, just— it's a lot."

Seong crossed to her side of the car. He wanted to touch her but refrained. "I think I know what is going on in your head; you can correct me if I'm wrong. You didn't use me, Liah. You didn't take anything that wasn't offered. As a matter of fact, any time you can't sleep, you're welcome to sleep with me. Um, lay with me? Uh, you know what I mean." His ears were on fire.

Liah suppressed a smile.

"Let's go." He gestured toward the store. Grabbing a cart, he entered the building with her following behind. "Did you need to get anything?" he asked her.

She stared at him for a minute. "Yes, but it's sort of personal."

He thought about it. "Do you want to split up and just meet at the front?"

She nodded. Grabbing a basket near the door she made her way into the large store. Seonghun began his own browsing. Picking up razors, deodorant, and conditioner, he rolled around until he saw the heating pads. "She wasn't kidding," he said aloud. There were different shapes and sizes.

In the end he bought fourteen boxes. One to replace hers, one extra for her, and twelve for him. He saw a display of electric heating pads as well. He picked up one for each of them. He didn't really need anything else but walked around the store to make sure. For some reason he paused at the craft section.

It was a small area of the store, but over in the corner he saw bins and barrels of fake flowers. Wandering over, he saw a bin filled with clusters of daisies. Looking around he saw an employee. "Excuse me?" They turned to look at him. "How difficult is it to remove the fake flowers from the stem?"

The employee walked over and showed him that it was easy. All it took was a gentle tug and the blossom popped off the stem. Smiling his thanks, he scooped up a few, along with a few other flowers. Heading toward the front, he saw her standing with two bags of her own. He hurriedly dumped his purchases on the conveyor belt while waiting for the cashier to ring him up. Sliding his card through the machine, he gathered his bags.

Liah's eyes widened as she took in all his bags.

"I may have gone overboard on buying patches," he admitted.

As she burst into laughter, Seong wondered what he had to do to get her to laugh like that again. She looked so much less guarded.

Liah popped the hatchback of her car so they could put their purchases in. She glanced at him once they got settled into their seats. "Do you want to pick something up to eat or would you rather eat inside some place?"

Seonghun thought about it. It was kind of a chilly day. "Let's eat inside."

"Any food suggestions? I'm not really p-p-picky."

"Burgers, please."

Maliah pointed the car in the direction of campus. A short drive later, they parked in front of the tall metal sign of the Triple XXX Diner. While the name made the place sound taboo, it was actually a family friendly restaurant on campus. It had cheap, good food that was plentiful.

Seonghun went with a burger that had a smear of peanut butter on it, while Liah opted for the breakfast menu of hashbrowns and eggs. As they ate, Seonghun spoke up. "Were the cupcakes okay?"

"I've only e-e-eaten the l-l-lemon one so far. It was really g-good. Thank you for that. I'd been feeling rough, it cheered me up." She smeared ketchup on her hashbrowns as she spoke.

"I'm glad." He took a massive bite out of his sandwich, savoring the creamy peanut butter.

She looked at his sandwich suspiciously. "How is that edible? It's peanut butter on a hamburger."

"I'm not sure, but it works. Bite." He held out the hamburger.

Maliah turned up her nose.

"Biiitttte," he cajoled, waving the burger in her face.

Tentatively she took a small bite. He watched as she chewed thoughtfully. "It's not horrible, but not something I'd ever order."

"When we first got to the program here, the Asian Student Union took all the new transfers here. I came back three more times by myself that week to eat this." He wolfed down his sandwich before starting on his fries.

"If you eat like this a lot, I see why Minjun worries about your vegetable intake." Liah ate a mouthful of eggs before speaking again. "Do you still do activities with the union?"

He shook his head. "I'm not a joiner. They were very helpful, but I don't need activities all the time. I know Yong goes every now and again."

She nodded. "I occasionally went to the Black Student Union. They were invaluable to me last year, but I'm embarrassed to see them now. I only told them the tip of the iceberg last year, but they heard everything in student court. It was humiliating."

"What is student court?"

"When you have a grievance or you do something wrong on campus and are caught by the campus police, you have to go to student court. It's to save students from having an actual record." Liah stopped eating, pushing the remaining hashbrowns around on her plate. "The thing is, if you agree to the terms in student court, it leaves you unavailable to press charges with the actual police. I didn't completely understand what I was doing. Because I didn't tell everything that happened, everyone suggested I go to student court. It's my fault she didn't get expelled."

Seong saw self-loathing rush across her face, along with something else he couldn't quite place. "You have to let that guilt go," he said. "I don't know what happened. I won't pretend to know, but you were hurt; you did the best you could with what information you had. The only person that should feel guilty is the person who hurt you."

She wouldn't meet his eye, but by her demeanor he could tell she wasn't in a great place right now. He reached out, grabbing both of their meal tickets.

"Why don't you wait for me in the car?"

"I-I-I-I-"

"I know you can pay for your own," he said gently. "You fed me spaghetti and got me out of my clothes without joking about how bony I am, it's fine. You can pay next time, I promise."

Staring at him for a minute, she nodded. Liah slid out of the booth, heading immediately for the car. Seonghun glanced out the window; Liah's head was down on the steering wheel, her shoulders shaking. Though he wanted to comfort her, It didn't seem like a great idea. So, he gave her what he could.

Time.

"Can I have two milkshakes to go? One chocolate, one strawberry please?" he asked his waitress.

She nodded, added it to his ticket, and went behind the counter to get them made. Resting his hand on his head, Seong pulled out his phone, sending a text to Yongjoon asking about the student court.

Yongjoon called him almost immediately. "Are you about to go to student court? I can't represent you, I'm a pre business law student. Not personal."

Seonghun snorted. "No. Are the records from the student court public? Like could I see the details of a case?"

"Mmm... drunk cases, yes. Some student versus student, also yes. But if a potential physical harm crime was committed against a student, then no. Those are sealed," Yongjoon explained.

The waitress dropped off his shakes. Seonghun juggled the phone a bit, reaching for his wallet. "Thank you, Yong."

"No problem. I'm going to offer you a bit of advice as well. Don't go digging. There are ways around sealed records, but if she hasn't told you and finds out you know, you're going to lose every bit of trust Liah has with you."

"I didn't say who it was about."

"Seonghun, you talk to exactly three people daily. I know Min and I

haven't been to student court. Don't invade her privacy like that."
Yongjoon sounded as firm as he had ever heard him.

"I won't," he promised.

"Will you be home for dinner?"

"Actually, no. Minjun requested my presence."

Yongjoon snickered.

"What?"

"I'll let Min tell you. Do me a favor, get Maliah's number. Ask her if it is
okay if I text her."

"Okay."

They said their goodbyes. Seonghun grabbed the milkshakes, before
walking out to the car. He could see from a distance that Liah had pulled
herself together, enough that she was composed when he handed over her
strawberry milkshake.

"Thank you," she whispered.

"You're welcome." He didn't say anything else except to navigate her to
the green garden lab he worked in. As she pulled into the parking lot, he
spoke up. "Yong wanted me to ask you, if you felt comfortable with him
texting you?"

She chewed her lip a bit before nodding slowly. "All three of you can
have my number." Reciting her number slowly to him, Seong quickly put it
in his phone before texting the information to Min and Yong. Her phone
immediately began to beep. He watched as Maliah opened her messages,
revealing she had three from Minjun, while Yong had just sent one. He
smiled as she stared in confusion. "No one ever really texts me. I keep my
phone mostly for emergencies."

"Minjun will text you constantly about every thought running through
his mind at the time. Just a warning," Seonghun said.

"Yongjoon?" she asked.

"Sometimes he'll send a photo of a plant, or bug in nature. He'll send it
to me to see if I know what it is. We have conversations during the day as
well. He finds out what's important to you, then makes it a point to
capture it if he sees it."

"What about you, Seonghun? What do you text about?"

"I talk about plants, food, or something funny I've seen. I'm not super talkative."

She glanced at her phone again before looking at him. "I'm glad you have good friends."

"They would be yours too, if you let them in." He began to feel odd as he noticed her staring at his mouth before looking in his eyes. "Come on, let's get you set up so you can have your therapy session, while I work in the field." He led her into a nondescript brown building, directly into a room with rows of lockers. Seong paused in front of the locker labeled with his initials.

"What is your last name?" she asked suddenly.

"Yu." Pulling out his apron along with his worn boots, he set them to the side as he shuffled things around, locating his gardening kit as well. He watched Liah as her hand hovered over his tools. Gently, he took her hand, placing it on top of his worn leather kit. "What's yours?"

"Evans." He took a moment, watching her stroke the soft leather before she peeled it open, looking at the things inside. He had two kits; this was the smaller of the two, as it included his handheld tools. The bigger one he would be selling before he left campus, as it would just be extra bulk for him to take home. Everything in his large kit was readily available on his farm. He technically had the things in his small kit as well, but he was partial to it.

Sliding the apron over his head, he turned his back to face her. "Can you tie me please? I normally tie myself, but I don't want to contort and possibly throw my back out of whack again."

She tied his strings. Her touch was so gentle, he barely felt it, only hearing the whisper of the fabric sliding against itself. "You're good." Seong sat on the bench to change from his sneakers to his muddy work boots. "Should I have worn other shoes?" Liah asked, looking down at her footwear.

"No. You'll be sticking to the stone path. It's pretty impossible to get dirty if you stay on it." Jamming his sneakers in his locker, he picked up his tools, sticking the leather pouch in the front pocket of his apron. "Can you grab my shake?"

She grabbed their drinks, trailing after him as they walked out of a side door of the building. He watched her face as they stepped outside into a different area, rarely seen by non-AG students.

"Oh!" she gasped.

"I did the same thing the first time we were brought out here." He grinned.

The whole area was basically a grid. Stone pathways led to dirt plots where flowers, plants, and vegetables grew. There were pumpkin vines packed with fat pumpkins. A lot of the flowers had died off or been picked clean. Some of the plots were bare, ready for fall/winter planting. Seong led them to a pretty stone bench close to where he would be working.

"You can sit here and have your session. The wifi from the building reaches out here. If you need me, just wave your hand, I'll just be three rows down," he explained.

"Should you be bending with your back sore?" Maliah asked.

He pointed. "Look down the rows." Further down were standing troughs filled with plants. "I'll be working from those today, harvesting as much as I can. Thank you for thinking of me though."

She nodded, pulling out computer equipment as she sat on the bench. Seonghun walked down to the area he needed. He was far enough away that he couldn't hear the private conversation, but close enough that she was easily able to grab his attention if she needed him. He began sorting through the flower remnants as well as pulling seeds from his hybridized lavender. Seong was deeply involved with his work. It wasn't the same as a harvest at home, but just as satisfying to know he created this. From it, more things would come. Forty-five minutes into his work, he saw something out of his peripheral vision. Seonghun's head snapped up; he saw Liah waving to him. Grabbing his harvest, he tucked his tools back into his pocket before making his way over to her.

Walking over he saw her eyes were swollen and sad again. He'd had on gloves while working, but his hands were still a bit dirty. Seong didn't think she'd mind as he reached his hand out for her to hold. Maliah pulled out an earbud, handed it to him, as she grabbed his hand. "T-t-t-this is Dr. S-s-s-t-t-t-" she paused, taking a breath, "Dr. Stewart."

Seonghun turned to the screen. A black woman with a nose ring, yellow head wrap and bright red lipstick sat there, seemingly observing their interactions. "Hi, I'm Seonghun."

"Hi Seonghun. I was just speaking to Maliah; she stated you've let her sleep in your bed a couple of times?"

"She was having nightmares, so she climbed into bed with me," he explained.

"How does that make you feel?" Dr. Stewart asked.

"She doesn't have a support system, so it seems like it is hard to ask for help. It makes me feel good that she feels comfortable enough to ask me," he answered honestly.

"That is a nice way of putting it. I will caution the both of you, not to use sleeping together as a crutch. Maliah knows she needs to deal with her feelings." Seong glanced at Liah.

She wouldn't look at him but instead was focused on her therapist. Dr. Stewart began speaking again.

"Seonghun, Maliah is going to talk to you about some things today. She wanted me to be here while she spoke as a support person. You will be in the notes of today's call. You have the right to request only the notes that are pertinent to you. Are you okay with this?"

He nodded.

"Maliah, it's your show." Dr. Stewart was quiet after that.

Seonghun watched as Liah took a shaky breath. "When I was accepted into Silver Leaf, my parents hit the roof. They didn't see or understand how hard I'd been working to get to this point. I was told I wasn't allowed to go. The problem with that statement was that I was eighteen years of age. There was nothing that they could say or do to stop me. When they realized that, I was immediately kicked out of my house." She paused for a bit. Seonghun squeezed her hand to reassure her. "I knew this was coming, I didn't have much in the way of material things, but I'd secreted a lot of items out of the house, into the trunk of my car. So I walked out, with seemingly nothing."

"I got into my car. I drove around at first, terrified of what just happened. It wasn't the happiest home, but I always had shelter. I was now homeless. Not knowing what else to do, I made my way over to my high school campus. There was a counselor who helped me fill out my forms for college and helped me to find scholarships. I broke down, admitting what happened." Liah licked her lips before she continued. "Turns out she had dealt with something similar with another student before. She worked with me to get me legally emancipated, because she knew after this year I wouldn't be going back to my parents. She spoke with contacts at Silver Leaf to get me into a dorm early. There is a program called Upward Bound for high school kids. I got hired to be a counselor. It meant I lived on campus, had three meals a day, while getting paid. It was one of the best times of my life."

She looked at Seonghun, faintly smiling. "Though I had responsibilities, my free time was my own. No one was putting me down. The kids liked me because I was close to them in age. I taught a few of them to play guitar. I picked up sketching; not only was I good at it, but it brought me a little peace. I used it to purge feelings, until I was capable enough to find a therapist to help me."

Seonghun glanced at the screen. Dr Stewart was listening intently, though he was sure she had heard all of this before. He turned his focus back to the young woman who was barely holding it together.

"Toward the middle of the summer, I got my roommate assignment. She seemed sweet; she came from a rich family so we really didn't have a whole lot in common. We talked about what each of us was bringing to the dorm room. I'd saved money while working in high school, also I had saved all my money from working that summer, so I could help to provide for the room as well. In the end she bought most of the things, said she had an 'aesthetic' for the room, and she wasn't sure any of the stuff I was going to buy would fit into it. That should have been my first clue."

"Your first clue as to what?" Seonghun asked.

"That the girl was batshit fucking crazy, Sorry, Dr. Stewart."

Dr. Stewart chuckled. "You don't have your therapy license yet, so you're still allowed to call people batshit fucking crazy."

Seonghun laughed, and Liah smiled a little.

"When she got to the room, she brought her parents. She seemed to boss her own mother around, her father was checked out, except when he was looking at my ass. We got our room set up then her parents took us both out to eat. I thought that was nice." Liah picked up her shake, handing Seonghun his as well. She took a sip before continuing her story.

"Things were good at first. She was snooty, wanting her stuff just so, but I could respect that. I kept my side as neat as possible. Then she wanted to go to parties all the time. I'd go with her a lot, but she would start pressuring me to drink. Even before I was on medication I didn't really drink. I don't like the taste, I didn't like the way it made me feel. Then s-s-s-she started p-p-p-pushing for oth-her t-t-t- stuff. T-t-t-that I s-s-s-s-should dress a c-c-c-certain way. If s-s-s-someone she l-liked took an interest in me, she'd start pointing out my flaws."

Seonghun's hand felt like it was being clamped by a vice. He gently rubbed his thumb on one of her knuckles, trying to force her to calm down.

"I decided t-t-t-that this w-w-wu-w-wasn't working anymore." Maliah took a deep breath seemingly focusing herself. "I stopped hanging out with her. I was hardly ever in the dorm. When I was, it was late; she was either gone or sleeping. That pissed her off, badly. I found out later that she has a habit of picking people to become her minions. I wasn't minion material, so things started happening."

Liah was silent for so long, Seonghun prodded her. "What things?"

"I only had o-o-o-one job at the time, it was a c-c-c-c-crappy minimum wage job, so I was on an extreme budget. Things like soap, shampoo, hair creams, began disappearing. My clothes would mysteriously have holes in them. I struggled to replace things, doing the best I could while continuing to ignore her. I think that made it worse." She looked at Seonghun as she grabbed a chunk of her hair. "Do you understand that this is not all my hair?"

He shook his head no.

"They are extensions, hair that isn't mine, twisted into my own. I had really pretty hair. When it was wet, it was to my waist. When it was dry, it was a curly ringlet afro."

"Had." Seonghun glanced at the screen.

The doctor nodded imperceptibly.

"I found out she had been putting hair removal cream in my shampoo. It caused my hair to fall out. I had chunks missing. Eventually I had to get it cut." The tears she'd been holding back during the story finally started to fall.

Seong wanted to cry with her. He saw the absolute heartbreak on her face.

"How much natural hair do you have, Liah?" he asked.

"You know how I just said it fell to my waist?"

He nodded.

"As of last month it just barely touched my shoulders."

His eyes widened. "Oh my God!"

"I found piles of dirty tampons in one of my drawers I didn't use. I couldn't figure out why it smelled so rank on my side of the room. The final straw that got her called to student court was she set me up to be raped."

"WHAT!?" he shrieked.

Liah immediately flinched back from him.

"Sorry, I'm sorry. I didn't mean to… Raped?!" He saw she had basically checked out of her body. The story was now being told on autopilot. There were no stutters, no life in her voice.

"She got some guy drunk as hell, brought him back to our dorm, pushed him in our room, shutting him in. He was so out of it, he thought I was her. He kept petting me while trying to yank at my pants."

Seonghun stared in horror.

"I screamed. I screamed as loud as I could, while fighting him. My RA burst through the door immediately pulling him off of me. I told her I didn't know who that man was, or how he got in, as I had locked the door. The guy started drunkenly saying her name. 'Casey, where is Casey'."

Seonghun's blood turned cold. "Stop."

Both Liah and Dr. Stewart turned to him.

"Maliah, you don't seem to be all here right now, but I really need you to focus. Does your former roommate Casey have green eyes, brown hair, and freckles?"

She nodded slowly.

Seonghun felt sick to his stomach. Briefly he told Dr. Stewart what happened in his class, how the woman wouldn't let go of his arm, causing him to wrench his back again.

"Her name is Casey Needler. She was my lab partner up until Monday. They threw her out of class."

Everyone was silent.

"Okay," Dr. Stewart spoke. "I think this is enough for today. Maliah, give me your self-care guide."

Maliah wouldn't answer. She was sitting there frozen.

"Maliah?"

No response.

Seonghun looked at the screen. "I have her. What do I need to do?"

"If she needs to cry, let her cry. Make her take a shower, have her journal her feelings or draw them if she can. Soft clothes. Just be there for her. If things get worse and she starts breaking down completely, my number is in her phone under Dr. S." She paused for a second, "I've been authorized by her to let you know that she has a prescription for anti-anxiety medication. It should be in her room in her top desk drawer if she needs it. If she isn't talking within the next three hours, she needs to take one." Dr Stewart looked at him. "This is a lot, young man. Are you sure you can handle this? If not, we may need to get her checked in for a 24 hour hold."

"I've got her. When she feels better, I will have her contact you." Seonghun began gathering her bag. Maliah still hadn't moved. He wasn't even sure if she had blinked.

"If either of you need anything at all please call me. I have an answering service that will contact me at all hours."

Seonghun nodded, thanking her before hanging up the call. Closing the laptop he pulled the earbud out of his ear as he looked at Liah. She was still holding his hand but barely. She didn't flinch as he pulled the other earbud out of her ear. He dropped them in his jeans pocket.

"Sweetheart," the endearment slipped out of his mouth without thought, "I know you're shaken up; I know you're anxious. I'm going to get us both out of here, but I need my hand back to pack up."

She let go of his hand and gripped the hoodie she had on. He quickly packed up the laptop. Standing up, he threw their cups away in the trashcan next to them. "Come on, sweetheart," he helped her up. Together they shuffled back into the brown building. He hurriedly put on his shoes.

Holding his breath, he reached behind to tug on his apron strings. They came loose without him hurting himself. He sat down on the bench next to Liah to take off his boots.

"She hurt you?"

He looked over Maliah looking straight ahead, trying desperately to keep it together.

"She did, yes."

It was silent for a bit and she spoke again. "It's my fault she's still here. If I would have pressed charges—"

"It's not your fault at all," he interrupted her, "she is responsible for her actions. It also sounds like her parents know she's trash as they are paying for your therapy. I do have a question though. What is to stop you from pressing charges now?"

"When you go through student court, you sign a form stating that you won't try to push the issue forward with the police; the student court verdict stands."

"Their verdict on that case." Seonghun thought out loud as he grabbed her bag. "What happens if I press assault charges? Because she assaulted me."

"I don't know," Liah whispered.

He glanced at her as he shuffled them both to the car; she looked awful.

"I know you don't know me that well, but you don't look in a place to drive. I have a license. I can drive if you don't mind?"

Maliah pulled the keys out of her sweatshirt pocket, handing them over without hesitation. She slid in the passenger seat, closed the door, and waited. He got in the car, immediately adjusting the seat, as his legs were once again by his ears. Once he was somewhat comfortable, Seong pulled out his phone to call Min.

"Min, I know we're supposed to go out to eat for dinner, but I'm in the middle of... something. Can we have dinner in the dorm?"

"Uh... I think so, but we need to be in my room."

"That's fine. Can Liah hear this? I can't leave her alone right now."

"It's not a problem if she's there. I'll bring dinner, what do you want?"

"Hold on." He glanced at Maliah who was looking out of the window. "What is your favorite comfort food?"

"Mexican. Anything Mexican."

"Min—"

"I heard. I got it."

"Use my card. Also use it if you take a ride share."

"I'll talk with you soon." Minjun hung up the phone.

Adjusting the seat, Seonghun turned on the car and began to drive back to the stadium. He reached for Maliah's hand, relieved when she squeezed his tightly. Pulling into the stadium, he looked at her. "What do you need?"

"A nap, a shower, time to process." Her voice was barely a whisper. "I'm sorry you had to cut your lab time short."

"Not concerned about it. I got the seeds I was looking for. I was hoping to grab a pumpkin for the dorm, but they were red tagged anyway, so I couldn't."

"Red tagged?"

Seong slid out of the car and came around to open her door. She seemed sort of weak so he reached in to help her out.

"I'm fine, I can walk, I promise. What does red tagged mean?"

"They are part of a project, not just something you can take. They shouldn't leave the area." He popped the trunk to begin pulling out bags. Her bag of purchased items was open so he could see inside.

"Um, I have a mom. I've also had a girlfriend before. I'm not bothered by these products, just letting you know." He handed her the bag before grabbing all of his. "If it's personal because it's embarrassing to you, that's fine, but don't think any of us in the dorm are going to go 'pads gross' and freak out. We're all grown men."

"Casey made fun of me, called me an infant because I can't use tampons very well."

Seonghun was baffled. "What infant has a need for a tampon?"

Startled, Maliah looked at him. He was absolutely confused, which caused her to burst into laughter. "I never thought I'd laugh about any of the shit she pulled, so thank you."

"No problem." They began walking to the bus stop. "Are you feeling any better?"

"Not really. I'll be better after I shower, take some medication, and a nap."

"Do you want some company?"

Maliah turned to look at him. "Are you asking to shower with me?"

Seonghun choked on air. "No! I was asking if you wanted company while you were sleeping, which possibly sounds worse."

"No, you're fine. I'd actually like that." They sat on the bus and didn't speak until getting back into the dorm. Seonghun took a good look at her once they were back in the dorm room. She looked exhausted.

"Why don't you get your shower? I'll be in my room reading. If you change your mind and decide you want to be alone, that is fine too, just let me know."

Maliah shuffled to her room as Seong went to his own. He changed into his sweatpants before reaching over to turn his music on softly. Picking up his book, he wondered if he was ever going to finish it. Soon he was enthralled with beings from another planet when he heard a soft knock. "Come in," he called out.

Maliah walked in. She had on pajama pants, a long sleeved t-shirt, with his sweatshirt over her shirt, unzipped.

Seonghun took off his new glasses, carefully laying them on the night-stand, along with his book. "Did you take your medicine?"

Liah nodded. "I'm probably going to be asleep in ten minutes as a result."

"That's fine. That's what you're in here for."

She slipped off the sweatshirt and climbed under the covers with him. He didn't know what to do. He'd held her last night, but that happened while they were asleep. Seong decided to lay on his side as he had been, facing her. Liah laid flat on her back, closing her eyes. Studying her profile for a moment, he closed his own eyes.

CHAPTER 15

Once again when his eyes opened, Liah was wrapped in his arms. Seong was half tempted to set up a camera to see how they ended up like this. She probably wouldn't agree to that though. He was still on his side but she was backed into him, with his arm around her tightly. He put his nose on her shoulder, breathing in her scent.

"Mmm, why are you smelling me?" her sleepy voice said.

"You always smell really good," he admitted.

Liah turned to face him. She looked a little groggy still. "You aren't skinny." He watched her stretch as much as she could with his arm still around her.

Seonghun was confused at her statement. "What?"

"You said something about me not making fun of you being skinny earlier," she whispered. "You aren't skinny, you're really built."

Seonghun froze slightly as he observed her face. She kept her eyes on his, fidgeting slightly. His heart was in his fucking throat. Taking a deep breath he did the only thing he knew to do, be completely honest with her. "I don't know if I'm reading this situation right; I don't want to scare you or make you feel bad," he said quietly.

"I don't think you're reading it wrong." She kept her eyes on him.

Seonghun's heart was racing. Why on earth was liking someone this nerve wracking? It was never like this with Jia. His fingertips felt swollen and clumsy as he went to cup her cheek. He immediately stopped as Liah flinched away. "Don't touch my face please." Seong remembered her telling him that the guy kept stroking her face. Seong gently brought his mouth to hers. It was brief, a light peck before he pulled away to gauge her reaction.

"I'm okay. I promise," she said quietly.

He kissed her again, slowly. It was a somewhat chaste kiss, but it lit every nerve ending aflame for Seonghun. The feel of her, combined with how she smelled and tasted, was making him slowly lose his mind. He wanted more. He pulled her flush against him causing him to moan.

Liah pulled back slightly. "I'm sorry, I'm feeling a bit overwhelmed," she admitted.

"It's okay. Don't apologize for seeing to your needs. I'd never get angry at you for caring for yourself. Can you tell me what else you're feeling?"

"I just kissed my only friend. I feel kind of dumb, but also…"

"Also?" he prompted.

"I want to do it again." Liah looked at him fully before casting down her gaze.

"Well, we can parse through your feelings now, or we can kiss now and talk about feelings later."

"I've honestly had enough of feeling like shit, which talking about my feelings always makes me feel."

He kissed her nose. "Okay."

Seong adjusted so she was laying on the bed as he hovered over her. Dipping his head down, he kissed her lightly before lingering a bit longer on her mouth. Liah's hand slid down his chest, to his waist, gripping him tightly. Seonghun felt her play with the edge of his shirt, as if she were scared to lift it. He pulled back, focusing on her eyes. To him, Maliah looked unsure, but not as fearful. He could ease a little of that for her, at least he thought so. "You can touch me anywhere you like. I have times where I can't really stand being touched, but this definitely isn't one of those moments."

Seong delighted in the fact that she tugged lightly on his shirt, pulling his face to hers. He kissed her again. Liah's hand slid under his shirt, coming to rest gently at his waist. Seonghun was more vocal than her with grunts and soft moans. As they continued, Liah got braver, gently trailing her hands across his stomach. He honestly didn't want to stop kissing her, but he was hard as a rock and about to lose his mind.

All of a sudden she arched up against him. "Oh god!" he cried. Grabbing her firmly by the hips, he pushed her down into the bed, quickly moving away from her.

"I'm sorry, what's wrong?" Liah looked ready to bolt.

He grabbed her hand gently. "Nothing is wrong, everything is absolutely right, a little... too right," he sighed. "I don't take pretty much anything lightly, including this," pointing from him to her, "but I'm still a human being, with, um, desires." His ears turned red.

It was quiet for a minute.

"It's going to be a while before I'm ready for anything else I think. I like kissing you, but I'm not in a mindset to go further anytime soon," she admitted.

"Text your therapist, let her know you're okay. I'm going to see if Minjun is home." He meant to only give her a quick kiss before he got up from the bed. It devolved into more. When she gently touched the tip of her tongue to his, his eyes rolled into the back of his head. "Liah, I have to stop."

She slowly backed up, blinking at him. "Sorry, you came in for a kiss and I thought—"

"I know, me too." He stood up. "I'll be right back."

Walking out the room, he saw a pile of Mexican food on the countertop in the kitchen. Crossing over, he knocked on Minjun's door before opening it to see his friend studying on his bed. "Why didn't you tell me food was here?"

"I went to knock on your door, but heard you moan. I figured you were having a little alone time. I thought Maliah was with you, though? That was the whole point of us eating here. The door to her room is open."

Normally when Seonghun got embarrassed, the redness in his ears and face was gradual. He immediately turned scarlet, nearly purple.

"Why are you so re— Oh shit!" Min's eyes widened as he connected the dots.

"Minjun..." Seonghun warned.

"Are we both banging the roommates!?"

"I'm not banging anyo— I'm sorry, did you say both of us?" He stared at his best friend.

"I mean, we haven't had sex, but he kissed me."

"Yongjoon kissed... you?" Seonghun felt something pop in his head. He prayed he wasn't having a stroke. "Let's go grab Liah, sit on the couch, so you can spill your guts." Seong leveled a look at Minjun. "No jokes, Min. She's had a shitty day. We both have. If she says it is okay, I'll give you details." Min followed Seonghun out of the room and began to fill his plate. Walking into his room, Seonghun opened the door. "Are you hungry?"

She was looking down at her phone. "Yeah. Dr. S warned the both of us about starting something during an emotional moment." She kept looking down, not meeting his eyes.

"We will go as slow as we both need. Okay? This isn't an emotional moment. I've wanted to kiss you for a while," he admitted.

"The day I ran into you when you came out of the shower, I wanted to kiss you." She glanced at him, before focusing on the bed again.

He patted her hand. "Let's grab food before Min eats it all." Pulling her up, he held her hand until they got to the food.

Minjun had gotten chips, salsa, tacos, tamales, burritos, beans, and rice. Everyone served themselves. Once seated on the couch, Seong spoke. "Go ahead, Min." Biting into his taco, he waited patiently.

For once in his life Minjun hesitated. He looked at Yongjoon's door. Both men knew he was at the gym. "Min?" He looked over at Seonghun. "No one here is going to judge anything you say."

"I—" Min was quiet for a moment before trying again. "I've had a crush on Yong for a while. I never said anything because, well, I've seen him with girls."

"Minjun, he could say the same for you."

"I know. That's not important. This morning I woke up to make sure you took your pain pill."

Liah's head snapped up at that.

Minjun smiled softly. "It's okay, I saw you were in there and walked back out. I went to bug Yong instead. We talked for a minute, but he was sleepy, so I left. He came into my room because he caught me in a lie."

"What was the lie?" Seonghun asked.

"I told him I was going to study at the library this morning."

Seonghun snorted. Liah looked confused.

Min looked at Maliah. "None of us wake up early except for classes or to check on one another. I would have been asleep, had I known that Seonghun was okay," he explained. "He asked me for the truth, so I told him that I liked him. He told me he was aware then he kissed me. He said he refused to be treated like the girls I'd hurt." Min looked at Seonghun. "I've always been clear with everyone I've ever dated or been with that I wasn't looking for forever."

Liah spoke up for the first time. "Have you, ever been with someone that you were well aware that they wanted more, but ignored it for your own pleasure?"

Minjun turned red.

"J-j-j-j-just because you outline the rules, doesn't mean you don't have to follow them." She pointed out quietly. "You have a responsibility to your partners, you know? It's n-n-n-not on you to manage their feelings, but if you can tell they want-t-t-t more than you, you have a responsibility to ack-ack-acknowledge that."

Seong looked at her astounded. It was the most she ever said to Min in his presence. "Maybe you're right, but I don't know where to go from here."

She was quiet as she bit into a burrito. "Do you like h-h-him?"

"Very much so," Minjun admitted.

"Show him. Show him in a way that makes him feel special. I think for a lot of people, it's simple things that make you feel ch-ch-cherished."

Seonghun listened to what she was saying, knowing the advice just wasn't for Min.

His friend nodded as he took a bite of tamale, chewing before asking, "You guys had a rough day?"

"I can't tell the story again, Seonghun." Liah's voice quavered. "There is still so much to it, I just can't right now."

Seonghun looked at Minjun. "Her former roommate, a person that was supposed to be her friend, hurt her badly. The same person that grabbed my arm causing me to reinjure myself."

Minjun choked on a chip. "Casey!?"

Seonghun nodded.

Min looked over at Maliah, who was slowly folding in on herself. Setting his plate down he walked over to her. Kneeling at her feet, he held out both of his hands, palms facing up. Slowly she placed her hands in his. "We aren't her," he said simply. "We won't hurt you. Not physically, not mentally. None of us. It's not who we are. It's definitely not who he is." He glanced at Seonghun who was watching. "I know it is going to take time for you to understand that, but if you do want to talk, any of us are here."

Seonghun nodded at her.

"Yeah."

Three heads turned to see Yongjoon standing at the entrance. "I can't promise I won't accidentally hurt your feelings, because sometimes I stick my foot in my mouth, but we'd never do anything malicious."

Tears were starting to fall onto Maliah's cheeks.

"You don't have to say or do anything right now. But we would love to go to the drive-in with you this weekend." Minjun squeezed her hands. "Yongjoon has an SUV, so you can sprawl in the back with Seonghun. Will you give us a chance?"

"I'm petrified," Maliah admitted.

Yongjoon walked over, sitting with Minjun in front of Liah. "Let's make a deal. Come with us to the drive-in on Friday night. You get anxious, you feel uncomfortable, we leave immediately, no questions asked."

Seonghun watched them both, his heart full. How did he get so lucky with such great friends?

Maliah glanced over at him. "This means a l-l-l-l-lot to you?"

"I'd like you to get to know us, yes."

"Okay, I'll go. If I get anxious you'll bring me home?"

"Without question," Minjun said.

Liah nodded and began to focus on her chips. As she slowly ate her chips, Seonghun wolfed down a tamale, a burrito, and two tacos. She watched in amazement as he ate.

"D-d-d-do you always eat like this?"

Seonghun turned red. "I'm always hungry."

"Ever since he was a kid, he's always had a huge appetite." Minjun scooped up a forkful of rice. "With the farm work and now working out, he stays lean, but his metabolism is high."

"H-h-have you ever been full?"

He nods. "I'll be full after I eat for about thirty minutes, but then I'll be hungry again."

Finishing most of her food, Maliah got up and put her plate in the sink. "I have to study," she looked at Seonghun, "I also need a little time alone."

"I understand. In my top desk drawer, there's a letter I didn't finish. You can have that." He walked into his room to grab it along with the things he got her at the store.

"You only used one box, you didn't have to buy me extra, but thank you very much," she said. "What's this?" She held up a medium sized package.

"A heating pad. You said you used the patches for your cycle. I thought this would help too. I got one for my back."

"Thank you, that was very nice of you."

"You're welcome. Will you be staying in my room tonight?"

Liah shook her head. "Dr. S doesn't think it's a good idea for us to spend every night together. She's worried I'm using you to get rid of the nightmares, instead of working through what is causing them."

"I understand, but if it gets too bad, come in, okay?"

She nodded and started to walk away.

"Liah?"

She turned to face Seonghun. Minjun and Yongjoon were eating, pretending not to look at them.

He walked the two steps to her, hesitating before kissing her briefly. "Goodnight."

"N-night." She walked into her room and closed the door quietly.

"Did I just see Seonghun kiss her? I didn't just see that, did I?" Yongjoon asked Minjun.

"Yeah, it happened. It's been an interesting day for all of us I think," Minjun said.

"You know, I can hear you two clearly, right?" Seonghun said.

"Oh yeah, we're aware," both men said at the same time, before dissolving into peals of laughter.

Seonghun rolled his eyes and began to wrap up the leftovers, putting them in the fridge. "Yongjoon, did you get anything?"

"I didn't know there was going to be a gossip session tonight, so I stopped by the cafeteria to grab something." He stood up, patting Minjun's leg absentmindedly. "I have a little studying to do before crashing."

Minjun stared at him as Yong walked into his room.

"What are you going to do?" Seonghun asked quietly.

"Listen to Maliah, figure out how to make him feel cherished." Tossing his plate in the sink, he squeezed Seonghun's shoulder. "Thank you for listening."

"Anytime." He smiled at Min as his friend closed himself in his room. Alone, Seonghun began to run water for the dishes while happily humming a tune. Finishing up, he turned out the light. He was headed to his room when he stopped. Walking up to Liah's room he pressed his ear to the door. Hearing music, he tapped softly.

When Maliah opened her door, she looked up at him. He towered over all women with his 6'4 frame, but she was even tinier than most women. He knew now more than ever that he needed to be careful how he approached her. "Hi, I know you need some alone time, but I just wanted to ask for one more kiss before I retire for the night."

"Oh. Sure." She grabbed his hands and pulled him into her room. All the lights were on today, as she was studying. Her hair was pulled up into a haphazard bun, with pens stuck in it. He didn't notice earlier, but she had on mismatched socks again. One yellow striped and one blue striped.

"You're cute," he blurted.

She chuckled and looked down. "Thanks."

He slowly leaned down, kissing her cheek. She flinched slightly. "Is it your whole face I can't touch or kiss?"

"I don't mind you kissing my cheeks like that at all, I was just startled because I didn't think it was where you were going to go. To answer your question, I don't mind my forehead being touched. I just— I woke up to that man petting my face, and I-I-I-"

"I'll respect it, but I'd mention it to Min if I were you. He's touchy feely; I don't want either of you to be hurt because he made a misstep."

Liah nodded.

He skimmed his hand down his waist, pulling her closer before kissing her. He meant to keep it brief, he really did, but he got caught up in her scent, her softness, just being with her.

Liah finally came up for air, gasping. "Seonghun, I really need to study."

"Yeah, I do too." Letting go of her waist, he took a step back. "Goodnight, Liah."

"Goodnight." She grabbed her textbook before getting into her bed where a notebook already sat.

He saw her hands trembling as she opened the textbook. "I'm not— This isn't too much for you is it? I'm not overstepping boundaries, am I?"

"I've been in therapy for a while, Seonghun. I'm also going to school to be a therapist. If you cross any boundaries, you will know. I'm very clear in what I cannot tolerate. You've always checked in with me before you do anything; I appreciate it."

"Why are you shaking then?"

"I'm trying not to violate your boundaries." She sighed while looking up at him. "I've never been with anyone. I like kissing you. I want more, but even I realize this is entirely too soon. So I'm just struggling? I'll deal with it a little later."

"Deal with it?" Seonghun repeated.

"Goodnight, Seonghun." Liah smiled softly, ignoring the question.

Seonghun walked out of her room in a daze.

CHAPTER 16

Seonghun woke up, immediately running to the bathroom before his roommates got in there. Brushing his teeth, he decided to forgo shaving, hopping into the shower. As he scrubbed, he thought about Liah 'taking care of it' and was instantly hard. Moaning, he grasped himself firmly, trying to stifle his moans as he took care of his own needs. It didn't take long, soon his hand was pressed against the shower wall as he struggled not to cry out as his orgasm. Leaning his head on the cool tile, Seong let the water pour all over his back. He wanted to take things slow. They both needed to take things slow. He also wanted to bury himself inside her. It had been so long since there was a woman who made him feel this way.

Turning off the shower, he dried himself, continuing to think. He was a patient man; Seonghun liked Liah, really liked her. He owed it to both of them to get in control. Throwing on his clothes, he cleaned up before leaving the bathroom. Maliah's door was closed, but there was a note, thicker than normal, on his door. Seong stuck it in his backpack, before putting on his shoes. Heading to the nearest dorm that had a food hall, he grabbed two plates of food, before sitting down to read Maliah's letter. When he opened the envelope, three granola bars fell out. He picked them up, shoving them in his bag, as he began to read.

Seonghun,

After our talk about your metabolism last night, I had a feeling you don't snack during the day, so I've enclosed some granola bars. They won't fill you up or anything, but it should get you from meal to meal. You should probably pack snacks during the day.

The idea of you and Minjun growing up together is heartwarming. I think if my mom had someone to lean on during those times, maybe she would have liked me more. She had me before she graduated high school. I ruined her life. I don't say this to cause pity or make you feel bad, but it is true. She wanted to be an actress, which I know sounds like a cliche, but she was actually really good. She did community theater around our area; I watched the videos growing up. She could have probably done it if she would have just left me behind with my dad. But she didn't. I never knew why. She hated me so much, Seonghun. Why didn't she just walk away after my grandmother died?

Sex. Phew, okay. So as we discovered last night, though Minjun's sex was consensual, both parties didn't always leave the situation positively. Like I said last night, it isn't his job to manage someone else's feelings, but if you see that they want more, it's best to part ways before even entering that territory. I'm with you in the fact that having sex with someone is important. I haven't really cared about anyone enough to have sex with them. I'm not against it, but that spark has to be there. They also need to feel in the same ballpark as I feel, so that no one is hurting after. Which leads me to you. Us? Me? I don't know.

I like you. There, I've said it. I think you're handsome, sensitive, and smart. I like the fact that even though we're both quiet, it isn't awkward. I really like kissing you. However, I'm still healing. I'm still dealing with the emotional abuse from my parents as well as everything that happened last year. As you guessed, I hold a lot of guilt. I'm a little worried about leaning on anyone or even being close to someone enough to allow them to hurt me. But I'm trusting you. I'm trusting all of you, but especially you. I have a lot of baggage, but I'm also a good person, I like to think I'd be a good friend. I'd like more, but we'd both have to take it incredibly slow.

You said something kept happening every time you tried to break up with your girlfriend? What on earth kept happening to stop that conversation? I'm sorry it took hurting your mom's feelings for you to finally break up with her, but at least it is done, right?

When you go home, will you go back to your family's farm, or will you strike out immediately on your own farming venture? Is there a particular crop you want to farm? Have you been to Fair Oaks Farms before? I think you would like to see it. I've gone there solely for ice cream before. It is so good. There is a farm in Indianapolis called Traders Point Creamery that makes some of the best chocolate milk I've ever had. They sell it in stores around here too.

I really liked the poem you chose. It sounds like us. All four of us. We were strangers that are slowly becoming friends. Thank you for the cupcakes as well. I haven't eaten the yellow cake one yet, but I will. What is your favorite meal and dessert? Also, when is your birthday? What about Minjun and Yongjoon? It is 6 in the morning. Minjun is texting me. I have to go see what he wants. Have a good day at class.

-L

Seong stared at the letter in shock. She liked him? He didn't really understand why he was so surprised, she didn't seem like the type to randomly kiss someone. *Wait—*

He frantically thought back to the first letters and conversations. He knew she was a virgin, didn't she say something about never being kissed before? He pulled out his phone.

Seong: *Was I... was us, I mean me...Was that your first kiss last night?*
Liah: *Yes. Could you tell?*
Seong: *No. I just remembered from our earlier letters or a talk we had, a brief mention. If I would have remembered, I would have made it more special.*
Liah: *Not everything has to be an event, Seonghun. And who's to say it wasn't special? It was, to me.*
Seong: *No regrets?*
Liah: *None.*
Seong: *Good. Do you really think I'm handsome?*
Liah: *Bye, Seonghun.*

Chuckling, he put his phone in his pocket so he could finish his breakfast.

HIS CLASSES WENT SMOOTHLY that day. He found that having something to eat regularly did help. Seong felt more alert, easily able to focus on his classes. He walked into the lab, meeting briefly with his teacher, who apologized again for Monday. Seonghun waved him off. Since Casey was gone it wasn't an issue. He took his seat next to Shiwon.

"Thank you again for taking me home," Seonghun said as he pulled his book out. "I was able to rest well."

"It wasn't a problem at all. Everyone needs a little help sometimes. You could help me by putting in a good word with your roommate, she's really cute." Shiwon rested his head on his hand as he smiled at Seong.

"Ahhh..." Seonghun blushed.

"Interesting. You actually made a move then. How did that go?"

"She kissed me back."

"That's good. Are you going to take her on a date?" Shiwon asked.

"I haven't gotten that far. We've been out together a couple of times. We're going with the other roommates to the drive-in this weekend."

"You should take her somewhere nice at some point. Girls like that." Class started up so Shiwon and Seonghun both focused on the tasks at hand.

He wondered if she would like to go somewhere nice? What was considered nice? Did she want a fancy meal? He wanted to text her, but he needed to focus on the lab. Shiwon was an amazing partner. They worked in tandem, anticipating what the other person needed. There was the added enjoyment of actually staying focused on the task rather than also trying to avoid purposeful hand caresses.

"You're a pretty good partner," Shiwon said, helping to wash beakers. "My last one was okay, but only put in bare minimum work."

Seonghun smiled. "I have to keep my grades up. There is also the fact that I like my courses. Are you busy? Do you want to go get something to eat?"

"I'd like that." Together the two of them walked over to the student center. It was full of not only restaurants, but where a lot of the student unions were housed. Shiwon and Seonghun sat, chatting about their other classes over sandwiches. Eventually Shiwon had another class, but they exchanged phone numbers before he left. Seonghun was throwing away trash when he saw something that made him pause. Walking over, he entered the door for the Black Student Union.

A girl was at the front desk clicking away at the computer. "Can I help you?" she asked him.

"Can I talk to someone that deals with student court?"

She nodded, picking up the phone. "What is your name?" she asked, looking at him.

"Seonghun Yu."

After a bit longer on the phone, she looked up at him. "Go back, take a left and Keisha will be right there."

He thanked her. Following her instructions he was soon greeted by a tall woman with light brown skin. Her dark brown eyes stared at him curiously. "Seonghun? Hi. What can I do for you?"

Now that he was here, he was at somewhat of a loss as to what to say. "I have a friend that employed your services last year. She was grateful for the help that she received. I think she wants to reach out, but she's embarrassed about how things went. I thought if you reached out to her, it may help." He paused for a minute. "She's a good person but she's alone; I want to show her she doesn't have to be."

Keisha looked at him for a moment. "Who's your friend?"

"Her name is Maliah Evans."

"I figured as much. She is a good kid. It should have never ended up the way it did. That girl should have been kicked out. I felt so bad, but we did what we could. Has she had any issues that you know of?"

Seonghun hesitated. "Not her." He proceeded to tell Keisha what happened.

"If we can get her on one more thing, we can actually press charges to the actual police. I don't think the hand grabbing will do it, but keep in mind, if something does happen, to the point we get the police involved, we can get her student court record opened to show that this is a pattern. She was such an ass during the proceedings. She knew she was going to get a hand slap." Keisha shook her head. "I'll reach out to Maliah, I promise. I'm guessing I shouldn't mention you stopped by?"

"I would really like it if you didn't. We just started becoming friends. She just started to let me in. I don't want to diminish progress between us," Seonghun explained.

"I'm glad she's talking to someone. She's a brilliant girl. She's one of those people you hope good things happen to."

Seonghun nodded in agreement. "Thank you for meeting with me."

"You're welcome here anytime. Bring Maliah by sometime if you can." Keisha smiled.

He shook her hand before walking back out, heading back to the dorm.

CHAPTER 17

Arriving at the dorm, Seonghun was treated to an amusing sight. Minjun and Liah were on the floor with her foot in Min's lap. Min was hunched over her foot with a tiny brush in his long fingers carefully painting aqua polish on her toes. Liah looked up when she heard the door close. Seonghun was trying hard not to laugh. "He said he wanted to bond; this is how he wanted to bond," she explained.

"This is kind of hard," Min said as he dabbed a bit of polish onto the bottle. "I don't feel like I have a stable grip on the brush."

"Your hands are probably sweaty. Put the brush back in the paint and go wash your hands," instructed Liah.

Minjun stood up to go do what she said as Seonghun walked over. He brushed a kiss on her forehead. "Hey."

"Hi."

"Dinner tonight?"

"I can't, I have to work."

"Will you sleep with me tonight?"

Liah looked at him for a long moment before he realized what the problem was. "Not sex, actual sleep."

She relaxed slightly. "I'll have some studying to do when I get back, so I will be in there late."

"That's fine, just come in, I'll probably wait for you since I don't have hardly anything to do tomorrow." He touched her shoulder before kissing her gently. "Have fun with Min."

"She will!" Minjun came strolling out of the bathroom. "Go away, we're bonding."

Seonghun pat Min on his head before going into his room. Turning on music, He pulled out fresh stationary, immediately writing.

Liah,

Do you have any happy memories of your family or childhood? Any at all? How do you feel around children when your life was so difficult growing up? Maybe you should ask your mom, Liah. Ask her why she didn't run away. You speak mostly of your mom, what about your dad? You don't go home or visit, so I'm assuming your relationship isn't great with him as well.

I never really thought of Min actually hurting someone with the way he operated. I liked the advice you gave him. Make them feel cherished. I think that is what anyone would truly want. I like you too, Maliah. I like when I get to hold you in bed. I like talking to you or reading your notes. You're working your way through darkness, trying to use what you've learned to help other people. That's admirable. As fast or as slow as we go is between us and as Minjun has probably told you, I'm kind of turtle-like in my speed. I tend to overthink everything. Which leads me to your question about my ex. It's not really something I'm comfortable putting down on paper. If you ask me outright I'll tell you.

I have a sweet tooth. I love chocolate; the thought of chocolate milk is heavenly. I'll look for it the next time I go out. My favorite American dish is hamburgers (You could probably tell). My favorite Korean dish is something called jajangmyeon. It's a noodle dish. My birthday is also June 8th. I'm going to leave you to ask Min and Yong their favorite foods, but I will tell you that Yongjoon's birthday just passed (September 9th) and Min's is coming up (November 20th).

I had a question I have been thinking about for the past few days that doesn't really add up for me. Last year was your first year of college. This is your second year, but you're graduating in the spring? How did you get so many credits so fast?

There was a knock at his door. "Come in!" he called out as he put the paper in his desk. Maliah walked in. She had on a simple black dress with a white collar. Jeweled hearts were clipped to each collar, attached by a chain. Black tights and black high heeled Mary Janes completed her outfit. "You look pretty," he said.

"Uh, thanks. I'm getting ready to go. I'll talk to you this evening?" she asked.

"Yes. I'll be here." He stood up, gently brushing his mouth against hers. She kissed him back, sliding her hand up to his chest. Grabbing her wrist he pulled her to the bed. Skimming his hands down the sides of her dress, Seong slowly slid his hands underneath. A soft whimper came from her. "Good or bad?" His voice sounded deeper than normal to him.

"Good, really good." She continued kissing him as his hands explored under her dress.

Tentatively, Seonghun ran his thumbs over the cups of her bra. Though he couldn't see, he could feel the thin fabric; her nipples were hard. Lost in the feel of her, he forgot where he was and that his door was wide open.

"Do you want to go get din-Oh! Sorry!" Minjun walked right back out, shutting the door behind him.

It was enough to break them apart. "I'm sorry." Seonghun began to smooth her dress down.

She grabbed his wrist. "Don't be. T-t-t-that was n-n-n-n-nice."

"Are you sure you're okay? You're stuttering."

"I-i-i-it comes out in ext-t-t-treme emotional reactions," she took a breath. "I'm not angry, or scared."

"Then what are you, Liah?" He scooted closer to her.

Gently she touched his face, kissing him one last time before getting up. "Goodnight Seonghun, I'll see you this evening." Liah left quickly.

He covered his head with his pillow, laying there, wishing for heaven only knew.

"Are you okay? Should I leave?" Minjun entered the room.

"I'm fine. Sorry, Min." Seong's voice was muffled under the pillow.

"It's ok, you've seen me in worse positions." It was true. Minjun sometimes wasn't careful about where he started things. "Do you want to go to dinner?"

"Will you come to the gym after?"

Min wrinkled his nose.

"You can just peddle on the bike. I haven't really spent much time with you, or Yong."

"You've been a little preoccupied. It's okay, we don't begrudge you. But yes I'll go to the gym with you after we eat."

Seong stood up to prepare for the gym. "Minjun, how are things between you and Yongjoon?"

"They're fine." He gave a small smile as he walked out of the door.

CHAPTER 18

Throughout much of the meal, the boys tried to prod details of Seonghun's relationship. "There's not much to talk about. We enjoy being around each other, we talk."

"That was more than talking I walked into earlier," Minjun noted getting up to throw his trash away.

"Yeah, we got a little carried away." Seonghun blushed.

"Minjun!"

As Min was walking back to the table, he looked up to see Ashley walking over with Casey following behind. Seonghun wasn't someone that was quick to anger; however, everything he'd learned in the past two days had him staring daggers at Casey.

"Hey, I haven't seen you in a while! What are you up to?" Ashley smiled at him, fluttering her lashes.

"Hi. I'm hanging out with my friends." Minjun edged closer to Yongjoon, hoping for a save. Yong merely smirked before walking off to throw away his trash.

"Do you maybe want to get together later?" She looked at him hopefully.

"Uh—"

Seonghun, can we talk?" Casey walked up to him speaking softly.

"No. I have absolutely nothing to say to you." He walked past her with his tray, trying not to snap.

"Seonghun, wait!" She grabbed his hand; he jerked away as if she had burned him.

"DO NOT TOUCH ME!" he roared. Conversation in the cafeteria stopped; you could hear a pin drop. "Who the hell do you think you are?!"

"There's no need to get loud," she snorted.

"No need? NO NEED!?" He heard his voice getting louder, but couldn't tamp it down. He was enraged. The red haze over his vision told him he needed to leave immediately. He worked hard not to get angry, as he was a large man that was easily intimidating. Usually he'd never want to hurt anyone, but this was all beyond the pale. "IS THAT WHAT YOU SAID WHEN YOU PUT HAIR REMOVER IN HER SHAMPOO CASEY!? OR HOW ABOUT BULLYING HER OR SETTING HER UP TO BE RAPED!? WAS THERE NO NEED FOR HER TO GET LOUD!?"

Min shook off Ashley. "Seong, let it go. Let's leave." He grabbed his arm trying to pull him from the room, but it was like trying to move a boulder.

"How in the world do you know anything about that? Let me guess, that bitch has been telling stories. It wasn't that big of a deal. If you just come with me, we can talk about it. She was such a fucking stick in the mud, I was trying to liven her up." Casey looked bored at the whole idea.

By this point Seonghun was vibrating with rage. "If you come near me, Min, Yong, or Liah, I will personally see to it that you're arrested. She didn't know better, but I do."

Casey stood there, staring at him. Seong didn't like the look that flashed across her face. "You could try," she smirked. "I'm a little harder to get rid of than that, cutie."

Seonghun had never called a woman out of her name, but he was beyond through. "You're an absolute bitch. I can't believe I ever thought for a moment you were nice. Stay away from me. Stay away from all of us."

Yongjoon grabbed Seonghun's other arm. "She wouldn't want her business spread like this. Let it go, come on."

"I will see you later, Seonghun." He saw nothing but malice in the girl's eyes. Turning his head he walked off.

It was silent as they walked to the gym. Finally Yongjoon spoke up. "I've missed a few steps here. I'm going to be honest."

"I've heard some of it and I'm still missing steps," Minjun said.

Seonghun stopped and sighed. "I'll talk with Liah and ask if I can share what she told me with you, but you heard most of it. She hurt Maliah. Physically and emotionally."

It was silent until Yongjoon spoke up again. "Did—"

"No. She fought him off." He sighed as he stopped walking, looking at his friends. "I'm not really feeling the gym tonight. Can we just go get ice cream?"

"That sounds like a great idea." Minjun grabbed both their arms before Seong could change his mind, pointing them in the direction of the little corner store.

Inside, Seonghun picked up a pint of chocolate for himself and strawberry for Maliah. Walking down the aisles he paused briefly as something caught his eye.

"What are you looking at?" Seong jumped. When he turned around, he saw Yongjoon staring at him.

"I uhh—" Seonghun started to look everywhere but what he was looking at. Unfortunately Yongjoon beelined on them.

"If you think you're going to need them, buy them."

"Isn't it presumptuous of me?"

"From what I saw this evening, Seonghun, it isn't presumptuous at all." Min came walking down the aisle.

"I'm not ready for that step," he admitted quietly.

"That's fine, but it's okay to be prepared," Yong said. He slid a box of condoms off the rack, handing them over. Seonghun silently took them before walking to the front, grabbing four boxes of granola bars on his way. Minjun eyeballed the same display while Yong shook his head. "We're nowhere near there. If we ever are, I've got it," Yongjoon said, wrapping his arm around his friend's shoulder, pulling him to the front where the register was.

As they arrived, Seonghun had finished paying, waiting patiently on them. Setting out back to the dorm, Minjun spoke up.

"You're going to need to tell her what happened, Seong."

He sighed. "I know. I didn't mean to do it. I just— She doesn't care that she damaged someone's life."

"You sensed something wasn't right with her while she was in her class. Now you know your gut wasn't wrong," Yongjoon pointed out.

Seonghun nodded as they continued walking back to the dorm. The guys ended up playing video games while eating their ice cream. Eventually, Seonghun stopped playing, grabbed his stationary from his room writing, while his friends raced.

Liah,

By the time you get this note, I'll have already told you about the incident with Casey. I'm going to apologize again. I was so angry, Maliah. She didn't care who she harmed. She treated everything she did like a joke. Like it didn't matter, like I shouldn't care. She still thought I would see things her way, that this was just a bump in the road.

Blatant disregard of people is not something I'd ever tolerate, which is why I'm feeling guilty for my outburst in the cafeteria. I know you wouldn't want that, once again, I'm sorry. Is there anything I can do to make it up to you?

Seonghun heard keys jingling in the door. Maliah walked through the door and walked up to the couch where everyone sat. It was a marked difference to a few weeks ago where she would come in and immediately go to her room.

"Hi," she said quietly to everyone, squeezing Seonghun lightly on his shoulder.

"Was work okay?" Yongjoon asked.

"Yeah. A bunch of snooty people came in for a private tour. I'm not great with remembering the details of art, but we've had the exhibit for m-m-m-months, so I know it like the back of my hand. There isn't a question you can throw at me about it that I c-c-c-can't answer. But they tried and failed." Her stuttering was becoming less pronounced around her roommates.

"What kind of things do you get asked?" Minjun turned his attention away from the tv screen.

"Mostly about t-t-t-the art, what it is supposed to represent, where it was painted, how it was painted."

Seonghun grabbed the hand still resting on his shoulder, squeezing it tightly.

"I have a badge that indicates that I'm a student trainee, so you get people trying to stump me or make me nervous. Problem is, with art or music, I'm in my element. If I like something enough, I'll research it to the ends of the earth. I went down a three month rabbit hole with the musical Hamilton. Did you know that no one really liked Charles Lee because he expected to be paid? Also he smelled."

Everyone looked at her blankly. Liah smiled awkwardly. "Okay. I'm going to go." She made her way to her room before Seonghun stood up.

"Wait. There's ice cream for you in the freezer. Also, can I talk to you for a second? Privately?"

"Sure." Liah walked into her room, grabbing the note left on the outside. He pulled the ice cream from the freezer, before walking into her room. She was pulling out pajamas to sleep in when she looked up, smiling at him. Noticing his demeanor, her smile dropped instantly. "What's wrong?"

He handed her the ice cream. "We went out to dinner today before going to the gym. Minjun ran into Ashley, who's friends with Casey. Who happened to be with her."

"Are you okay?" Liah asked.

"No. I'm still pissed. I kind of got loud. About everything, about you. I'm sorry."

"Loud? What do you mean?"

"She didn't care how she'd hurt you."

Maliah looked at him baffled. "I-I don't understand. Why are you so upset? It didn't happen to you. It happened when you didn't even know me."

Seonghun immediately saw the problem. "You're my friend. I care about you. One of those things that comes with being friends."

"Shut the door," was all she said.

He did as she asked before walking back to her.

"No one has ever defended me unless it was their job. It feels nice." She walked up to him, tugging on his shirt. He bent down to her level so she could kiss him. She slid his hands up his neck, drawing him in deeper.

Seonghun moaned, happily continuing where they left off earlier that day, sliding his hands under her dress. After a brief hesitation, he slipped his hands into her tights. He began to stroke her outside of her underwear, gauging her reaction before deciding to push further. Sliding his hands into her panties, he choked back a cry as he touched her skin.

Liah let out a soft moan, gently biting his lower lip. "More, please," she whispered, trailing her hand down his chest.

He parted her folds and gently swiped his finger, immediately noticed something. She was reacting, but she didn't seem aroused to his level. She wasn't wet, at all. He wasn't very experienced, but he knew a little bit. Using his fingers, Seong gently rubbed small circles. Though she seemed to be enjoying herself, there was no physical evidence, nothing. After about ten minutes, he tried sliding a finger inside her.

Liah pulled away from his mouth, "Stop please," she said.

He immediately removed his hand. "Was it not okay?" he asked self-consciously.

"I liked everything you did, but there are a few things I should probably tell you. It's nothing bad, but it's going to take me a little bit to work up the nerve. So I'm going to ask you to let me study for an hour; I'll come over and sleep with you, or you can come back here and sleep with me." Liah's mouth was swollen from the kissing. She was looking like she wanted to devour him.

He supposed he didn't do too bad if he made her look like that. "I'd like to sleep over here tonight."

"Okay, give me an hour of study time. You're actually welcome to stay while I work." She pointed at the bed.

"That would be nice. Let me get my books." He opened the door to see their roommates still playing. "I'm going to go study with Liah for a while."

"Anatomy?" Yongjoon started laughing at his own joke.

Maliah stuck her head out of her door. "Perhaps physiology," she said softly.

"DID SHE JUST MAKE A JOKE!?" Min shrieked. He threw his controller before launching himself at her.

"Oh god!" Her eyes widened as he came in for a hug.

Seonghun was ready to pull him off if needed.

"Trust your friend, Seonghun," Yongjoon murmured.

Minjun gave her a gentle squeeze, bouncing back over to his game. Seong continued the walk to his room to pick up his books. He bid his friends good night before walking back into Maliah's room, shutting the door.

"Lay on the bed, I'll stay at my desk." She was already working on her laptop clicking away, eating the ice cream he bought her.

He climbed into the bed, smiling again at the twinkly star lights she had strung above the head of the bed. Giving up almost immediately at trying to study, he went to his book. He was so enthralled in the story that he almost missed when Liah shut her book. Almost.

Looking up he saw her stretching her neck and rolling her shoulders. "Are you okay?" he asked.

"Yeah, I'm good. I'm going to go to the bathroom, then we'll talk." Grabbing a small bundle of clothes, she left the room.

Seonghun took a look around her room again. There were no personal pictures, only art. Over by her desk was a collage of black pinup models. They were all curvy, in seductive poses.

"Are you looking at my ladies?" Liah walked in, putting everything back where it belonged.

"They are beautiful," he said. "I like this one the best." It was a picture of a dark skinned pinup, dressed in a yellow bikini. She had on black gloves with jeweled bracelets. Her hands were by her head as if she were flipping her hair while she laid on a small cushion with yellow heels on. Seonghun looked over; Maliah was wearing a long sleeved t-shirt with no pants. He blinked.

"Mmm, she's pretty," Liah agreed. "Seonghun, what would happen with your ex to stop the conversation?"

He blushed slightly. "I would always bring it up when we were in a private place, I didn't want to break up with her in public, it seemed rude. But I'd bring it up, she'd begin kissing me, touching me; eventually, she'd have her mouth on me. I really couldn't function much after that happened. At the end I would drop it because it just felt bad that this girl just gave me a blow job while I was trying to break up with her. It was just a cycle." He shrugged.

"You realize she was manipulating you, right? She didn't want to break up so she found a way out of it. You were a bit to blame as well because you couldn't stop thinking with your dick."

He startled at her saying dick so matter of factly.

"I know now. But in my defense, she was the first person I'd ever been with. The feeling was— I liked it a lot. But I learned my lesson. I'm generally cautious about how I deal with people."

"That's good."

"So what was it that needed explaining about earlier?"

"Yeah, that." Liah sighed as she went to a drawer. Seong watched her pull out two bottles. One was a pill bottle while the other looked like a lotion bottle of some sort. Sitting on the bed with both, she looked at Seonghun. "What do you know about antidepressants?"

"You take them when you're sad."

"Something like that." She tossed the bottle to him. "I'm on a high dosage. With that comes side effects. The pills affect my sex drive. I don't have a high sex drive most of the time. I hardly get wet, or sometimes don't get wet at all. I still get aroused, I just need help so that it doesn't hurt." She handed him the bottle. It was lube. "I still orgasm, it's just not as intense as it used to be when I wasn't on the pills."

"So it wasn't me?" Seonghun asked self-consciously.

"No. I like kissing you, I like it when you to—mmph!"

Seonghun didn't let her finish before his mouth was on hers again. Gripping her thigh, he laid on top of her as they kissed.

"C-can I take your shirt off?" he asked.

"If you take yours off too," she replied.

He whipped his shirt off quickly before helping her with hers. Her breasts were larger than he initially thought. A lot of her clothes were baggy, so he honestly had no clue. Skimming his hands up her chest, he brushed his thumbs over her nipples. Hearing her gasp softly, Seong smiled against her mouth as Liah slowly touched his chest, trailing her hands to the hair on his stomach that led to his pants. Sitting up, she leaned in to gently flick her tongue against his nipple. Seonghun moaned loudly as

Maliah began to flick her tongue rapidly over his nipple while alternating sucking. He wanted more.

He slid her panties down, immediately touching her. Seong softly stroked the dark thatch of curly hair before gently spreading her lips. Gently rubbing, Seonghun realized she was wetter than before, but still not very. Grabbing the bottle of lube, he smeared a small amount on his fingers before he tried again. As he began stroking her clit in small circles, she trailed her tongue to his neck. Trailing her own hand down, she slipped into his shorts, and began to stroke him outside of his boxers.

"Is this okay?" she started tugging at his pants.

"God yes."

She yanked at his pants. He began to kiss her, laughing as she struggled with his clothes. Finally she succeeded, wrapping her hand around his dick.

"I'm going to be a h-h-h-hundred percent honest r-r-r-r-right now and tell you I don't know what the hell I'm doing," she admitted. Seonghun paused what he was doing to look at her. She didn't really seem into what he was doing to her.

"Wait a minute." He brushed his hair off his forehead. "Are you getting any pleasure out of this?" he asked.

"I'm enjoying watching you," she said honestly.

"That isn't what I asked you though."

"Seonghun," she sighed, "I've never been with anyone, but I know my body. What you're doing feels nice, but I struggle to get myself off at times. I had a feeling it would be the same with a partner." The hurt he felt must have shown on his face because she elaborated further. "Okay, I want you to imagine a roller coaster. You see it?"

At his nod, she continued.

"I think of foreplay as that first climb on a rollercoaster, where you're slowly inching your way to the top." Her hands weren't touching him, but demonstrating the climb. "You get to the very top, and your orgasm is when you h-h-h-hit that drop on the coaster. I consider myself lucky if I get the drop. What tends to happen to me, is I get to the t-t-t-t-t-top; before I can hit the drop, the coaster starts sliding back to the beginning point where I have to start all over again. This can happen a couple times; I may get to the d-d-d-d-drop, or I have to give up for the time being because I get sore."

"So you come close to orgasm, but it just stops?"

"Yes."

"But sometimes you can orgasm?"

"Yes."

He sat back on the bed, with his back resting against the footboard. "Can you show me?"

She looked confused. "Show you what?"

"Show me what makes you come, how to help you achieve that," he requested.

She got quiet. "I've never—"

"We're both naked on your bed, Liah. No one is judging."

"I'll touch myself if you do the same."

"Okay."

Patting the bed, Liah searched for the lube and set it by her leg. She began to slide her hand down her chest, touching, then pinching her nipples. Avoiding eye contact with Seonghun, she picked up the lube, squirting a small amount into her hand.

Seonghun began to stroke himself slowly, twisting his wrist as he moved his hand up and down while he watched her.

She returned to touching her nipples with one hand, while using three fingers on the other hand to rub her clit. Slowly she began to inch two of the fingers inside herself.

Seonghun was about to lose it. All of a sudden, he noticed her hand wasn't moving, her wrist was. "What are you doing?" he asked her, trying to focus on not spilling too soon.

"Hitting my g-spot," she moaned out softly. He could tell Liah saw the confusion in his face. "Come here," she ordered, stopping what she was doing.

He crawled closer to her.

"Let me see your hand."

Seong held his hand out, watching as she trailed her own over his fingers. "Your fingers are thicker than mine. Use one finger, touch me inside, but don't thrust in and out."

She had used plenty of lube so he slid in easily. "Rotate your wrist and do the 'come here' motion with your finger." She demonstrated the motion with her own finger.

He did as she asked, immediately feeling a small patch of flesh that was spongier than the rest.

"I-I-I-I-If you keep stroking it like th-th-th-that I might come." Her voice wavered as he applied more pressure to the stroke. Tentatively adding another finger, Seonghun was delighted to hear a quiet whimper from Liah. Swiping his thumb down her clit, the sheer delight he felt as she clenched her teeth to keep from screaming was unmatched. Seong dropped his mouth to her chest and began to flick his tongue across one nipple before drawing the other into his mouth, sucking lightly. Liah cried out softly, gripping his thighs as she struggled not to disrupt the other roommates. Straightening up, he kissed her, tasting the toothpaste she must have used while in the bathroom.

She began to rock against his hand, quietly keening. Seong watched as Liah suddenly went rigid. Her orgasm was faint; he barely felt her walls flutter, but the look on her face said she'd gotten it. Removing his fingers, Seonghun gave her thigh a squeeze, leaving slightly damp fingerprints along her dark thigh.

It was silent for a moment before she spoke up, "Show me how to do the same for you."

Seonghun wrapped her hand around him again. Starting with an easy up and down motion, he then showed her how to rotate her wrist as she moved. Seong leaned back on his elbows, watching as Liah was intently focused on what she was doing. Leaning over, he kissed the tip of her nose, causing her to look up at him. Seonghun kissed her fully, enjoying her soft lips as she touched him. All of a sudden he felt his own orgasm building. "Can you move your hand faster, sweetheart?"

Liah increased her speed.

"Shirt, grab shirt." Seonghun's speech was garbled, but Liah understood, reaching down to the floor to toss him his shirt. He caught it, covering himself in time. The orgasm was hard, making Seong see stars. His body involuntarily jerked in the bed as waves of pleasure overcame him.

Maliah laid on her side, observing curiously.

Cleaning himself up with his shirt, he tossed it on the floor before looking at her. "If I hadn't been here, how long would it have taken you to come?" he asked.

"Anywhere from an hour to an hour and a half," she replied. "I can cut that to thirty minutes if I use my vibrator."

He perked up. "You have a vibrator?"

"Yes."

"Why don't you use it every time?"

"Because it has the unmistakable sound of a vibrator. I live with three men," she pointed out.

"Oh."

"Yeah."

"Can I see it?"

"Later, I'm getting sleepy."

"Liah, have you thought about lowering your dosage of antidepressant?"

"Not particularly. It's the same dosage I've been on since I got out of the hospital. I'm still a mess when I talk about the things that happened. I don't think it's time yet. I can't justify lowering it for more sexual satisfaction."

"Do you have other side effects?"

"Mmm, I become 'wooden'," she used finger quotes, "sometimes things that should have an effect, don't. You screaming at Casey should have provoked some sort of reaction. The only thing I thought was that it was nice that someone stood up for me. I lose my appetite from time to time. That's it."

"I'm about to ask a really personal question," he said.

"You've seen me naked," she said drowsily, pulling the blanket over her. "What is it?"

"Are you on any birth control?"

"No, I haven't had a need. I also take quite a few pills in my daily life. I'm not trying to add to it." She cuddled into him. "I'm going to go to sleep now. Goodnight, Seonghun."

"Goodnight, sweetheart."

CHAPTER 19

Seonghun awoke to Liah gone. Feeling where she was on the bed, it had long grown cold. Sitting up he stretched and saw a folded note on her desk with his name on it. As he opened the two sheets of paper, he gasped. It was a drawing of him again, from the waist up. Seong was topless. With the perspective of the drawing, it was as if he were above something, staring intently.. He realized it was probably him hovering over her last night. How did she draw so quickly this morning? Looking at his phone, he realized it was noon; no wonder he was ravenous.

Quickly putting on his shorts, he grabbed his shirt from the floor before leaving Liah's room. Walking across the suite, Seong noticed everyone else's doors were open. The silence in the suite was encompassing, letting him know that he was the last one to leave today.

He changed clothes, not bothering with a shower as he was going to the gym after he ate. As he walked, Seong's hair on the back of his neck stood on end. Looking around he didn't see anything unusual, but couldn't help glancing behind him occasionally. Eventually Seong told himself he was being silly. As soon as he got his breakfast, he opened Liah's note.

S,

I have roughly two good memories of my family. The first one was when I was small, about 5 or 6. I got to play in the sprinklers with the neighborhood chil-dren. I was probably allowed to go because there were so many kids. The neigh-borhood always wondered about me. I wasn't seen very often, and didn't participate in other activities with neighborhood kids. After I got done running through the sprinklers, one of the moms lumped me in with her kids, buying us all ice cream from the ice cream truck. There's a picture of me standing in line excited with everyone else, while my parents were there, looking somewhat happy. I stole it. It's not like they are going to be looking for it.

The second memory was in high school. My parents came to my senior choir concert. I typically shy away from solos and like to stay in the back, but my choir teacher heard me singing by myself one day and forced me to try out. So I did, and I got it. The catch was I got paired with boys (it seems like I'm always getting paired with boys). Have you heard of a song called 'In the Still of the Night'? Boyz II Men remade it, but it is a much older song. Listen to their version.

My parents barely knew where I went to school, much less that I could sing, so it surprised them. I think it floored my mother a lot. I was doing what she wanted to be doing (to an extent) in high school. I found out later on that several faculty members came up to them and told them how I was a bright student and they couldn't wait to see what I did with my life. Any praise on me, felt like praise on them (they raised me after all, so why shouldn't they take the praise /sarcasm), so they were super proud of me. They took me out to eat and everything. They even refrained from arguing for a while. It was nice. I don't talk about my dad because, well, there isn't much to say. He was less about the verbal abuse, but he didn't stop it. He simply wasn't present there for me. My most vivid memories are of my mother screaming at me and my dad just watching tv ignoring it. Above it all. It didn't matter. The screaming didn't matter.

Seonghun never wanted to fight a pair of adults more in his life than when reading this note about her parents. She was still hurting. He felt it in the letter. She wrote about it in a clinical manner, but all of this hurt her. He continued reading.

A turtle-like speed is fine with me, Seonghun. We didn't really go turtle speed last night though. Are you okay? Are you overthinking? I enjoyed being with you last night, so if that was a worry, please don't let it be. Thank you for being honest about your girlfriend. I know it is hard to talk about things in your past (I think you know that I know that), but sometimes I need to hear them. I'm going to be honest with you right now, last night was kind of hard for me as well. It takes a lot to get me to orgasm; you respected that. I appreciate it. However, I'm probably not going to be ready for sex anytime soon. It sort of feels like we should have a rhythm together before we even get to that piece of the puzzle. If we get there. It seems kind of odd. A month ago I didn't have any friends. Now I have two, and you. I'm sorry, I don't really know what to classify you as. A friend with benefits?

I wondered if you would ask about my schooling situation. Before I got scholarships, I knew that college was going to be a hard road for me financially. Even if I got grants given to poor people, Silver Leaf is an expensive school. I'd been planning for college since I was in 7th grade. From freshman year to senior year of high school 90% of my course load were college credit classes. I could take them discounted through the local community college. As a result, I technically have a degree already. I have an associate degree in general studies. I graduated from high school and college at the same time.

Seonghun gawked at the page. This woman was incredible.

The community college has a deal that high school students who complete a particular program start out as juniors if they go to certain college campuses in Indiana. Silver Leaf is one of them. So last year I was a junior. This year I'm a senior; I'll graduate at the same time as you three.

Do you realize how deep of a sleeper you are? The light is on in my room while I'm writing away and you're dead to the world, naked, under my comforter. I'm going to be honest, and say I'd like to climb back in and maybe snuggle you for a bit, which is not something I've ever actually wanted to do before. But I've already missed class this week. While I do have documentation on file that allows me to miss classes, I don't like to take advantage of that fact. Plus I have a couple of music lessons today. Have a good day and make sure you eat something in between your meals. I'll talk with you soon.

-L

The weird feeling he had earlier dissipated, so after he finished reading his note, he walked to the gym. To his surprise both Minjun and Yongjoon were there. Minjun was sitting beside Yong on a stationary bike, with the hood of his sweatshirt up and sunglasses on. Yongjoon was lifting weights while talking to him. Stowing his bag in the lockers, he walked up to them both. "Is it too soon to ask her to be my girlfriend?" he blurted out, in lieu of a hello.

His friends looked at each other before staring at their tall friend. "Seonghun, did you have sex last night?" Yongjoon asked.

"No. I'm not ready for that, I told you," he blushed hotly.

"Okay, is there a particular reason why you want to ask her right this second?" Yongjoon continued to lift weights while looking at Seonghun through the mirror.

"You know how we send notes?"

Both of his friends nodded.

"She mentioned in one how a month ago she didn't have any friends; now she has two, and me. She didn't know what to classify me as, mentioning something about friends with benefits. I don't want just the benefits. I want all of her. She's the whole benefit." Seonghun was nearly shouting as Minjun struggled not to laugh at him.

"If you're asking if I think you would scare her off if you asked, I'm going to say no. She may pick it apart, but it wouldn't freak her out, I don't think," Minjun said.

Yongjoon wasn't paying them any attention. He was squinting in the mirror. "What's wrong?" Seonghun asked as he began to stretch thoroughly.

"I thought I saw—" He kept staring. "I'm just seeing things, never mind. But yes, what Minjun said. Just ask. It can't hurt."

"When I was with my ex, we just kind of agreed that we were dating. Should I take her out on a date before asking?"

"You're asking us? Minjun doesn't really date. I haven't had a serious date in years," Yongjoon said.

"Years?" Seonghun asked. "Any reason why?"

Minjun lightly peddled the machine as he listened.

"Dating someone seriously is a form of intimacy to me. It's letting someone in on a whole other level, sharing emotional scars. If I'm in that deep, they need to be too; I haven't found anyone that I'm interested in getting that deep with," Yongjoon explained.

Seonghun slid his eyes to Minjun who seemed to be deep in thought.

"So yeah," Yongjoon said as he dropped the weight, "I don't know if we're the ones you should be asking. I will say though, that asking her on a date couldn't hurt. Who doesn't like to go on a date?"

Seonghun nodded, wandering off to another machine. Yong went to follow when he saw Min standing between the men, looking uncomfortable.

"When we were younger I had a small crush on Seonghun. I would imagine kissing him all the time. I wondered if he felt the same way. He was completely oblivious to relationships though. It faded away though fairly quickly because even though he's my best friend, he's also the weirdest man I've ever met." Minjun chuckled quietly. "It was around that time I realized that most people don't want to kiss both boys and girls." He began to walk away when Yongjoon grabbed him by the arm.

"Do you lean toward one or the other?" Yong asked.

Minjun shook his head. "I don't lean toward any gender really. Someone could be gender fluid; it's about who they are as a person, not really their gender."

Yongjoon was silent for a moment. leaning in, he kissed him on the cheek. "Thank you for sharing, Min." He followed after Seong to spot him.

Minjun beamed. He proceeded to roll on a yoga ball until the other two were done.

Seonghun wanted to show them the place Maliah had taken him for breakfast so Yongjoon drove them across the bridge to Lafayette. As they walked in, they saw the owner behind the counter. As he saw Seong, he smiled. "Hi there! I remember you. You were with my friend that gets a BLT all the time."

"Yes. I brought some more friends with me today." His friends waved at him.

Just then a bag was brought to the counter by a waitress. "Speaking of her, this is her lunch order. A little late today. She's normally here before 12:30," the manager said.

Seonghun looked at his watch. To his surprise it was already three. "Can I pay for that?" The manager agreed so Seonghun glanced over at his friends. "Go find a table, I'll be there in a second," he said as he pulled his wallet out. Once Liah's meal was paid for, he joined his friends in the booth. As he sat down, Min opened his mouth to say something, but quickly closed it when he saw Seong.

"Min, I don't have secrets from you two. You can ask what you want," Yong said as the waitress came over to fill the coffee cups.

"Were you in a relationship with a man or a woman?" Minjun asked.

"I've had both, but my most serious relationship was with a man," he replied.

"Did your mother take it okay?" Seong spoke up.

Yongjoon chuckled. He then burst into a full belly laugh. "My mom is perfectly fine with it. She shows up at the Pride parade in Indy, with a t-shirt that says 'Free Mom Hugs'. She loves people, end of story."

Yongjoon's father died when he was a baby, so all he knew was his mother. He protected her with his life. She moved to the states as a young bride, but became a widow all too soon after. Cho never remarried; as far as the men knew, she never dated. She doted on her baby boy without being overbearing. Yong was a straight up mama's boy, not caring what anyone thought about it.

"What happened with your relationship?" Min asked.

"A few things actually," Yongjoon said.

They were interrupted by the waitress coming to take their order. Seonghun ordered a burger and fries (with a side salad to minimize Min's glare), Yongjoon ordered a BLT, while Min got the spaghetti.

"Go ahead, Yong," Seonghun said.

"He was a bit older than me; he saw me as someone he could mold into what he wanted. Which isn't a thing you can do. When we started dating he asked me for a poly relationship."

"Poly?" Seonghun asked.

"He wanted our relationship to be open to multiple partners. I didn't want a relationship like that. He was free to leave, but he said he would be okay with just me. He lied." Yongjoon took a sip of his coffee. "He'd been seeing several other people, not just me. I had to go get tested for STDs. I thought Mom was going to cut him."

"You seem very calm about all of this," Minjun noted.

Yongjoon smirked, one of his dimples showing. "I am now. But then, I was an absolute basket case. My trust was destroyed, my heart was broken, I had been lied to so many times, about so many things, I didn't know which way was up. My mom said I had a choice to make. I could dwell on why this happened, letting my heart soak in bitterness, or I could 'chalk this one up to the game'." Yong laughed. "She said that I needed to take a step back to think really hard if this was all truly a shock, or I had been lying to myself the whole time because I wanted to be loved. If the latter was the case maybe I needed to be alone for a while because that relationship wasn't love."

"Cho gives good advice," Seonghun said.

"She should follow her own advice sometime," Yongjoon snorted. "She found the guy, immediately kicking him in the nuts. I didn't find out until much, much later."

They all started laughing as they heard the bell at the door indicating that it had been opened. Seonghun glanced over to see Maliah walk through. "She is so pretty," he said without thinking. Her glasses were crooked again. She was still wearing his sweatshirt, with the arms covering her hands.

Minjun glanced over. "She is, but she wears that sweatshirt all the time."

"It's mine. I loaned it to her when we went to the park, but she never gave it back."

They watched as the owner explained her meal had already been paid for while pointing to their booth. When she turned to look, all three of them started waving at her. She thanked the manager before walking over with a small smile.

"Hello."

"Hey," Seonghun said, scooting over so she could sit. "I wanted to show them this place." Just then their food arrived. After everything was placed on the table, both her and Minjun spoke at the same time.

"Eat your salad first."

She smiled at Minjun before staring at her lap.

"Now there's two of you? Are you going to be ganging up on me?"

She glanced at Min who grinned widely at her.

"Maybe," they said together. Both of them started giggling.

Seonghun smiled at the two of them. "Do you have time to eat your lunch with us or do you have to get back to work?"

"I can eat with you." She unpacked her bag. At the bottom was a slice of cake. "Is that—"

Seonghun glanced over to see what she was looking at. Over a mouthful of lettuce, he replied. "It's lemon pound cake with lemon cream cheese icing." Maliah stared at the cake.

"Are you okay?" Yongjoon asked.

She looked up at him. "I fucking love lemon everything." Everyone was startled at the expletive.

Min choked on his spaghetti.

Yong started laughing.

Seonghun shook his head, going back to his salad, trying to hurry up so he could get to his burger.

"I didn't even know they sold this. Thank you." Ignoring her sandwich she went straight for the cake.

She moaned, startling Seonghun. "I really love lemon cake." Licking her lips of errant icing she was solely focused on the cake.

Seonghun gawked at her, before laughing hysterically.

"What's so funny?" Minjun asked.

"Two things. One, we could have all been friends quicker had we left a lemon cake outside her door."

"This is probably true," Liah admitted.

"What is two?" Yongjoon asked.

"Two is personal," Seonghun said, leaning over to whisper in Liah's ear. "You moan louder for the cake than you did last night."

Liah choked. "Sorry? Cake trumps..." She looked up to see the roommates staring at her expectedly. "Cake will always trump that," she amended.

They continued eating. Seong watched as she finished half of her sandwich. She pushed the other half toward him, to his absolute delight. "I gotta get going, I have another student soon." She lightly kissed him on the temple, since his mouth was full of sandwich before taking a sip of the water he'd left untouched. "I will talk to you guys this evening." She slid out of the booth. "I forgot to ask, do you take anything to the drive-in?"

"Sometimes we bring snacks, other times we eat there, it just depends," Yong said.

"Will you make spaghetti for dinner?" Minjun asked suddenly.

Liah wrinkled her brow. "Didn't you just finish a plate of spaghetti?"

"Yours is better," he admitted, "also you have cinnamon rolls."

"I can do that. I'll send you a list of stuff you need to check for in the kitchen. Let me know if we don't have it."

Minjun nodded, pushing Yongjoon out of the booth. He gave her a hug, which Yong joined in on. Min began then rattling them all around which made Maliah laugh.

"Bye, guys. Thank you again for lunch."

The three men watched her leave.

CHAPTER 20

L,

Can I see the picture? I'd love to see what happy baby you looked like. I listened to the song. Do you have a copy of the video of you singing it? I love the song, it's sounds like old school doo-wop, which is what I think that group was going for.

I'm sorry for everything that happened to you growing up. No wonder you were cautious of all of us. You don't really have much of an example of friendship, do you? None of us are malicious, I promise. I won't say that I don't get angry; I do. I wanted to fight your parents as I read your letter. I don't lash out, though. I'm a big guy, it can come off as frightening due to my size alone. Lashing out can terrify people. Also, I try not to make choices in anger. You can end up hurting the people you care about. So I may get mad, but I hope we can talk it through.

You asked me earlier in another letter what I want to farm and what's my plan. My family owns a large amount of land. Surprisingly large. My plan after college for now is to take what I learned and go back to them. While I was in school in Korea, I also had a small house built on one of the further plots of land. It's enough for me to work and have a small harvest from. I'll take that over and save money. Eventually my parents will retire. Maybe to the city, maybe build a new house on the land, but I'll take over completely. One side is focused on rice. We also have standard crops like barley, potatoes, and small groves of apple trees. We have a lot of land that isn't utilized, and from talking to my father, our neighbors are giving up, so he may be acquiring that as well. I didn't understand why he was accumulating so much land, when we have so much we don't use (we rent quite a bit out to other farmers to use as pasture grounds) but my mom explained that he just wants me to be able have the space to use my education. It's another way for him to show his love I suspect.

Friends with benefits? I don't like that phrase at all. I don't know why; it just makes my skin crawl. I'll analyze that feeling another day. We're friends... That kiss? I dunno. How about we're friends, trying to figure out if there is more? That sounds about right. With that being said, I wanted to ask you on a date, but it's an odd request because I'm asking you on the date, but I'm also asking you to take us somewhere that only you know.

Seonghun banged his head on his desk at how awkward he was sounding. He continued to plow on.

I was wondering if you could take us roller skating next weekend. We could do that and maybe dinner? Let me know.

So, you graduated college... in high school?! That is amazing! How did you find time for your studies and work? I still don't understand how you're working two jobs along with having a full course load. It seems like a struggle to keep up every day on homework.

One of the things about being a farmer is the early rising. It is a thing I struggle with. I love to sleep. There is nothing like sleeping in a nice bed with soft sheets, waking when you want to. It is probably one of my most favorite things in the world. My dream day would be never leaving the bed, except for bathroom breaks of course. But all meals would be served in bed. There would be nothing but reading, or tv or other things.

He turned red at the thought of other things with her.

It was nice to have lunch with you today. I'm glad you seem comfortable with us. Also anytime you want cake, sweetheart, I'd make it happen, just to see that look of pure bliss on your face.
-S

He honestly wished he could get that look of bliss on her face in other ways, but that was probably going to take some time. Seong didn't mind, he was a hard worker. Sealing the letter in an envelope, he poked around the bag of flowers, finding a sprig of lavender. Trimming the sprig, he taped it diagonally to the envelope. He walked into the common area to see Min frantically scrolling his phone.

"Are you okay?" Seonghun asked him as he taped the note to Liah's door.

"I asked Yong out on a date. I don't know where to go." He was staring at his phone in distress.

He shrugged. "Take him somewhere out of town. Take him to St. Elmo's."

Minjun looked at Seonghun. "How did you think of that so easily off the top of your head when I've been sitting here for an hour an absolute mess?"

"Because you tend to freak out easily." He opened the fridge, pulling out a couple of bottles of water, before sliding one to Min.

"If you took Maliah on a date, you'd freak out?" Minjun asked.

"No," he responded slowly, "I don't think so. I don't tend to panic like you do."

"Are you going to ask her out?" Seonghun pointed at the note on the door. "That's good." Minjun looked at him. "Are you doing something fancy?"

"Maybe some other time. I thought I would keep it simple."

They heard keys jingling in the door. As it opened, Maliah waddled in. She was holding a pumpkin between her legs and bags in her hands. "You should have called, we would have come to help," Minjun chided her as they grabbed the bags from her. Seong didn't think it was a great idea to grab anything from between her legs, pumpkin, or no.

"I forgot I could ask someone," she said embarrassed. "I'm used to doing things by myself, though I typically am not dragging around a pumpkin."

"Why do you have it?" Min asked, confused.

"Seonghun said he wanted one, so I got him one." She handed it over to him.

He smiled at her as he set the pumpkin down. "Thank you. Do you want to cut it on Saturday?"

"I've never made a jack o' lantern before. Sounds like fun," she said as she unpacked the bags. "Min, do you want to help cook again?"

At his nod, she instructed him to go wash his hands before turning to Seonghun.

"Thank you again for lunch, it was nice. I love cake."

He hid a smile. "So you've said several times." He watched her pull multiple boxes of cereal out of the bags. "Were you craving cereal?"

"No, I'm going to make Chex Mix for the drive-in."

"Chex Mix?"

Liah handed him one of the boxes of cereal, tapping the side of the box before washing her hands at the sink.

He read through the recipe. "This sounds interesting."

She looked at him. "I know it sounds weird, it's okay. But it is really good. Also I use the recipe as a jump off. I don't follow it completely. It doesn't give me enough coating if you follow it to the letter." She dried her hands before opening cans of tomatoes.

Minjun came out of the bathroom and Maliah handed him a packet of hot sausages. "Do you remember what to do?"

"Cut the casing off, before frying the meat in the pan," he recited as he got to work. Maliah started to dump crushed tomatoes, herbs, and other seasonings into a pot.

"You make sauce? Why not buy the jarred kind?" Seonghun asked.

"I doctor up jarred sauce so much, it just makes more sense to make it from scratch." She threw in a parmesan rind.

"Where did you learn to cook?" Minjun asked as he struggled with the first casing.

"TV mostly. It was either cook or starve. My parents thought I was too chubby, so there wasn't a lot of food kept in the house. When I started earning my own money, I bought myself a small amount of groceries every week. Spaghetti, jarred sauce with no meat, is an inexpensive meal."

Seonghun looked at her. "You aren't chubby."

"Yes I am."

"No you aren't," chimed in Minjun.

She looked down at herself. "I wear baggy clothes, so you wouldn't really be able to tell, but my hips and butt are big. There's nothing wrong with being chubby—"

"No, there isn't," Seonghun agreed.

"So I embrace it. I am what I am." She shrugged.

Seonghun walked up to her, grabbing her gently by the shoulders, before unzipping the sweatshirt. "You aren't chubby. You're shaped like a woman with curves." He had her so that her back was facing Minjun. Seong took the opportunity to skim his hands along the sides of her chest, down to her waist. "If you were chubby, it wouldn't be a big deal either, but I've heard you mention your 'fat ass' before; I wanted to set the record straight." He could tell it would take her time to come to terms with something she'd heard her entire life.

Opening the fridge, Liah handed two cans of cinnamon rolls to Seonghun. "Can you open these? But wait until I'm in my room?"

"Why wait?"

"I can't take the pop." She scurried off into her room, grabbed the note before shutting her door as Seong stared after her baffled.

"She did the same thing the other night. It's not a loud noise, but I can see how it would be startling," Minjun explained.

He followed the instructions; both men jumped as the can popped open. Solidly prepared this time, he popped the second can easily. Setting the cans on the counter, Seong knocked on her door. No answer. Biting his lip he opened the door just a crack. "Liah?"

Maliah was passed out on her bed asleep with the pages from his letter in her hand.

"Oh, sweetheart." He sighed. Poking his head out of the door, he called to his friend, "Min, can you finish the dinner from here?"

"Yes, why?"

"She fell asleep."

"I'll take care of it, go to her." With that, Minjun turned back to the stove to finish dinner.

Seonghun closed the door behind him. "Liah," he said cautiously, sitting at her desk.

He watched as she opened her eyes, staring confused at her bed. "I've never dozed off that fast in my life, I'm sorry." She set his letter under her pillow, trying to sit up.

"Maybe it's your body telling you to slow down." He patted her leg. "Minjun is going to finish dinner. Take a nap with me." He went to his knees, helping her take her shoes off. Liah's socks were a delight. One was pink, one was yellow; they both had a big red heart on them. "I love that your socks never match."

She chuckled. "It's silly, but it makes me smile. I know everyone sees me as this nose to the grindstone person, but it's like my little secret." With her shoes off, she went to get under the covers, but stopped. "You should probably get in first. You sleep longer than me."

Seonghun climbed in with Liah following after him. For the first time, things felt awkward to him. They were pressed back to back in the small bed. He turned so he was facing her back. "Are you still awake?" he asked softly.

"Yeah," she whispered.

"Did we do too much too soon?" he asked. "I'm getting a weird vibe."

"I don't know how to just be after the other night," she explained, turning her head to him. "I don't know if that is what you expect every time we're in bed together. I'm not— that's not—" She seemed at a loss for words.

"Okay." He sat up, observing Liah. She had a sleepy look on her face with her hair splayed across her pillow. "We're adults, right?"

She nodded.

"As adults, we set the pace for what we want. I like you a lot, Liah. I think you're fun to be with. If you want to be just friends, that's fine. I have boundaries with that, however. I don't kiss my friends like I do you. Hugs, yes, and even us sleeping together platonically, is fine. But that would be the end of it." He moved one of the twists off of her forehead, tucking it behind her ear. "If we pursue whatever it is that we're doing, I don't 'expect'," he used finger quotes, "anything at all. There are two people on this journey; we have to figure out what works for us. For the record, I agree that we moved a little too fast the other night, but I really wanted to touch you." His ears bloomed red.

"I like you too. I know it's more than friendship that I feel for you, but I'm not ready to explore the physical side of that, you know? It feels like a level of intimacy that, well, we aren't at yet," she said.

"So we explore what's between us, and we wait until we're both ready for that step again. Deal?" He looked at her.

"Deal. Does that mean no more kissing? I'm comfortable with that, but if you aren't…" She dropped the sentence.

In response he leaned in and nipped her lip. "We can kiss as much or as little as you want. I'm going to be honest, I may pull away before you want me to, because, well, I want you. But I don't want to make you uncomfortable." He shrugged.

"I get it. We're good?" Liah looked up at him.

"We're good. Get some sleep." He kissed the tip of her nose before lying back down. She rolled back to her side. Seong followed her, wrapping his arms around her.

Seonghun woke up to an empty bed with a note beside him on the pillow.

S
I'd love to go skating with you.
-L

He felt giddy. He was also hungry. Looking at his watch, he saw that he had slept for three hours. Scrambling out of the bed he walked into the living room. Maliah was by herself doing homework with the tv playing softly. Looking up she saw him stumble out of her room.

"Hungry?" she asked.

He nodded, so she closed her book.

Standing up, Liah walked over to the fridge pulling out a plastic wrapped plate heaped with spaghetti, green peas, and two cinnamon rolls. Maliah removed the plastic and popped it into the microwave for a few minutes.

He walked over to her and kissed her gently. "Thank you." Seonghun's voice was rough from sleep. "Where is everyone?"

"Party on Frat Row," Liah murmured as Seonghun nuzzled her face.

He brought his mouth back to hers. Liah's hand automatically went up his shirt, resting on his waist as he continued kissing her. The microwave timer sounded.

"Uh…" Liah's voice was muffled. "Seonghun, dinner?"

"In a second, this is nice." He pulled away from her mouth, dragging his own down her neck, biting her before lightly sucking.

"Oh god," she moaned. "Stop for a second."

He released her neck, looking at her. "Are you okay?"

"That was— I'm-I'm good. I just— you bit me and I—"

Seonghun smirked. "You have a spot."

"A what?"

"A spot. A place that feels better than most."

"Where's your spot?" she asked, pulling the plate out of the microwave.

"It's one of those things better discovered together, rather than me just telling you. You'll find it sooner or later." He took the plate she handed him. "Thank you."

"Don't thank me, I barely did anything. Minjun did a really good job."

"Who put the plate up for me?"

She looked down at her feet, avoiding his gaze.

"Min is sweet, but he would have tossed everything in the fridge, so, thank you."

"You're welcome." She went back to focusing on her homework.

While Seonghun ate, he watched Maliah work. She was so intent on absorbing the content of her materials, she seemed to forget he was there.

"Liah?"

No response.

"Maliah?"

"Yeah?"

"Do you want some ice cream?"

She looked up at him confused. "Huh?"

He gave her a kiss. "I'll be right back. Keep studying."

"Okay." She went back to her work.

He chuckled, shaking his head. As he walked to the store, Seong had that odd hair raising feeling again. Trying to shrug it off, he kept moving. Standing on the corner, while waiting for the light to change, Seong saw someone out of the corner of his eye rushing toward him. As he turned someone, brushed past him hard, basically throwing him to the ground. His ankle twisted as he went down. As he hit the ground, Seong's new glasses skittered into the street.

"Are you okay?" A guy ran out in the street grabbing his glasses. Luckily, there was no traffic coming. The gentleman kindly helped Seonghun stand. It was a struggle, but together, they did it. Gingerly, Seong tested his ankle; it was sore, but walkable.

"Thank you so much," he said as the man handed him his glasses. His heart sank as he saw his brand new lenses completely scratched up.

"It's not a problem. Whoever did that, it was purposeful. They put their hands out to push you."

Seonghun was still dazed, not fully taking in what the man had to say. It was almost like static over his words.

"My name is James. Let me give you my number just in case you decide to talk to the police."

He exchanged information with Seonghun, making sure he was able to walk before he went on his way. Seonghun dug in his pocket, pulling out his phone. It was a little scratched on the sides, but no worse for wear. He scrolled until he got the number he needed. Shaking a little, he pressed the call button.

"Hello?"

"Liah?"

"Hi Seonghun, your voice sounds strange."

"Can you uh, can you come and walk back with me? I was pushed into the street. I don't feel very well."

"Did you go to The Den for ice cream?"

He nodded his head, not thinking clearly.

"Honey, if you're saying something I can't hear you. I need to know where you went, so I know where to go."

"Yes, yes I went to The Den."

"I'm on my way. Hold on, okay? I'll run."

"Please hurry." He hung up the phone. Slowly sliding down to the ground, Seong realized his shaking was getting worse.

CHAPTER 21

When Maliah found him, he was balled up, his knees to his chest with his arms wrapped around them. She knelt down on the sidewalk next to him, not touching him. "What do you need?"

"I just want to go home."

"Are you okay with me touching you?"

"I…" He looked at her, losing his train of thought. There was so much static in his head.

"Okay. We've got this." She held her hand out to him. Slowly, he gripped it. "I know how you're feeling right now. It may not seem like it, but I do. You're confused about who would want to hurt you like this, wondering if you did anything wrong, and how you can trust anyone right now." She put her other hand on top of his. "Those feelings aren't going to go away overnight, but you will feel a bit better once you're in safe surroundings. Come back with me to the dorm; we'll get you in bed. I can hug you, or not if you don't want to be touched. We will get this sorted out together, but you need to take the first step."

Seong stared at her for a long time before slowly rising to his feet. Liah went to let go of his hand, but he squeezed. Hand in hand they walked back to the dorm in silence. As soon as they were settled, Maliah checked him over for injuries. The palms of his hands were scraped up and his ankle was slightly swollen. "Go sit on the couch," she said as she walked into her room.

Seonghun complied robotically. "I don't know why I feel like this. I wasn't hurt badly."

Maliah didn't say anything to him as she sat next to him with a tiny first aid kit. "You're in shock."

He looked at her through his scuffed lenses. "I just got these glasses."

"I know. We'll get them fixed, I promise." She began cleaning the scrapes with alcohol. "Elevate your hurt ankle."

He watched her as she quietly doted on him; his heart tugged. "Thank you for coming to me."

"You would have done it for me." She glanced up at his eyes before focusing on his hand.

"How did you know what to say?"

Liah was silent for a little bit. "Because I had the same out of body feeling you had when that man was pushed into my room," she whispered. "I asked myself some of the same questions you were asking yourself." It was quiet as she finished cleaning the scrapes. "You don't need bandages or anything," she said. "How does your ankle feel?"

"Stiff."

"Why don't you go lay down?" she suggested.

"I don't want to be alone right now," he admitted.

"I could call Minjun." She looked at him with a straight face. He stared at her. "I'm sure him or Yongjoon will keep you company." She tried smothering a smile, but the corners of her mouth twitched.

"Will you stay with me tonight?" he clarified.

"Yeah, I will." She kissed him on his cheek before standing up. "I'm going to change. I'll be there in a minute." Seonghun shuffled to his room. He sadly took off his glasses, looking at the scratches. The scuffs were bad. He was taking his shirt off when she tapped on the door. Turning around, he put his glasses on to see her staring at him.

"What?" he asked.

"I want to draw you. You have beautiful lines," she said.

"I don't know what you mean by lines."

She walked over. "Turn around."

He turned, his back facing her while he looked over his shoulder at her. She traced his back with her fingers. "Your body is very defined. I want to draw it."

"Naked?"

"I've had some classes in that area, but I honestly don't feel comfortable drawing naked people. Topless is fine."

"Just let me know when."

Climbing into bed, Seong waited on Liah. She closed the door before joining him. "How are you feeling?"

"I'm upset that my glasses are scuffed. I'm confused as to who would hate me so much, they would push me into traffic. I'm grateful you were here." He kissed her.

"I feel bad that I was so focused on my work, I didn't go with you," Maliah admitted.

"You can't think like that. It could have been you pushed in the street."

She shrugged. "You need to file a police report."

"I know. I'll do it tomorrow." He slowly wiggled closer, kissing her again. She opened her mouth to him, sliding her hand up his chest. Eventually, Maliah pulled away.

"I'm sorry, I have to stop. I want—"

"I know, I do too." He gave her one last peck. "Goodnight, sweetheart."

"Goodnight."

When Seonghun's alarm went off the following morning, Liah was gone. But there was a blob sitting at his desk. Putting his glasses on, he saw Minjun. "Where's Liah?" he asked, slowly sitting up.

"She went back to her room. You were restless all night. Nothing she was doing was calming you down, so she went back to her room."

"Min, were you sitting here watching us sleep?" Seonghun asked incredulously.

"No," Minjun laughed, "I was getting out of the shower when she was walking back to her room."

Seonghun relaxed.

"So, were you going to tell me what happened, or were you just going to show up with scratched glasses?" Minjun asked.

"It's fine, Min. The more I think about it, the more I think maybe I stumbled," he said as he stood up.

"Seonghun." Minjun stared at him.

"Seriously, I'm fine." Seonghun gingerly tested his ankle.

"Seonghun." His best friend grabbed his arm.

"What?"

"Do you really think you stumbled?" he asked quietly.

Seonghun was silent.

"What are you scared of?"

"Who would do this, Min? What did I do?"

"I don't know. That's why you need to report it. If anything, maybe one of the cameras around the area caught something, so you can get reimbursed for your glasses."

Seonghun sighed.

"Go get your shower. You can go after your classes. There should be plenty of time to file a report before we meet everyone for the drive-in." With that, Minjun left, letting Seonghun get ready.

Once he was finished, he tapped on Maliah's door before he left. He opened the door when she said to.

Liah was in sweats, working on homework. "How are you feeling?" she asked, flipping her hair out of her face.

"My hands are okay, my ankle is a little sore, but nothing too bad," he said.

"Not what I meant." She closed her book, staring at him.

"Still a little shaken up," he admitted freely, "I don't want to go to the police. I'm worried they're going to think I'm making a big deal out of nothing."

Maliah stared at Seonghun for a beat longer before she got up. Opening her closet, she pulled out an old billfold. Inside there wasn't anything but a single card that she handed to Seong.

Looking down at the card, Seonghun saw that it had a name on it. "Who is Detective Krishna Drake?"

"She was the woman who came after everything happened to me last year." Maliah paused for a minute before she continued. "She was nothing but kind to me. Ask for her specifically. I know for a fact anything you say will be taken seriously by her. She pushed me to press actual charges, which is against their policy, but I didn't understand what she was trying to tell me." She hung her head as she tugged on her braids lightly.

"Hey, none of that." He lifted her chin so they were eye to eye. "It wasn't your fault. None of it was your fault."

"I know. At least, I'm getting there, but it still stings."

"What are your plans for today?" he asked.

"Guitar lesson, homework, and Chex Mix. Then the drive-in with a-a-a-all of you." She sat back on the bed.

"Still nervous?" he asked.

She nodded.

"Say the word and we come right back home. No one is upset, no one blames you, okay? I hope you will enjoy the movie though. Even if we don't like it, we always comment through it and point out silly bits." He grabbed her hand, gently squeezing it.

"N-n-n-none of you are going to hurt me, I'm in c-c-c-c-control, If I n-n-n-need to come back it is okay," Maliah repeated to herself quietly.

"Do you have a session with your therapist today?"

"Yes, why?" she asked.

"Talk about it," he said simply. "Talk about all of us. She's a nice person."

Maliah nodded. "I will. I do want to g-g-g-get better. It helps." She looked at him. "I'm doing what I need to do. I have a responsibility to myself. You have a responsibility to yourself to go to the police."

"I will," he promised her. "Can I kiss you before I go?"

She wrapped her arms around his waist, pressing her head to his chest. Well, as far as she could reach anyway. He was engulfed by her scent again.

"You always smell so nice," Seong murmured as he wrapped his arms around her gently.

"I don't have anything on now. Just soap," she said looking up at him.

He gave her a quick peck on the mouth, before sadly unwinding himself from her. "I have to get going. I will see you this evening though."

"If," she hesitated for a moment, "if you have a problem explaining yourself to the police, give me a call. I'd be happy to hold your hand through the process."

Seong was touched. He could tell it would cost her a lot to step foot in that police station; the fact that she would do it for him did fluttery things to his stomach. "Thank you, I will." He kissed her forehead before leaving.

Classes flew for Seonghun that day. Pretty soon he was on the opposite end of campus, where his roommates normally took classes. It was also where the campus police building resided. To his surprise the two of them were sitting outside of the station, waiting for him.

"You didn't have to come," he called out.

"Yeah we did," Yong said. "Maliah left us a note last night, worried you wouldn't come. She thought you might need a support system."

"We wouldn't let you do this alone anyway. You know that," added Minjun.

Seonghun took a deep breath before climbing the stairs to the police station. Walking in, it wasn't like the television cop shows Seong had seen. It wasn't gritty, there weren't people milling around with cups of coffee. It looked almost like a business office. People were typing up reports at gray desks. Right up front was a woman behind a long receptionist's desk staring at a computer screen. Seong walked over to her.

The woman looked at him. "Hi, can I help you?" she asked, waiting patiently.

Seonghun fingered the card in his pocket. "I was wondering if I could speak with Detective Krishna Drake?" He felt the confused stares of his friends at his back.

"I'll see if she is available. Take a seat, it shouldn't take long." The woman pointed to the bright yellow couch behind them. They took a seat while she picked up a phone.

"Who is Krishna Drake?" Yongjoon whispered.

Seonghun shrugged. "Liah said that she helped her with the last incident. She tried to get her to press charges outside of student court, which wasn't authorized. They are supposed to push the student court no matter what. It seemed like she had more of Liah's interests at heart, rather than following the letter of the law."

They watched as a tall Indian woman walked up. She was dressed casually in jeans with a little badge hanging on her belt. Her curly hair was held back by a yellow headband that contrasted with her bright blue shirt. Perched on the headband were glasses. "Hi, I'm Detective Krishna. One of you asked for me?"

Seonghun stood up, introducing everyone.

"It's nice to meet you. What can I help you with?" she asked politely.

"I—" Seonghun opened his mouth but closed it quickly, not knowing really where to start.

Detective Krishna smiled sympathetically. "Why don't you three come with me?" She led them to an office with a simple rectangular wooden table. Four metal chairs were pushed in. "This is where I do research sometimes, or where I go when I need quiet. I thought it may help a bit," she explained as she took a seat. "You seemed to be having difficulty talking, so how about I ask some questions?"

Seonghun nodded.

"I don't usually have people ask for me by name, unless I've helped them before; usually it is women I've helped. So I guess my first question is how did you get my name?"

"Uh, you helped a friend of ours last year. I told her I was worried about someone taking me seriously so she gave me your card. Her name is Maliah, Maliah Evans," Seonghun said.

Detective Krishna's face went from pleasant to worried in a split second. "How is she?"

Minjun spoke up. "She's okay." He thought for a minute. "She doesn't talk much, but we're slowly making friends with her. She's nice."

Detective Krishna nodded. "She is a very nice girl. None of the things that happened were her fault. I wish—" She sighed. "What I wish for isn't relevant I guess. I'm glad to see she has friends. Now, are you here because of her?"

Seonghun shook his head. "Things have felt weird lately. I didn't mention it to Liah because I didn't want to worry her. But it feels like someone has been following me from time to time." He told the detective what happened last night.

Detective Krishna held up a hand. "Can you hold on just a second?" She stood up before Seonghun could say anything else, leaving the room, coming back shortly with a laptop. Pulling her glasses to her eyes, she began typing. "Did anyone see?" she asked.

"Yes, a guy saw the whole thing." Seonghun pulled out his phone to give the information to the detective.

"There is a camera near The Den, I can have the tape pulled to see if anything was caught on it." She looked at all three of them. "Are any of you in a fraternity or pledging a fraternity? Could this be considered a prank?"

They shook their heads no.

"Have you had issues with anyone lately? Any threats?"

Seonghun shook his head no again, while his friends nodded.

"Maliah told Seonghun what happened last year," said Yong. "The person who caused all the trouble was his former lab partner. Minjun was seeing her friend for a while. Both Minjun and I listened to her go on about how she wanted Seonghun. It was obsessive language. Seonghun reported it to his lab teacher; his lab teacher switched everyone's partner's around, so as not to make it suspicious that it was just for him. He should probably tell the rest." Yongjoon glanced at Seonghun.

It dawned on Seong what Yong was saying. Seonghun cleared his throat slightly, speaking of the events that led to Casey getting kicked out of their lab.

Detective Krishna was typing steadily into the laptop. As she was typing she spoke up. "Anything else happened?"

"It was after this, I found out what happened to Liah. She mentioned the first name; I put two and two together. A few days later, the three of us were eating dinner in a cafeteria when the girl Minjun was seeing came up to talk with him. Casey was with her. She grabbed my arm to ask me to go somewhere to apologize, I just lost it." He looked at Detective Krishna sheepishly.

"Lost it how?" Detective Krishna asked.

"I started yelling." Seonghun turned red. "She didn't care. She didn't care how she had hurt this sweet woman. It was a game to her. I was so angry. I'm still angry. Everyone has failed Liah. And this bitch gets to walk off scott free."

There was silence in the room except for Detective Krishna's typing.

Once she finished she slid the laptop to the side. "I don't know if Maliah told you how I worked, but I'm as honest as I can be. I urged her to go outside of the student court as best as I could. I couldn't be overt with it because I could have lost my job. She didn't understand what I was saying at the time. So this is me being honest with you. From what you've told me, either Casey pushed you in the street, or she got someone to push you. I don't have proof of that; I can't run around accusing people without proof. You've given me enough that I can pull the camera near the area. Also—" She pulled the laptop toward her again, pressing a few buttons before turning the laptop to him. It was a map of the school. "Where is your dorm? Touch it on the screen; a dot will appear," she instructed.

Seonghun did as she asked.

She turned the screen back around to herself, pressing a few more buttons before turning the screen back to him. She had zoomed in the area from his dorm to The Den. "Drag your finger along the trail you took to the store." He looked at the screen before dragging his finger as she asked. A blue trail started to form. When he finished he handed back the laptop.

"There are cameras all over campus, especially in areas where the students walk a lot. Maybe we can see if someone was following you," she looked at him. "If there is an issue, you call me. Understood?"

He nodded.

"I don't care what time it is. The card I gave Maliah has my cell phone in it. Did she explain there's a restraining order?"

Minjun spoke up, "She mentioned it briefly."

Detective Krishna explained, "They are in different majors. There is no reason Casey should be anywhere near the buildings Maliah is in. If she sees her in public, Casey is to leave. I don't care if she is in the middle of a meal. She lost that right. If she is within fifty feet of Maliah, you call. I will have her arrested."

"Is there anything else I can do?" Seonghun said.

Detective Krishna sighed. "I've been a detective on campus for three years. Maliah was my first serious case. She broke my heart. She didn't cry, at all. She just kept asking why someone would do this to her. I didn't have an answer for her then."

"Do you have one for her now?" Yong asked.

"There are shitty people out here. Darkness preys on light in order to dim it." The detective paused for a minute. "I hope she hasn't let darkness snuff her out." She looked at Seonghun. "If I find anything in the videos, I'll be in touch. Otherwise, give me a call if anything happens." She stood up, shaking each of their hands, before leading them back out to the front.

Outside of the building Seonghun looked at his friends. "What now?" he asked.

Yongjoon spoke up. "We go to the glasses place, to see if they can get the scuffs out of your glasses. If not, we leave them there to fix while you use your contacts for a few days."

Seonghun groaned.

"Come on. I'll buy both of you food." Yongjoon pulled out his keys while walking toward the parking lot. At the thought of food Seonghun perked up, following his friend.

CHAPTER 22

Luckily, the shop was able to buff all the scuffs out of his glasses, making them look brand new. After a meal, they went home, but were currently scared to open the door as music was screaming outside of their door. Yong looked around but didn't see anyone outside their rooms or complaining. Shrugging, he opened the door.

Everyone was nearly knocked back by the loudness of the music. They all hurried in, quickly shutting the door before they got complaints. Seonghun looked over to see Maliah pouring something from a sheet pan onto paper towels. Setting the pan down, she looked up, jumping slightly at seeing the three men staring at her. Grabbing her phone, Seonghun watched her turn the music off. The silence was more unnerving than the music.

Minjun spoke first. "How is your music that loud from your phone?"

"Uh, I have speakers and a subwoofer under my bed. It's small, but powerful," she said quietly.

Minjun looked at her for a minute before she nodded her head in the direction of her room. He took off running with Seonghun at his heels. Sure enough, a small rose gold Bluetooth speaker set was under her bed.

Seong walked out of the room. "You know, you're welcome to have it hooked up here in the living room." He saw her hesitation. It was then he remembered that Casey started her mental torture by ruining the stuff that she worked hard for. "Or if you feel more comfortable, keep it in your room, that's fine too."

She nodded as she began to scoop the contents of the pan into plastic bags.

Seonghun wandered over to look over her shoulder. "Is this the Chex Mix?"

She nodded again as she focused on not spilling it everywhere.

Scooping up a handful, he put it in his mouth. Maliah looked up in time to see him about to dive head first in a pile of the cereal mix. "Freeze, back away from the Chex Mix," she said calmly.

"It's really good," he whined, "let me have one more bite. Please?" He tried to give her puppy dog eyes.

Rolling her eyes, she grabbed a coffee mug. Scooping up a pile, Liah handed the mug to him. "You need to share."

His friends heard her orders, immediately looking up. Seonghun took off at a sprint out the door while eating as they chased after him.

"She said you have to share!" Yong yelled.

"It's really good!" Seonghun was shoveling it in his mouth as fast as he could.

Min came up to the side of him, grabbed the mug, before turning in the opposite direction. He grabbed Yongjoon, pulling him into a study room before locking the door. Seong began banging on the door.

"You've eaten half of what was given. You can wait until this evening for more," Minjun called out.

"Fine," Seonghun grumbled.

Yong unlocked the door and Seonghun sat on the couch as they tried the treat.

"This is good," Minjun said through a mouthful.

Yongjoon nodded in agreement as Seonghun sulked.

"You had half the mug Seonghun, you have to share," Min chided him.

"I know," he pouted as he stood up, heading back to the dorm room. When he got back, the bags of cereal were nowhere to be found and Maliah's door was closed. He tapped lightly on the door, opening it when he heard her soft 'come in'. She was seated on the bed sketching quietly. Closing the door, he sat beside her.

She glanced up. "Did you share?"

"Yes." He sat next to her attempting puppy eyes again.

"You can wait until this evening," she said. "How did the police visit go?" She was looking down when she asked so she didn't see his face change.

When he didn't answer she looked up at him. "Did—" Seonghun hesitated before plowing forward. "Do you have a suspicion that Casey pushed me into the street?"

She closed her sketchbook, placing it on the nightstand. "You denied her something she wanted. She doesn't forgive or forget that easily, so yes, I have my suspicions."

"Why didn't you say anything Liah?"

"When? When you were going into shock? When you were crying out in your sleep? When you were so worried that someone wasn't going to take you seriously you didn't even want to go?" She pointed all of this out, not unkindly. "Me telling you my suspicions wasn't going to do anything for you."

"I wouldn't have hesitated to go to the police at all if I thought it was her," Seonghun protested.

Maliah was silent for a moment. Standing up she stood over him, straddling his lap. "This okay?"

He nodded.

She kissed him, softly at first, but soon opened her mouth to him, letting him slide his tongue in. He moaned slightly as he tried to pull her closer. She broke away as he tried to slide his hands under her sweatshirt, but stayed in his lap.

"I appreciate your need to protect me. But there is nothing to protect me from at this point. She can't hurt me anymore. There is nothing she can do to me. She can hurt you though. I would like for her to get caught before she escalates into lasting harm for you or your friends."

"Your friends too," he said.

"What?"

"They're your friends now too," he repeated. He slid his hands down her waist, onto her thighs, rubbing lightly.

"Oh." She seemed deep in thought, so Seonghun kissed her.

Squeezing her thighs he slowly ran his hands up her back. She stopped kissing him to trail her tongue up his neck. Seong reciprocated, nibbling at her neck. Liah's tongue trailed the shell of his ear. Seonghun's eyes rolled in the back of his head as she sighed softly before nipping at his earlobe.

There was a smile in her voice as she whispered, "I think I found your spot."

"Yeah?" he whispered back, "how can you tell?"

He knew how she could tell, he was just curious what she would say. But Maliah didn't say anything. Instead, she rolled her hips against his erection. He whimpered, not knowing if Yong or Min were back.

"That wasn't there before," she said quietly. She rolled against him again, watching his face as his eyes rolled in the back of his head again.

"I thought," his voice shook slightly, "that we both agreed to go slow."

"I'm fully dressed, you're fully dressed. Neither one of us is touching underneath our clothes. I'd say we're going fairly slow. Wouldn't you agree?" She slowly gained a rhythm to her movements, though it was clumsy.

He put his hands on either side of her hips to guide her movements. "You have a point." His voice still shook. "God!"

"Shhh, shhh," she whispered. "You've got to be quiet. There's other people."

His breathing was getting heavier. "I can't help it. It feels—"

"I know. Let me make you feel good." She continued to ride him, with him guiding her movements. As he cried out again she quickly put her mouth to his, silencing him. His grip on her thighs became firmer as he began to move her faster, basically slamming her over his erection.

"Liah I—" he panted.

"I know, sweet boy, let go. It's okay." She trailed her tongue to his ear, gently sucking his earlobe.

He put his mouth into her shoulder, muffling his cries as he spilled into his jeans. They sat like that for a while, their faces buried in each other's necks.

"I want to make you feel like this," Seonghun said.

"As you saw, it's not something that can happen over clothes. It also takes a lot of time. Time that we," she looked at her watch, "don't have. I like doing this with you. It makes me happy. It doesn't have to be a tit for tat situation. I like knowing I can do that to you." She slid off his lap.

"I like touching you. I want to... make your roller coaster drop." He gave her a soft smile. "I understand what you're saying though, when you're ready to go further, I will be as well." He kissed her again. "I'm definitely going to need a shower before I go. Your room is closer to the bathroom. Can you grab my shower stuff? Ask Minjun where it is, he can show you."

She nodded. Both of them exited the room, with Seonghun slipping into the bathroom.

CHAPTER 23

The car was somewhat silent, so Yong turned on the local pop station. Maliah was in the back seat looking like a cornered animal. Seonghun was trying his best to keep her calm, but there wasn't a whole lot he could do in a moving vehicle but hold her hand.

"What is your favorite animal?" Seong asked desperately. The look on her face was horrifying.

"E-e-e-e-" she sighed. "Elephant."

"Why?" he asked.

"They are a m-m-m-matriarchal societ-t-t-ty, f-f-f-family orient-t-t-ted, a-a-a-and cute."

Minjun turned to look at her from the passenger seat. "So a woman led family is what you like about them?"

"I-I-I-I-I don't believe a man should lead a f-f-f-family just because he has a d-d-d-dick," she said simply.

Seonghun choked on air.

"In all honesty, a f-f-family should be a unit. Making decisions together." Maliah looked out the window. "Everyone's opinion should count."

Seonghun looked at her. "Even the kids?"

She nodded firmly. "Especially the kids. Give kids as much autonomy as you can. They are just tiny p-p-p-people with feelings but not a whole lot of agency to do anything about them."

Min glanced at Seong as the next question came out of his mouth. "Do you want kids?"

"I-" Maliah was quiet for a moment. "I don't know."

"What makes you unsure?"

"The argument of nature vs nurture."

Seonghun was confused, but Yong answered instantly. "You're scared you won't be a good mom."

"I'm more scared that history will repeat itself with any child I have."

"You turned out fine," Minjun pointed out.

"I had to take part of a Xanax to get into this car. I still want to run out screaming," she said flatly.

Seonghun looked at her. "Are you going to fall asleep?"

"Eventually, but not any time soon. I didn't take enough for that."

It was quiet as Yongjoon pulled into the drive-in. Liah searched through her purse, pulling out a ten dollar bill to hand to him. Seong gently pushed her hand down before handing Yongjoon a twenty.

"Oh, thanks," she said quietly.

"I wouldn't ask you to come some place then make you pay, that's rude," Seonghun said.

"I don't want to assume anything," she replied.

Seonghun sighed. Glancing over at Min, he communicated wordlessly. His best friend gave him a slight nod. They had selected a lighthearted movie for the first round. Some comedy that was fairly new. As Yongjoon pulled in, Minjun hopped out to go to the concession stand. Maliah went to follow when Seonghun touched her leg. "Can you stay here with me? I need to talk to you."

Maliah nodded. "Yeah, sure."

"What did you want to eat?" Seong loved drive-in food. It was cheap, trashy, and absolutely filling.

"Just a coke and popcorn," she said.

"You haven't eaten dinner." He realized she didn't eat a whole lot, but he wasn't fond of her skipping meals. He saw that she looked uncomfortable, so he spoke up. "Is it because I'm paying?"

"No, you've paid for me before. I— my stomach is kind of knotted up," she admitted.

He glanced over at the roommates who were waiting patiently. "Popcorn, two cokes, and just buy a whole pizza." He looked over at her. "If you do get hungry for actual food later, cold pizza isn't bad. Min, use my card for everything, that's fine."

Min nodded, tugging Yong away. They watched as their two roommates walked away holding hands.

"Gosh they're cute," Liah said. She turned to Seong. "You wanted to talk to me?"

It wasn't quite dark yet; he could still see her eyes behind her glasses. She looked a lot less fearful with him. "Seonghun?"

"You know how I feel about you, right?" He stared at her.

"Yes."

"I don't want to be just your friend, Maliah."

"You understand being with me isn't a sprint, right? It's a marathon. I'm going to have bad days."

"I get that."

"There are days where I just cry. Living is hard sometimes."

Seonghun started laughing. "Are you trying to talk me out of liking you? Because it isn't going to happen. I see you, Maliah. I see what's in here." He pointed to her heart. "That means more to me than any bad day. I want to be there for your bad days, to help you through it, if you'd let me."

Maliah looked at him nodding slowly.

"Do you want to be my girlfriend? I'm sometimes moody. I need solitude at times."

"I can respect that."

He reached out a hand to brush her hair but stopped short. He went to pull his hand back but she grabbed it, gently skimming her face, only flinching slightly.

"So, do you want to be my girlfriend?"

"Yes."

"Can I kiss you?"

"Also yes."

He immediately slid over to her side of the car. He meant for it to be a quick kiss, but it was anything but that. Pretty soon he was on top of her, moving slowly.

Tearing his mouth from hers he whispered softly, "I want you."

"I want you too, but, we agreed to go slowly. I'm not having sex in your friend's car. I'm not having sex in my car. We're entirely too old for car sex." She gasped as he hit a particularly sensitive spot with his grinding.

"Yeah, slowly. We said slow," he repeated as he kissed her again, continuing with his movements.

Someone beating on the window startled them and broke them apart.

"I'm opening the damn door, you two better be decent, I swear to god." Yong flung the door open.

Maliah sat up, looking a bit like Cousin It, with her hair in front of her face. She looked stunned. Seonghun slid to the opposite side of the car.

Yong stuck his head in the car, next to Maliah, sniffing. "It doesn't smell like sex in here."

At that Liah looked mortified.

"Did you two—"

"Yongjoon."

He turned to look at Maliah. Leaning over, she whispered in his ear. "Oh. Okay."

She continued whispering.

"Really? That's sweet."

She finally sat back. He handed her the two Cokes and a bag of popcorn. She passed one of the drinks to Seong. Minjun handed them a pizza before shutting the door, still giggling.

Seonghun glanced at her. "What did you say to him?"

She dug in her bag on the floor, pulling out a giant bag of Chex Mix, which she set on the front arm rest. Everyone could reach it. She then grabbed a small blanket, covering herself up before sliding over to him, setting the pizza on the opposite side of her.

"I explained to him that I'm a virgin. I wouldn't have sex in any car. I also said that I had agreed to be your girlfriend and we both got a little carried away." As she spoke, the roommates climbed in the front seats. Yongjoon turned the car radio on as they waited for the movie to start.

There was nothing but noises from everyone eating. Maliah nibbled on her popcorn while watching as Seonghun put away half a pizza.

"If I eat, it will only be one slice, so if you want to continue eating, that's fine," she told him.

One of the things that Seong got embarrassed about a lot was the amount of food he consumed. He couldn't help it. He was a big guy with a massive appetite. Liah never said anything derogatory about it at all, instead she insisted he didn't eat enough while trying to feed him. He smiled as he grabbed another slice.

Out of nowhere Minjun asked a question. "Who are Jack and Rose?"

Yongjoon choked on his slice of pizza.

Maliah immediately looked at the window, which was fogged up with a massive handprint. She laughed so hard, she began snorting, then there was no sound at all. The boys stared at her in amazement. It was the hardest anyone had ever seen her laugh. As she tried to compose herself, she spoke up, "I-I-I-I'm sorry, Yongjoon."

"That isn't your handprint," he pointed out.

They all turned to look at it. Seonghun's hands were as big as hers were small; it was very obvious it wasn't hers. Liah lost it again. She pulled out her phone while snorting. Handing it over to Min, she pressed play on a video.

"Oh. OHHHHH!" Minjun said.

Seonghun looked over; you couldn't see anything but an old-fashioned car rocking. All of a sudden a hand pressed to the window of the car.

He blushed. "Sorry, Yong." Just then the sound of advertisements in the car cut off and switched to movie previews.

"Shhh, it's starting," Minjun said. They all settled in to watch. The movie turned out to be bad. Not even a little funny. So everyone began to talk.

"Give me something you wish you could have right now, big or small," said Yong.

"A funnier movie," Minjun deadpanned.

"More pizza," Seonghun said longingly.

Maliah handed him the last slice, laughing as he inhaled it in three bites.

They looked at her as she stared out the window thoughtfully. "More life experience I guess."

Seonghun looked at her. "What do you mean?"

"I've focused on getting to where I need to be for so long, I've missed out on so many things someone my age has probably done, you know?" She let her eyes wander to the handprint. "I never went to prom, I couldn't have afforded it anyway. Never danced with anyone. You're the first person I've ever kissed. I just... I feel behind sometimes."

It was quiet for a little bit when Minjun turned around. "You could kiss me?"

Maliah and Yongjoon spoke at the same time.

"What?"

"Pardon?"

Seonghun just rolled his eyes as he grabbed a handful of Chex Mix.

"We all know it wouldn't mean anything, you'd get your life experience, maybe you'd feel better."

"Thanks, Minjun, but I don't think that's a good idea."

"Why not?"

She pointed her thumb at Seonghun. "He's fairly calm about it and doesn't seem like he would get jealous."

"It's Min," Seonghun said. "I expect him to slobber on you at some point."

"But," she paused, looking at Yongjoon, who was struggling to control his breathing. "Words have consequences, Minjun. I know it was an offer that was made out of the kindness of your heart, but you're standing on the cusp of something very important. Don't ruin that." It was quiet for a minute when Seong saw Yongjoon look back at Liah with a gleam in his eye.

"What about me?"

Maliah looked confused. "What about you?"

"Why don't you kiss me?"

She cast a sideways glance at Seonghun, who rolled his eyes again before leaning in to whisper in her ear, "This isn't going to go like he wants it to. By all means, if you want to, have at it. I'm fine with it." Both of them glanced at Minjun who was looking a little hurt.

"I don't want to cause problems. I don't think this is a good idea. So no. I'm not going to. Thank you for the offer though."

Yongjoon nodded before going back to the cereal.

Maliah piped up again, "What is one thing you wish you could avoid?"

"Homework," Seonghun said.

"Putting my foot in my mouth," Minjun said sheepishly.

"Himbos," Yongjoon said.

Min turned red.

"What about you?" Seonghun asked Maliah.

"Right now? The holiday choir concert."

"Why?"

She sighed. "I like to sing as part of a group. One of the rules of choir is that by the time you're a senior at your last concert, you have had to have taken a solo." She took a sip of her drink. "It's not a big deal normally. If you're in choir during your senior year, you're probably going on to perform, so typically everyone jumps at the chance to try for a solo. I'm not a performance major. I have no desire to be, but I still have to take the solo. I've tried wiggling out of it, I can't."

"When is your concert?" Seonghun asked.

"Thursday before semester break."

"Can I come?" he asked.

"No one's ever shown up for me except once.. That would be nice. Thank you," she said quietly.

"What do you mean?" Yongjoon asked.

"I don't have anyone," Maliah explained.

"Parents?"

"Uninterested. They kicked me out when I was accepted into Silver Leaf."

"Grandparents?"

"Dead."

"Aunts or uncles?"

"My parents are only children."

Yongjoon stared in disbelief. Seonghun understood his shock. Yong's family was small, but he still had his mom no matter what. He also knew that his father loved him very much before he died. To have no one was unfathomable to him, to all of them really.

Liah must have seen the look on his face as she rushed to reassure him. "Yongjoon, it's fine. It's always been this way; I'm used to it."

"It isn't fine, nor is it something you should get used to, but I'll leave it alone." Yong quickly dropped the matter.

Min looked at him before carefully grabbing his hand.

They talked quietly for the rest of the movie. Seonghun maneuvered Maliah until he was cuddled with her under the blanket. He was relaxed as he listened to the quiet talk between the roommates. There was nothing really lingering over their heads right now since he'd asked her to be his girlfriend. Life was good. Shortly into the second movie, Maliah fell asleep with her head in Seong's lap. He covered her up, watching her face as she slept peacefully through the movie. Seong heard shifting from the front; looking up, he saw his friends had turned to face him again. "You know we're coming to Liah's concert too right?" Yongjoon whispered.

"I figured. You looked heartbroken when she said she had no one," he murmured, looking down at Liah.

"I knew because you told me, it's another thing when she says it. It doesn't even phase her. Like family bonds aren't a thing with her," Yongjoon said.

"That's because they aren't. Her family is trash." They all looked down at her as she slept.

It was quiet for a while before Yong spoke again. "Do you think it's presumptuous to ask her to come home for Thanksgiving? What does she do for the holidays normally?"

"She stays in the dorm, I believe. I never really asked," Seonghun said.

"If I ask her, you know Mom won't let her stay in the same room as you right?"

He immediately started pouting. "Why not? We're adults. We aren't... doing that." Seong struggled not to shift at Yongjoon's stare, lest he wake up Liah.

"Seonghun, I came back to my car rocking with a Titanic handprint on the window." Yongjoon stared him down. "Anyway, it doesn't matter. Mom isn't going to let any of us sleep in the same room as her."

"What about you two?" Seonghun whispered.

"What about us?" Minjun asked.

"Is Cho going to separate you two?"

"No," Yong said.

"That's not fair," Seonghun pointed out.

"It isn't," he agreed. "Her reasoning is sort of sexist, but it's the way my mom rolls. I was always allowed to have girls sleepover, whether we were dating or not, but once I hit a certain age, I wasn't allowed to sleep in the same room as them. 'Girls can get pregnant' is what Mom always said." He shrugged. "I always thought it was nice she let my friends sleep over, so I didn't really argue about it. Her house, her rules, you know?"

"I don't know why we're even talking about this. We don't even sleep together every night," Seonghun said.

"I just wanted you to know. I also need to ask Mom to make sure it is okay. I know it is, but it's a matter of respect." He pulled out his phone and sent a quick text. He received one back almost instantly. His phone kept going. "Uh," Yong looked at the increasing alerts. "Do either of you know if she's girly?"

"What do you mean?" Min asked.

"Does she like doing girl stuff? Shopping, nails, whatever the hell it is girls do when guys aren't around," Yongjoon explained.

"She studies," Seonghun said flatly. "She paints her toes, and Minjun's fingers on occasion."

Yong pulled at Min's hand to see black sparkly polish.

"She collects pinup girl pictures; judging by her room, yes, I'd say she's somewhat into the girly stuff," Seong said.

"That should be good enough for Mom. She'd love to have another woman to hang out with." Yongjoon responded to his mother. They continued to watch the second movie, which was better than the first. When it ended, Yongjoon turned on the light in the car to gather the trash, which caused Maliah to sit bolt upright. She looked like she was ready to run.

"It's me, you're here with me." Seonghun talked to her quietly. "No one here is going to hurt you. You're out with friends and you fell asleep."

"Seonghun?" She blinked at him.

"Yes, it's me," he said patiently. "I took your glasses off so you wouldn't break them, here." He handed her glasses back to her. Their friends observed the exchange as they cleaned up.

"Are you okay? Do you need to go to the bathroom before we go?"

"Yeah." She stretched for a moment, opening the car door.

"Do you want me to come with you, or are you okay?" Seong asked.

"I'm fine." Without another word, she headed toward the concession area.

"Do you always have to reassure her like that when she wakes up?" Min asked as he watched her walk away.

"No," Seonghun replied, "but you can tell when she's startled or out of it. The events that transpired happened when she was asleep, so sometimes she wakes up startled, especially if I'm with her. I understand it, but I hope it gets better as time goes on." He started to gather the trash in the backseat, quickly hiding the rest of the Chex Mix from everyone.

Yongjoon looked around. "Did we eat all the cereal mix?" They started searching for the bag.

"We must have," Minjun replied.

Maliah returned as Min spoke. "You must have what?" she asked.

"All the Chex Mix is gone. I guess we plowed through it," Yongjoon explained.

Maliah looked right at Seonghun who was turning red.

Nonchalantly she buckled her seatbelt. "If people don't learn how to share, they don't get to try Muddy Buddies later in the year which consists of chocolate, peanut butter, cereal, and powdered sugar." There was silence in the car as Seonghun sheepishly pulled out the bag of Chex Mix.

Minjun began snickering. "How did you know?"

"I saw the bag before I left to go to the bathroom. There was no way he could have gobbled it down that fast, his jaw would have been killing him." Her eyes began to close as she spoke.

"Go to sleep, Liah. I'll wake you when we get back to the dorm." He watched as she curled into a ball as best as she could in her seatbelt. Seonghun covered her with her blanket again before buckling himself in.

"I'm going to honestly miss this," he said.

"The drive-in?" asked Min as they got in line to exit.

"Yeah, I mean, we graduate in May. It won't be open again before we graduate. This was our last time here," Seong pointed out.

"You guys will visit from time to time," Yong said.

"Sure, but it won't be the same. We won't be living together," Seong said quietly. The silence was heavy as four years of memories washed over the men.

CHAPTER 24

When they got back to the apartment complex where Yong parked, Seonghun began to shake Maliah. She opened one eye to look at him, before closing it again, snuggling into her blanket. "Yong, give me your keys. I'll lock up after I get her out."

"Do not have sex in my car," Yongjoon said seriously.

"No one is having sex anywhere, give me the damn keys." Seong held out his hand, exasperated.

He tossed the keys to him, walking around to pull Minjun toward the dorm. As soon as they walked off, Seong began shaking her lightly again. "Liah, come on, sweetheart, we're back. We need to go in."

"Comfortable. Don't wanna move." She covered her head in the blanket. Looking behind him, he shut the car door.

"Maliah." His voice sounded different to his own ears, deeper. "Let's go inside." He kissed her forehead as he began to peel the blanket from her.

"Just stay out here with me. It's nice." She opened one eye again to see him hovering over her.

"Maliah."

Instead of responding, she pulled his body down to hers, snuggling him tightly. "You're warm."

"God you smell good," he spoke into her shoulder. "Liah, I really want to touch you."

"You are touching me."

"You know what I mean." He felt slightly faint at her smell, combined with the heat her own little body was throwing off.

"I know what you mean," she agreed. "But you've been touching me all day."

"Is it too much?"

"Mmm, no, but I don't know what has made you so earnest," she replied.

"I want to make your roller coaster drop," he admitted.

"I know you do."

"I also want to see your toy."

Under the parking lot lights, he saw her look a little embarrassed. "That's not coming out until we're by ourselves."

"That's fine. How about tomorrow?" He began kissing her neck softly.

"Mmm," she moaned softly, "what is going on tomorrow?"

"Yong and Min have a date." He slowly unzipped the hoodie that she had on. "Why on earth do you still have this?"

"It's soft, it's comfortable, and for a little while, it smelled like you," she admitted.

He smiled at her. "I have multiple hoodies in my closet. You're welcome to grab them." He peeled her out of the jacket. Liah's waist was small; Seong could fit both of his hands around it. She had on a striped tank top that he raised to plant a kiss on her stomach. Seong focused on her face as she began to shake a little.

"Scared?" he asked, concerned.

"Turned on, incredibly turned on." As she looked at him, he saw fear warring with desire in her eyes. She wanted this too.

"We have to leave the car, Liah, I can't touch you in here, I promised Yong." His voice cracked from need.

"Okay." Liah sat up as Seong helped her slide the hoodie back on, zipping it up before they climbed out of the SUV. Seonghun rounded the car, making sure the doors were locked. Grabbing her hand, he pulled her to the dorm, nearly running.

Maliah laughed the whole way. "Slow down! You have longer legs than I do."

He stopped abruptly, kissing her. It was late at night; The only people out were returning to their dorms from parties. The drunken revelers started cheering them. At the cheers, Seonghun came up for air, focusing on Liah's face. She was tired, he could tell, but the desire was still there.

"Let's go back to the dorm, Seonghun." She took his hand as they walked.

"Liah, what do you do during the holidays?" he asked suddenly

"I stay in the dorms. On Thanksgiving I watch the parade, a Charlie Brown movie, cook a Cornish game hen with some sides, then set up the small tree in my room. Christmas is pretty much the same way, only I give myself a really nice gift. Something I wouldn't normally splurge on because I count my pennies."

"What have you given yourself in the past?" Seonghun asked, interested.

"Well, you saw my small sound system, that was last year." Seonghun opened the door for her as they reached the dorm. "Thank you. The year prior I gave myself some pearl earrings. A lady should always have three pieces of jewelry. Pearl earrings, pearl necklace, and diamond studs. The other two are going to have to wait until I'm established in my career," she said.

"Why?"

"When I spend a large amount of money, I want exactly what I want. The jewelry I want is pricey, almost two thousand dollars each. I could swing it, but it would put a significant dent in the cushion I keep for myself." She pressed the button for the elevator. "On paper I look like I have money, but people don't take into account that I don't have a parental cushion. If something happens, it could wipe me out." Stepping into the elevator and pressing their floor she looked at him as he was deep in thought. "What do you do for the holidays?"

"We go to Yong's. Cho is very welcoming. I know it's early, but you're welcome to come with us."

Maliah snorted. "You can't invite me to someone else's house."

"Yong is going to ask you, he already asked his mom." They stepped out of the elevator, walking down the hall to their suite. "One thing though," he paused in the hallway, "We won't be able to sleep together."

"I don't know why you have sex on the brain, but I'm not having sex with you at someone's mama's house, if I get invited." Maliah looked at him wildly.

"I'm not the one with sex on the brain." He tried hiding a smile, failing miserably. "I mean we can't sleep in the same room. She won't let us."

"Oh. Sorry. That's okay, it's fine."

It wasn't really fine for Seonghun. He liked waking up next to her, even in the tiny twin bed. Opening the door he blinked. Maliah came around him to see what he was gawking at. It was one thing to know his friends were talking about dating. It was another to see them basically playing tonsil hockey on the couch. He looked down at Maliah who had a strange look on her face.

"Uh, why don't you get your pajamas and meet me in my room?" she whispered. She darted to her room, shutting the door quietly.

"Guys? Can you take it to one of your rooms? Please?" Seonghun pleaded.

"Sorry." Yong got up, taking Minjun's hand before pulling him into his room.

Seonghun rolled his eyes. He grabbed his clothes, before knocking on Liah's door. When there was no response he opened the door, chuckling softly as he saw she managed to at least get her pajamas on before she passed out cold. Setting his things on her desk, he began to take his clothes off. Stripping out of his jeans, he glanced at the pile of clothes he brought with him.

"Liah, do you care what I sleep in?" he whispered.

She opened one eye, "No."

Cutting the lights, he lifted the blankets, scooting her next to the wall as he climbed in. Maneuvering a bit, they finally got comfortable with Liah's head on his chest.

"Seonghun?"

"Yeah?"

"I don't know how to be a good girlfriend," she said quietly.

"How long has that been worrying you?"

"Since you asked me."

"Well, being a good partner, in my opinion, is sort of based on honesty. If something makes you uncomfortable you probably need to let me know; I'll do the same. With that, I'm going to tell you, I'm getting the feeling that you don't want me touching you intimately. You've avoided it since the other night. You had no problems getting me off, but you won't even let me try for you."

She sighed. Reaching behind his head, she turned her sparkly lights on. Liah rested her chin on his chest as she looked at him. "Truth? I saw the look on your face the first time we messed around. You looked crushed that you couldn't get much of a response from me. I can't help my responses, Seonghun. I can barely get off myself sometimes."

"I can't get to know your body unless you let me try, Liah. Our roommates are in Yong's room on the opposite side of the suite. They aren't going to hear anything. If you don't want to mess around I understand. I'll hold you, we'll kiss goodnight, and that can be the end of this discussion tonight. If you do, we could get out your toy." It was quiet between them for a while. He played with her hair, gently touching her while she thought about it.

"Hand me my phone please."

He did as she requested.

Liah pressed the screen a few times; music started playing softly from the speakers under her bed. "It will cover some of the noise," she explained. "Open the nightstand; there is a box in there, can you pull that out please?"

Seonghun did as she asked. The box was a small plastic tub, the kind he saw her use for her bathroom supplies. This one wasn't clear, however it was dark blue. He handed it over to her as he laid on his side watching her open it.

Inside the tub were two vibrators. One was a slender pink wand, with three metal balls embedded into the top in a triangle shape. The other was a softer, phallic shape with a curve to it that was a dark purple. She held up the pink wand first. "This is what I use when I don't know where everyone is or when they will be home. If I can't come using this, I'm probably not going to at all." Setting it down, she then picked up the purple one. "This one takes time; I use it in conjunction with the other one."

She turned on the switch, guiding his hand to the top of it, letting him feel it. To him it felt like almost a massaging motion. As he focused on the movement of the wand, Seong realized something. "It's doing what you had me do with my hand inside you."

"Yes. I'm assuming you want to be an active participant tonight?"

"Yeah." He nodded.

"So we won't need this one." She turned off the purple one, putting it back in the tote. "When you put that up, the lube is in there, though I have a feeling we won't need it."

"Why?" he asked as he looked around for the clear bottle of liquid.

"I was really turned on earlier," she explained. "I never know what I'm going to get on the horniness scale." Liah chuckled. "Pre-medication, this wasn't an issue."

"Really?"

"Yeah, I was pretty horny all the time with nowhere to expend it but by myself."

"Let's see what we can do, sweetheart." He kissed her, rolling her on her back.

He slowly eased her out of her top and stared at her. Liah's areolas were darker than her skin with a pink undertone. He gently put one of her nipples in his mouth, flicking it with his tongue. The moan that came out of her startled them both. He focused his attention on both her nipples, while trailing his hands down her torso. Liah kept letting out these small breathy gasps that were driving him wild. Seong watched her as he trailed his tongue down her body, slowly tugging her pants down.

"Are you okay?"

All of a sudden she lunged at him, kissing him. Their tongues teased each other as his hands gripped her hips tightly. Touching between her legs, Seong was pleasantly surprised to find her aroused. He began to kiss her neck as he gently rubbed her clit with his thumb. She began to moan while grinding against him like earlier.

"Baby, lay back for me please. I can't focus on you when you do that."

Seong laid Liah back down. Grabbing the vibrator he looked at and saw there were two settings. "Which position?"

"Turn it to the left," his girlfriend whispered.

Holy shit, he had a girlfriend.

Seong did as she instructed, immediately noticing that the vibrator wasn't moving at a constant speed. It went up and down like a…"Roller coaster." He smiled softly at her. "Show me what you like, please."

Maliah showed him how to position the vibrator against her. As he did so, he slid a finger inside her.

"God, you're wet," he moaned.

Seonghun saw that she was struggling to control her breathing, not really focused on what he was saying. He began stroking her like she showed him before while holding the vibrator firmly against her. "Oh god!" she called out loudly.

"Shhh, you've got to keep it down," he whispered.

"It feels— Shit!" she cried out again.

He inserted another finger, watching her writhe in pleasure. That nectarine blossom scent was intense along with her natural scent. Seonghun felt faint. Suddenly Liah let out a shriek as he felt her clamp down on his fingers. She pushed the vibrator away as she rode out her orgasm. Seong watched her, pleased that she looked even more enthralled than she did when she had cake. Smothering a laugh, he slowly removed his fingers from her, staring at the glistening wetness. Curiously, he put his fingers in his mouth, sucking on them. Yeah, he wanted more. Looking at her, Seong saw her observing his every move. He positioned himself so his head was between her legs.

"Can I taste you?" he asked.

He immediately saw the conflict in her eyes. "I want you to, but this just seems really fast. I went from never being touched to having your face in my—" The embarrassment was plain on her face.

"I've heard you say dick multiple times, you cannot be embarrassed to say pussy." He smirked as she started avoiding his gaze.

He snickered as he eased his fingers back inside her and began to stroke again. She sat up as he moved his fingers, meeting his mouth with hers. He pulled away. "Say the word, Liah." He grabbed the vibrator again, pressing it against her. She moaned, trying to yank him back to her. Seong resisted, moving his fingers as fast as he could. "Say the words, Maliah. Talk dirty to me."

She moaned against his mouth. "When you finally put your mouth on my pussy, it won't be in this tiny fucking bed."

This time he moaned as he kissed her. He drove her to orgasm again, her cries lost in his mouth. She collapsed on the bed, breathing heavy. As Seong lay beside her, she began to touch the bulge in his boxer briefs.

"Baby no. You remember earlier? No tit for tat. This was about you tonight, I actually got what I wanted." He reached over to turn off the vibrator.

"I don't understand, what did you get?"

Adjusting so that they were both under the covers, he snuggled closer to her. "I wanted to see you drop down the roller coaster. I wanted to be a part of it when you did."

"I went down the roller coaster twice, which is rare." Liah rolled over and looked at him. "It won't always be like this. There are days where I just can't. You can't get upset or frustrated when it doesn't happen. It makes me feel guilty, like I'm defective."

Seong swallowed. "I didn't mean to make you feel that way. I just like being close to you. I want to make sure you enjoy it as well, you know?"

"I enjoy the closeness of this. But I also just like being with you. There wasn't anything sexual to start with. I liked you before all of this." Liah yawned.

"I like being with you too." He kissed her forehead as he felt his own eyes get heavy. "Liah, should I put the toy back before I go to sleep?"

"No. I have to clean it in the morning. Good night, Seonghun."

"G'night."

The next morning Seonghun woke up in her bed alone. Putting on his glasses, he noticed a note on her desk with his initials on it. He grabbed it and curled back into the bed. As he opened it a picture fell out. He set it on the nightstand without looking while he read.

S,
Though the movie was kind of trash, it was nice hanging out with you three. I

hope I didn't start a fight between Yongjoon and Minjun. I don't think I did,
judging from what we walked into last night.
I also enjoyed last night after the movie with you. Yeah. I don't really know
what else to say about that. Maybe cake doesn't trump everything.

He grinned.

It also feels like we haven't slowed down like we said we would. I'm okay at this
pace, but what you asked last night, I'm really not ready for. I hope you understand.
I'm warring with a couple of things in my head regarding everything. I know you
won't hurt me, but my heart is fighting my head on that one. I'm worried about
moving too fast, letting you in, and being left with nothing. I'm also concerned about
pregnancy and the other things that go along with talking about sex.

"Other things that go along with sex?" he said aloud. He had no clue
what she was talking about. The rest he understood. It was a big change for
her. For him as well. Shrugging, he went back to the letter.

I'm still concerned about being a good girlfriend. I was half tempted to look up
to see if there were any answers. But then I felt like I was 12 years old looking
up 'how to kiss someone' again. Before you ask, yes I did look it up when I was
12. It didn't make sense to me that it was something you just instinctively
knew how to do, you know? Anyway, I haven't looked it up. Yet. I'm neurotic,
it may still happen.

He snorted. He kind of wanted to see her browsing history to see what
type of stuff she looked up.

A while ago you asked to see a picture of me happy as a kid. This is the ice
cream picture I told you about. Please be careful with it. I only have the one
copy and I'm not going back to my parent's house any time soon for anything.
When you wake up, they'll be donuts out front. I'll be sure to get chocolate.

Yours,
-L
PS: Check the fridge

He picked up the picture. One glance, and his heart instantly broke. A little girl sat with some other kids, but there was a clear space in between her and the others. Liah looked into the camera with her wide eyes. While you could tell she was happy, she looked so tired, even that young. He wondered if she suffered from depression even at that age.

Her parents were behind her in the picture; he was surprised that she looked more like her father than her mother. He had the same large eyes, freckly moles, as well as her nose. The only difference was the expression. He looked bored, not even smiling in the photo. Her mother's hair was a dark blonde color, bone straight. Her nose wasn't as wide as Liah's; it was almost pointy in comparison. The biggest surprise was her skin color. Liah's mother was only a few shades darker than Seong. She wasn't smiling either, just staring into the camera with a blank expression. Liah's mother was a beauty, there was no doubt, but the look on her face didn't do her any justice.

She had told him this was a happy memory. It was one of the only happy memories she had. Seong had seen her face when she was actually happy. This wasn't it and it hurt him all the more. It made him determined to show her what real happiness was. He crawled out of bed, throwing on his clothes from the previous night before stepping into the bathroom. He heard Minjun speaking enthusiastically over the TV. Finishing quickly, headed to the common area.

"So he thinks he's living in his sister's novel; that is the only reason he has attraction to Saifah. He also thinks that's the reason Fighter and Tutor are a thing." Minjun pointed at the TV as Maliah looked on in confusion.

"Why does Tutor owe all this money? How does he owe all this money but live in this nice ass apartment? How is his name Tutor, and he's a... tutor?"

Seonghun started snickering. Looked like Min had dragged her into a Thai BL drama. Liah was curled into a ball, tucked into Min's side, wearing Seong's sweatshirt with her own shorts. Walking over to the couch, he kissed the top of her head. "Morning."

"Hi. There are donuts. Soda is annoying," she said as she continued watching the TV.

"The drink?" he asked, confused.

"No, the person. FIGHTER DON'T WANT HER!" she yelled at the TV.

Min started giggling. They both had cups of coffee in front of them along with empty plates. Seonghun wandered over to the kitchen, spying the large box of donuts. Lifting the lid, he saw two jam filled donuts, two chocolate ones with chocolate icing, and two plain. Immediately diving for the two chocolate ones, he remembered her note, so he opened the fridge. In a large glass bottle was chocolate milk. After he poured himself a cup, he plopped down on the couch next to Liah. Taking a bite, he glanced at the two of them enthralled in the show.

"Do you have plans today?" he asked her.

"I've been summoned," she said dryly, glancing at Minjun.

"She's going with me to buy an outfit for tonight," he explained.

Seonghun winced. "Min, have you explained your shopping habits? No one should be subject to that by surprise." He looked at Liah who was staring back at him confused at the conversation.

"Min is the most indecisive person in the world. He will have you between stores for hours." Seong looked at Minjun who was blushing. "Wear comfortable shoes, force him to buy you a snack; once he has an outfit, drag him from the mall."

"You aren't coming?" she asked.

Seonghun snorted. "There is no amount of money that could convince me to willingly go shopping with Minjun if I don't have to. You're on your own with that, sweetheart." He took a bite of donut before watching the show.

She looked at Minjun. "You set me up."

"No one else will go with me," he whined.

"Based on this trip, I may never go with you again." Liah arched her eyebrow. "I'm going to get dressed." The two men watched as she went into her room.

Seonghun looked at Minjun. "Please don't run her around. She just got used to all of us."

"We'll be fine, stop worrying." Minjun turned off the drama. Running his hands through his dark hair, he looked at Seong. "What's important to you is important to me. Remember that."

He nodded. Minjun clapped him on the back as he headed into his own room to change. Switching the television to a documentary, Seong took a sip of the milk. Startled, he looked down at his cup. It was the richest, silkiest cup of milk he'd ever had in his life. Draining the cup, he immediately went back for more.

"Don't drink more than two cups of that in a single meal. You will be doubled over in pain." Liah warned as she stepped out of her room. She'd traded her shorts for jeans.

"Come here." He walked into his room with her following behind. Unzipping her jacket, he slid it off her shoulders. Underneath she wore a plain t-shirt. Opening his armoire he pointed to the side that held his shirts. "I keep all my sweatshirts here. You're welcome to come in any time to grab what you want."

She looked at the sweatshirts before reaching up to grab one. As she reached, her shirt lifted slightly; he saw a tiny bit of ink towards the back of her hip.

"You have a tattoo?" he asked as he lifted her shirt to see more.

"Yes. It's small." She tugged her jeans down slightly so he could see. He saw a star, roughly the size of a silver dollar pancake. "I wanted something easily hidden; it reminds me that I'm small in the grand scheme of things. So whatever I'm going through is not the biggest thing in the world and it will pass."

He skimmed his finger over the star and saw her break out into goosebumps. The skin felt odd there though, thicker, and slightly indented. "It's nice."

"I eventually want a small cluster of stars. I got this when I was eighteen. It was kind of a major thing to spend money on something I wanted but didn't need. I just haven't gone back. It's also cool because it's a star, not a super stylistic design, so I can go to another artist if need be to add to it." She hefted her pants back up before throwing on another one of his hoodies, this one the colors of their school, blue and silver. "It smells like you." She sniffed the collar.

He held up the other sweatshirt in his hand. "This one smells like you."

"I hope you know I haven't been running around with a musty sweatshirt on. It's been washed a couple of times."

"I figured." He brushed a kiss on her forehead. "Remember what I said about Min. Make him buy you food. It is the absolute least he can do for dragging you all over."

"How on earth do you make someone buy you food?" Maliah asked.

"I usually just point at whatever I want while I whine his name as he's running from store to store."

She snorted.

"If he gets to be too much, call me or shoot me a message, I'll come save you," he promised.

"I don't seem like it, but I'm an avid shopper myself. We'll be fine."

"Maliah! Are you ready!? Stop kissing Seong, let's go!" Minjun hollered from the living room.

"I'm not kissing him!" she yelled back.

"Not yet anyway." He grabbed her waist. She startled a bit but calmed down instantly. "Have fun okay?" Seong gave her a soft kiss before releasing her.

"I will. Don't drink all that milk. You'll be sick. Do you want us to bring you back food?"

He arched an eyebrow at her.

Snorting, she walked out to the living room. "I'll bring something back. Have a good day."

"You too." He looked at Minjun. His friend nodded before ushering Liah out of the door. Seonghun sighed, sitting back on the couch to finish his breakfast.

CHAPTER 25

Thank you for sharing the picture with me. I'll be careful with it and I will return it soon. Can I ask you a personal question? Have you dealt with depression your whole life? I know you said it was one of the happier memories you had with your family. You're smiling, but something doesn't feel right. You look exhausted in the photo. Not sleepy, just emotionally tired.

Liah, as much as I want to, I can't promise not to hurt you. We're human. We're discovering who we are to each other. There are bound to be missteps. I can promise never to hurt you on purpose. That I can do. I promise to always take your feelings into account into every decision that involves us.

It does feel like we didn't slow down at all, did we? I like being with you in that way. I like touching you. I like figuring out what feels good to you and watching your face as we figure it out together. Let's just keep going as we are. We can figure it out along the way. I understood what you meant by pregnancy, but I don't understand what you mean by other things when talking about sex. You're going to have to elaborate. As far as pregnancy goes, I understand your distaste for taking pills. If we're ready for that step, I'm prepared.

H e felt his face heat as he wrote the last line. It also reminded him that he hadn't seen Yong today. He sent him a text before he continued with his writing.

I don't think you started anything between the two. Min has a huge problem with sticking his foot in his mouth. He's so used to doing whatever he wants to make himself feel good that he doesn't think about the consequences. I'm very glad he's always stayed away from drugs. While it is great to feel pleasure, he's going to have to realize that if he wants to be with Yongjoon, he needs to think about someone else's feelings other than his own. This is kind of making him sound like he's selfish. He isn't. He's a very giving man. It's just other than his friends, his top priority is his pleasure. He's never desired a relationship, so he's going to have to learn how to be part of one. He'll get there.

His phone beeped with a text from Yongjoon. He was getting his haircut before heading to the gym. Seonghun responded that he'd meet him at the gym in thirty minutes.

I would have never thought to look up how to kiss or how to be a good boyfriend online. I should probably take a good look at the latter to be honest. I don't think I was the greatest one last time. I'd like to be better. I think I'm doing better simply in the fact that I actually want to be with the person I'm with, not just going along with the flow. I think that's a good start. This is kind of long. I'm going to get changed and go to the gym with Yongjoon. What is a food you would eat all the time if you could? Random question, I know, but I'm trying to figure out where we can eat next weekend. Are we still pumpkin carving this evening?
Yours,
-S

He sealed the letter, attaching a giant sunflower to it before taping it to her door. Satisfied, he went back into his room to change.

AFTER MAKING sure he was thoroughly stretched, Seonghun spotted Yongjoon as he lifted weights. "Are you nervous about tonight?" he asked his friend as his hands hovered over the weight bar.

"Mmm, no. I've known for a while Min felt differently about me. I was waiting for him to realize it himself. I've had time to get used to the idea," Yong explained.

"You've said a lot about Minjun, but not a lot about your feelings," Seonghun pointed out.

"I like Min's heart. Always have. Some of his life choices have been sketch, but he almost always has the purest intentions. I admire him. When he's with your girl, he knows exactly what to say. He always speaks his feelings, never holding back. But he's never harsh unless he has to be." Yongjoon lifted the weight as he spoke.

"You sound like you love him," Seonghun said.

It was quiet for a minute, the only sound of Yongjoon's slight grunts. "I love Min, yes. But not like you're thinking. I could easily fall in love with him, but he opens his mouth sometimes and the craziest shit spills out."

"Like offering to kiss my girlfriend?" Seonghun asked.

"Like offering to kiss your girlfriend," Yongjoon agreed.

"In his defense, he didn't mean anything about it. He just wanted to help a friend feel better about themselves. Kissing is something he does well." Seonghun blushed.

Yongjoon abruptly set the barbell on the stand. "Not you too," he moaned.

"It's not what you're thinking. It was long before we had met. We were still kids. I was curious."

"About what?" They switched places.

"Min knew he liked both sexes by the time we were about twelve. He also had developed a slight crush on me. I love Min, but nothing like that. But I wondered if I could. So I tried. I don't. Once he kissed me, he realized he didn't either. I was just the closest person to him," Seonghun explained.

"I always wondered about you two," Yongjoon said.

"Nothing between us ever went further than that. He's my best friend," Seonghun said simply.

They finished with weights, walking over to the treadmills. Seong heard a beeping of someone activating the treadmill next to him, but kept focused on his run.

"Hey cutie."

Both men's heads snapped up. looking over, Casey was running right next to Seonghun. Subtly Yongjoon turned the voice recorder on his phone before setting it back on the treadmill. He needn't bother being sneaky. Casey only had eyes for Seong.

"What do you want?" Seonghun kept running, looking straight ahead.

"I told you I'd see you again. You still hanging with my loser room-mate?" She wore nothing but a tiny sports bra and tinier shorts. Her pace on the treadmill was somewhat slow.

"She's not your roommate, she definitely isn't a loser; she's a better person than you'll ever be." Seonghun refused to look at her. He kept his head straight as he ran.

"Please. Ms. Goody-Two-Shoes, always studying or working. All I asked was for her to hang out." The pace on her treadmill picked up, but her breathing stayed the same. "She fed me some lines about goals. We're young! Who has time for all that? All she had to do was what I asked. Nothing had to escalate."

"You understand she's not a soldier, right? Liah doesn't have to listen to a word you say. She was just trying to live her life." Seonghun stopped the treadmill, finally looking at her. She kept increasing her speed.

"And you," she ignored his words, "we would be great together. We're both smart. You're a little quiet for my tastes, but that's okay. We're both gorgeous—"

Seonghun snorted.

"So why don't you take me out sometime?" She turned to face him. Her eyes were unusually bright; her pupils were like pinpricks. It was creepy.

"I'm seeing someone."

"Liar," she hissed.

"He isn't lying," Yong said.

"Even if I wasn't seeing anyone, there is no way in hell I would ever agree to date you. Ever. You need help. Stay away from me." He started to walk off to the shower area.

"You look good," she called out, "I heard you had a little accident. You should watch where you walk." She hopped off the treadmill, staring at Seong as he turned around slowly, facing her.

"I don't know where you would have heard that from." Seonghun stared her down.

She smirked as she got close to him. He resisted the urge to back up, staring into eyes that didn't quite seem all there. "I hear what I want to hear when I want to hear it." Her eyes roved over him hungrily. Seonghun felt like he was being appraised. His skin crawled as he fought every urge not to back up.

"Stay. Away. From. Me. I won't tell you again," Seong warned her.

"Ask your little friend. I'll do what I want. I want to see you. I will be seeing you again, cutie." She gave him a little finger wave before walking off.

Seonghun wheezed out a breath. "You got all of that right?" he asked.

"Every last word," Yong said.

"Send it to me so I can send it to Detective Krishna."

Yongjoon did as he asked.

Seonghun forwarded the message before looking over at his friend. "Don't you have a date to get ready for?"

When the two friends got back to the dorm room it was relatively quiet. Maliah's door was open, but no sound was coming out, not even music. He nodded at Yongjoon before heading to her room. Tapping on the door, he waited until he was granted access.

"Minjun Chin, if that is you I swear to god I'll learn how to fight so I can uppercut you."

Seong peeked in to see Maliah laying on her bed with a washcloth covering her eyes. She was back in her shorts with her requisite mismatched socks.

Holding in a chuckle he sat at her desk. "Tough day?"

"Oh my god!" She tossed the washcloth to the side before turning her head to him. "We get to Macy's; things are fine at first. Then about an hour in, he gets twitchy, decides he wants none of the things we've seen so we should go to another store." She sat up on a moan and began rubbing her feet. He pushed her hands out the way, kneading the arch in her left foot.

"Thank you," she said, sighing. "So, then we go to Von Maur. Same thing, pile of clothes, flipping through everything, then the twitchiness starts. Noticing it happening again, I suggest we take a break from looking. Maybe he could help me find a dress for the holiday concert. That way he can parse through clothes while I try stuff on."

"That's smart. You took him out of his head for a bit." Seonghun was impressed.

"Yeah, I thought it was smart too, but I just shined a big ass light on me. Do you know how many dresses he had me try on? Take a guess." She looked at him.

"Ten?"

"Multiply that number times four then add three," she said dryly.

Seong winced.

"After trying on all of those dresses, he decided the third one I tried on was the best, which I agreed with THE FIRST TIME I TRIED IT ON!" she hollered at the wall that separated their rooms. "Then I made another mistake. He asked what shoes I was going to wear with it, so I told him I had a pair of black heels that would be fine. Apparently black is too harsh for such a delicate pink. I tried to explain to him that the dress was long; no one would see the shoes. He said I would know." She whimpered when he hit a sensitive spot. "So now I have shoes that I will wear maybe twice because I don't have anything else to match. I whined about it so he bought the shoes. I took that in exchange for a snack."

"He would have bought you both if you whined for it."

"It felt like taking advantage, having him buy the shoes. The snack would have been double guilt," she explained. "The good thing though is that while I was trying stuff on, he figured out his outfit. He's pleased, I'm exhausted; I hope to never see another mall again." She collapsed on the bed.

"I warned you."

"You did. I have never seen anyone shop like that. Did you know there is a difference between French cuffs and regular cuffs on a shirt?"

"French cuffs you need cufflinks for. Regular cuffs don't necessarily need cufflinks. I've hung around Min my whole life, sweetheart. If I didn't know the difference, he'd accuse me of not paying attention to him." He patted her leg to scoot her over so he could lay with her.

"Ah, makes sense. Anyway, I picked up chicken for us to eat this evening. It's in the fridge. After they leave, we can start carving the pumpkin."

"Can I see your dress?"

"Maybe later, I don't even want to look at it right now," she admitted.

Seong started laughing as he kissed her. "Poor thing. Imagine if I had let you go without warning you?"

"I would have searched 'how to box' and everyone would have caught these hands." She waved her fists around feebly. "Except maybe Yongjoon. He was not party to this. He was already gone when I woke up this morning."

"He claims to not be an early riser, but he's almost always out the door before us," Seong explained. "Also, do you actually research everything?"

She blushed. "If I don't know it, someone on the internet does."

Seonghun prayed that his face didn't betray a smile. "So I know you researched kissing. Have you looked for anything else related to that?"

"No." She responded quickly, but her face betrayed her.

"I won't make fun of you, if that is what you're worried about," he said.

"The things I searched came up with weird sites that I'm not sure I want to click," she explained.

"Do you want to just ask me? I can provide some perspective, I suppose?"

"I—"

"LIAHHHHHHHHHHHHHHHHHHHHHH! HELP!" a yell came from Min's room.

"Minjun, I'm not getting out of this bed!" she shouted back.

"Please!?"

Maliah sighed, climbing over Seonghun. "I'll be back." She waddled slowly toward his room. As Seonghun laid on her bed he heard her scream. "OH MY GOD WHAT DID YOU DO!?"

Min's voice was fainter. "I was trying to do something to my hair."

"You did something alright. You're going to have to get in the shower and rinse... whatever this is, out."

Seonghun heard her shuffling back to her room. As she walked in he saw a brief glimpse of Minjun before she shut the door. His hair looked white.

"Did I just see Min with white hair? How the hell did Min get white hair?"

"As dark as his hair is, he had to have bleached it. I'm assuming none of you know about bleaching?" she asked.

He shook his head no.

"Jesus. I hope he looked up some instructions, otherwise he's going to lose all his hair." She went to crawl back over Seonghun when he grabbed her hips and sat her on top of him.

She arched a brow as she looked at him. "I'm nowhere near in the mindset for anything you may be thinking of while I'm on top of you."

"I figured, but I wanted to continue our conversation. Did you want to ask me something?"

Liah rolled her lips; her mouth was in a straight line. "No."

"I'm more than happy to answer anyth—"

"This is embarrassing and I'm not above using everything I know to stop this conversation," she interrupted.

"I don't think it's embarrassing, I'm fascinated by your mind and I want to know what you want to kn—oh god!"

Maliah began to roll her hips on top of him; the friction was enough to make his eyes roll. "Liah wha—"

"I'm done talking about this, okay?" She slid her hand under his shirt, lightly skimming his belly.

"O-okay."

She immediately stopped what she was doing, rolling to the side of the bed. "Thank you."

It was quiet for a minute before he spoke up. "Please don't do that again."

She looked at him confused. "What?"

"Please don't use sex to manipulate me. I told you that in confidence. Not for you to use it against me." He was looking up at the ceiling.

"I didn't know what else to do to get you to stop talking."

"That's fine. I get it; I'm being nosey because I want to know everything about you, but I told you my ex used to do that to get her way. You told me it's manipulative, so I'll ask that you don't do that again, okay?"

"I won't do it anymore. I'm sorry," she said quietly.

"You're forgiven," he said.

There was a tap at the door. "It's open," she called out.

Minjun opened the door.

Seonghun blinked.

Minjun was blond. White-blond. He was dressed in a lavender shirt with sleeves folded and cuffed. The cuffs were white, held in place with silver cufflinks. Black slacks with shiny black shoes completed his outfit.

Seong watched as his girlfriend sat up, staring at his best friend, blushing. "Why do you look like that?"

"L-like what?" She tried to look innocent but the quirk to her mouth gave her away. He narrowed his eyes at her.

"You look nice, Minjun," she said. Climbing over Seong again, he watched his girlfriend observe his best friend. "Turn around."

Min did as she asked. Seong watched as she inspected his hair. "So, it's not bad, the ends of your hair are slightly yellow, because they weren't toned right, but they are also split. You need a trim."

He turned back around, smiling at her. "Thank you."

"You're welcome, have fun. Both of you be careful."

He patted her on the head before shutting the door. She turned back to Seonghun who was trying hard not to laugh.

"What?" she asked.

"You thought he was cute, admit it."

She was quiet for a moment. Finally she looked him in the eye. "Dark haired Minjun is adorable. Almost sweet in a way. Blond Minjun is a demon. There is no reason for him to look that good."

Seonghun laughed. "He tends to have that effect on people. Would you get all red in the face like that if I dyed my hair?"

"Please don't. Your hair is beautiful." She walked over to touch his bangs.

He tugged on one of her twists. "I'm curious to see what your hair actually looks like."

"These will stay in for a little bit longer. By the time it is time for them to come out, my hair should be at a length I'm comfortable with."

That reminded him of the gym. Sighing, he put his hands on her hips. "Liah, something happened. I can tell you or you can hear it for yourself, I don't know which would be less traumatic."

"It's fine, I can listen." Seong fished his phone out, pressing play on the file he sent to the detective.

"So she basically admitted to pushing you into the street. Jesus she's dumb." Liah shook her head.

"You don't seem as affected by her."

"I'm affected by the past. By what she has done already. That's what I have nightmares of. I don't worry about her in the present. She can't come near me. It's you I'm mostly concerned about." She looked at him. "I have nightmares that I didn't stand up for myself, that I could have prevented her from messing with you or anyone else if I'd been brave enough."

"You can't think like that. You can't put the burden of someone else's behavior on yourself," he argued.

"That's what the good doctor says too, but there was a phrase I learned a while back." She looked off into the distance trying to remember. "Ignorance of the law does not excuse."

He smiled. Seong wasn't much of a debater like Yong, but he knew a thing or two. "Do you know the explanation around that saying?" When she shook her head, he broke down the phrase. "It's believed that if something is common knowledge, you can't use 'I didn't know' as an excuse. Nothing about student court is common knowledge. That saying doesn't fit this situation."

"I—" She opened and closed her mouth. "I'm not used to being outthought if that makes sense."

"I hope you'll think about it." He stood up and stretched. "Wanna go eat? I'm hungry."

"Sounds like a plan." Together they walked out of the bedroom.

CHAPTER 26

"Okay, so do you want a face or something else?" Maliah twirled a marker in her hand.

"What can you do?" Seonghun asked.

"Pretty much anything you can put your mind to. I'm still new to drawing but anything you want on a pumpkin I can do, I think." She watched as he grabbed another chicken leg. "Have you eaten anything but those donuts today?"

"I had a bowl of oatmeal," he said.

"You have got to eat more than that, otherwise you wolf down mass quantities at odd times." Pursing her lips, she stared at him thoughtfully. "When was there a time you felt well and truly full?"

He thought about it for a minute. "I went to an all you can eat buffet once and stayed full for a really long time after. I also couldn't move much for an hour or two after I ate."

"What about large holiday meals?" she asked.

"Yeah, I stay full after big meals like that," he said. He reminisced briefly about Cho's epic dinners.

"I wish I had your metabolism. I'd be skinny."

"You are skinny. You'd be too skinny because there's no way you'd eat enough to maintain any type of shape," he pointed out, looking at her over his glasses.

She rolled her eyes. "Anyway, back to the pumpkin. What do you want?"

"A face I think."

"Scary face?"

"No, happy face."

Maliah stared at the pumpkin for a minute. "I got it. Hold on." She began to draw. The face was simplistic but when she got done, Seonghun realized she had done two designs in one. The happy mouth was a bat.

"That's cute." He looked on as she admired her handiwork. Liah walked around the kitchen, searching in the cabinets until she found a pie tin. "What's that for?" he asked.

"I'm going to make you a deal."

"I'm listening."

"I'll carve the pumpkin, but you have to scrape the insides out. Seeds go in that pie tin. You do it, I'll make Chex Mix tonight while you're cleaning the insides," she offered.

"DONE!" He handed her the knife.

He watched as she cut the top of the pumpkin. As she yanked it off, some of the pumpkin guts attached to the top slapped at her skin making his girlfriend wince.

"You okay?"

"I have issues with textures. No problems eating different textures, but touching them, meh." Setting down the top, Liah began carving the front of the pumpkin, trying to make sure the chunks she sawed out fell on the outside of the pumpkin. Using a tool kit she got from the grocery store, Seong watched in amazement as Liah carved the delicate details she had drawn. She even shaved lines on the sides of the eyes to resemble crinkles.

"This is really cute." She was talented. He went to stick his hands in the pumpkin but she stopped him.

"Go wash your hands first please," she said as she pulled out ingredients.

"Why?"

"I'm going to roast the pumpkin seeds."

He did as she asked. As he began digging into the pumpkin, she turned on classical music that softly played through the speakers in her room. They worked companionably in silence, letting only the music fill the air.

"Hey."

She looked up at his call.

"Can I hear you play the violin?"

"Let me get this in the oven and yeah, sure. I was actually tapped to play in the concert this year. The other senior soloist is singing a song that requires band back up. He's always been very nice, so I volunteered." She started laughing. "He found a very clever way to do his solo when he really didn't want to."

"What did he do?" Seonghun started separating the seeds from the pumpkin guts, placing them in the pie pan.

"Mmm, you'll see if you come." She washed her hands in the sink.

"I asked you if I could come," he said, confused.

"You did."

"So why wouldn't I come if I asked to come?"

She was silent while she cleaned up her mess. Walking into her room, Seong saw her come back out with a violin. Liah looked at him as she fiddled with the strings. "Do you want to hear classical or something else?"

"I'd like to hear an answer to my question." Seong was a gentle man, but he wasn't a pushover. Part of him was feeling a bit insulted as it seemed as if Liah didn't believe him.

"Because with the one exception I told you about, no one has ever shown up to a concert for me. I'm honestly not expecting that to happen for me." She looked at him. "I'm enjoying my time with you, I just—" She hesitated for a minute. "I don't have faith in anything good for me lasting. It never does."

He picked up the pumpkin guts, tossing them in the trash before washing his hands. Wiping them on a paper towel, he walked over to her, holding out his hand. She took it.

"Seems like we were in opposite places a few days ago," he said.

"Yeah."

"Did you have a chance to read today's letter?"

She nodded.

"Like I said, I can't promise to never hurt you. Life doesn't work that way. We make mistakes. Even you. But the promises that I do make, I keep. I will be at your concert. Nothing would keep me away. Understood?" She wouldn't look at him, or respond. "Liah?"

"Yeah, I understand," she said quietly. She felt off to him. as if she was just saying it to placate him. All of a sudden he heard a persistent beep. Seong watched as she robotically walked over to the stove. Opening it up, she stirred the cereal mix. He waited as she reset the timer. Liah seemed to be struggling with her words, so he was quiet as she gathered what she needed within herself to speak. "I'm not used to people saying they will be there for me, truly meaning it. I've never been able to talk to someone without anything I say being thrown back in my face." Tears started to well up. He saw her take a ragged breath as she gripped the counter, trying to get her bearings.

"I-I-I-I'm not u-u-u-used t-t-t-to th-th-th-" Liah shuddered as a sob overtook her.

He walked over, gently wrapping his arms around her. Seong rested his head on hers as his girlfriend gripped him tightly. After about ten minutes the sobs stopped. All he heard was soft hiccups.

"Better?" he murmured.

"Sort of. It's been building since last night I think. I felt safe with you guys. I don't just fall asleep anywhere."

"I could tell. You hardly stuttered after you calmed down."

"You guys are nice. You don't say bad things about other people. You have funny conversations."

Seonghun chuckled. "Yeah, we do. Someone always has a question that needs to be answered. It's worse when we go camping. Sometimes we spend all night talking about random things. As a result we end up sleeping half the day away."

"That sounds like fun," she said softly. Liah slowly let him go, continuing to cook. Looking over at him she asked, "Do you prefer sweet, or savory things?"

"Yes."

Snorting, she opened the cabinet, pulling down sugar, salt, several other spices, and some oil. Maliah lightly coated the seeds in oil before dumping a little of each seasoning into a bowl. Stirring it together, she carefully dusted the seeds in seasoning. When she got done, her phone beeped again. She stirred the cereal, tossing the seeds into the oven alongside the mix. "I wonder how Yongjoon and Minjun are doing?"

"Min is probably on his second glass of wine, while Yongjoon is probably pushing water on him so he doesn't get trashed," Seonghun said.

Walking around the counter, she picked up her violin. "What did you want to hear?"

"Can you play me something that makes you feel proud?"

Liah tapped her lip for a minute thinking. Putting the violin under her chin she closed her eyes before she began playing a fast song. It was intense and from what Seonghun saw with her fingers she had to be precise. She finished it quickly as it was a short tune, before putting her violin back up.

"What was that called?"

"Flight of the Bumblebee. When I got it I knew I could be good at this." The timer went off again. Once again, Liah stirred the cereal before pulling out the pumpkin seeds. Dumping them into a bowl, she handed them to him.

"Want to watch your Thai drama and eat seeds with me?" he asked.

"I promised Minjun I wouldn't watch without him. But I'll watch Jeopardy with you." She looked up at him.

"Done," he said. They snuggled into the couch together.

SEONGHUN WAS WRAPPED around Maliah with his tongue down her throat when Yong and Min returned.

"Uh, Seong?" Yong called out awkwardly.

Maliah snapped back first. She stared at the two men who were holding hands. "Hi. D-did you have a nice time?"

Without responding, Minjun let go of Yongjoon's hand. He grabbed Maliah, pulling her into his bedroom.

"Is there a particular reason why my best friend has kidnapped my girlfriend?" Seonghun looked at Yong while trying to tuck something in his pants pocket. Yongjoon pounced, drilling a finger into Seonghun's side, causing him to scream while trying to shove his friend off of him. Taking advantage of the fact his hands were busy, Yongjoon reached into his pocket, pulling out…

"Her boobs are bigger than I thought." Yong dangled the bra in between them. "She's got good taste in bras."

"Give me that!" Seong snatched the bra from him, shoving it quickly into his pocket. "She'd be mortified."

"Shouldn't be out in the main area like this if you don't want to get caught. Hasn't that been the rule for a while?" Yongjoon smirked.

"I didn't even know it was a rule. It hasn't really applied to me," Seonghun said.

"True," Yongjoon said. "To answer your initial question, it's a date recap I think. He needed someone to talk to."

"I'd say he could talk to me, but I don't think Minjun has ever had an actual date." Seonghun thought about it. "He's just had… assignations? Is that the right word?"

"It's as good as any. I've had dates. I know you've had at least a date or two." Yongjoon pointed his thumb at the door. "She hasn't, so she can possibly relate. Also, some things happened that she can explain better than I could."

Seonghun felt guilty. "I should have taken her out this weekend. We have plans next weekend."

"What did you guys do tonight?" Yongjoon asked.

Seonghun pointed at the pumpkin. Liah had a votive tealight that was actually battery powered. There was no flame, but it gave a flame appearance that she set in the jack 'o lantern. "We carved the pumpkin, made pumpkin seeds, made Chex Mix, she had a minor breakdown, played a song on the violin for me and we watched Jeopardy."

Yong stared at him. "You both are so fucking weird." He shook his head. "You technically had a date. It was just an at home one."

Seonghun thought about it for a minute and nodded. "Maybe. How did yours go?"

"Did you know he was taking me to Ruth's Chris?"

"I might have had an inkling." Seonghun smiled.

"It was nice. We're friends so we didn't run out of things to talk about. After his first glass of wine his nerves calmed down." Yongjoon turned slightly pink. "He took me to a play. It was at a small theater house. The seats were close enough that you felt immersed. The play though—" He paused.

All of a sudden there was a small crash as they heard Maliah's voice. "THEY DID WHAT!?"

"He must be telling her about the play. He didn't quite understand why I was horrified."

"Wait, what happened?" Seonghun asked.

"Well, the play started out with a teacher getting in trouble because she let her students play slave and slave owners, to try to make the kids feel empathetic toward each side. How well do you know about slavery in American history?" Yongjoon asked.

Seonghun shrugged.

Yongjoon pointed at Maliah's door. "I could be wrong, but chances are her ancestors were enslaved in Africa then brought over in chains to this country, forced to work on farms. It's a lot of history, I'm not going to get too deep into it, but it was bad. A whole war was fought about it. Anyway, bottom line is no one should be empathizing with slave owners." Seong watched him put his head in his hands. "The whole play was a mess. Then someone came out in a KKK outfit and 아이씨."

Yongjoon rarely mixed his languages. He stayed solidly in one lane throughout the conversation, so Seonghun could tell he was frustrated by his exasperated comment in Korean.

"Keep going, did you guys stay?"

"We were toward the front so we couldn't leave without attracting attention. Min was confused as to why I was so upset. When the play ended, we walked back to the car. He was worried I was mad at him, but I assured him that wasn't it at all. I tried my best to explain that while the play was billed as a comedy, it wasn't very funny. Also the fact that there wasn't a single black person in the audience was very telling." Yongjoon sighed.

"OH MY GOD! WHAT!?"

Both men turned to Minjun's door as they heard Maliah yelp.

"He must be at the part with the KKK robes." When he saw Seonghun's face he held up a hand. "Just, look it up, use incognito on your browser, please make sure she is nowhere near you when you do."

Seonghun nodded.

"I took him for ice cream to console him, also to let him know nothing was ruined. We spent the rest of the evening talking. Besides the play, I had a great time with him. Also the blond hair is something." He hid a smile.

"The blond hair made Maliah take a second look at him. She called him a demon." Seong laughed, remembering the look on her face at a cleaned up Min.

"He is lethal, that's for sure. I'm going to go to bed. You good?"

Seonghun nodded.

"Good night then." Yong walked into his room.

Seonghun waited patiently. Ten minutes later, Maliah came out of Minjun's room shell shocked with her hair in two buns.

She looked over at Seonghun. "I-I don't know what the hell just happened. I don't even know how my hair is in buns."

Seonghun tried not to laugh. "You okay?"

"If you plan a date for us, please run any possible history issues through Yong. He's Korean American, correct?"

Seonghun nodded.

"So he's been through several Black History Month presentations. I—" She paused and stared at nothing. "I want to burn the playhouse to the ground."

"Well, don't do that," Seonghun said gently.

She walked over and gave him a kiss. "It never occurred to me that you don't really have a reference for my history. Not just my personal history, but my ancestors. I guess it makes sense, I mean, I don't have a reference for yours."

"It seems like yours is a little fraught," he said quietly.

"Yes. I'm going to go to bed. I'm not angry or anything. Just a little shell shocked. I need some time alone."

"Okay. If you get lonely, come see me." He gave her a half-smile.

"Okay. G'night, Seonghun."

"Goodnight, sweetheart. Oh!" He pulled her bra from his pocket. "Here."

She laughed at him. "Thanks for attempting to preserve my modesty."

He blushed. "It didn't work. Yong saw."

"It's okay. It's just a bra, it's clean. G'night." Liah walked into her room.

He walked into his room, closed the door before firing up his laptop. After going to an incognito browser he typed in 'What is the kkk'.

CHAPTER 27

When Seonghun woke up the next morning, he laid in bed for a while. His initial search led him down a rabbit hole of facts he had no clue about. Eventually he landed on an article that had a long list of books to help him fully understand what he had been reading. Seong ended up putting a hold on a few of them from the campus library. They should be ready for pick up this morning.

Padding out to the common area, it was quiet. On the weekend, he was rarely up this early, so it was surprising not to at least hear someone's music floating faintly through the suite. Min's door was open, but Yong and Maliah's were closed. After using the restroom, he knocked on her door. There was a bit of shuffling behind the door. Seong was surprised as she cracked the door, poking her head out. Normally she just told him to come in.

"Hi, Seonghun. It's really not a good time," she said sleepily.

He took a good look at her. She was swollen in her face as if she'd been crying. But there were no tears and her eyes weren't red.

"Are you okay?" he asked.

"I'm fine mentally if that's what you're asking."

"Why all the mystery? What's wrong?"

"I have a stomach ache. I'll be alright tomorrow." She went to shut the door, but he held his hand up, blocking it.

"I'm not trying to be rude, but how do you specifically know you'll be better tomorrow? Have you taken anything? Do you need anything?" He'd never seen her look that tired. It was concerning to him. However, it seemed like he asked too many questions because she burst into tears.

"Oh." Seonghun stepped back startled. "I didn't mean to upset you, I just didn't want you to suffer in silence."

"It's not you," she sniffled, "I'm just sort of emotional right now."

Seonghun thought for a minute. "You're swollen, you have a stomach ache, and you're emotional. Okay." He looked at her for a moment as she stood there. "Do you have one of the patches on?"

"How did you—"

"I've had a girlfriend, like I told you. We didn't get that deep into it, but she was on birth control, so her times were fairly scheduled, I know the signs," he explained.

"Oh." Maliah blinked. "Well, yeah. I have two patches on, as well as the heating pad you gave me. I'm just in pain; it drains my energy."

"Let me in."

She opened the door to him. She was in his sweatshirt paired with men's basketball shorts. They hung long past her knees. Liah had taken her hair out of the buns, pulling it back into a low ponytail.

"You're cute," he blurted out.

"I'm a mess. I need to lay back down." With that, she plopped in the bed, sticking the heating pad on her stomach.

"Where does it hurt most?" he asked, sitting at her desk chair.

"My stomach hurts, but with my back it radiates down my legs," she explained.

"Do you want me to rub your back?"

"I don't think so." Her voice was slurred as she was dozing back off. He sat there waiting for her to fall back asleep, before getting up and creeping out of her room. Immediately he knocked on Yong's door.

Yongjoon opened up, staring at his friend. "May I borrow your car?" He opened the door wider, motioning him inside. Seonghun walked in, stopping short at the sight of Minjun asleep in his bed. "Oh."

"Don't get weird on me, Seong."

"I'm not. It's just, you're moving a little fast," Seonghun said.

"Not what you're thinking. He just slept here last night." Yongjoon grabbed his keys from his armoire. "Where on earth are you going this early?"

"Grocery store and the library. Do you need anything?"

"I'll text you." Yong handed his keys over.

"Thank you, I'll be back soon. If Min gets up, let him know to leave Liah alone. She isn't feeling well."

Yongjoon saluted as he climbed back into bed. Seonghun's heart warmed as Min rolled over in his sleep, immediately laying his head on Yongjoon's chest. Seonghun walked out of the room. As he left the dorm, he pulled out his phone, making a list.

A COUPLE HOURS later he walked back in the suite to see his two friends studying while music played in the background. They looked up as Seonghun walked in with several bags, watching as he put everything away. Ice cream, cans of soup, and several types of chocolate were the main things he'd purchased.

"That is the weirdest grocery haul I've ever seen," said Min.

Ignoring his friend, Seonghun walked over to his room, dumping the books on his desk. Coming back out, he grabbed a candy bar before tapping at his girlfriend's door. At her soft 'come in' he entered. "How are you feeling?" he asked.

"The pain meds kicked in, so it's not as bad." She was still lying in bed, flipping through her phone. She set it down to look at him. "Thanks for asking."

He handed her a candy bar. "I don't know what kind of candy you like. I also don't know if you're allergic to nuts, though, you ate the Chex Mix, so I guess you aren't."

She looked down at the candy bar. It was a king sized Milky Way. Liah immediately burst into tears.

"Uh, I have other candy out front if you don't like that," Seonghun said slowly.

"N-no t-this is f-fine." She wept as she opened the candy bar. Splitting it in half, she gave him a piece. Seong watched as she cried quietly, eating the candy.

"Are you okay?" he asked cautiously, biting into the chocolate bar.

"This was just really nice of you." She looked up at him as a fresh torrent of tears started, "I'm an emotional wreck during my period. I can't help it, everything sets me off for at least a day or two."

He nodded as if he understood. He didn't really. He'd never had to deal with this. His mom would have some pain, that was about it. The same with his ex. They never had emotional outbursts around this time, but he supposed every woman was different.

Liah finished her candy. Hunched over, she pulled out her bathroom kit. "I'll be back," she said as she walked to the bathroom. Seonghun got up, running out to the kitchenette to heat her some soup. He asked his friends if they were hungry; they both shook their heads, watching as he stirred the soup.

"Is she still not feeling well?" Yong asked, concerned.

"Not very, no," was all Seonghun would say. He knew she felt kind of awkward about the whole thing.

"I hope she feels better. If she needs anything from us, let us know," Minjun said.

Yong nodded his agreement.

Seonghun gave them a half smile before carefully carrying a bowl of soup into the room. He was flipping through one of her textbooks when Liah slowly walked back in.

"Is it time to change your patches?" Seonghun asked.

"Yeah. I don't need the front one anymore, just the back one. That's what hurts now." She unzipped the hoodie before lifting up the shirt underneath to pull off the patch. Reaching behind her she went to grab the back one when he brushed her hands away.

"Where's the replacement?" he asked.

She handed him a patch. He removed the old patch from her skin, reapplying the new one in the same spot.

"Thank you."

"You're welcome. I brought you soup." He held out the bowl to her. He saw her look up at the ceiling to prevent tears. "Do you always weep like this during your period?" he asked, astounded.

She nodded.

He rubbed her back as she sniffled. "Come eat some soup."

She sat on the bed, eating as he rubbed her back. "There are other chocolate bars in the fridge along with other cans of soup in the cabinet. I figured you wouldn't want anything heavy," he said softly.

"I need to study, but I'm going to be down for at least another three hours," she said. As she stood to take her bowl in the kitchen, he intercepted, gently pushing her back down on her bed. When he walked back in she was laying down.

"Do you want company or do you want to be left alone?"

She hesitated for a moment. "Please stay with me." She curled into a ball.

"I'm going to get my text books. I'll be right back and stay with you until you fall asleep." He left the room, grabbed his books and was unsurprised to come back to her crying. At this point he was pretty sure she was going to be dehydrated from all the tears. "Okay, scoot over." He closed the door, taking off his clothes. She slid over, watching him as he stripped down to his t-shirt and his boxers. Once situated in the bed, he pulled her over. She laid her head on his shoulder as she sobbed quietly. He rubbed her back, comforting her as best as he could until she fell asleep. He looked over at his textbooks before looking down at her. He could easily slide out, but honestly, he didn't want to. Kissing her forehead, he closed his eyes as well.

SEONGHUN FELT her trying to crawl over him. He grabbed her waist and arched up. She cried out, loudly. Opening one eye he looked at her. "I'm sorry, did that hurt?"

She shook her head. "Opposite. I'm super sensitive." She laughed without humor. "Nature's little joke, it's probably easiest for me to enjoy myself sexually right now, but I'm an absolute mess; I don't want be touched." He gave her a sympathetic smile while patting her thighs gently as she slid across him to get to the bathroom. Grabbing his textbooks, he walked out to get a snack. After fixing a sandwich, Seong started to focus on his studies. As he started typing, he heard her slow gait as she walked across the suite, finally landing at his door.

"Thank you for staying with me," she said quietly. She seemed less swollen in her face.

"You're quite welcome. All you ever have to do is ask."

She nodded, before leaving him to his studies.

He began to work on his homework. He sent a text to Shiwon asking if he wanted to work on the lab report after class. He replied back, agreeing. They held a short conversation and talked about hanging out some time during the week. He liked Shiwon. The only problem he had was him asking Maliah out, but he took the no in stride.

He went back to his work, wrestling with statistics for a few hours before his stomach began to growl. Grabbing a granola bar from his desk, he ate it as he wandered over to Maliah's side. Knocking, he opened it up to find her sitting in the middle of her bed. Liah had papers scattered everywhere with her laptop in front of her. As the door opened, she looked up at him, slightly unfocused.

"Are you hungry for something other than soup?" he asked.

She nodded.

"Do you want to go find a cafeteria?"

She shook her head no. "I don't eat in the cafeterias."

"Why?"

"It feels weird eating there alone."

"You wouldn't be eating alone, you would be with me." He sent a text with his phone beeping almost immediately after. "Also our roommates."

"Oh, okay then." She stood up, stretching. As she raised her arms, her shirt lifted, showing a slightly pooched out belly. Seong reached a finger out, poking the softness. Looking down at her stomach, Liah covered it with her hands quickly. "I get really bloated."

"Don't hide, it's cute. You look—" He stopped speaking abruptly.

"It's okay, I already know what you're going to say. I look pregnant. It will go away by the end of the week."

"I didn't mean anything bad by it." Seong knew she was more than a little sensitive about her weight.

"I know, I realize I get puffier than normal during this time. It doesn't really bother me."

She grabbed the things she needed, looking around the room before her eyes landed back on him. "I need you to step out." He left the room quickly, shutting the door. Walking over he sat on the couch, waiting patiently for everyone. Yongjoon's door opened; both his friends came out while putting on light jackets.

"Are you about ready?" Yongjoon asked.

"Waiting on Maliah, she's coming," he said. As Seong sat there, he had an idea. Dialing a number he pressed the phone to his ear.

"You miss me already?" Shiwon asked.

"We're all going to eat in one of the cafeterias, come with us," replied Seonghun.

"I can do that. Where are you going?"

Seonghun went through the cafeterias mentally realizing there was only one close to them open right now. He told Shiwon, agreeing to meet him in about fifteen minutes. As he was hanging up the phone, Maliah came out of her room. He noted that she seemed a bit better, even her glasses were on her face straight. "Sorry," she said as she saw everyone waiting.

"You're fine. Are you feeling better?" Minjun asked, grabbing her hand while tugging her out of the door.

Yongjoon hid a smile. "Hope you're ready to share your girl."

Seonghun rolled his eyes as the two men followed behind. Outside of the building, Seong spotted Shiwon. He waved to his lab partner. Both Yongjoon and Minjun stopped short.

"He's—" Yong said.

"Yeah," Minjun agreed.

Seonghun and Maliah looked at Shiwon leaning casually against the building. He was Asian, skinny, and tall; taller than Seonghun by a little bit. His hair was long, not quite reaching to his shoulders. Seong watched as he pushed his dark bangs off of his face. His features seemed perfectly proportioned with a full wide mouth that seemed to be his defining feature. Though he was attired in simple black skinny jeans, they accentuated his long legs. Shiwon was skinny, but seemed as if he took up more space.

Maliah looked at the roommates before she started giggling. "They're a little surprised by how cute he is."

Seong grabbed her hand. "Are you really supposed to notice other cute people when you're seeing someone else?" he teased her.

"I'm not blind, he's hot. But he didn't bring me a chocolate bar or soup," she pointed out.

He smiled while squeezing her hand.

"You didn't tell me Shorty was coming," Shiwon called out.

As they got closer, Seong watched as Shiwon sort of squatted, making himself smaller as he addressed Liah.

"You gave him a chance?"

She nodded.

"Good, I thought he might have punched me had you agreed to coffee that day." He smiled at her.

Minjun choked on air at his smile.

"Jesus." Yongjoon stared at Shiwon.

He glanced over at Yongjoon and Minjun. "Hi, I'm Shiwon."

Min was frozen, not even blinking. Yongjoon quietly said hi back.

Maliah's face was buried into Seonghun's back, laughing so hard she was shaking. Seong was trying incredibly hard not to burst into laughter himself.

"Are you guys ready to eat?" Shiwon asked.

"Yeah, let's go." Seonghun pulled Maliah to his side. Together, they walked into the cafeteria. Everyone separated to get what they wanted to eat. Seonghun blazed through, his tray a pile of sandwiches, fries, chicken strips, cake, and at both Minjun and Liah's reproving looks, two vegetables. He sat down first, immediately cutting into a chicken strip, when he heard something he was praying he wouldn't hear while Liah was around.

"Fancy meeting you here."

He set his fork down, glaring at Casey. "Go away."

BACK AT THE DORM, Seonghun began fidgeting. He was back in Maliah's room studying at her desk as she sprawled out on her bed.

"Liah?"

She grunted at him.

"Can I ask what medications you're on?"

She looked up at that. "Why?"

"You never talk about them, except to say you're on them. I was curious."

She closed her book, sighing. "To be honest, I've been tapering down, so it's nowhere near the pill cocktail it was when I left the hospital. Fluoxetine, Xanax, and buspirone. Xanax I only take as a last resort."

"What do each of them do?" he asked.

"Fluoxetine is for depression and anxiety, buspirone for anxiety, Xanax for anxiety." She ticked them off her fingers.

"Which one messes with your sex drive?"

"Fluoxetine."

"You can't go off it?"

"You know how I've been a mess all day? Crying at the drop of a hat?"

He nodded.

"Multiply that times ten plus add me not getting anything done because I'm too emotionally taxed to get out of the bed. It's not pretty or productive. My dosage has been lowered slightly. It was so high at one point that literally nothing affected me. Happy news, sad news, I'd just sort of sit there. That screaming I just did at dinner? Wouldn't have happened."

He watched as she rubbed her lower back.

"Your back still hurts?" he asked.

"Yeah."

"Clean up your books."

She looked at him questioningly.

"Trust me. Clear off the bed." He shut the door while she did as he asked.

Piling her laptop and books on the desk, she sat back on the bed.

"Scoot forward," he ordered. He slid in behind her, getting comfortable as he unzipped the sweatshirt she wore today, sliding it off of her shoulders. Lifting her shirt slightly, he looked at the patch. "Is it about time to change this?"

"Close enough to time," she said quietly.

He took the patch off, tossing it in the trash before kneading the muscles in the small of her back.

"Ohhhh." She dropped her chin down to her chest.

He smiled behind her as he heard her soft grunts when he hit a particularly painful spot. He put more pressure into his rubbing when she moaned, loudly.

"Shhh, they're going to think we're doing something else." He kissed her neck softly.

"It feels so good," she moaned.

He started laughing. "You have got to be quiet."

There was a light tapping at the door. "Can you two keep it down just a little please?"

"Nothing is happening, Min, you can open the door," Maliah called out.

Minjun opened the door cautiously, "You two okay?"

"F-f-f-f-OH GOD!" she cried out as Seong's thumb hit a sensitive spot. "Sorry, Min, I'm sorry, I'll try to keep it down."

He nodded, closing the door.

Seonghun began an assault on her neck as soon as he heard the door click.

"I can't, Seonghun."

He felt her panting. Easing up on his affections, Seong continued to rub her back. "Sorry."

"S'okay." She was quiet for a minute. "I can't really participate, but that doesn't mean you can't." She turned around in bed, kissing him. He wrapped his arms around her, trying to rub her back as best as he could.

Liah slid her hands under his shirt, tentatively touching his shoulders, caressing his chest. Moving her mouth to his neck, her hands drifted lower. Seonghun had given up rubbing her back; he was just touching Maliah as much as he could. As she was touching him, he gently lifted up her shirt.

"I'm not good with this, but we're going to give it a try," Seong said as he reached around behind her to unhook her bra. After struggling for a moment, he felt the clasps give way. Sliding the cups up, he rubbed his thumbs across her chest. Instantly, he felt her stiffen.

"Sensitive," she whispered in his ear. "Please be gentle."

He began to caress her all over, stopping short of her face. He felt as she slowly reached inside his pants, grabbing him firmly. Biting back a strangled moan, he stopped touching her long enough to yank his pants lower.

She bit his shoulder gently before lifting her head to look him in his eyes as she touched him. He thought she looked a little unsure of herself as her hand moved up and down. Kissing her, he wrapped his hand around hers, reminding her how he liked to be touched. Soon their kisses became frenzied as her movements picked up speed. Seonghun moaned in her mouth as he came, his body arching slightly off the bed, as he spilled all over both of their hands.

Liah got up and grabbed the towel hanging on the back of her door, cleaning her hands. Seonghun held out his hand for the towel, but instead, she began cleaning him up as best as she could. Finishing up by wiping his hands, she handed over the towel in case there was something she missed.

Pulling her arms out of her top, she slid her bra off and tossed it on the desk, before pulling her shirt down and walking out of the room into the bathroom. Seong heard her turn on the sink. She quickly came back into the room as he walked out to wash his hands as well. When he came back into her room, Liah was laying down with tears running down her face. Quickly closing the door he walked over to her and sat on the bed.

"Did we move too fast?" he asked cautiously.

She shook her head.

"What's wrong?" He was a little nervous.

Liah was just sitting there crying. "You're really nice," she hiccupped, trying to compose herself, "I like being with youuuu." She burst into louder sobs.

He rubbed her arm as she continued to cry. "I like being with you too. I don't know what to do," he said helplessly.

"I'm a wreck, I don't know why you would even want to be with me." She turned on her side, facing the wall.

He watched, mystified as her shoulders shook. "Hold on. I'll be right back." Walking into the common area, he opened the fridge, pulling out another candy bar. Retreating back to her room, he sat on the bed, dangling the treat in front of her face. "I know you said you cry a lot, but I don't know what to do. I know when I get sad, food helps sometimes."

She quietly took the candy from him, unwrapped it, giving him half before nibbling. "That's one of the reasons I like you, you know?" he said as he bit into the candy bar. "You always give, no matter what. You're sick, I bought the candy bar for you, but you still split it."

"I like sharing. Things seem nicer when they're shared," she whispered.

"You're smart, you've been through some shit, but you try not to let it stop you. I'm pretty sure if something happened between us, I'd lose my best friend to you." He saw the tears had subsided.

"Minjun would never," she said, calming down.

"Min is loyal, but he really likes you. He makes friends easily but they aren't—" Seonghun waved his hand around as if he was trying to grasp the word out of the air, "they aren't forever friends. They're people that after we leave school, they may drop a 'hi' or 'what's going on' from time to time. He's going to bug you for the rest of your days."

"I don't know whether to be thankful or petrified." Maliah sniffled.

"A little bit of both is probably wise." He began rubbing her back. "Can I sleep in here tonight?"

"I'd like that a lot." They both finished their candy before cuddling under the blankets, slowly drifting off.

CHAPTER 28

The next morning Seonghun's alarm woke him up. A testament to how tired she was, Liah didn't even move at the sound of the loud music. He gathered his things, creeping out of her room to get ready. As he was collecting his books, he realized he still had the picture of Maliah as a child. He stared at it for a minute before carefully placing it in his wallet. Once he had everything, he ran to breakfast.

As he ate, he began reading one of the books that he had checked out from the library. Slowly reading the book, he was beginning to understand why the play was so horrifying to his two American born roommates. Taking out his phone, he sent a text to Min, letting him know the name of the book. He knew that Minjun understood it was bad, but like himself, he struggled to understand exactly why. This would help. Finishing up breakfast, he was walking out of the door when he remembered what Maliah said about Casey. He called the number Detective Krishna gave him.

After exchanging pleasantries, he explained what happened yesterday. "I'm a little concerned that she saw us together. She's going to escalate."

"I took a look at the videos; sadly, I can't get a good look at the person who pushed you. They had on a big coat. They were half your size height-wise though." The detective paused for a moment to give Seonghun the chance to absorb the information. "I also looked at the cameras starting from the day you had the incident in class. The person in that same coat has been following you."

"What do I need to do?" Seonghun asked.

"There is a bulletin going out via email to the school about some unusual activity. There will be officers stationed in several areas across the campus," she explained. "The thing is, all of the officers will be marked, except in your area. They will be plain clothed. I've given them a picture of you and Maliah. I will also need pictures of your roommates, so they will observe anyone that is following you, especially in that coat."

"Thanks, Detective." Seonghun knew he sounded dejected.

"I know it isn't much, but she's getting sloppy. She's going to get caught," the detective assured him.

"I'd like her caught before she causes more damage," he said. With little else to say they disconnected the call. Seonghun headed out to class.

BEFORE HIS LAST class he stopped by the large hot house on campus to clip some flowers. Though it was fall, they generally had all sorts of flowers in the warm building all year round. He'd chosen daisies, pink roses, and little sprigs of lavender. As he was leaving, one of the girls that was in there stopped him, asking if he was giving them to someone. At his yes, she dragged him back in, showing him how to make a bouquet using filler leaves. He thanked her profusely. Seong knew how to arrange flowers; he went to a workshop on it, but rarely used the knowledge.

"All I ask is that you pay it forward. We get a lot of ag major guys in here that cut flowers for their girlfriends or moms. Some of us that work here teach them. We hope that they do a good deed in kind," she explained as she placed rubber bands around the stems. Seong promised her that he would before heading into his lab. Shiwon was already there, clipping his hair out of his face.

"You know, you could cut that; it would be less of a hazard," Seonghun pointed out.

Shiwon looked mock offended. "You saw how your roommates reacted to my hair. I would never. It's my best feature, one of them anyway." Once his hair was out of his face, he donned the protective gear of the lab. "See, you even found it attractive, you brought me flowers!"

Seonghun's backpack was open; the small bouquet was visible. He blushed furiously.

"Shorty will appreciate the flowers though. Seems like a nice girl, except when she was yelling at the crazy pants. Then she looked like she was going to tear that girl limb from limb. Which is kind of hot."

"She was kind of an emotional wreck yesterday due to circumstances out of her control. I haven't seen her since I left this morning, I thought it would be nice." He donned his own goggles. "I just want to—" He paused.

Shiwon glanced at him before he spoke, "I know something is different with Shorty. I also know it isn't your story to tell. But the way she looks at you makes me think you're making her very happy."

Seonghun looked surprised at his observation.

"I'm not just a pretty face." Shiwon shrugged. "I'm fairly perceptive; there has been a change in her eyes from when I asked her to coffee to yesterday. She's still very guarded, however. If I asked her to go anywhere with me, be it two steps from you, she'd say no, probably while running in the opposite direction. But she's less hesitant to touch you now. When I brought you back to your dorm, she maneuvered away from both of us. She also looks for you, even when she was conversing with the blond guy."

Seonghun was silent for a moment, focused on mixing chemicals. "It's not my recital, but I don't think she would mind if I invited you. She has to sing for the holiday concert. You want to come?"

Shiwon was checking off the list of things they needed for the lab. "Send me a text or an email with the information. If it's at the end of the semester, it will be a bit of a time crunch, because I'm going home for Christmas."

"Where's home?"

"Seoul."

Seonghun looked startled. "Your English is perfect."

"So is yours." Shiwon looked at him confused.

"No, you sound like Yong. You sound Korean American. You have no accent."

Shiwon laughed. "I've had English lessons since I was a child. I kept up with them. I'm guessing you stopped, but picked back up in high school?"

Seonghun nodded.

"That's why. My initial teacher was British. For a while I had a weird British accent, but before I came to Silver Leaf, my teacher was American. I still pronounce some words with the British accent like 'schedule' and 'aluminum', but it's mostly an American accent."

They began to focus on their lab, staining parts of plants, before mounting them to slides. The work in this class would be used to teach entry level biology. As they finished the last of their slides, Seonghun began to clean up. Out of the corner of his eye he saw Shiwon look at him, as if he wanted to say something.

"If you need to tell me something, just say it."

"Do you have any sisters?" Shiwon asked.

Confused, Seonghun shook his head no.

"Girl cousins, an ex-girlfriend, anyone female in your life?" Shiwon persisted.

"I had a girlfriend a while ago before Maliah."

"Did she participate in any performing arts?"

Seonghun shook his head again.

"I have six sisters," Shiwon said.

"That is a lot of girls," Seonghun said, smiling.

"That's why my hair looks as good as it does." Shiwon smirked. "I asked because out of the six sisters, two play piano, one plays the flute, and one is a ballerina. Every recital my parents went to, my sisters were presented with flowers. Every single one. At my sister's graduation piano recital they got her a small gift as well as flowers because it was her last time playing as a child." He smiled at the memory. "Mom got her a pin for any outfit she was wearing. It was a treble clef covered in diamonds. She wears it when she dresses up."

"That's really nice of your parents," Seonghun said, confused at where this was going.

"I'm not saying you should get her something covered in diamonds. That would be a little weird for the short time you've been dating, but make sure you at least show up with a small bouquet of flowers."

Seonghun thought about it briefly. "Her birthday is right before the recital. She's gracious about some things, but I think it would be overwhelming if I presented her with anything other than flowers so soon after her birthday."

Shiwon clapped him on the back. "That's fine. I just wanted to put that in your ear. I know you'd feel bad if you showed up with nothing but saw people around Shorty getting flowers."

"Why do you call her Shorty?"

"Have you seen her? She's pocket sized compared to either of us." Shiwon snorted. "If it bothers her though, I'll stop."

"She's never made mention of the fact. She typically works hard letting people know if her boundaries are crossed, so I would assume that she would tell you if she wasn't pleased." They stepped out of the lab. Seonghun immediately searched around his bag for a granola bar. Waving goodbye to Shiwon, he headed back to the dorm. As he was walking, his phone rang.

Looking around, he saw a bench to sit on. He wasn't too keen on walking while on his phone after being pushed into the street. "Hey, Min."

"Hi, um, did you have a fight with Maliah?" Minjun was whispering into the phone.

"No, not at all. Why?"

"I've been home for an hour. She has been crying the entire time. I knocked on her door but she asked me to leave her alone. She sounds awful."

Seonghun sighed. "Grab dinner for all of us, Min, Mexican please. I'll be back in about fifteen minutes."

"Do you know what's wrong?" Minjun whispered.

"Yes I do; she'll be fine in a day or so, but right now she's a little emotionally raw. I'll be home soon." He disconnected the call before running to the dorm.

At the dorm, it was mostly quiet except soft music floating through Maliah's door. Yongjoon was gone. Min was as well, presumably picking up dinner. Seong grabbed the envelope taped to his door before crossing the common area. Tapping lightly, he called out, "It's me."

She opened the door; if it were possible, she looked worse than she did yesterday. Her face was swollen and tear stained. Liah just looked worn down. "This isn't from your period," he said slowly.

She shook her head, opening the door wider, allowing him in. He pulled out the flowers from his backpack. "These are for you. I clipped them at the hot house." He saw her welling up again.

"Thank you." Her voice was hoarse.

"Do you want to talk about what happened?" he asked quietly.

She was touching the petals of the flowers in the bouquet as if she'd never seen flowers before. He remembered the daisy he put in her hair.

"I had therapy today. Lots of painful stuff got brought up. Stuff that I had forgotten, but was just pushed down." She looked at him with her big brown eyes, filled with tears. "My parents had to love me at one point, right? You don't bring a baby into the world absolutely hating them, you can't." Liah started sobbing again.

The sounds tore at his heart. He reached for her, crushing the bouquet between them. There was silence in the room except for her gut wrenching sobs. He held her while stroking her back quietly, allowing her to cry. When she calmed down a bit, he finally spoke.

"I do believe your parents loved you. You said that your grandmother wouldn't allow your mom to get an abortion. But that was something she could have done, easily hiding what happened. Miscarriages happen all the time. I don't know what went on between the time you were born to what you can remember, but you're probably going to have to get those answers from them, sweetheart." Seong kissed her forehead.

"My therapist wants me to set up a meeting with them. A group therapy session. I'm terrified," she whispered.

"What are you scared of?"

Liah was quiet as she leaned into him. "That I'm worthless. That I'm a waste. That everything that happened growing up was my fault. If I had been better, none of the stuff that happened on campus would have happened." She began weeping again. "I don't even know if they will agree to meet me, Seonghun. I haven't spoken to them in almost two years."

"How do you plan on getting in touch?" he asked.

"I'm going to write a letter. They've had the same phone number for years, but I don't think I can speak to them verbally without breaking down," she admitted. "Will you read it after I get done?"

"Sure. Now I have a proposition for you. Why don't you grab a shower, put on something comfortable, come out and eat dinner with us? We're getting Mexican." He stepped back, pulling the flowers from her hand, setting them on the desk. "We'll watch a movie to take your mind off of it for now."

She dashed the tears in her eyes, nodding. Liah gathered soft pajama pants, a t-shirt, a green and a purple sock. "Do you have a pullover sweatshirt I could borrow?" she asked quietly.

"It will be on your bed when you get out of the shower." He kissed her cheek, pleased she only flinched slightly. He went to walk out of the door, stopping. "Liah?" She looked over at him with her eyes and nose red. "Nothing about you is worthless. You're worthy of love. I'm sorry they never showed you that." He gave her a half-smile as he walked out.

Seong laid his bag down in his room before he grabbed the requested sweatshirt, laying it on her bed. Returning to his room, he sat on his bed as he opened the envelope. Inside there was a drawing that made him snort with laughter. Minjun was overloaded with bags, dragging her as she lay on the floor. There was a bubble above his head that said, 'Just one more store!'. He set the picture aside.

S,

It was a good catch, about the emotionally tired. Knowing what I know now, I would say yes, I've probably always been chronically depressed. However, I didn't receive treatment for it until I was much older with the ability to access it on my own. I'm fortunate in the fact mine wasn't severe enough that I felt the need to take my own life for the most part. Between us, I did have days where it felt like it would be better if I wasn't here. I still have days like that. But I try hard as I can to work through the darkness. Sometimes it is so hard to fight.

I promise to take your wants, needs, and feelings into account as well. I'm not used to this however; I'm asking you to give me grace to make mistakes. Both Minjun and I are a little lost at this juncture. We'll figure it out. I always do at least.

We're going slower than most people would, I think. All the stereotypes I ever heard about college was that everyone was hopping into bed with each other. That's what you see in every college movie. I'm okay with the pace we're setting. When I talk about other things, I mean doctors' visits with testing. You're the first person I've had any sort of experience with, but it was time for me to make my annual doctors' appointments. I have one for my primary care doctor; she said this year I'm due to have a pap smear. I have no need for STD tests.

Seonghun stopped reading briefly to grab his phone to look up what a pap smear was. He immediately wished he hadn't. It sounded painful and unneeded.

It is nice that you're prepared for if (when?) we have sex. I am as well. I pretty much try to stay prepared for all aspects of my life. You never know when you're going to be thrown out your house, or find out someone is literally chemically destroying your hair. That's a little maudlin humor there.
Minjun cares about Yongjoon a lot. Like, more than you probably think. I don't know if you guys talk about all of that (feelings), but he word vomited on me. I won't betray his confidence, but he's working hard to be what Yongjoon deserves. I reminded him that there are two people in a relationship (sometimes more, I'm not judging) and that it's okay to have expectations for himself as well. Which brings me to you.
You have written sweet, incredibly moving endearments about going slow, being there for me, and whatever it is I need. Seonghun, what is it that you need? I don't want to be neglectful to your feelings. I'm a lot. I'm emotional for no reason (as you saw this weekend), I overthink, sometimes tuning everything out around me. But I will always try to be the best person I can to you.
Things I could eat all the time? I love Mexican food, steamed broccoli, steak (sirloin), tacos, mushrooms, and of course lemon cake. I had fondue once; that was pretty cool, but it was a lot of money for not a lot of food. I love chicken wings. There was a bar in Indianapolis that would look the other way when I came in. They knew I was under age (I was 16 at the time) but all I wanted to do was order chicken wings, an iced tea, and study. The owner said as long as I didn't draw attention to myself, sitting in a corner unseen, he would continue

to serve me. I think it was because I never tried to give him a fake ID or bull-shit him. I was literally there just for the wings. Sometimes he would give me my tea for free. I thought that was nice.

I know you're planning the date, but would you like to go on a walk after we're done? I know a place. I used to walk there a lot, but then I realized it's kind of dimly lit, isolated; walking there by myself was a recipe for a bad time. I'd like to show you though if it isn't too cold. I'm going to end this here. I have in-person therapy today as well as a guitar lesson to give.

See you soon,

-L

Seonghun folded up the letter before dropping it into his box. He walked out to the living room to find an amusing scene. Minjun sat in the middle of Yongjoon and Maliah. Both of them had claimed one of his shoulders as Minjun flipped through the channels.

"Have you guys eaten yet?" Seonghun asked.

"No, we're waiting for you," Maliah said. She stood up, walking to the kitchen to grab plates.

Seonghun picked up the bags of food, setting them on the coffee table. As he sat down, he took a good look at his girlfriend. Her face was still slightly swollen but the tear stains were gone. While she looked comfortable in his sweatshirt, her face showed signs of exhaustion.

"Can you ditch class tomorrow?" he asked as she spooned rice on her plate.

"I'd really rather not. I try not to abuse that as much as possible. Why?" she asked.

"You look exhausted."

"I am. But I studied quite a bit today, finishing my homework for the week. I'll probably turn in shortly after we eat." She bit into a taco. "I wish you guys would let me buy dinner once in a while. I feel funny accepting free food all the time."

"Free food is the best food," Yongjoon stated as he started eating rice. "If you like, you can buy next time, we won't stop you."

Seonghun opened his mouth to protest, but Yongjoon gave him a look. He closed his mouth, going back to his burrito. It wasn't that he was against her paying, it was just that he could afford to pay for her, so why wouldn't he? It felt good to provide for her. He felt a hand on his thigh and looked over.

"You know your thoughts basically telegraph across your face?" Liah asked him.

He shook his head.

"You aren't a chauvinist, so I'm not sure why you think you need to pay for everything. I appreciate you paying for me from time to time, but I would like to treat you guys too occasionally. I like sharing things when I have someone to share them with," she said simply. "I have the means to buy meals. I work hard to be able to do things with my money."

"Are you going to try to pay at the skating rink?" Seonghun asked.

Minjun turned to them. "When are you going skating? I want to go."

"Not this time, Min, we'll all go another time, I promise," Seong said. He looked over at Maliah who was staring at him. "We didn't actually set a day. We just said this weekend."

"Friday? Do you have anything on— wait, I have a gallery tour." She opened her calendar on her phone. "I'll be done by 7:30, back to the dorm by 8. It won't take me long to get changed."

"Why do you have to change?" Yongjoon asked.

"I'll be dressed up for the gallery tour. I can't skate in my work dress," Maliah explained, opening a small container of jalapenos.

"Will you have enough time to skate if we go on Friday?" Seonghun asked.

"Yeah, as long as you don't mind having dinner after. If you get hungry there are snacks at the rink." She popped a pepper in her mouth before proceeding to dump the entire container on her tacos.

"Hear me out," Minjun said. "Why don't you two go skating on Saturday, and we can go bowling on Friday? We can eat there once you get off work." Seonghun didn't see an issue with that, but when he looked over at Maliah, she was quiet.

Finally she cleared her throat. "I've never been bowling before. I don't know how."

"You chuck a ball down an aisle," Minjun deadpanned. "You listen to music as you chuck said ball, while making fun of your friends for their form. Also we'll be in time for cosmic bowling!"

The other two men groaned.

"What's wrong with cosmic bowling?" Maliah asked.

"Do you have an aversion to really loud music?" Yong asked.

Maliah arched her brow.

"Good point, you'll be fine. It's really loud. There are strobe lights while you bowl." He scooped a glob of cheese onto a chip.

Seonghun turned back to Maliah who had stopped eating. He noticed her hand scrubbing up and down her leg. Putting his plate down, he turned to the guys. "I'll be right back." Taking her hand, Seong pulled her into her room. Shutting the door, he turned and looked at her. "You're on the verge of an anxiety attack. Do you need time alone?"

She nodded as tears started forming.

"Don't cry, it's okay. We'll get the rest of the date stuff sorted out this week. You've had a rough day, I figured you may need some quiet time." He remembered his conversation earlier with Detective Krishna. "Also I have some stuff I need to talk to you about when you're less overwhelmed. It isn't good or bad, just informative." He watched as Maliah crawled into bed, curling into a small ball. His heart broke as he looked at her. "Do you want me to stay?"

"Spend time with your friends, Seonghun. They need you too."

He nodded and tucked her in, kissing her forehead. "If you need me in the middle of the night, come over okay?"

"Okay."

"Goodnight, sweetheart." He cut the lights before closing her door, walking back out to the common area. He sat back down, finishing his food.

"Is she okay?" Min asked as he looked at her door.

"She had a really bad day. I thought therapy was supposed to be helpful? All it seems to do is make her spiral," Seonghun said.

It was quiet for a minute before Yong spoke up. "Have you ever seen someone with a splinter that's gotten infected?"

Seonghun and Min both nodded. "We had a classmate in high school that was so scared to have the splinter removed he waited too long," Minjun said.

"So you have the surface wound, then you have the infection underneath. Both have to be healed for the finger to get back to normal. A lot of times, the infection is more painful than the surface wound, because you can easily pick the splinter out." He looked at Seonghun. "Think of therapy as the antibiotic to the infection. The infection is painful, it's persistent, but with the right treatment it will get better. You don't know if the infection will respond to the initial medicine, so it may take a few different types to get better. But if you do the work, it does get better."

"In this analogy, what's the splinter?" Minjun asked.

"The initial problems that caused the need for therapy," Seong said, clearly understanding.

Yongjoon nodded. "In her case, Liah knows why she is the way she is, but it caused damage that she's trying very hard to heal. She's going to have setbacks. That is the way therapy is. It's not always linear. It sometimes leaves you with questions you don't always get the answers to. You have to find a way to get the answers or learn to be satisfied without them."

"How do you—" Minjun looked at him. "The analogy was way too concise. You've been through this before."

"Not to her extent, but I've been to therapy a couple of times. A few times when I came out to my mom. She wanted to make sure I felt supported, so we had a few group sessions. I also had to go when I the bad breakup. It messed me up for a while," Yongjoon explained.

Together they began cleaning up the dinner mess. It was Yong's turn to do dishes. He spoke up again. "She is trying to be a friend. We need to let her, so she needs to be part of the dish rotation."

Seonghun opened up his mouth but Yongjoon held up his hand to preempt him. "I get it. You want to do things for her. But doing that is going to isolate her. Don't you think she's isolated herself enough? Liah is perceptive. She's going to notice you not letting her pay for things, or help clean up."

"I want more for her," Seonghun said simply. "I want her to be treated —" He paused, frustrated not knowing how to explain it in English, so he switched to Korean. "그녀는 항상 사후 생각으로 취급되어 왔다. 나는 그녀가 내가 그녀를 그렇게 생각하지 않는다는 것을 알았으면 한다."

Yongjoon continued in English without missing a beat. "You've never treated her as an afterthought, Seong. You don't have to pay or do everything for her to get that point across. She's independent; you're trying to take that from her."

He sighed.

"She's never had friends, Seong. Let her learn what it is to be in a positive relationship."

Seonghun nodded, before picking up the towel to help dry.

Min started giggling. Yong looked over at him questioningly. "If he ever becomes a dad, he's going to be one of those helicopter parents, trying to wrap his kid in bubble wrap."

"No, I won't."

"Yes, you will," both friends said, collapsing in giggles.

Seonghun rolled his eyes, continuing to dry. They spent the rest of the night catching up on what's been going on. He mentioned that Shiwon said hi. Both boys turned beet red.

"He's just a guy," Seonghun said.

"He is that. Just a guy, a gorgeous guy," Minjun said.

"I want to touch his hair," Yongjoon blurted out.

"I told him to cut it, because it was getting in the way in labs."

Yong grabbed his chest before falling to the floor.

"Don't worry," Seonghun chuckled, "he said it was one of his best attributes."

They laughed as they cleaned the small number of dishes, before putting the food away. Yongjoon quickly retired as he had some studying to do. Seong was grateful because he needed to talk to Min.

"Min, have you ever been tested?"

"We're in school, I have a test every other day it seems." Minjun stared at his friend confused.

Seonghun started laughing. "No, I mean tested for STDs. If I needed to do that, where would I go?"

"Oh! Well, it's been a while since you were sexually active, so I don't think you need to, but you can go to the student med center. That's where

I've gone. It's probably time for a check-up for me as well. You can make the appointment online." He looked at his friend. "Are you two having sex?"

"No." Seonghun began to turn red.

"But you want to," Minjun guessed.

"I do. But I also want her to be comfortable. I think negative test results would go a long way to making sure she is comfortable once we—" He paused. "When we do it." At this point he was scarlet.

Minjun patted him on the back. "It's okay, I know what you mean. Make an appointment on Friday after your last class for both of us."

Seonghun agreed. Using his laptop, he did as he was told. Shutting off his laptop, he read a few chapters of his book before calling it a night.

A few hours later he felt a tapping on his shoulder. Opening his eyes, he saw a blurry figure. "Liah, what's up?" He knew he sounded gruff, but sleep was a thing he couldn't compromise on.

"I can't stop thinking, I need to stop thinking," she whispered.

He lifted the blanket so she could sleep next to him. Sleep wasn't what she wanted though. Climbing under the blanket, she climbed on top of him.

"Oh," he moaned softly as he grabbed her hips. "Are you still on your period? Can I touch you?"

"Yes, still on my period." She skimmed her nose down his cheek, gently biting his neck. "I'm still not comfortable with you touching me while I have a crime scene in my pants."

"Fair enough." He slid his hand to her neck before slowly placing it on her face, drawing her into a kiss. Liah stiffened momentarily but allowed him to do so. When their mouths met, he touched his tongue to her full bottom lip, happy when she responded eagerly. Slowly, he moved her body over his, pleased at the tiny gasps he heard from her.

"Shhh. Yong is a light sleeper," he said. Something began niggling at the back of his head through the arousal. Before he could express it, she descended on his mouth again, rolling her hips, while trying to quietly muffle the sounds she made. "Wait, stop. Stop, Liah." He gently picked her up and laid her beside him. Stretching his arm, he turned on his light while grabbing his glasses. "You said you can't stop thinking. Stop thinking about what?"

"I really don't want to talk right now." She began to stroke his stomach.

Seong grabbed her hand, preventing her from touching him, before he spoke again, "Didn't your therapist say something about doing other things rather than facing your feelings head on?"

"Please don't do this. Don't make me talk about this." Liah's eyes watered and he almost relented.

"You don't have to talk about it with me."

She immediately scrambled, trying to climb back on top of him.

"But I'm not going to let you bury your feelings or try to hide from them." He blocked her as she tried to touch him. "I like you a lot, but you need to face this if we have any future of intimacy beyond this. I can't make love to you wondering if you're just having sex with me to chase the thoughts out of your brain. I deserve more than that; you do too." He reached over inside his nightstand drawer because he already knew what was coming. Sure enough she burst into tears. He quietly handed her the tissues. As she mopped her eyes, she took a shuddering breath. He wasn't expecting the next question that came out of her mouth.

"Why do you keep tissues in your nightstand? Why not just keep them on your desk?"

He thought she was whispering before, but he realized her voice was going out from all of the crying. "I don't need them when I'm at my desk," he said simply.

"I don't underst— oh. Ohhhh." If he wasn't so sleepy, he'd laugh at the wide-eyed look on her face.

"Yeah." He placed his glasses back on the nightstand before sinking back down in the bed. "We can talk tomorrow, but I'm tired. Are you staying?"

She looked at him, as he blinked sleepily. Turning out the light, Liah laid next to him, resting her head on his shoulder. He brushed a kiss on top of her forehead, going back to sleep instantly.

CHAPTER 29

The next morning when Seonghun woke up, there was a note on his nightstand. Liah was gone. Putting on his glasses he peered at the note. It was a three paneled cartoon. There were two animals, a bear, and a sheep. The sheep was blowing up a balloon in two of the frames while the bear looked on. In the final frame, the sheep was handing the bear a fully blown-up balloon. Below the picture were three simple lines.

S,
I'm sorry.
-L

Seonghun sat back in his bed, sighing. Speaking with Yong yesterday, her behavior made sense. However, he had more questions. Picking up his phone, he sent a message.

Seong: *Can I have Dr. Stewart's number?*

The blinking dots in the message went for a long time, stopped, then started again. Finally, a message came through.

Liah: *Can I ask why?*
Seong: *Do you have a minute for a call?*
Liah: *My voice is gone mostly so I won't be able to say much.*
Seong: *That's fine. Call me when you can.*
Liah: *K. Give me 10 minutes.*

Seonghun ran to the bathroom, hurrying so he could climb back into bed. As soon as he walked back into the room his phone rang. He picked up before getting comfortable.

"Hi," he said.

"Hey." Her voice sounded hoarse.

"I know this is a busy day for you, so I won't keep you. You don't have to say much. Liah, what happened last night wasn't cool. I appreciate the apology, however. I want to talk to Dr Stewart, because I want to figure out how I can best support you in times like these. There won't ever be an instance where I just allow you to try to bury your hurt. It isn't healthy or fair to either of us." Seong heard her sniffling on the phone, immediately feeling bad. He hoped she wasn't in public. She wouldn't like to be crying where people could see.

"You asked me in your note what I needed. I want to be able to support you properly. I need Dr. Stewart's number to do that as well as your permission to call her." It was quiet on the phone. He heard her moving around, possibly trying to find a tissue. He knew he was right as he heard her blow her nose.

"I won't give her permission to talk about what we discuss. I can't. There is so much—" She started coughing.

"I understand, I'm not asking to take a deep dive into your notes. I just want to be there for you. Right now, I don't know how."

She was silent for a while. "Okay."

"Okay?"

"I'll text it to you. I have to go, I have class," she said softly. He barely heard her.

"That's fine. I'll talk to you soon." Disconnecting the call he sent her a text as the requested number came in.

Seong: *Do you have a break at all today?*
Liah: *I'll have time in between my last class and work at the gallery this evening. I'll be back at the dorm to change.*
Seong: *Could I convince you to ditch work?*
Liah: *I can't, I'm sorry.*
Seong: *It's fine, I'm just worried about your voice.*
Liah: *I've never cried so hard I lost my voice. But we're dealing with a lot of heavy shit in therapy.*

There was a tap at his door as Yong appeared. Seonghun sent one last message.

Seong: *I'll see you when you come home.*

He looked over at Yongjoon. "What's going on?"

"Gym, then lunch. Come on."

"Give me ten minutes to make a call." Seong stood up, changing his clothes

Yongjoon closed the door. Calling the number Liah gave him, Seong explained why he was calling, that he would be busy for the next couple of hours but would be available to talk after that. Hanging up the phone, he finished dressing, put his ball cap on backwards, put a granola bar in his mouth before going to let Yong know he was ready.

They were lifting weights at the gym as he talked about what happened last night. Min was once again in a sweatshirt with the hood pulled up, rolling around on a yoga ball. "Remember, I told you therapy isn't linear. She's going to have awful days," Yongjoon said.

"I know, but I also know that her trying to bury how she feels in other activities is going to get her in trouble," Seonghun explained.

"I'm not saying she wasn't wrong," Yong grunted as he lifted the weight, "I'm saying you're going to need to extend her as much grace as you can. I had a hardcore support system in my mom. She was there for me no matter what stupid thing I did while trying to build myself back up. Maliah knows what she did was wrong. She apologized; if I understand her, which I feel like I'm starting to, she's going to give you a verbal apology when you see her."

"I feel helpless," he finally admitted.

"You sort of are. These are her demons, her fight. The best you can do is to be there to catch her when she stumbles. We all will be." He looked at Minjun rolling around the ball, grinning at his boyfriend. "I'm going to be honest with you, I think you jumped into a relationship with her a little too fast. I saw how you looked at each other though; I knew it was inevitable. I'm a little concerned about both of you handling this situation. That said, I think you're doing fine. You set boundaries. Everyone stating their boundaries is always a healthy thing."

Seonghun smiled at him. "You sure you don't want to be a therapist?"

"I like to argue way too much to be a therapist. I'd be the worst therapist ever." He walked over to spot Seonghun on his weightlifting. "Besides, what I'm telling you is basically everything that was told to me. I'm not giving any nuance to her situation. This is generalized."

It was quiet in the gym as he lifted. It was the middle of the day, usually there was a crowd around this time, but luckily the amount of people was sparse, with no one in their part of the room. All of a sudden, they heard a shout. Setting the weight back on the platform, the two men looked over at Minjun. He was curled up, the yoga ball bouncing away. Rushing over, the men squatted to check on their friend. "Min, what happened?" asked Yong.

"Someone kicked me off the ball, hard." Minjun lifted his sweatshirt to show a red mark on his stomach. "They ran off, all I saw was hair."

"This place has cameras. I'll be back." Seonghun ran to the front desk, crossing his fingers that the camera caught something. He reached the front quickly, asking the perky receptionist for security.

After explaining what happened, a member of the staff went to his friend, to make sure he didn't need medical treatment. "Whoever it was just winded me," Minjun explained.

Seong saw that he looked very uncomfortable with the attention. Yongjoon's arm was slung around him, lightly rubbing his back.

"I'm fine. I'd just like to know who it was."

"You didn't see anything?" Seonghun asked.

"I was rolling around on the ball having a good time. I wasn't paying attention except to make sure I wasn't in anyone's way. It's pretty quiet here so I was able to roll around freely."

"If you three will come with me, we can review the footage," the lanky security guard said. The three men followed behind him to a small office. The guard sat at the desk where several monitors were. "You need to look at this one right here." He pointed to the monitor closest to them. It was silent for a moment while everyone watched the screen. Minjun blushed as he saw himself rolling around. Then they all saw it.

A sharp hard kick to Minjun's abdomen. The foot was booted with a pointy toed shoe. The girl's brown hair fell in waves as opposed to the straight sheet it always was. There was no mistaking that profile: Casey.

Seonghun looked at his friends as he picked up his phone. "Hi, Detective Krishna. I'm sorry to bother you, but you need to get to the gym right now. I think there's enough evidence to have Casey arrested."

Detective Krishna showed up, watching the security footage that was queued up for her. She looked as confused as Seonghun. "You've never had any interaction with her, correct?" she asked, looking at Minjun.

Min shrugged. "I slept with her friend for a time. But we didn't really talk, no."

"You," she pointed at Seonghun, "were right there. Why did she go for your friend? None of this makes sense."

"She called me her boyfriend when we were all at dinner on Sunday. I think whatever façade she uses to present as normal to the world is cracking." Seong looked at the screen. "I don't think she is thinking strategically like she normally does."

The detective nodded. "We'll pick her up. Please tell me you aren't going to do this through student court?"

Minjun shook his head. "I want to press charges. All the charges, even charges that I can't press, I want to press them."

Yong smiled as he ruffled Min's hair. "Are we done? I want to get him back to the dorm."

The detective looked at her laptop. "Yes, we're good. I'll give you a call when we've got her in custody." The boys trooped out to the car. As soon as everyone strapped in, two things happened. Seonghun's stomach let out a loud protest at the lack of food and his phone rang.

"Take your call. I'll go through the drive thru," Yongjoon said.

As he connected the call he spoke up, "I wanted to stop for ginger tea for Liah's throat. Hello?"

Yongjoon nodded, making sure Min was okay before pulling off.

"Hi, Seonghun, this is Dr. Stewart returning your call. Is this a good time to talk?"

"Yes, hello."

"So what exactly happened?" she asked.

Seonghun quietly explained how the night went from the time Minjun called him. He turned red when he got to the bedroom portion of it.

"She left earlier than I got up this morning, leaving me an apology note."

"You did a good thing. Thank you for not giving in to temptation. I know it can be hard sometimes. Now, I can't give you any information about her treatments, diagnosis, anything without a written note from Maliah, which she has not given me. So I'm going to ask you, what is it that you want from me?"

"I want to know the best way to support her when she has days like this. I don't know how to help."

"What do you want when you're sad?" asked the doctor.

"I don't understand," Seonghun said.

"It's a very simple question. You've had a bad day, everything has seemed to go wrong, you're being blamed for things that aren't your fault. What gives you comfort on those days?"

Seong was silent for a moment. Finally, he understood where she was going. "Comfort food. My mom's jjajangmyeon, talking with my friends, maybe a funny movie."

"Maliah is no different than you or I. Her sadness just runs deeper. You know things that make her happy. Use them. It may not take her out of her funk, but it will make her feel wanted, which is all anyone wants."

Seonghun nodded even though Dr. Stewart couldn't see him. "I understand."

"Good. Anything else?"

"That's it. Thank you, Dr. Stewart."

"Anytime. Maliah is a good girl. Nice to see someone noticed it too."

Seonghun had an idea. "Is it against the rules for you to interact with her outside of meetings?"

Dr. Stewart laughed. "No. What did you need?"

"Will you come to her winter concert in December?"

"I can do that, do you have date?" Seonghun gave her the information. "I have it marked down. I'll be there. Thank you so much for calling."

"Thank you, Dr. Stewart. Talk to you later."

During Seong's conversation, Yongjoon had picked up fast food. Seonghun looked over and saw that Minjun was asleep. "Do you think we should have taken him to the hospital?"

Yongjoon glanced over at his boyfriend briefly. "He said he was fine. He wouldn't lie about it. If he ends up feeling worse, we'll take him."

Seonghun nodded. Pulling into the store, Yongjoon put the car in park. "I'm going to stay out here with him."

"Do you need anything?" Seonghun asked.

"Nah. We have plenty leftovers for dinner."

Seonghun left the car, running into the store. Pausing at the wall of tea he found lemon ginger, along with something called 'throat coat' before going on a search for honey.

"Fancy seeing you here."

Seonghun's blood chilled. Turning around he saw Casey. It was chilly out, but nowhere near cold enough for the thick heavy coat she was wearing. Looking down at her feet, Seong saw that she had on the boots that kicked his friend earlier. Seong felt a haze of red cover his vision as he glared at her. He wanted her to pay, badly. "Surprised they haven't arrested you yet."

"I don't plan on being arrested." She walked up to him, running her fingers up his arm. "If I'm arrested, how do I get to see you lifting weights? Super stimulating view."

He snatched his arm away as she smirked. "Why did you kick my friend? What did he ever do to you?"

"Do you know how much you dote on those two guys? It's as if you are in a relationship with them. I'd honestly believe that over you actually fucking Eeyore."

"Fuck you," he spat, walking away.

"I keep my promises, Seonghun. You will be seeing me a lot more. I feel like once you get to know me a little more, you'll just adore me. Everyone does."

"Who's everyone? Your friends? Don't see anyone. Your boyfriend? Don't see that anywhere. Looks like you're alone. As alone as you made Maliah feel. But joke's on you. She isn't alone. You are. She fucking won. You lost. You will always lose, you crazy bitch." He walked away, not even looking back at her. Quickly paying for the tea, he ran back into the car. "Drive, Yong. Now."

As Yongjoon pulled off they got a glimpse of Casey looking at them from the store. Her eyes were dark as she smirked and waved at them.

"How the hell did she even know we were going there?" Yongjoon demanded.

"I don't know. Let's just get back to the dorm. I will feel so much safer when we're back there." He pulled out his phone.

Seong: *I know you're still in class. Please walk with someone to your next class. Casey attacked Minjun. It's on tape and they are going to arrest her, but she found me at the grocery store.*

It wasn't long after he hit send that his phone began to ring. "Hey," he said softly.

Though her voice was nearly gone, she sounded hysterical. "Are you okay!? Is Min okay!? Is Yongjoon okay!?" she began coughing uncontrollably.

"Calm down, sweetheart, calm down. We're fine. Min said he's okay. He's sleeping in the car and we're coming back to the dorm."

"I'm calling in. I have dinner. I'll be home after class." She hung up the phone before he could say anything.

"Well, that's one way to get her to actually care for herself," Seonghun said to himself. He looked in the rearview mirror at Yongjoon. "She's calling into work and bringing dinner."

"She is going to freak out," Yongjoon said. "Min is her first actual friend."

"Hey!" Seonghun said, insulted.

"No, buddy, she had your number almost immediately. She knew you were attracted to her, though I think it took her awhile to realize she was attracted to you. Minjun was her first actual friend. No strings. Just offered himself." He pulled into the apartment complex. "Take the food bags, I got Min."

Seonghun grabbed everything while he waited for them. Yongjoon woke up Minjun, wrapping his arm around his waist, encouraging him to lean on his shoulder.

"Yongjoon, I'm fine, I promise. It's just a little sore," Minjun protested.

"Indulge me just a little okay? Just let me take care of you for a bit," Yong murmured. The three men made their way to the dorm.

Once there, they situated Minjun on the couch. After he ate, he laid down with a blanket, quickly going to sleep. Seonghun grabbed a quick shower, went into his room, and picked up the book he'd been reading about Black history. Yongjoon met him back in the common area with his homework, and they both sat quietly with the TV on low. Pretty soon Seonghun felt himself dozing off. It had been a stressful afternoon. Closing his book he looked at Yongjoon. "I'm going to take a nap. Let Liah know she can come wake me when she gets in."

Yongjoon nodded before going back to reading his textbook, occasionally notating. When he wasn't writing, his fingers were running through Minjun's hair. Seonghun went into his room, crashing instantly.

He was woken by a page turning in his book. Slowly he reached over and grabbed his glasses. He saw Maliah slowly flipping through his library book. "Hey, sweetheart. You check on Minjun?" Seonghun stretched.

"Mmm? Yeah. He said he's fine. Happy I brought pizza home." She glanced at him as he rolled to his side.

Using his arm, he pulled her back so he could wrap his arm around her waist. He buried his face into her side, smelling her.

"Are you sniffing me again?" He heard the smile in her voice.

"You always smell good. Sue me." He shrugged.

"Seonghun, I owe you an apology." She closed the book, setting it on his nightstand. "It's not an excuse, but I was in a really bad frame of mind last night. That's no excuse to basically molest you to forget." Her voice was still creaky, fading out when she spoke.

"Hold on," he rested his chin on her side, "molest means it was unwanted. It's very much wanted, believe me." He gave her a half smile. "Whenever we mess around I'd prefer both of us be in the present, with the other person. Not trying to drive away memories of the past or awful thoughts." He kissed her. "I want you here with me, not stuck elsewhere, using my body to get out. That's all. I—" He paused. "I care about you. Any chance we have of this being a long term thing, hinges on the fact that we're mindful of each other's boundaries. As far as your apology goes, it is accepted. We both know better now." He scooted over. "Can you lay with me for a bit?"

She lay beside him and turned to face him. "I really am sorry." Her voice cracked.

"You're forgiven." He moved some braids out of her face, pleased when she didn't flinch. "I meant to make you a cup of tea when you got home."

"I'd like that very much."

"In a minute." He kissed her again.

"Wait. Wait a second, Seonghun." She tapped his shoulder before reaching over to his nightstand. "I meant to ask, is this assigned reading for you?" She held up the book on Jim Crow laws.

He shook his head, explaining, "Yongjoon explained what happened at the play."

"That fucking play."

Seonghun hid a smile. "Yeah, he mentioned KKK outfits. When I was about to ask, he told me to look online because he didn't have the strength to get into the history. So I looked it up. Then I kept looking deeper until I ran across a list of books to read. I checked three of them out of the library." He looked at her. "Do you know your family's history? I read that a lot of it is lost."

"Pieces. On my mom's side someone was a house slave but was also the doctor for a lot of slaves, due to the fact she worked in healing. I don't know anything about my dad's side. There's a bible with my ancestors' life spans written in it. Can you trace your family?" she asked.

"My mom has a book that she worked with my grandma on before she died. It has a lot of our history in it, I don't know if it is complete or not."

There was a tapping on the door before it was opened. "Are you coming to eat?" Yongjoon stuck his head in the door.

"Yeah, we're coming out," Seonghun called. Yongjoon shut the door.

"We're okay then?" Liah looked at him.

"We're more than okay." He kissed her softly before pushing her gently out of the bed. "Let's go! Pizza!"

Maliah snorted as she slid out of the bed. "Always food with you. Will you let me plan the next date?"

He shrugged "Sure. Did you have something in mind?"

"Actually, I do. I know it will be an action packed weekend, but how about Sund—" She paused and her eyes lit up. "Minjun!" she hollered. Her voice cracked, but it was enough that he heard.

"What?" He sat on the couch blinking sleepily.

"Can you just—" She grabbed his arm attempting to pull him to his feet. Min groaned as he got up. She pulled him into his room, shutting the door behind them.

"What's going on there?" Yongjoon asked as he opened the lids to the pizzas. She'd gotten four. Pineapple and ham, Sausage, pepperoni, along with a combination.

"She was getting ready to ask me out somewhere, but changed her mind, yelling for Min instead." Seonghun sat down, scooping up half the combo pizza.

Suddenly Minjun's door burst open. "Absolutely not." Maliah stepped out.

"Those are my terms." Minjun followed behind her.

"I don't need any new clothes though!"

"You can always use new clothes, especially for a date." The two men on the couch watched them while inhaling pizza.

Liah sighed. "Two hours, two fifteen minute breaks, and you buy lunch."

"Three hours, a thirty minute break, and I'll buy you a snack along with lunch. You have to come with me to get a haircut as well," Minjun countered.

"Add two fifteen minute breaks." Liah held out her hand. Minjun shook it. Maliah turned to Seonghun. "Do you want to go on a date with me—" Min elbowed her, "Sorry, with us, on Sunday?"

Minjun looked at Yong. "You too. You want to go out with us on Sunday?"

The two roommates looked at each other, confused. "Are you asking us out as a group?" Yongjoon asked.

"No, we're botching asking you two out on a double date," Liah said.

"Oh," Seonghun said.

"Okay," Yongjoon replied.

Seonghun nodded in agreement.

Seong watched as his girlfriend sat on the couch, diving into the pineapple pizza. Everyone watched TV until she spoke up. "Is anyone going to tell me what happened today?" Her voice was crackly. Seonghun got up to make her tea as the other roommates filled her in on what happened.

Maliah tugged on Min's shirt. Minjun nodded as she lifted it. A bruise was beginning to form. "Oh no." She brushed it gently with her fingers. "Why didn't you go to the hospital?"

Min looked uncomfortable. "The police took pictures as evidence. It felt really intrusive. I didn't want any more attention. If I start to feel bad, I'll go. I have a doctor's appointment on Friday for something else. I can bring it up then." He tugged his shirt down, seemingly embarrassed at her attention before going back to his pizza.

Seong walked over with a cup of tea for her. She thanked him, sipping the fragrant brew before Minjun spoke up again. "I was asleep in the car, but I was under the impression that something happened when you stopped for tea." He looked at Seonghun.

Seong stopped eating to explain what happened in the store. "I don't understand how she knew where we would be."

"She probably didn't. I'm going to assume it was a coincidence. Like she was near the store and saw you enter. You didn't go anywhere close to the gym, correct?" Maliah asked.

"No, we were closer to the dorms." Yongjoon grabbed another slice of pizza.

"There isn't much near our dorm, so maybe she was just taking a chance."

"Maybe," Yongjoon said. "How does she end up where we always are though?"

"Well, didn't Detective Krishna say she saw someone following you guys for a while in the videos? You basically have a routine. Not hard to figure out where you would go next," Maliah said thoughtfully.

"I don't want to talk about this anymore," Minjun whispered.

Everyone glanced at him. He was pale.

Seong watched as Maliah looked at Yong, angling her head to his room. Yongjoon got up, pulling Min to his feet. "I'm kind of sleepy, why don't you come lay with me for a bit?"

"The dishes—"

"I've got them, Min. Go get some rest." Maliah gave him a small smile.

Min nodded. Yong grabbed his hand, leading him to their room.

She began carrying the boxes into the kitchen. Seong brought the plates over for her to wash. "If you wash them, I'll dry."

"Okay." While she packaged up the leftovers, he left their suite to dump the boxes in the trash room. Coming back, he saw she was up to her elbows in suds.

Taking advantage, he walked behind her, wrapping his hands around her waist, burying his nose in her neck. "Are you feeling any better?"

She shrugged. "I'm still pretty emotionally raw." She paused for a minute. "Do you want kids, Seonghun?"

"Right this second!?" He craned his neck to look at her.

She started laughing. "No, do you want kids eventually?"

"Yes, more than one. I was lucky I had Min, but there were times I wondered what it was like to have an actual sibling. I would get lonely. Kids are little sponges. They soak up all the love you have to give them. I think I have a lot of love to give," he said thoughtfully.

"We talked in therapy about my upbringing. I don't want to put another kid through what I've been through. Also, depression can be hereditary."

"Isn't being careful that you don't want to hurt anyone a bigger step than either of your parents took? Also, you're going to school to be a therapist. You recognize the signs of depression. Hell, you just saw something wasn't right with Minjun and got him to lay down." He turned her around. Liah's hands were wet, dripping onto the floor. "You can't judge yourself with your parents measuring stick. It doesn't fit. You aren't your parents."

She gave him a sad smile. "That's close to what Dr. Stewart said."

"Listen to her, she's a smart lady." He kissed her before whirling her back around. Grabbing a towel, he started drying the plates. As Seong dried, he noticed her cup was nearly empty. "Do you want some more tea?"

"Yes please. Are you going to tell me what you and Dr. Stewart discussed?"

"She didn't tell you?"

"She told me that nothing from our sessions was spoken of, nor did she give out personal information. That's all."

"We talked about alternatives to provide comfort while not deflecting the feelings you're having." He brushed a kiss on her temple before setting down the dish towel. Seong flipped the switch on the electric kettle. "Like, I know you love lemon flavored everything. I know you like to roller skate. What's your favorite movie?" he asked.

She smiled shyly. "Anything in the Marvel franchise."

He wasn't expecting that. "Really?"

"I want to be Princess Shuri, messing around in a lab with technology." With her squeaky voice, he could barely hear her.

"That's cute." He grabbed her mug. Putting a bag of the Throat Coat tea in, he filled it with hot water. "What else do you like?"

"Summer storms, I think I might like the beach but I have never been, cherry popsicles, music, art. Oh gosh, speaking of art," she turned to look at him, "Yongjoon's mom. Do you know her favorite colors?"

He shook his head.

"Okay, how about her house? What are the colors she uses in her house?"

"Her bedroom has a dark purple wall."

"Okay, I can work with that." Drying her hands, she pulled out her phone, making a note. "What does Wednesday after your classes look like?"

Seong shrugged. "Studying, reading, spending time with you three."

"Want to come to the art studio with me? I wanted to draw you, but I think I want to get you on film more."

"I can do that, what do I need to bring?"

Liah took a small sip of tea. "This feels really good on my throat." She sighed happily. "Do you have a white button down shirt, and black slacks?"

"White button down, no. Black slacks, yes."

"Plain white t-shirt?" she asked.

"Yes. It's a v-neck."

"That's good. Wear that with your oldest rattiest jeans please."

He nodded. "You've never been to the beach? Can you swim?"

"I had to take swimming in high school. It was my lowest grade; the swim teacher took pity on me because I wanted to be valedictorian. I should have had a C, but she gave me a B. I can doggy paddle," she said.

"We'll go to the beach in the summer before I leave. I'll teach you."

"You swim well?" she asked as she motioned him into her room.

"I qualified for the Olympic trials in high school for swimming. Didn't make it though."

She stared at him, "The Olympics. As in the thing I watch every four years? As in the march of the athletes?"

"Same Olympics, yes." He grinned at her.

"There are so many facets to you. I'm tickled when I find another one," she said. "Do you want to go grab your books? I'm pretty far ahead, but it couldn't hurt to study some more."

"No."

"No?"

"I want to share the tub of ice cream in the freezer, then kiss you for a while." He looked at her and was pleased when he saw her smile.

"Okay."

CHAPTER 30

The next morning Seonghun woke up in Maliah's bed with his boxers on. He glanced over at her; from what he could see, she was topless. Last night was good. Her period was gone so she let him touch her. It took a bit of effort, but he was able to make her orgasm again. Quietly slipping on his pants, he walked out of her bedroom, right into a cluster. Minjun was on the couch, his face blotchy, while Yongjoon was sitting next to him trying to soothe him.

"What's going on?" he asked.

"They went to Casey's dorm to arrest her. Her room was cleared out with no trace of her. Turns out she hasn't been attending classes since she got kicked out of your lab. They don't know where she is," Yongjoon said while rubbing Minjun's back. "We're ditching classes for the rest of the week. We got permission from the police and the school. You two did as well. All of your work will be emailed to you. We're going to go to Mom's. You're both welcome to join us."

Seonghun sat down on the couch next to Minjun. "You okay?"

"I can't stop crying," Minjun sniffled.

"You were okay yesterday, Min," Seonghun pointed out.

"He was in shock," a voice croaked out.

They all looked over and saw Maliah. She had a blanket around her.

"Things don't process right until you come out of shock. I'm assuming you had a rough night?"

He nodded. Seonghun got up to fix her a cup of tea.

Maliah took his place on the couch. "Did I hear right, we don't have class?"

"Yeah. They said to keep an open eye. The restraining order isn't going to stop her if she has flown off the handle," Yong said.

Seong looked at her; there was a look on her face he hadn't seen before. Liah had a face of pure rage.

"I refuse to let her take anything else from me," she croaked. She gave Seonghun a grateful smile at the cup of tea he handed before looking back at Min. "Get your mind right. We still have a shopping date."

"Will you come to Indianapolis to shop?" he asked.

"I'll even take you to the fancy confusing Fashion Mall," Maliah promised.

"Why is it confusing?" Seong asked.

"It has a weird layout. If you don't know any better, you think the mall is half the size it actually is. You have to go all the way to one end then take an escalator to reach the other side. I spent hours searching for Lush one day until the nice lady at Coach pointed it out," Maliah explained.

"What's Lush?" Min asked.

Maliah looked at him with huge eyes. She glanced over at Yong. "Does your mom have a tub?"

"Yeah, huge jacuzzi tubs."

"Everyone get dressed. We're going to Lush." She slammed her tea like a shot, took off to her room, shutting the door.

The men all looked at each other. "I think we may have activated her shopping gene," Minjun said.

They drove in separate cars. Though Yongjoon offered them both rooms at his mom's, Maliah declined. Seonghun wasn't going to leave her at their dorm by herself, so he declined as well. The plan was they eat lunch before splitting up to shop. As they arrived at the Fashion Mall, Maliah made a beeline for Lush. Before stepping in, she looked at the three men. "Do any of you have a sensitivity to heavy scents?"

They looked at her confused.

"Okay, well, I warned you," she said as she walked into the store.

Seonghun followed her but was immediately stopped in his tracks. It was as if he were punched in the face by multiple fragrances.

"Is this where you get your perfume?" he asked, slightly dizzy. He tried to get it together; he refused to faint in a store.

"No, that's Sephora. Which reminds me, I need to pick up another pen." She sniffed at a huge ball.

"What the hell is that?" Yong eyeballed her.

"It's a bath bomb, Min, smell." She handed it over to him.

Minjun took a big sniff. "It smells nice."

Maliah put it gently in the basket while grabbing his arm, pulling him to different displays to smell things.

"Liah, I need to leave this store. I'm dizzy," Seong said.

She glanced over at him. "You look a little green. We'll meet you in the food court in thirty minutes."

He nodded, grabbing Yongjoon, who looked a little out of it himself.

"There were a lot of smells," Yong said as they exited. "Did you want to go straight to the food court?"

"No. Her birthday is coming up. I wanted to get her the perfume she wears. She only gets the pen because it's the cheapest. She said I could find it in Sephora. What's a Sephora?" Seonghun asked him.

He shrugged, pointing to the mall directory cube. They walked over, scanning the large map. "It's five stores to the left," Yongjoon said, pointing. They rushed through the store, finding what they needed when they got a text from Min asking to meet up. "Liah had to go to the lingerie store; she didn't want him along." He held Seong back laughing as he tried to walk out of the story.

Min showed up, swinging a large brown bag as they were making their purchases. Seong dropped his obvious striped bag into his friend's.

"What on earth did you buy?" Yongjoon asked.

"Nothing. Maliah bought it for me. Said it would make me feel better. She explained how to use everything."

The men continued chatting as they walked the mall. When Seong looked up, he realized they were in front of a jewelry store. "How much time do we have left, Yong?" he asked.

"About twenty minutes, it can't hurt to look around."

"What are we looking for?" Min asked.

"Birthday and Christmas presents I guess," Seong said.

They walked in, peering into each of the cases. Seonghun felt pulled to a corner of the store. When he got there, he realized it was pearl jewelry. All of a sudden, he saw a bracelet. The pearls were slightly uneven, adding to the charm. A small silver pendant with a pink jewel was attached to it. He waved the guys over.

"That's pretty," Yongjoon said. He called over the salesclerk that had been helping him. "My friend would like to see this please." The clerk took it out of the case while giving facts. It was strung on a platinum chain. The little charm was platinum too, while the pearls were naturally occurring. The bracelet had an adjustable clasp.

"How much is it?" Seonghun asked, bracing himself.

"It's actually on sale, seventy-five dollars before tax," the clerk said.

"I'll take it please." They walked over to the register to finalize the sale.

"Yong! Come here," Minjun called. He pointed at the jewelry case.

"Oh, that's lovely." It was a beautiful silver butterfly necklace. It was in the locket section, which was confusing. They waited for the clerk to finish with Seong so he could retrieve the necklace.

"I don't understand why they put it in the locket section," the clerk said. "It doesn't hold pictures or anything like a traditional locket, but it does open." He demonstrated. The butterfly was silver with delicate lacy wings. It was attached to a thin chain.

"SOLD!" both men shouted. They looked at each other. "Do you want to split the cost?" Yong asked.

Min nodded; together they walked to pay for the piece. While he waited for them to finish, he spoke with the salesclerk about other jewelry. He was still talking when his friends joined him again. "We have about five minutes to get to the food court," Min said. "Are you getting her more? She'll be overwhelmed."

"No, I was looking to get an idea for Christmas. She said something about a lady having three pieces of jewelry. I know she plans on getting a pearl necklace—"

Yong started laughing, quickly coughing to hide it. Seonghun looked at him confused. The clerk was also smothering laughter.

"I'll just—" The clerk locked up the jewelry before taking off toward the back, laughing.

"Did I say something wrong?" Seong asked.

"Ah no. I'm just being immature. I'm sorry, continue." Yongjoon covered his mouth to stifle his giggles. They began walking to the food court as he explained that he didn't know what length she wanted in a necklace, so he thought the studs he may be able to handle.

Everyone placed their bags in Minjun's large one. As they were standing in line for sandwiches, Min looked at him. "You're going to have to purchase something today so that you can hide your bags until you get back to the dorm."

"I know. I'm not sure what to get," Seonghun said.

"While I'm shopping with Liah, go to Express. Find a nice sweater for Sunday," his friend ordered.

Seong picked up the tray with their food on it. "Slacks?" he asked.

"You can get away with dark jeans. No rips or tears."

"Sneakers?"

"Ehhh." Minjun scrunched up his nose. "One of the two pairs of dress shoes you have should work. Just base it on whatever sweater you buy."

Seonghun nodded, taking a massive bite of his chicken sandwich, before setting it down. Searching for the term 'pearl necklace', Urban Dictionary was the first hit, so he clicked it, choking as he read.

"YONG!" he yelled, coughing.

"I'm sorry!" Yongjoon started laughing again. "Anytime I hear about a pearl necklace it's what comes to mind!" He slumped over the table laughing uncontrollably.

Maliah walked up, set her bags down and looked at Yongjoon. "Are you okay?" Only a slight squeak came out. "Okay then, I'm going to go get tea." She left her bags with them, walking over to the coffee stand. Seonghun's fingers turned itchy as he stared at the pink striped bag.

"Leave her stuff alone, if she wants you to see, she will show you," Min warned.

Seong pouted. He was still pouting when she came back with her mug of steaming tea. Sitting down next to him, she leaned her head on his shoulder. "Why are you pouting?"

"No reason." He shoved a fry in his mouth, "You get what you need?"

"Yeah, got my refill on my pen; they gave me so many free samples of face creams. They gave me more than what I normally get, so that's nice." She sipped her tea. "Victoria's Secret was having their annual sale, so I stocked up on underwear, and I got a body scrub from Lush." She glanced over at Minjun. "We don't have to do this right now. You look like you could use a nap. The deal doesn't expire."

"No, I'm fine. This won't be a three-hour trip though." He stood up from the table. Glancing at Yong, he held out his brown bag. "Will you carry my bag? We will meet you two back here in—" he looked at his phone, "an hour and a half?"

Yong nodded, kissing his temple. "Slow down if you need to. Don't run yourself ragged."

Min whispered in his ear, "I don't actually need anything. I'm going to get her out of these god-awful sweatshirts." Giving him a quick kiss, he grabbed Maliah's hand, pulling her from Seonghun who was trying to suck her tonsils out.

"I'm coming." She grabbed her bags, following Minjun into Sak's.

Yongjoon stole one of Seong's fries. "So, Express?"

"Yeah, it should take me about ten minutes, then we can wander." He pushed the fries between them so that they could share. After finishing, the two of them trooped to the store Minjun told them about. Seong immediately beelined to a sweater.

"I like this." He held up a dark blue cable knit sweater that zipped all the way up. It was simple. He grabbed it in an extra-large, heading to the cashier.

"Hold on," said Yong. He went through the rack until he found a size large, "try this on."

"But I'm an extra-large," Seonghun protested.

"Humor me." Yongjoon shook the sweater at him.

Rolling his eyes, Seonghun traded his sweatshirt for the sweater. "See, it's too tight." He stretched his arms toward Yong to show him the sleeves.

"Push the sleeves up. Does it feel uncomfortable?" Yongjoon asked.

"No, but it isn't loose at all," Seonghun complained.

"Buy the sweater in this size, wear it Sunday; watch your girl's face. If you don't get the reaction I'm thinking, I'll personally return the sweater." Yongjoon smirked.

Seonghun agreed. He also found a cable knit sweater in white that Yongjoon relented, allowing him to get it in his actual size. Both shirts were on sale, so it wasn't expensive at all. While walking to the front Yongjoon tossed a bag of t-shirts at him. "You need a smaller shirt to go under that sweater. All your t-shirts will be baggy underneath."

Seonghun went to the cash register. "You didn't get anything," he said.

Yongjoon held up his hand. He was holding a rust-colored button-down sweater. "I didn't need anything, but this looked nice."

Seong's phone beeped. Checking his messages, his jaw dropped at the picture he opened. "Whoa."

Yongjoon circled around to take a look.

Maliah was standing on a platform in front of mirrors. They could see Minjun in the chair snapping the picture off to the side. With her attention on adjusting the strapless black dress, she didn't notice Minjun's phone. The dress hugged her curves, showing one of her legs through a split in the side.

Min: *It would need tailoring, but I'm trying to convince her to buy it. She said has no place to wear it. Could you find a place for her to wear it?*
Seong: *Do whatever you need to do to get her to leave with that dress. I'll find something so that she has to wear it.*
Min: *Consider it done.*

"Your girl has a body; you'd never know with all the stuff she wears." Yongjoon stared at the picture.

"I think the stuff that happened last year messed with her body image. I don't know how she dressed before that, but she had issues from her parents telling her she was fat as well." He shrugged. "I keep trying to tell her she's shaped like a woman, but she just looks at me confused."

"She wears dresses to work though."

"Yeah, but her top half is always covered up by a jacket or sweatshirt plus the dresses always hit at her knee or below. If she has class or therapy, she's in sweatpants. I leave her alone about it because as long as she's comfortable, what do I care?" He paid for his purchases, taking the brown bag from Yongjoon while he paid. He pulled out his previous purchase, stuffing them into the bottom of the bag holding his new sweaters before handing the bag back.

"Do you want to wander around?" Yongjoon asked. "We've literally been to the least expensive stores in this mall."

Seonghun nodded. He stopped in a tea shop to look around, picking up a custom blend for Maliah. It smelled of spiced oranges. He also picked up a jar of honey since he was interrupted from doing so yesterday.

After wandering through multiple stores, it was time for them to head back to the food court. They sat down, waiting with drinks. "Oh shit, I think he pushed too hard." Yong was staring off toward the entrance of the store.

Seonghun looked up from his phone. Maliah looked pissed. Minjun looked worried. Seong opened his mouth.

"I don't wanna talk about it, I want to go back to the dorm please," she interrupted him.

"Lunch?" Seonghun asked hopefully.

"You haven't eaten?" She looked irritated.

"I was waiting on you," he said quietly.

Her face softened a fraction. "Fine. Let's go to Cheesecake factory, I can take my dessert home." She stomped off in the direction of the parking garage.

"What did you do?" Yong stared at Min.

"You saw how pretty she looked in the dress!" he whispered desperately. "I just thought that I could show her how much prettier she looked in things that actually fit her."

"Oh, Min." Seonghun sighed.

"She's seen me in my boxers, I didn't think she'd get upset with me walking into the dressing room."

"Min, I know she's your friend, you don't really see her gender. But she's a girl. A woman that's been through some shitty stuff," Yong said.

"Yeah, I—" He sighed. "She started screaming while covering herself."

"Min." Seong groaned.

"Needless to say, uh. She's pissed." Minjun looked down at his feet.

"We need to catch up with her before she decides to just drive back to the dorm by herself." Seonghun grabbed his bags before he started jogging in the direction she went. He didn't have to worry because she was stopped, staring in a storefront window.

He walked up to her. "See something you like?"

"Mmm." She tapped the window. "One day I'm going to dress like an actual lady."

He looked at the display. It was a designer bag, of that much, he was sure. He'd seen those C's before. It was light pink and quilted.

"I could get you it for Christmas?" he offered.

She choked. "I don't know what your finances are, but please don't give me a four thousand dollar bag for Christmas. Especially since we'd only have been dating like three months at that point."

"F-four THOUSAND!?" he shrieked.

She nodded. "I'll own one someday. The rational person in me says to get it in black, that way I can wear it with many different outfits. But the wannabe frivolous person in me wants it in the pink."

"You should get whatever makes you happy." He gave her a kiss on the temple.

She dug around one of her bags, handing him a medium sized box. "These are my favorite cookies in the whole world. I thought you might like them too."

"I'll share one with you this evening over a cup of tea if you like," he said, tucking the box into one of his bags.

"I plan on having cheesecake."

Min walked up looking remorseful.

"Minjun, I'm really— I have a complicated relationship with my body. I'm not comfortable in my skin a lot of time. You can't just barge in on me. Yeah, I'm your friend, but I'm not one of the guys, understand?"

He nodded.

"Also. I dress how I dress. You don't have to like it because I don't dress for you. I dress for myself, for my comfort."

"I'm sorry," he whispered, "you're just really pretty, but you don't do anything with it."

"Well, it's my pretty to waste." She glanced one more time at the purse on display. "Let's go eat so I can get back to the dorm." Walking into the restaurant, it wasn't busy; they were seated quickly.

"I forgot their menu is a chapter book," Yong said as he flipped through it.

Maliah looked at Seonghun. "Have you been here before?"

He shook his head.

"I know generally in your case, your stomach is bigger than your eyes, but it will be the reverse here. The portions are huge. That's why I fully intend on just taking my dessert back to the dorm." Not minding her warnings, they ordered an appetizer of the deep-fried mac and cheese balls. Seonghun split a gooey fried ball in half, scooping a portion of it onto her plate.

"Thanks." She began to nibble at it.

"What did you end up getting?" Seong asked.

"Just a gray sweater dress. It's a little low cut, but I have a tank top or something I can wear underneath it," she replied.

Minjun opened his mouth to say something.

"You made your opinion known in the dressing room," she said acidly, "I explained to you how I felt. For the last time drop it."

Minjun quickly shoved a bite of the appetizer in his mouth.

Yongjoon observed her. "You're being firm."

"I've been firm in my boundaries since starting therapy. I've never had to be forceful in them because you three never pushed them."

Yong stared at her so long she began to fidget. "Do you know how to fight?" he finally asked.

She looked at him confused. "No. If I knew how to fight, I'd just beat Casey's ass."

Seonghun snorted.

"Text me some dates during the next few weeks that you have openings in your schedule. I'm going to teach you how to throw a punch." She agreed as their meals came out.

Seonghun's eyes widened at the massive steak on his plate, along with the mountain of mashed potatoes and green beans. He looked over at Maliah's plate. Seeing how good her salmon looked, he began to pout, giving her the saddest eyes he could muster.

"Really?" she asked.

He nodded. Sighing, she cut her salmon in half, putting it onto his plate. He did the same with his steak. Their roommates were doing the same thing.

"Yongjoon?" He was still looking at his plate but arched a brow to indicate he heard her. "What is your mom's favorite color?"

He thought about it for a moment. "Purples, blues, greys. The colors you see in a summer sunset. Why?"

"Thank you gift for Thanksgiving," she replied, before popping a piece of salmon in her mouth. She eyeballed Seonghun's plate in disbelief as he proceeded to demolish everything while eating half her rice too.

"I'll be right back." Walking over to the dessert area, Seong peered into the glass.

"Can I help you sir?" A young woman behind the counter walked up.

"Can I get a slice each of the two lemon cheesecakes you have, two of the chocolate ones, and two red velvet? Also, can I pay my portion of the bill up here?"

The young woman nodded. "Which table are you at?"

He pointed to the two seats at their booth. Thanking the server, he walked back to the table. "Are you ready to go?" he asked Liah.

"I haven't paid my bill or gotten my cheesecake yet," she said.

"Bill paid, cheesecake acquired." He waved the plastic bag at her.

"How did you know which cheesecake to get?"

"I got you one slice each of the lemon ones they sell. Did I do good?" He held out the bag for her to see.

"Yes. Very good, thank you." She looked over at Yong and Min. "Are we still bowling on Friday?"

"Would you mind coming back up here?" asked Yong. "We can go bowling in Indianapolis. I don't see us coming back to West Lafayette until Sunday morning."

"That's not a problem with me." Maliah looked at Seonghun who was staring at the cheesecake slices. "I don't think it's a problem with him either. We'll see you guys on Friday."

"You two be safe and keep an eye out. Since I won't be there, I'm going to send the people a text message letting them know your car will be in my spot. You can park at the apartment complex until Sunday morning."

"Thanks Yong." Seong watched as she looked over at Minjun who was avoiding her eye. She looked at Yongjoon; he slid out of the booth, allowing her to sit next to Min. "You're still my friend, I still care for you, but you need to understand that I'm a girl; there are some things that will be uncomfortable to me. Okay?"

He nodded.

She kissed him on the cheek. "Take some time for yourself. You'll feel better in the morning." Sliding back out of the booth, she gave Yong a side hug, waving at both men as they walked out of the restaurant.

Maliah looked at Seonghun as they were driving back to the dorm. "Do you want to go straight to the studio?"

He was peeking in the bag, drooling at the cheesecake. "No. I want to go back to the dorm for a bit. Plus, you asked for my rattiest jeans. These aren't them." He pointed at his pants.

"Do your oldest jeans have holes in them?" she asked.

"Yeah, in the knees and thighs." He reached in the bag, pulling out one of the chocolate cheesecakes.

"Why don't you wait until we get back to the dorm? That's going to be messy. The cookies won't be that bad though," she suggested.

He looked at her. "You have a problem with mess?"

"I like things tidy if that is what you're asking. I'm not a naturally neat person. I'm actually very messy, but when Casey started her bullshit, it was easier for me to notice what had been tampered with if I kept everything in its place."

"You don't seem messy."

"Oh, I work at it. When I did the Upward Bound thing, I had a dorm to myself for six weeks. It always looked like a bomb went off."

He laughed as he set the cheesecake back in the bag before placing it in the back seat. "I know you said elephants are your favorite animal, but what about domesticated animals?"

"I like all animals. I think I like dogs more though. They don't seem standoffish like cats. They tell you when they want affection." She took the exit to West Lafayette as she spoke. "It would be nice to have a dog. Maybe when I start my masters, I'll look into it."

"When I milk the cows, the barn cat, Doongi, follows me."

"Is Doongi a boy or a girl?" she asked.

"A girl. She is tiger colors."

"Sounds cute. Do you share milk with her?"

"She gets a small pan, yes."

"Other than the pictures you have sitting in your room, do you have pictures of your family?" She glanced at him quickly again before focusing on the road.

"Yeah, I have an album."

"Can I see?"

"Sure, let's get everything in the dorm, I'll show you." He directed her to the apartment complex that Yong parked at. Once she pulled into the space, she popped the trunk.

"Wait."

He came around the back, looking at her. "What's wrong?"

"I have an extra bag. I only bought the sweater dress at Saks." She opened it up to find a glittery long black dress. "Oh." She looked at Seonghun, baffled. "I tried this on, but I didn't buy it. I don't have anywhere to wear it."

"We'll figure out a place for you to wear it. It's too pretty not to be worn."

"We're college students. Where the hell are we going to go that requires a formal gown?" She looked down at the dress.

"If I figure it out, will you go with me in that dress?"

She glanced up at him. "Anywhere that you take me that requires me to wear that dress, is going to require a suit or a tux from you."

Seong shrugged. "I can buy a suit or rent a tux. I have no issues with either of these things." He put his hand on her neck, gently sliding it up to her face, watching her for discomfort. There was none. "Say yes? Let me take you somewhere in a pretty dress." He kissed her.

"Does it mean that much to you?"

"Yes."

"Why?" She pulled the rest of the bags out of the trunk while she waited for his answer.

"Sometimes it feels like you don't really understand how pretty you are." Liah opened her mouth to protest but he interrupted her. "You asked me a question, let me finish please. You don't know how pretty you are, but you're also intimidated by how you look." Seong grabbed the bags from her as they started walking. "I have no problems with you wearing sweatpants, or my shirts. I like seeing you in my shirts, I think it's cute. But I also think that you have this awful image of yourself. I want you to see what I see, what apparently Min sees as well."

"I don't have a bad image of myself," she protested.

"Do me a favor," he stopped walking, "the next note you write me, include a drawing of yourself."

"Okay." They continued their walk. Once they reached the dorm, there was a surprise. ID cards were always needed to access the upstairs area, but now there was a guard.

"IDs please?" The security guard stared at them both. They handed them over, waiting as the guard scanned them into a machine. As he looked at the pictures, his face softened. "I have notes for you two." He handed over envelopes to each of them as he handed their cards back. "Have a good day."

Maliah walked over to the wall of mailboxes. When she opened it, three giant envelopes spilled out. Seonghun looked over at her; she was staring at them shaking. "What's wrong?"

"C-c-c-" She couldn't get it out.

"Put them in your bag; you can tell me when we get upstairs, okay?" He rubbed her shoulder as she hastily shoved them in her bag. They walked to the elevator. Seonghun was getting worried about how deep she was breathing. "You need to calm down, you're going to hyperventilate." He kept rubbing her back.

"M-m-m-masters p-p-program," was all she could say as she was breathing deeply.

"Your responses from colleges!?"

She nodded.

"All of them?"

She shook her head and held up three fingers. After an eternity, the elevator opened. He looked at her. "Hold on, okay?"

She looked at him confused until he handed her the bags, lifted her up, running to their suite. Maliah burst into giggles as he fumbled with his keys, getting them into the door. Setting her down, he searched through the bag for the envelopes, handing them to her, picking her up again, tossing her on the couch as she snorted with laughter. Seonghun then pulled out his phone, quickly video calling Min.

"Hey."

"MALIAH'S MASTER PROGRAM PAPERS ARE HERE, GET YONG RIGHT NOW!" Seonghun screamed at the phone.

Maliah was in hysterics, laughing so hard she nearly fell off the couch. They heard Minjun screech. Yongjoon yelled back. When Min explained why he was screaming, there was a loud clunk in the background; soon three people were in the video frame.

"Hello there, sweetheart, I'm Cho Pae." A woman's face appeared. When Seong first met her, he thought she looked like Yong in a wig. "I'm Yongjoon's mom; I was told you'll be joining us for 추석?"

"Uh h-h-hi. What are the words you just used? 'Chew sock'?" Maliah looked a little frightened.

"추석. Think of it as Korean Thanksgiving," Seonghun explained.

"Oh. N-n-n-nice to m-m-meet you. Yes. I h-h-h-hope that's o-o-ok."

Seonghun saw her balling her fist. Gently, he took her hand.

"The more the merrier! You have some papers to open right now though, don't you?"

Maliah nodded, pulling out the first envelope. University of Hawaii at Mānoa was on the corner of the envelope. Opening it up she slid the first paper out.

"Dear Maliah Evans, Congratulations! We are pleased to offer you admission to the University of Hawaii at Mānoa—" Tears started running down her cheeks.

Minjun, Yongjoon, and Cho started cheering. Seonghun wrapped the arm not holding the phone around her. "It's okay. You did it. Keep reading."

She took a shuddering breath and continued. "Due to your academic achievements and personal endeavors, it is our privilege to offer—" Her voice trailed off as she burst into loud sobs, startling Seonghun. She waved the paper at him. He took it from her, finishing up the letter.

"Due to your academic achievements and personal endeavors, it is our privilege to offer you a scholarship covering your full tuition for the next two years of your studies. Holy shit."

"Language!" he heard a yell from the phone.

"Sorry Cho." Seonghun looked at the camera sheepishly for a moment before turning to Maliah. "Oh my god. Your tuition is paid for. You can go to school for free!" She was sobbing uncontrollably. "Sweetheart, you have got to calm down. You still have two other envelopes to go." He handed her the next envelope. It was from a college in England.

She opened the letter. "It is our honor to offer you admission to University College London." Tears were running nonstop. He was amazed that she could even see.

"Full ride again?" Yongjoon asked. Behind him Minjun was twirling Cho around while cheering.

She read further. "No. Half tuition is covered. Which would be a problem, because I'd be on a student visa, probably not allowed to work. I'd have to take out student loans." She made a face as she set it down with the other.

Seonghun handed her the last one. "Where is USC?" he asked her.

"Uh, University of Southern California." She opened the final one. Scanning the letter, she started screaming. She threw the paper at Seong before taking off running around the room. Liah was about to lose what little voice she had again. Minjun and Cho came back to the phone.

"What is going on over there?" Minjun asked.

"I don't know. Hold on." He glanced at Liah who was doing a weird jerky dance while yelling. "Tone it down, baby, you barely have a voice as is."

She calmed a bit but kept doing her dance.

Seonghun looked at the letter. "She got accepted," he scanned further. "Holy shit."

"Language!"

"Sorry, Cho." He read a little more. "She's accepted, full tuition scholarship for the next two years, housing as well as books for the next two years are covered as well. Oh my god!" He looked at Maliah in astonishment. "What kind of grades do you have!?"

She sat back down on the couch, smiling brightly. "I'm a straight A student, but it's not just my grades. I have volunteer hours that I've done in the past, I work two jobs, I also write my ass off on those entrance essays. I'll be a college graduate with no student loans because I work two jobs to make sure I don't have to take them out. I'm also a minority. I'm a poster child for most universities." Her eyes began to well up again. "I'm going to grad school!" She jumped on Seonghun giving him a smacking kiss. "I'm gonna help people!" When she kissed him deeper, he moaned, grabbing her hips.

"Uh, we're gonna go, guys. Congratulations, Liah! We'll see you on Friday." Yongjoon hurriedly hung up the phone.

"Liah-mmph!" Her lips covered his as she pushed him to lie back on the couch.

"Very happy, don't want to talk, want to kiss." She pulled away from him slightly to speak before she claimed his mouth again.

Seonghun wasn't stupid, so he went with whatever she wanted. Pretty soon they had fallen off the couch. Giggling, they continued their assault on each other's mouths. Maliah's sweatshirt came off. So did Seonghun's. Pretty soon, all of their clothes were scattered around them.

"Ah, stop. Stop please." Seonghun gritted his teeth at the effort it took to say anything. He wasn't inside her, but he was really close to being so. "We don't have protection right now."

Maliah snapped out of her haze slightly. "I'm not sentimental about things, but I really don't want my first time to be on the dorm floor."

"Are you opposed to other firsts being on the dorm floor?" he asked.

She shook her head. "I don't think so."

"Hold that thought." He stood up and walked to his room. Opening his nightstand, he looked at the box he purchased weeks ago with Yongjoon. Opening it, he pulled out a condom and grabbed his comforter before walking back to the common area. He saw Maliah naked, sitting on her jeans. She looked up when she heard him.

Holding up the condom so she could see, he explained. "This isn't to pressure you or anything, but if you change your mind, it's here." He set it on the coffee table.

She nodded. "Thanks for thinking of that."

"I'll always try to protect you. Last thing you want right now is a baby, seeing as how you're on your way to graduate school," he smiled at her, "I'm so proud of you."

Maliah's smile was so big, it looked as if it would split her face.

"Stand up for a second."

She did as he asked. Seong spread his comforter out on the floor. Pulling her back down to the floor, he began kissing her again. Softly kissing her neck, Seonghun worked his way down her body, letting his tongue trail to her breast. When he flicked her nipple with his tongue, she arched up against him. "You are so beautiful like this," he whispered.

She let out a strangled moan, trying to keep quiet.

"There's no one here, sweetheart," he hovered over her other breast, "you can be as quiet or as loud as you want to be. It's just us." He covered her nipple with his mouth, teasing her with his teeth and tongue. Sliding his hand between her legs, Seong stroked her. "I really want to make your roller coaster drop," Seonghun whispered. He really didn't want to wait, but he was forcing himself to be patient. Wrapping his hands around her ribcage, he used his thumbs to stroke her breasts. "You have freckles." He ghosted his fingers across the small patch of them under her left breast.

She looked at him, her eyes slightly unfocused. "Yeah. I have them in a couple places."

"Hmm. I'll find them later." He continued caressing her, briefly coming back up to kiss her before beginning his descent again. He gently swiped his thumb down her clit causing her to arch against him again.

"Seong," she called out. "It's never felt like this," she whispered. "I don't know what to do."

He took off his glasses and set them on the coffee table. "You remembered what you said to me, when you first showed me how to get you off?" She was blurry, but he saw her shake her head no. "You said, and I quote 'when I put my mouth on your pussy, it won't be in this fucking tiny bed'." He smiled down at her. "We aren't in bed, sweetheart."

"Oh god," she moaned.

He lowered his mouth to her, taking a long lick. "God, you taste as good as you smell," he moaned. As he took a second lick, she froze. Seong lifted his head to ask if she was okay, and he realized she was screaming. Her voice was shot again so he couldn't hear it. He put his head back down focusing on her. He began lapping at her, while gently pushing his finger inside. Turning his hand like she taught him, he stroked as he devoured her, listening to her squeaks and moans. He couldn't wait to do this again when he could actually hear her. As he continued his ministrations, he felt her walls grip his fingers. Rolling his eyes up to her, she was still calling out and gripping the blanket. Liah wasn't quite there but seemed close. With his free hand, he gripped her thigh tighter as his mouth moved against her. Pressing down hard on that spongy patch, he moved his fingers as fast as he could.

Minjun thought that Seonghun was bashful about sexual activity. He was just uncomfortable discussing it with other people. He enjoyed sex; it was natural. He liked giving pleasure as much as receiving it; seeing Maliah writhe above him made him impossibly hard.

"Seong," she squeaked out. "OH GOD! Seong!"

He felt her clamp down around his fingers before arching off the blanket. It was the one of the most intense orgasms he'd ever felt from her. As she came down, he gently removed his fingers, while laying his head on her stomach. "I wonder if this is going to be the foolproof way to get you over the hump. I'd be happy to do it any time you like."

She began toying with his hair quietly. "I want you," she rasped. "I want you so much it hurts to think about sometimes. But I'm not mentally there."

"I'm not pressuring you, but can you tell me what's holding you back?" He rested his chin on her lower stomach while he looked at her.

She was silent for a minute, stroking his hair. "The one thing my mother imparted to me was that sex fucks you up, no pun intended. That it makes you believe in things that aren't real like love. It will always have its consequences, be it a baby, a broken heart, or whatever." She sighed, looking down at him. "I'm realizing my mom's full of shit; her experiences are not mine, but when something has been hammered into you for so long..." She paused.

"It makes it hard to overcome the voices telling you that this is bad," he finished.

"Yeah. There's a part of me that wants to run in my room to shut the door. There's another part that wants you to do that again."

He smiled as she looked bashful.

"There is another part of me that wants to feel you inside of me."

It was quiet again. She kept stroking his hair. He sat up on his knees. "How about for now, we just listen to the middle voice." He leaned down and gently bit the inside of her thigh. "Hey! I found another patch of freckles!"

Maliah's laughs quicky turned to moans as his mouth made contact with her again.

CHAPTER 31

After a shower, the couple walked to the art studio on campus. When Liah gave her name to the front desk, the receptionist rounded a corner. Coming back, he handed her a camera with several lenses as she handed over her id card. They also gave her a key to the studio she'd be working in.

"Typically, you can't get access like this unless you're a fine arts major. Turns out, with all the extra classes I took in the summer, I'll be graduating with a minor in fine arts. So, I get access," Liah explained as she unlocked the door.

Seonghun looked around. There was a white backdrop on a stand in the center of the room, with a bucketful of what looked like umbrellas. The whole place was dimly lit. He watched Maliah lock the door.

"It's going to take me a minute to get set up," she said. "Put on music; don't be scared to make it loud. The room is basically soundproof." She still sounded like she had swallowed glass.

He set the speaker she requested he bring on a table. "When we get back to the dorm, you need to have a couple cups of tea."

Liah was distracted by the umbrellas. "Okay." She pulled several of them out, setting them around the backdrop. As she fiddled with them, he realized they were lights. She studied the backdrop before looking at him.

"What's wrong?" he asked.

"I'm not ready for the light test yet, but can you come here and stand on the backdrop?" He did as she asked. "You aren't pale, but I don't know if I like this white shirt on white backdrop. I'll light test it, changing the backdrop if I need to." Liah focused on his face. "Eat your snack, I'll be ready in a bit." He pulled out two of the cookies she'd bought from the mall. They were a soft sugar cookie with a rich cream cheese icing and blue sandy sugar sprinkled on top. He tried to savor their rich sweet flavor, but they were so good; he ended up wolfing them down.

He watched her put together the camera, pulling an SD card from her purse. "They don't provide a memory card?"

She made a face. "They do, but I went to the data security lecture once; the lecturer showed us how she used the software that the school claims to use, that overwrites your data so it isn't retrievable. She then used open-source software she found on the internet, to retrieve the data easily. So I don't trust it. An SD card is cheap, it works on all the cameras here."

She pulled out a tripod. "Are you ready? Remove your shoes and socks before standing on the backdrop. These are testing photos. I'm using them to test the lighting. You can do whatever you want."

Seonghun wanted to make her smile, so he made the goofiest faces. He jumped in the air as she shot him. Liah giggled, adjusting the equipment along the way. "So, the white backdrop is not what I want." She walked over to the backdrop roll, pulling down a blue one. "Test shots one more time." After three shots, she smiled. "I'm ready." She walked up to him, standing on her tiptoes to remove his glasses. "I haven't really learned how to shoot without getting a glare on glasses. Will you be okay without them?"

"You may have to push me where you want me if it is far from the spot I currently am," he warned.

"Noted." She set his glasses on the table, calling out instructions as she snapped photos. Seonghun thought it was all very simple. The main problem was hearing what she was saying with her voice being squeaky.

"Can you turn down the music a bit? I can barely hear you." She walked over, disconnecting his phone from the speaker, adding hers. A voice crooned about a girl being always worth it. Seonghun thought the music took a strange turn. It felt sexy. She had him sit on the paper cross legged while she shot above him. He looked up at her as she instructed. Everything was blurred, but Seong saw her nearly drop the camera.

"You okay?"

"I— yeah. I'm good. Can you stand up? I want you to turn your back to me. Act like you're going to lift your shirt over your head, but you're going to only lift it halfway."

He paused before he did as she instructed. "Did that song just say, 'pussy for breakfast'?"

She avoided eye contact. "It's one of my favorite playlists to listen to while creating art."

He shrugged, turning as she asked, lifting his shirt slightly. But the bulbs didn't go off. "Liah?" He turned slightly to try and see her.

"Hmm?"

"Liah, are you staring at my back?" He tried to hide his amusement.

"Oh gosh, I'm sorry! I sort of— you're beautiful." He heard the camera click. "Do you feel comfortable taking your shirt off?" He slowly took off his shirt, tossing it to the side. She continued to take photos, instructing him which way to move. "T-t-turn around."

"You cannot be nervous about taking my picture. I was in between your legs just a couple hours ago. There's nothing to be nervous about."

"It's n-n-not anxiety." She continued snapping.

"Then what is it?"

She shifted him slightly. He grabbed her arms gently as she pivoted his waist.

"What is it, Maliah?"

She was silent. He squinted until he saw the table where she set his glasses. He put them on. When he turned to look at her, Seong saw what the problem was.

"It's okay, you know," he said softly. "To feel that way."

"I don't want you to think that I want you just for your body. I'd feel this way if you had a s-s-s-soft tummy or a bald spot."

"I know, but I don't have either of those things. I like that you look at me like that." He looked at the tripod. "Do you have the ability to shoot without having your hand on the camera?"

"Uh, yeah, I have a remote that can take p-p-p-pictures."

"Set the camera up and come over with me." He stood back on the paper.

"I haven't done test shots for my skin tone," she protested.

"It doesn't matter how these come out. No one else is going to see them but you or me." He looked at her. "Lose the sweatshirt, set up the camera, and come here."

She took off her sweatshirt, revealing a yellow shirt underneath. Liah set the camera on the tripod, grabbed the remote before walking to Seong.

"Hand me the remote." He held out his hand. Slowly she dropped it into his hand, searching his face. "Trust me. Anything you aren't sure about, tell me to stop."

She nodded. He wrapped himself around her. "Look at the camera, baby," he whispered in her ear. Seonghun was pleased to see goosebumps appear on her arms. He heard Liah's gasp as he lowered his mouth to her neck.

click

Wrapping his hand around her waist, he sucked the sensitive part of her neck as he lifted her shirt slightly. His arm covered the soft flesh he'd exposed. Seong couldn't help the slight smirk as he heard her hoarse moan. He didn't know what had gotten into him, as this was completely out of his norm. He didn't feel like an awkward giant with her at that moment. No, he felt powerful.

click

All of a sudden, he whirled her around, so he could see her face. She was breathing so hard her chest was heaving. "You don't have a bra on." Her nipples were at attention.

"It's just us. I had no intention of taking my sweatshirt off," she rasped. He brought his mouth down to hers gently. He teased her with his tongue before opening up and letting her slide her tongue against his.

click

Standing on her tiptoes, she ran her hands up his face, through his hair and pulled him closer, sighing softly as she nipped at his mouth greedily.

click

He felt her hands slide lower, down his chest, to his stomach, before unbuttoning his jeans. "What are you doing?" he whispered against her mouth.

"Having another first." She continued kissing him while slowly unzipping his pants. Reaching in she slowly pumped him a couple times before dropping to her knees.

"Oh god!" he cried out. She looked up at him while sliding his pants down.

click

She stiffened as the lights flashed.

"It's your SD card. You can do what you want with the pictures," he reminded her. "I'll stop if you want me to."

She wrapped her hand around him, slowly teasing him as she looked him in his eyes. "I'm trusting you a lot right now."

"I know."

"You can't tell anyone we did this. Not even Minjun or Yongjoon."

"I won't."

She was silent for a moment longer. He was about to hand over the remote when she nodded. "Take whatever pictures you want," she said before putting her mouth on him.

He cried out loudly, louder than he ever had.

click

She slowly tried to fit as much of him in her mouth as she could. It was doing absolutely nothing for him.

"Will you let me guide you?" He looked down at her.

She nodded. Slowly Seonghun slid his hand to the side of her face. He gave Liah a moment to get used to his hand before slowly rocking her head.

click

"Oh god that's it," he moaned. Seong wanted to slam into her badly, but that wasn't the first impression he wanted to make. When the urge became too much, he let go, letting Liah set her own pace. Seonghun was so used to sneaking around that his own cries startled him. Her mouth felt so good, he couldn't help it.

click

Liah found her rhythm, bobbing on him rapidly while looking up at him. His head was thrown back as he breathed heavily, poorly attempting to stop his moans.

click

He couldn't stop the moans or the garbled Korean coming out of his mouth as his balls began to tighten. "Baby, I'm going to come, you need to get off," he whispered hoarsely. Instead she tried to take him deeper.

click
click
click

His orgasm was intense. It was too much for Liah to handle at once, dribbling out of her mouth slightly. Seong collapsed to his knees, trying to catch his breath. Looking over, he saw her studying him silently. "Where did you spit it out at?" he asked.

Maliah looked confused. "I didn't. There's nowhere to spit." He went semi erect instantly. She looked down. "How is that even possible?"

He blushed. "I have a fast rebound time. I can be fully aroused again in ten minutes or so after the first time. The time it takes extends the more I come." He stood up to put his pants back on.

She stared at him wide eyed. "Are you an Avenger?"

He snorted as he sat down on the backdrop. "What kind of superpower is that? The power to drill through a building with my dick?"

Leaning over, Seong kissed his girlfriend who was looking a little bashful. "I'll tell you what it means." He kissed her again, slowly laying her down on the backdrop. "When I finally do make love to you," he unbuttoned her pants, slowly sliding them past her hips. "If I can't make your roller coaster drop that first time." She lifted her hips to help him. "It won't take me long to try a second time." He laid his glasses off to the side. "Or a third time." He spread her legs, lowering his mouth to her as Liah let out a strangled cry.

click

CHAPTER 32

Seonghun wanted to lay on that studio floor with Maliah forever, but there was a time limit they were close to hitting. He helped her put away the lights while watching with amusement as she searched for scissors.

"The backdrops are disposable; if it gets dirty, you're supposed to trim away as little as possible," she explained. She eyeballed the slight sticky stain they'd left on the bottom of the backdrop as she carefully trimmed it off, before tossing it into the trash. Seong cut the music, pocketing his little speaker.

Liah did a thorough once over. When she was satisfied, she popped her SD card out of the camera sticking it into her purse. "We can look at the pictures on my laptop when we get back to the dorm." Walking up to the door, she paused.

"What's wrong?" he asked.

"I l-l-l-l-locked this," She turned to him looking panicked. "Y-y-y-you s-s-s-saw me lock it."

"I did see you lock it." He looked at the door; it was cracked slightly. "Who has keys to the doors, Maliah?"

He saw her shutting down. "Sweetheart don't do this. We didn't do anything wrong. Focus. Who would have a key besides us right now?"

She touched the doorknob. "Reception."

"Let's go." He took her hand. He didn't know if she was shutting down or going into shock, but either way it wasn't good. It also wasn't how he wanted to end this experience. Pulling her to the reception counter, Seonghun opened his mouth to speak but felt her gently tap his leg. Looking down her expression had changed. She wasn't panicking. She was pissed.

"H-h-how many people are i-i-i-in here right n-n-now?" she demanded.

The receptionist smiled. "Hardly anyone, two including yourself."

"Who did you let in, that had either a m-m-m-master key, or a k-k-k-k-key to my room?" She glared at the receptionist.

"No one would have a key." He wouldn't meet her eyes.

"Seonghun, call the police. Call Detective Krishna right fucking now." Stepping to the side, he did as she asked.

"Wait! Wait, don't call the police. Please. I need this job!" The receptionist looked at her with wide terrified eyes.

"P-p-p-p-p-police are getting called r-r-r-r-regardless because we have a bit of a s-s-s-s-s-stalker problem. How much, you tell me between now, and when they arrived determines h-h-h-how willing I'll be to p-p-p-p-plead for your job." She glared at the man.

"A cute girl came in; said she was surprising her friend. She had balloons. She didn't want me to call the room but wanted to surprise you. I loaned her my key. She was out in like five minutes." He started babbling.

Seonghun came back over as he hung up the phone. "Detective will be here shortly."

"D-d-d-d-did you see any b-b-b-b-b-balloons outside the d-d-d-d-door?"

He walked back toward the hallway. "They aren't right by the door we were in," he yelled back at her. Walking further down the hall he noticed something. "Yeah, there's two; they are heart shaped and say, 'I Love You'."

Liah burst into tears. "Seonghun, what if she has pictures of me like that? It could ruin my career before it starts. Who's going to trust their kid's well-being to m-m-m-me?" She put her head in hands sobbing quietly.

He wrapped her in his arms, glaring at the receptionist who was trying to make himself very small. "Do you know how to operate the security cameras?" Seonghun barked.

The receptionist gave a short nod. He led them to the back where the cameras were. Slowly he began clicking keys on the console. "This is when she came in." He pointed at the screen. It was Casey in that big coat. Her hair was wild. She stood there holding the balloons. "I gave her the key; there she is walking down the hallway."

The three of them watch her as she unlocked the door, peeking in for a moment. She let go of the balloons, pulled out her phone, taking a few pictures. Leaving the door cracked she walked back to the front. Then they watch as she did the oddest thing. She walked past the security camera, backed up, blowing a kiss before leaving. "Rewind it to where she is looking in the door." Seonghun ordered. The receptionist did as he requested.

"Where's the time stamp?" He looked all over the screen.

The receptionist pointed in the corner. The time read 6:55 p.m. Seonghun breathed a sigh of relief.

"Sweetheart, look." He pointed at the time stamp, and then pulled out his phone. It was 7:15 p.m. "Our time was up at seven. She didn't see anything she wasn't supposed to. We were putting away equipment at that point." The sheer relief on her face had him feeling beyond guilty. This was his fault. It wasn't supposed to turn sexual.

"It's okay?" she asked softly.

"It's fine. I really want to get you home so we can put on sweats. I'll make you a cup of tea."

"We have to wait for the detective." She walked over to him and laid her head on his chest.

He held her as she began to shake. Seong felt her tears through his shirt. "I'm so sorry, Maliah." He stared at the receptionist, inclining his head toward the door. Taking the hint, he left, closing the door quietly behind him.

"I-I-I'm not sad, Seonghun. I'm p-p-p-pissed." She looked at him with tears running down her face. He used his thumbs to wipe them away. "T-t-t-that was sp-p-p-pecial to me, I feel sick."

"Baby, she saw nothing. Nothing was ruined. We still have that, okay?"

"Why is s-s-s-she doing this?" she demanded. "You s-s-s-saw that dude. He w-w-w-wanted her, why not go for someone that wants her?"

"I don't know. I do know that I don't want her. I'm with the person I want to be with. We're going to wait for the detective, then I'm going to take you back to the dorm, feed you leftover pizza, cheesecake, and tea."

"What an o-o-o-odd combo."

"Eh, we're kind of an odd combo. It works." He kissed her before leading her out of the room to wait for the detective.

Detective Krishna gave them a ride back to their dorm since they walked to the studio. "I would appreciate it if you two drove wherever you go from now on," she said as she pulled into the parking lot.

"I have the stadium parking pass, the bus stops running after a certain hour," Maliah explained.

"What is the total number of cars in your dorm?"

"Two," Seonghun said.

"Email me license plate numbers when you get in. I'll have someone courier over upgraded parking passes in the morning. You will be able to park behind your dorm." The detective looked at them. "Did you read the envelopes I sent over today?"

Maliah fidgeted while Seonghun explained, "We got sidetracked. She got acceptance letters to graduate school; we sort of forgot everything else."

"It's okay. Casey is on the run. She's hiding out on campus, though we can't figure out where. We raided her sorority; they kicked her out when they found out what happened in her biology lab."

"It seems odd they would kick her out for a dust up in biology," said Liah.

The detective shook her head. "The sorority is on thin ice anyway, about to get their charter snatched for hazing. They're trying to keep their nose clean for the time being. Anything that can remotely look bad on them, they are coming down on hard." She looked at Seonghun, "We also found multiple pictures of you in her dorm room, walking with your friends mostly. We saw two pictures of you with Maliah, her face was scratched out."

The couple looked at each other nervously.

"Are you guys in the same major?"

They shook their heads.

"Have classes near each other?"

Again, the pair of them shook their heads.

"I would advise that you both find a buddy to walk to classes with. If you see her, call the non-emergency line."

Maliah thanked her before leaving the car, slowly heading inside the dorm.

"Did I say something wrong?" Detective Krishna asked.

"She just started making friends. As of right now, she has two, and a boyfriend. None of us have classes anywhere near her or during the time she does. But I have an idea. It'll be fine."

She nodded. "Don't forget to send me license plate information so I can get you set up with parking passes."

Seonghun thanked her before walking into the dorms. The security guard from earlier was still posted. After he showed his ID, he ran upstairs. When he opened the door to their suite, Maliah was perched on the couch, staring at the SD card she held between her fingers. After filling the electric kettle, he sat beside her.

"Could you imagine if she had seen what transpired earlier?" she rasped.

"I don't want to imagine that, thank you very much." He arched an eyebrow. "I didn't take you as someone would appreciate a voyeur."

She avoided his gaze, staring at the card. "You've watched me before. That wasn't bad, a little uncomfortable."

"Go get your computer. Let's see what we made. I'll make your tea." He squeezed her arm before standing. She followed suit, walking into her bedroom, coming out shortly with her laptop.

He busied himself making cups of tea, plating cheesecake while it steeped. He also sent a text to Min with his idea while requesting Yong's license plate number. He received a message while spooning honey into the tea.

Min: *On it. Check your email for his number.*

Sitting back down, he looked at her as she focused on her laptop. "Can I ask you something?"

"You can ask me anything." She turned to look at him.

"You have a... taste for expensive things," he said slowly.

She flipped her hand back and forth. "There are some things I want that are expensive, yes. I'm also fine with things that are inexpensive if they hold up. That wasn't a question though."

"No, I suppose not." He handed her a cup of tea. "Do you imagine yourself living in a huge mansion or something?"

"No, not really. I don't need large spaces. I would like a house of my own." She looked off and squinted. "I'd like a fireplace."

"That's all you see?"

"I've never thought of the design of a house. Just different elements. I want a big bed. If I do end up having kids, I want them to be able to climb in when they are scared. I want a fireplace, like I said, to drink tea or hot chocolate in front of in the winter while reading a book. I want a nice tub."

"What qualifies as a nice tub to you?" He liked listening her dreams.

Instead of answering, she pulled up a real estate website. "This is what a lot of tubs look like in houses now. I hate the material they are made from."

Looking at it, he saw it was a beige material, running up the wall. It was okay, but nothing fancy.

"If I had my way, the shower would be separate from the tub. Like this." She showed him a picture of a massive house. The tub could probably fit all the roommates in it. The shower was nice as well. It was large and tiled in a neutral sand color with chrome dual shower heads. Off to the side was a wide seat.

"You could have sex in the shower," he blurted out.

She looked at him. "Have you ever had sex in the shower?"

"I've only had sex in a barn." He turned red.

"I—" She looked at him. "I don't know how to respond to that."

"We were in high school. My mom is a housewife, so is hers. Every moment we had was stolen," he tried to explain. "If someone would have seen my parent's car somewhere in a deserted area, there would have been questions. The barn was near the house; we could go into a quiet corner.

It's not like we did it a whole bunch. I don't think she really liked sex." He picked up a fork to hold out a bite of lemon raspberry cheesecake to her.

"What makes you think she didn't like sex?"

"It could be she didn't like sex with me, I don't know. She didn't respond a lot of the time. Sometimes she looked bored but didn't want to say stop. I would try to initiate but would be turned down. So, I waited for her to come to me, which wasn't often. I liked touching her. Looking back on it, it felt she would use oral sex to just placate me." He ate some of his chocolate cheesecake, brooding slightly. *You hurt me, Seong.* He tried to shake off the memories.

"Wait. You told me she'd go down on you when she wanted to avoid something. Did you ever reciprocate?" Liah asked.

"I'd try. She didn't want it. I maybe was able to go down on her two or three times in the years we were together."

"But you're good at it. Like really good. Like you know how my sex drive is, but if you wanted to do that I would immediately say yes."

"That makes me feel good, thank you. I've listened over the years to friends talking about those kinds of things. It could be boasting or bragging, but the stuff I retained seemed to satisfy you."

"Yes." Liah looked down at her cup of tea before sipping.

"Don't be embarrassed. My only regret is that you don't have your voice, so I can't hear you cry out like I want to."

"What about me?" she asked.

"What about you?"

"I feel dumb asking this. I'm a grown woman, I shouldn't be comparing myself to a teenager. Was everything I did okay?"

He politely took her laptop, along with her cup of tea before pouncing on her. Kissing her thoroughly, he looked at her. "I have absolutely no complaints. This also isn't a contest. It felt good to be wanted, to be touched by you. I get scared that your lack of sex drive has to do with me."

"Absolutely not. If I could help it, I would. I've been debating talking to Dr. Stewart about it."

Seong was surprised at that. He knew she wasn't willing to lower her dosage just because her sex drive was shot, so he wondered what on earth could be done. He got up and refilled her cup again.

"This tea is good. It smells amazing too." She wrapped her hands around the cup.

"They didn't have anything lemon based at the shop in the mall, but I saw this citrus blend. I thought you would like it."

"I do."

"Are we stalling about looking at the pictures?"

"A little."

"Liah, let's take a look."

She sighed, before taking her computer off the Wi-Fi. At his puzzled expression she explained, "I'm paranoid as shit right now. I won't look at this with an internet connection until I know she's caught or something."

"Fair enough."

Together they started going through the photos. He reached out and almost touched the screen. "That's…"

She smiled at him. "It's you. I told you, you're beautiful."

They laughed at the test shots while gasping at the back shots. "It's why I'm always staring at your back, your lines are beautiful," she explained. As they went through the shots, she edited the lighting, never editing his body.

They got to the pictures of them. Seong watched Liah's expression darken as she went through them. Instead of lightly retouching the pictures like she did with his, she began to thin her legs out or smash in her hips.

"Liah, no, stop!" He started to grab her hands.

"You didn't say anything when I retouched your photos," she pointed out.

"You changed the lighting in mine. You're literally taking chunks out of your body, stop." He took the laptop from her, quickly hitting the undo button. Seong sat the laptop down, pulling her to him. "What made you hate your body so much?"

"I don't hate my body, hold on." She went into her room, coming back with a photo album. "I still need to get the other picture back from you."

"I keep meaning to go get a copy of it to keep, but I haven't made it to the store. It's in my wallet, but it's not bunched or anything. I keep it nice; I promise."

"Why do you want a copy?"

"Baby Maliah is adorable with her ice cream."

She smiled at him. "I'll make you a deal. Get me a picture of baby Seonghun; you can keep that."

"Deal."

She opened the photo album; Seonghun saw the problem immediately. "Wow," he said quietly.

"You caught it huh? I look like my dad's mom. Mom HATES his mom, even more so than she hates me." She flipped through the photo album. Her mother was mostly in the background of any pictures Liah was in, while Liah's nose was frequently in a book, writing, or studying, not paying attention to her surroundings. You could smell the dysfunction coming off the pages.

Maliah's mother was tall and slender. She had none of the curves of his girlfriend. While Liah's eyes were wide, her mother's were constantly narrowed as if she was trying to figure something out. Her mother didn't look happy or at peace in any of these photos. Liah bore no resemblance to her that Seong could outright see. There was something else.

"Who's taking all of these photos?"

"Pops. I don't really know why though." She closed the book, setting it down. "I have a hard time remembering that my body type is okay when it was something that would set her off. She'd have me on constant diets."

"Stand up." He stood, waiting for her.

"Why?"

"Just, please stand up." He pulled her to her feet. Undoing her jeans, Seong slid them halfway down her hips, he also lifted her shirt. "Even if you suddenly lost twenty pounds, you wouldn't be doing anything except making yourself skeletal." He gripped her hips, tugging her closer. "You're beautiful as you are. I truly wish you would see it. There are women that pay money to look like this." He noticed she was giving him a look. "Really? Again?"

She gave him a half smile. "You unbuttoned my pants; I lost track of everything."

He kissed her. "Do you want to stay here on the floor tonight? We can camp out. Between the both of us, I'm sure we have enough blankets to keep warm."

"I'd like that. I want to grab another shower though, I'm kind of crusty from earlier."

"Same. I'll shower when you're done. I'm going to look through the pictures though."

Liah pulled her pants back up, buttoning them. "That's fine. Don't connect my computer to the internet as long as that SD card is in the slot, please." She walked into her room to grab her things before closing herself in the bathroom. He sat cross legged on the comforter, flipping through the pictures. The one she tried to change her body was the first one where he had her shirt lifted. He didn't even recognize the look on his face. They looked amazing together. She'd dropped to her knees; he was just looking at her. Seong laughed at the next one because he snapped it as he let out a moan; you can see the pleased smirk on her face.

They were very erotic. The biggest surprise was the shot of him going down on her. You saw the contrasts in their skin with his arm on her thigh, but you couldn't really see her face because it was shadowed. Her arms were stretched over her head with her back arched. It looked almost like a high art shot. He wanted to blow it up to hang over his bed. Seeing as how he was sworn from telling his friends, it probably wasn't a great idea.

Maliah stepped out of the bathroom with warm flannel pajamas.

"Can you come here for a second?"

"What's wrong?" she asked.

"Nothing. This photo," he pointed to it, "I want this one; I want to display it."

"Display it where?" she asked worriedly.

"In my room. It looks like art. You can't see our faces."

She stared at it for a minute before taking the laptop from him. Working quickly, she managed to shade some other areas as well as turn the photo black and white. "Oh!" He stared in shock at the photo after she finished. "It looks like a professional artist did this."

"If you're okay with this, I'll get you a copy made. What size do you want?" she asked, looking at him.

"Poster sized?" Seong suggested, smiling.

"How about a nice 8x10? Bigger than the pictures in your room, but small enough that it's not plastered above your bed."

"That's fine. How are you going to get it made?" he asked curiously.

In response she dropped that one file to her desktop before pulling the card out of her computer. "If you ever want to look at them, that's fine. All I ask is that until everything is settled, you don't insert the SD card anywhere that has an internet connection." Liah waited until he nodded. "You're welcome in my room at any time; I'll keep it in my top desk drawer."

Seong walked over to the kitchen, putting the pizza into the tiny oven before grabbing his pajamas. Before he walked into the bathroom, he turned to her. "Why didn't we take a shower together?"

"Well, one, that shower is tiny as hell. Two, we're not at a level of intimacy that I would willingly let you watch me wash my ass," said Liah.

He snorted as he closed the door.

Full of pizza, they talked for a bit before Seong brought out his small speaker. "Can we listen to the music you played in the studio?"

"Sure. Hold on though, I need to send the detective my license plate number." Liah brought up her email typing in the information. "Do you have Yongjoon's?" He checked his phone for the email, barking out a laugh. She looked over at him. Seong handed over his phone. The license plate number was there, but there was also a picture of their roommate's legs on a coffee table with a note.

Don't do anything we wouldn't do! <3

Liah had a devilish grin on her face. "Do you want to flip them out?"

He nodded as she brought up the camera on his phone. Picking up the condom she tore it open with her teeth. Liah tossed the condom at him, throwing the packaging on the table, quickly snapping a photo. Hitting reply to their message, she attached the photo, writing a quick note.

Too late. <3

She pressed send before handed his phone back while setting hers on the coffee table. It was silent in their common area until their phones began to go off at the same time. They broke into loud peals of laughter as their phones rang and vibrated.

"How do you want to play this?" Seonghun asked her.

"As far as they know, I don't know you've sent the message. Treat it like that." She picked up her phone, "Hello?"

"OHMYGODWHATTHEHELLISGOINGONOVERTHERE?!" a voice screamed at her.

She held the phone out from her ear. "Hello to you, Minjun," she said dryly.

Grinning, Seong picked up his phone. "Hey Yong."

"Hey buddy," he said cautiously. "You two okay over there?"

"We're perfectly fine." He looked over at Liah. She was face down in a pillow laughing as Minjun's voice screamed from her phone. She popped up, quickly turning on the speaker. Connecting her laptop, she began playing the playlist from the studio.

"Uh, so, the picture you just sent m—" Yongjoon paused, "I'm sorry did that song just say, 'pussy for breakfast'?"

Seonghun collapsed next to Liah trying not to burst into laughter. "I'm sorry, Yongjoon, did you need something? I'm kind of busy."

"Nooo, I was just checking on you and—" Yongjoon paused again, "what are you listening to?!"

Seonghun opened his mouth to say something when he felt Liah hovered over his shoulder. Right by the phone she made her voice breathy. "Come back to me please. We weren't done." Her voice was recovering slowly, but she made it sound sexy; the sound went straight south on him. "Yong, I must go. I'll call you tomorrow. Or you can call me. I don't care, but I need to go."

"Seonghun yo—" Seong hung up on one of his dearest friends.

She was cracking up, laying on the comforter with her arm over her eyes. "Min was freaking out, sputtering about safe sex." Liah realized he wasn't saying anything. Removing her arm, she jumped slightly as Seong had come to hover over her. "Hey." She smiled up at him.

"I'm not," he swallowed, "someone who thinks with his dick. I'm careful about how I approach people."

"I know all of this." She cocked her head to the side as if trying to figure out where he was going.

"That being said," he licked his lips, "I want to bury myself in you."

She choked on air.

"I want to touch you, I want to taste you, I want you to scream my name over and over again." Seong lowered himself slightly.

Her eyes went wide.

"When you're spent, and don't think you can take anymore, I want to start all over again." He kissed her.

"All I'm asking is that you give me time to get my mind right, so that I'm mentally healthy enough to give back what I get. Oral sex was a huge step for me; even now, my mind is fighting me on how it was a misstep."

He kissed her again. "I'm going to be honest with you right now, I don't want to take a step back. I don't want to stop tasting you."

"It makes me feel powerful that I make you feel that way. I'm not taking a step back, Seonghun. I'm just asking for a little time before we make that next step."

"I understand." He kissed her one more time and then rolled off her. "Do you want to watch Jeopardy?"

"Sounds like a plan." They cuddled on the floor, watching TV until they dozed off.

CHAPTER 33

"Are you ready?" Seong grinned devilishly as they both heard the knob quietly turn. Liah was on top of him, making fake breathing moans as he slowly moved her around. From the doorway, It would look like they were having sex. They both heard the door open. As they did, Liah let out a fake cry. Seong covered his mouth, as they heard the door quietly shut.

The two of them giggled as they waited a moment, then left the room tiptoeing down the hall. They heard Yong, from talking from the study room.

"What the hell do we do!?"

Seonghun stifled his giggles as Liah doubled over.

"Send a text. We'll say we're ten minutes out while we hide in here."

"You know, if you two minded your business, you wouldn't walk in on things like that." Liah came around the corner smothering her laughter.

"OH MY GOD!" Minjun jumped a mile.

"We were laying there talking. We knew it was you; since we're supposed to see you tomorrow, we figured you were just being nosy. So a little prank never harmed anyone." Seong followed behind her.

Yongjoon was laughing, but Minjun bubbled over. "Can you blame us!? You sent Yongjoon a picture of a condom wrapper, Liah was evading questions yesterday, you HUNG UP THE PHONE ON Yong!" Minjun shrieked the last part.

Maliah was doubled over laughing. "It hurts!" She dropped to her knees, chortling.

Seong looked down at her grinning before looking over at Minjun. "Min, we're both adults. Even if that happened, you wouldn't be privy to it."

"Also, use your noodle." Maliah gasped out. "We're both private people. Why on earth would either of us indicate that we were having sex unless it was a joke?"

It was quiet except for Maliah's snickers as the roommates realized they were played. "Man, you made me miss Mom's pancakes for this!" Yongjoon complained, shoving Min.

"She'll make you pancakes tomorrow, calm down." Minjun rolled his eyes. He looked at the two of them. "Do you guys want to go get breakfast?"

Seonghun nodded and Maliah looked at her watch. "Eh, I have a lesson and a late afternoon tour at the gallery."

"What are you doing after that?" Yongjoon asked.

"I need to do my homework."

"Bring it with you, come stay with us in Indy," he offered. "We could go bowling; you could have your date up there as well."

Maliah looked uncomfortable. "I have laundry to do."

He was relentless. They were coming with them. "Bring it with you."

"I can't stay, Yongjoon." Seonghun spoke up, "I have an appointment on Friday."

"Is it the same appointment Minjun has?" Yongjoon asked. Seonghun turned purple. Yong rolled his eyes. "Cancel it. There's a place near the house where you can get it done."

"Are you getting tattoos?" Maliah asked.

"Uh, no," Minjun said. "Doctor's appointments."

"So what's the next excuse you're going to throw at me that I can knock down?" Yongjoon stared at Maliah.

"I work on Friday, most of the day. That's the reason we're going bowling on Friday. Because I'll be in time for... space bowling."

Min giggled. "Cosmic bowling."

"Whatever. Intergalactic travel bowling."

"Fair enough, but you can spend the night. Come back tomorrow," Yongjoon pointed out. "It isn't that far of a drive."

She sighed, looking at him.

"Okay, enough of this," Yong stared at Liah, "What do you have against my mom?"

"I don't have anything against your mom, I don't know her."

"You were hesitant to accept my Thanksgiving invitation, you refuse to come over. It's either me or my mom; you seem mostly fine with me. So spill. We aren't leaving this room until you do." He crossed his arms, waiting.

Seong didn't realize there was an issue up until this point. Liah's excuses were seamless. "This seems like this is between you two. We're going to let you talk." Without waiting, he pulled Min out of the study room, closing the door behind them.

He was fully dressed when they walked back into the suite. Seong was in the middle of folding the blankets when Liah walked up to help. "I got it but thank you. You have your voice back."

"Yeah. It still feels a little scratchy." She grabbed her throat.

"Go get ready for work; I'll make you a cup of tea before you go." He grabbed the bedding off the floor.

"Thank you." She ran to get ready.

"Will we be able to leave right after she gets done?" Yongjoon asked. "Mom is beyond curious about her."

"She'll need to pack a bag so she's ready. She's running a bit behind right now," Seonghun said. He picked up the dishes, put them in the sink, and closed her laptop, making sure the SD card wasn't in the slot. He walked into her room, placing the SD card in the top drawer of her desk before setting her laptop down. Yong was staring at the condom wrapper as he walked out. He looked up as Seong started roaring with laughter.

"Look, there was too much going on in that call. I heard a song say, 'pussy for breakfast that's how I start my day', then there was the condom picture, then you hung up the phone on me," Yongjoon said.

"The song was part of the joke. She turned on the playlist to freak you guys out a little more. The condom, well, things were happening; if they progressed, I wanted to be prepared. Finally, the hang-up was accidental, but she uh," his cheeks turned pink, "I had to attend to something."

"Fair enough. If you two decide to have sex, I'll keep my nose out of it."

"I appreciate it." Seonghun turned on the kettle. "What about two?"

Yong laughed. "I think his interest in your sex life is because of the decline in his own."

"You two haven't?" Seong was shocked.

"He's holding back. I'm not sure why; I haven't broached the topic because I'm comfortable where we're at. If it starts to hinder the relationship we'll talk," Yongjoon explained.

Maliah walked out of her room; Seonghun handed her the tea mug.

"Thank you."

"You're welcome. I was wondering, would you feel comfortable with me packing an overnight bag for you? I know it's about time for you to go; Yong would like to leave as soon as you're done with work." He poured himself a cup of the fragrant tea.

"Normally, no, I wouldn't have an issue, but his mom told me to bring my dirty clothes to wash. I uh, don't want you in my dirty clothes."

"Pack the stuff you don't want me to touch, I'll take care of the rest. Do you have an overnight bag?"

She nodded.

"Pack, then leave the bag on the bed when you're done. You can shoot me a text of everything else you need." She ran in the room, making quick of the things she needed.

His phone went off and he saw the small list. She came out of the room. "If you drop me off, you can pick me up and just drive to Indy."

"You don't mind me taking your car?" he asked, surprised.

"You've driven it before, I don't think you'd be joyriding." She drained the last of her tea, rinsed out her cup before setting it to the side. "I need to go."

He grabbed his wallet as she tossed him her keys.

"I want to go. Can we go to that diner for breakfast?" Minjun asked as he came out of his room.

Seonghun shrugged. "Sure. Yong, come get breakfast."

"I'll meet you there, I need to grab a few things."

Maliah looked at him. "Detective Krishna said we should be using the buddy system."

Yong grinned widely, both dimples showing. "No offense, but I'm really not concerned about that girl on my behalf."

She looked at Seong for an explanation.

"You'll see later," he replied. "There is a reason he's the one that offered to teach you how to throw a punch. Come on."

CHAPTER 34

Seonghun dropped Maliah off in downtown Lafayette at an office building. "The art gallery is literally two buildings down, so I don't need a ride there." She pointed at the building. "Pick me up at quarter to three."

She moved to get out of the car, but he tugged her arm. "Have a good day." He leaned over to give her a quick peck.

"Thank you. You guys too." She waved at Minjun in the back seat before shutting the door. He waited until she got safely in the building before pulling off to the diner.

"Seong?"

"Yeah?"

"What's going to happen with you two when we go back to Korea?" Minjun looked at him in the rearview mirror.

"We've been together for barely a month, Min, I'm not really thinking about that right now." He pulled into the parking garage by the diner. "What about you and Yong?"

"I know he applied to law school in Washington D.C. I applied to the US diplomatic office in Korea. If I get the job, I'll have to travel to Washington." Once the car stopped, Min got out.

Seonghun got out as well. "It's that serious?"

"It is for me," he looked at his friend of over twenty years, "I love him."

"Oh, Min." He slung an arm around his friend. "I'm happy for you."

"It's scary. I haven't told him yet. I don't know when or how. It seems fast."

"Well, we've known each other for years, your relationship just shifted, that's all."

"I know he thinks I'm frivolous and I don't think before I speak. I want —" he paused briefly. "I want him to know that this isn't me just going on a whim. I haven't figured out how to tell him that though."

"You'll sort it out and make it special. I believe in you." Seonghun opened the door. The owner was sitting at the cashier's stand again.

"Hello there! Your friend just walked in." He pointed over to Yongjoon who already had a mug in front of him. Minjun wandered over to him. "When we get ready to leave, can I get a tea to go? My girlfriend's throat isn't feeling that great," Seonghun asked him.

"Is your girlfriend the nice young woman that gets the BLTs?" he asked.

Seong nodded.

"I like that very much. Nice to see she isn't alone. Yes, I'll get you squared away. Any particular kind? We have black tea, raspberry, lemon ginger, and orange pekoe."

"Lemon ginger please, with honey."

"I'll have it ready for you when it's time to pay."

Seonghun smiled at the man before making his way over to his friends. "Did Liah get off to work well?" Yongjoon asked.

"Yes. She looks a little tired though," Seong noted.

"Did you keep her up?"

"No, we watched Jeopardy and crashed."

Minjun laughed. "You sound like an old married couple."

He thought for a minute before he spoke. "She's always on the go. I think she likes just sitting there when she has the chance. Also, it's an opportunity for me to learn more about her. We talk a lot when we're sitting there like that." Just then a waitress came up to take their order. Seonghun didn't even bother looking at the menu, ordering The Challenge. His roommates ordered pancakes.

"They aren't my mom's pancakes." Yongjoon sighed.

"Why did you two rush back up here anyway? I mean, even if we were messing around, what were you going to say?" Seonghun asked.

"Nothing. We were just absolutely confused at what was going on," Minjun said.

Seonghun then filled them in on what happened last night in the photography studio, leaving out some of the details.

"So wait, she found you, charmed her way in, took pictures, then left?" Yongjoon asked. "What did she get pictures of?"

"According to the timestamp from what we saw in security, nothing. Just us cleaning up."

"What were you taking pictures of?" Minjun asked as he grabbed his boyfriend's coffee.

"Hey! You ordered orange juice."

"Because you already had coffee," Minjun explained. He took a sip before handing it back, waiting for Seong's answer.

"Initially, Liah wanted to draw me, but she changed her mind, taking photos instead." He'd practiced this; since it wasn't an actual lie, he didn't turn red or look suspicious.

"That's nice. You think she'd take a professional picture of me?" Min wondered.

"She may be a little wary about going back to that place, but it couldn't hurt to ask," Seonghun said. The plates of food came out. His friends eyeballed Seonghun's massive messy breakfast. "I have been dreaming of this since the first time I had it." He began cutting into the gravy topped breakfast.

"When did you have it?" Yongjoon asked.

"A month ago when I took Liah to the park. She brought me here for breakfast; we split it. It was more, she ate like a quarter of it, while I ate the rest."

"You know, I knew something was up that day. You're never out the door on a non-class day. I was so baffled," Minjun said, dumping syrup on his pancakes.

"I would have told you eventually. You see how she is. I didn't want to have her running in the opposite direction. I like talking to her. Every time she opens her mouth, she surprises me. Did you know her favorite movies are the Marvel movies?" he asked his friends.

"Well, that's cool. We can do a movie marathon over Thanksgiving break. I wonder if she'd make the cereal mix for that?" Yong asked. He pulled out his phone, sending his mom a text. "Mom said she'd make sure the ingredients were at the house for it."

"What did you two talk about in the study room?" Seonghun asked casually.

"I called Mom. She now wants Liah to have my babies," he said matter-of-factly.

Seonghun choked. Minjun started giggling. "How did that conversation happen?!" Seonghun set his fork down.

Yongjoon explained the conversation. "She wasn't allowed to have people over at her house. She was scared to death about my mother's reaction. Have you seen her tattoo by chance?"

Seong stared at him. "Yes, and I hope you haven't. Her pants have to be extremely low or off for you to see it."

His friend rolled his eyes. "No, I haven't seen her tattoo, it was just something she said. Something about tattoos covering up scars. Is it a big design?"

"No, it's about this big," He demonstrated with his fingers. "I touched it; it feels different from the skin around it. I didn't want to make her feel weird, so I didn't ask."

"I know it is her life, but I think whatever happened to her at home is worse than she is letting on," Yong said.

Minjun looked at him. "Her parents threw her out of the house as soon as she became an adult. For all they knew she had nothing to help her. I'm not sure it could get much worse. Why would you choose to make your kid homeless just because they got into college? Nothing makes sense."

"She's working with her therapist to confront them, to get some answers," Seong said.

"Why not just go ask?" Minjun drained the rest of his juice.

Yong spoke up, "When you're in a scary situation," he paused as he tried to figure out how to put it, "when you've had things in your life that have traumatized you, made you cautious how you move, how you talk to people, you want as much control as you possibly can get. She needs to feel safe to ask her questions. She needs someone there with her to redirect the conversation if it gets heated."

"Also, some people are master manipulators. The situation with Casey has her twisted up inside. She blames herself for not knowing her options. But how was she to know if the school was only pushing the student court at her?" Seong took a sip of coffee before continuing. "I don't know if she feels any responsibility for what happened as a kid, but if she does, they would know how to manipulate that to make her feel worse. This way, there is a neutral party there to stop things if it goes off topic."

"Are you going to be there?" Yong looked at him.

"I'd go if she asked me, but the only thing she's asked of me thus far is to look at the letter she's going to send when she's ready. She has to figure out how to write the letter without basically pouring her pain onto the page. It has to be neutral. She also needs to figure out what she wants to accomplish with this meeting I think."

"What do you mean?" Minjun asked as he grabbed a bite of Seong's breakfast.

"Well, is she angling for reconciliation? Does she just want reasons why her family treated her poorly? She needs to sort that out." Scarfing down the last of his food, he looked at his friends. "Those are questions only she can answer." He stood up, "I'm going to go take her a cup of tea before I go back to the dorm to pack for both of us."

"Please be mindful of your surroundings," Yongjoon said. "I honestly don't feel comfortable with you going back to the dorm by yourself."

"I know. She won't be expecting me to be driving, I don't think." Seong was fully capable of defending himself, but only Minjun was aware. As far as Yong knew, Seonghun was a pacifist. His stature was imposing; the last thing he wanted to do was scare people when he came out swinging. He waved to his friends before walking to the counter. Paying the bill, the friendly owner held out the tea along with two bags.

"I put honey packets and ginger candies in the one bag. In the other is a slice of lemon pound cake. She seemed to enjoy it the last time she was here with you."

"She loves lemon everything." Seong thanked him. Driving quickly back over to the building, he carefully parallel parked before walking into a beige lobby with people sitting around waiting. An older woman seated at a large gray desk watched as he walked up.

"Can I help you?" she asked.

"Hi, I have a drink for Maliah Evans."

The woman's eyes flashed. "Can I tell her who is here?" Seong gave her his name as she picked up the phone. He could only hear her part of the conversation.

"Maliah, there is a gentleman here with a drink for you." She paused, looking at him. "He's cute." Seonghun blushed. "He's a little nerd chic. I swear if I were twenty years younger…" She teased the younger woman on the phone. "Okay, I'll let him know. Should I show him the video of you headbanging at the Christmas party last year while we wait? Guess you better hurry then." She hung up the phone.

"I will give you twenty dollars cash right now with a slice of lemon pound cake for that headbanging video." He gave her his biggest smile.

She chortled. "Oh, honey, that's my good blackmail. It would take a lot more than that."

Suddenly Maliah came flying out the back with a guitar strapped to her. "Hey, hi, hello. No videos need to be shown, thank you." She turned, looking at Seonghun. "Hey, what's up?"

"Nothing. We just finished eating breakfast; I wanted to bring you tea. I also brought you a slice of cake that I tried to trade for a video but was shot down." He glanced at the woman in front of the computer.

"Diane has been holding onto that video for her moment in the sun. Cake ain't gonna do it." She took the items from his grasp. "Thank you. This was nice."

"Anytime. I'm gonna—" He pointed at the door.

"Okay. I'll talk to you this afternoon." They both stood there awkwardly, not knowing what to do, while Diane watched with amusement from her chair.

"For land's sake, kiss the girl!" Diane called out.

He looked at her, grinning. "You're a handful, aren't you?"

"Nonsense, I keep everyone in line." She smiled at him.

Seonghun brushed his mouth against Maliah's cheek, just as she turned, so he ended up kissing her mouth. *We're in public, keep it toned down,* he thought to himself. He kissed her, briefly before pulling back. "I'll see you this afternoon."

"Bye," she smiled as she headed toward the back.

"You aren't kissing cute men in my lobby and not giving me details, Maliah Evans! Get back here!" Diane trailed after her. He chuckled as he left the building.

When he pulled the car into a space near the dorm, he took a moment to look around. He didn't see anything. Walking toward the building, he continued to assess everything around him. His friends were in Minjun's room with the door closed when he arrived. He walked into his room, immediately pulling out a fresh sheet of writing paper.

L,

It was kind of nice to see where you work, even if it was brief. With all the issues we've been having lately, I'm also relieved that you aren't in plain sight and that someone has to call for you to come up to the front.

About the testing you were talking about in your last note. I have an appointment on Friday for that. It's been a while since I've been sexually active, but if it puts your mind at ease, I have no problems doing it. I was supposed to go with Min, but since he's staying in Indy, he is just going to go somewhere up there. I figured I would drive back with you on Friday, do my appointment here, staying in the dorm until you're ready to go.

Speaking of Indy, since we aren't going out here in West Lafayette, you can't show me your walking trail. Is there some place you like to walk in Indianapolis? I'd like to go on a walk with you. I would also love to take you for wings. I need to find a wing place in Indianapolis though.

Before I continue this note, I had to drop gossip to you. Minjun is in love! He's in love with Yong. It's very exciting. I'm happy for him. I'm also terrified for Yongjoon, because Min does things very big; I'm worried that he's going to show up with an amp outside his classes singing classic Korean love songs. I also want him to show up with an amp outside his classes singing classic Korean love songs. I think I want that for Christmas. In all seriousness though, it is very sweet. He's even started to rearrange his life a bit for him. He applied to the US consulate building in Korea because Yongjoon applied for law school in Washington D.C. He said he would have flights back and forth in the job he applied for. It would be a way to see him.

I knew Min wouldn't be returning to the countryside where we grew up after he graduated and I'm trying not to take it hard. He's been my best friend for so long and he has always been there, I don't know what a day without him is really like. I don't live far from Seoul, about two and a half hours, but it's just odd to not think of him popping up for dinner, or to talk.

I feel a little shaky writing this, but I think it needs to be said. I haven't mentioned plans for the future for us because everything is so new. I hope you don't think that I don't take us seriously, because I do, but at this point it seems weird to talk about it. I have to go back to Korea. You have graduate school. It's been a month. I just felt like something had to be said because I just spent half this letter gushing over our roommates.

Speaking of Yongjoon, I heard you were going to have his babies? I would like to object.

In your last note, you asked me what I wanted with our relationship. Firstly, I need you not to have Yongjoon's babies. That is a hard line. I can tolerate many things but having intercourse with one of my friends is a hard line for me (I'm snickering as I'm writing this). Seriously though. I just need someone I can talk to and laugh with. I like the fact that when we talk you take an interest in my ideas for the farm for the future. You aren't afraid to ask when you don't understand what the hell I'm talking about. I also need you to respect me.

We've already had the discussion, so I won't beat you over the head with it, but yeah, using my body to try and wipe away your pain is a no go for me. When you're with me, I want you with me, not lost in your head. If you're lost in your head and you need me to hold you or listen, I have no problems with that.

I need to pack for both of us. I have your list here and I'll make sure I take care of everything. One more question. Can I show the non-sexual photos to the guys? I told them about those pictures; I think they are going to ask you to take pictures of them. I told them you may be a little shy about shooting at the studio since we have a nutbag loose.

I hope the tea was nice.

Yours,

-S

He sealed it in an envelope, taping a tulip to the front. Seong made his way to her room. Her bright pink duffle bag was sitting on the bed. There was a small compartment to one side that was already stuffed. He assumed those were the things she didn't want him in. Opening up the main compartment, he saw her shower things, bras, socks, and underwear neatly stacked. Smiling, he sent her a text.

Seong: *I would have been more than happy to go through your underwear drawer to get what you needed.*

He went through the list and pulled out everything she requested. Liah mostly hung her things, so he took them off the hangers, folded them neatly, before putting them in the bag. He was packing her schoolbooks when he got a response.

Liah: *I'm sure you would have, but in case you haven't noticed, there is nothing super exciting about my underwear.*
Seong: *Does that mean I can take a look?*
Liah: *Go for it. Second drawer in the closet.*

Dumping the rest of her books into her backpack, he beelined over to her underwear drawer. Most of her bras were simple cotton with pretty designs, same with her panties. He still ruffled through to see if there was anything, and he hit the jackpot at the very bottom. He snapped a picture of the black lacy boy shorts.

Seong: *These are pretty.*
Liah: *I thought so too. Unfortunately, because of the way they are cut, my butt hangs out the bottom. I have a lot of butt, so if it isn't contained, it proceeds to eat my underwear, then I have a permanent wedgie. Not comfortable at all.*
Seong: *Why not try a larger size?*

He packed her laptop and opened the desk drawer. The SD card was missing.

Seong: *Please tell me you have the SD card.*

He tossed the letter in before zipping up her overnight bag. Pulling down her roller skates, he smiled at them. She had white skates that had some sort of cover on each of the toes of the skates in pink. The laces were pink with pom poms. The skates were clipped together with a rainbow suspender. He piled them on top of the bag.

Liah: *Yes I have the SD card. Down the street is a photo shop where I can get the print you wanted, along with prints of the solo photos. I will have those for you today. Also, I just never tried for other underwear. No one usually sees them but me, so the cotton ones worked fine.*
Seong: *Would it be presumptuous if I bought you underwear? Is that a creeper thing to do?*
Liah: *You're allowed to do whatever you feel. However, if you show up and put something like an edible g-string, crotchless panties, or any type of a thong in my face, it won't get worn.*
Seong: *No thongs? At all :)*
Liah: *I'll make you a deal. I will wear whatever thong you buy for me, if you wear a banana hammock when I do.*

Seonghun did a quick search to see what exactly a banana hammock was. After staring at his screen for a moment, he wrote back.

Seong: *Got it, no thongs.*
Liah: *Glad we could come to an agreement. I have a tween crying. I gotta go. I will see you in a few hours.*

He laughed as he pocketed his phone, dragging all of her stuff out into the common area. He walked into his room, grabbed his things, dumping them into his carryon bag. His laundry was already done, so he wasn't worried. He remembered the sweater he bought, along with jeans for Sunday. Fully packed, he set an alarm on his phone for two before taking a small nap.

When Seonghun woke up, he tapped on Minjun's door. Yongjoon

answered, looking drowsy. "I'm going to go pick her up. We'll go to Cho's right after."

"Alright. We'll head out in about fifteen minutes; I'll see you there." Yong closed the door to get ready.

Seonghun gathered up all the bags. As he stood to his full height, he felt a small twinge in his lower back. Setting them down, he walked into his room and grabbed a box of the heating patches. Tossing them into his backpack, he picked everything up. Packing the trunk of the car, he felt like someone was watching him. "I don't know if you can hear me, or if you're even here, but I'm not concerned with you." He spoke in a normal voice. "You're nothing to me, just like you're nothing to her. A bad dream, a memory. That's all you are and all you'll ever be." He closed the trunk. Once inside the car, he locked the doors before putting on his seatbelt. All of a sudden his phone beeped with a message. It was from an unknown number.

Unknown: *Can't be a memory if I'm always around.*

There was a picture of him putting away the camera lights, smiling at Liah. Screenshotting the message, he sent an email to the detective, explaining he was headed out of town, but would be happy to hand over his phone on Monday. He pulled off from the parking lot, refusing to look back.

CHAPTER 35

He stopped at a local coffee shop, picking up an iced americano for himself along with another ginger lemon tea for her. Pulling up to the building she pointed to earlier, he saw her standing outside talking to an older gentleman. Not wanting to interrupt, he put the car in park, waiting. Liah nodded at the gentleman, pointed to Seong, before patting his shoulder gently. Holding out her arm, he took it. Together they shuffled inside the building. She came back out shortly, climbing into the car.

"Hey."

"Hi." He kissed her cheek before handing her the cup of tea.

"Thank you. Is everything okay?"

"Fine mostly. I felt a small twinge in my back. I brought the patches so I can apply later. Who was that guy?"

"My boss, the main curator. He knows what's going on. Lord knows what he would do if someone attacked, but I appreciate the gesture just the same. He's a nice guy, always eager to show me what he knows." She breathed in the steam of the tea. "He's always trying to convince me to change my major to art history. He almost had me at one point. I love art, but it's not where I want to be."

He pulled off, heading toward the highway. "Will you work in a gallery when you go for your graduate program?"

"I think my days at the gallery are done. Dr. Mays is great, but the art world is very snooty. I don't want to perpetuate a system like that. I'd work in a gallery if it were down to earth, but I think I may just find a music store to give lessons while doing the music therapy lessons for a local therapist, wherever I land."

They talked the whole drive to Indianapolis. Seonghun wasn't surprised to see she was leaning towards USC; it was an amazing opportunity. She still had three letters she was waiting on however, so it was still too early to decide.

She listened to the changes he hoped to implement on the farm. He had learned about hybridizing in his classes; it was something he really enjoyed and was planning on eventually putting a greenhouse on his property. He also told her that he'd decided to switch houses with his parents when his father finally retires.

"Why switch?" she asked.

"Well," he blushed slightly, "my house is small, built for a single person. It's not tiny, but not conducive to a family. Their house is. There are updates I would want to do, but it's a really nice house, I think at least."

Thankfully, she glossed over the family part. "What updates do you want to make?" She listened as he spoke of heated flooring, kitchen, and bathroom updates.

"I think your house should be comfortable and inviting. Something you want to come back to at the end of the day," he explained. "My parent's house is fine, but it's theirs. I want to make it my own."

"I can understand that. I'm kind of excited to have an apartment to myself, to hang art while upgrading my old things."

He imagined for a moment them blending their lives and things together. Would they argue over colors? Would she want input on everything?

Too soon, too soon, too soon.

"Are you still considering a pet?" he asked as turned onto 86th street.

"Yeah. Both my therapist and I think it would be good for me to be responsible for something other than just myself. It will keep me from getting into my head too much." She began scrubbing her hands across her pants.

He looked down. "Why are you in jeans? Don't you normally have to wear a dress or dress up at the gallery?"

"Yeah, but I changed back into my normal clothes before you got there. It seemed odd meeting someone in my work clothes." Seong gave her a sideways glance as Liah was breathing deeply, seemingly trying to calm herself. He pulled over into a church parking lot before cutting the engine.

"Take your time," he said quietly.

"Will you tell me a little about her? It helps having as much knowledge as possible going into a situation."

He told her how Cho had taken a very homesick man under her wing, making him feel as much at home as possible. How at one point he missed his mom so badly he just cried. She never judged, just sat with him, listening to everything he missed. She contacted his mom to learn the exact recipe to his favorite meal, making it every time she saw him, no matter what else was on the table. It wasn't a hundred percent his mom's, but it was so close it didn't matter.

"I didn't realize you were so homesick," Maliah said.

"It's not bad now, but the first few months were the worst. I'd never been far away from home; all of a sudden, I was a whole ocean away." He saw the sympathy in her face. "I love my life at home. I love farming. It may sound silly—"

"Why would it sound silly for you to love what you do?" Liah interrupted. "That sounds like a pretty happy life."

"I don't know," he felt bashful, "your career goals seem more like a calling, less self-indulgent."

"One, you can't compare our goals. We're different people. Two," she paused, looking down at her hands before looking back at him, "my goals are self-serving. I'm trying to make lemonade out of lemons as it were. That the abuse, the shame, the cruelty that I faced will bear fruit, making an easier way for someone else. It's trying to somewhat justify it. That it's okay because look what I did with it." She flourished her hand for emphasis. "I helped someone through their pain by calling on my own."

"That sounds painful, to keep bringing it up," he pointed out.

Liah smiled at him. "It may seem like that. But it's not reopening the wound. It's touching the scar tissue. One day it will no longer hurt. But it left its mark; I won't forget."

"I hope—" He turned to face her as much as he could in the little car. "I hope I've left a mark on your life as well. A better one."

"You have. Very much so," she whispered, staring at him.

He kissed her. "You ready?"

She nodded. He turned the car back on and pulled out of the parking lot, turning onto Springmill Road.

He winced as he pulled into the driveway. He probably should have warned her.

"Uh, Seonghun?"

"Yes?"

"None of you told me that Yong or his family were loaded." She stared wide-eyed at the house.

Seong looked at it, remembering the shock, the first time he saw it. Though Yong said it wasn't a mansion, he wasn't sure he believed that. The front of the house was white brick with nine windows and a giant door. The driveway was long and curved, having two entrances. The door was a light-colored wood with black trimmings. The whole property looked as if it could be in a movie. The trees had lost their leaves for the fall, but still were impressive on the side of the house. He honestly loved Yong's home, especially the backyard.

"Would you believe that I forgot?" he asked sheepishly.

When she turned to look at him, he saw the understanding in her eyes. "He doesn't act like the snooty prep school kids I went to school with, so I get it."

"He's used to people wanting to hang with him because he has money, so he doesn't mention it," he explained to her.

"I got it." They grabbed their things. He felt the twinge in his back again; this time she noticed. "I'll put a patch on you shortly." She looked at him, making sure he was okay to carry his stuff. He headed toward the door with her following behind. When he opened the front door, he heard her make a noise. Seong turned around.

"Y-you're not gonna knock?"

He was confused. "Why would I knock? They're expecting us." He shrugged as he stepped inside the large foyer, dropping his bags before removing his shoes. She followed suit.

"Hello?" Seonghun called out.

"Kitchen!" Yong called out.

They walked in to find him face first in a plate of pancakes. Seonghun laughed but when he turned around he saw Maliah staring at the stove range like she saw a ghost.

"Are you okay?" He looked at her worriedly.

"T-that's a Bertazzoni professional series stove." She looked at him. "I've only seen it in magazines."

The boys turned to look at her. "What kind of magazines are you reading that have stoves with their specific names?" Minjun asked.

"I like magazines on house design. When I was a kid, I would cut the pictures out, making the houses I wanted to live in. I don't cut out pictures anymore, but I still look at the magazines. I have a subscription to one," she explained, still staring at the stove.

"You can touch it if you want," a woman's voice said.

Maliah turned away from Minjun, looking at the newcomer in the kitchen. Unconsciously she slid closer to Seong.

Cho Pae looked like she made a copy of her face, putting it on Yongjoon's body. They had the same dimples, same mouth, and same small eyes. Her eyes were a lighter brown than his with none of the gold flecks. Her cheeks were chubbier, making her look younger than her son.

"Hello, you must be the woman that is having my grandchildren. I'm Cho."

Maliah snorted.

"Ma, she's not having my babies. She has no interest in having my babies. She's dating the tall one she's trying to strategically hide behind. So, if any babies were to be had, they would be his." Yong took another bite of pancakes, smacking Minjun's hand as he tried to reach over with a fork. "It's your fault I couldn't have these sooner."

"H-hi. I m-made you a thank you gift, but I wasn't expecting to come this soon, so it isn't ready yet." Maliah finally spoke. "Also, I'm n-n-not having anyone's child. It's hard enough taking care of myself."

"That is very nice of you. I'm sure I will love it." Seong saw the look in Cho's eyes as she stared at Liah who was trying to make herself look smaller. "Why don't you come with me? I'll show you where you're staying and where the laundry room is."

"Okay." She looked at Seonghun to see if he was coming. A quick glance at Cho indicated he was not invited on this tour. "I'll be right here, eating pancakes."

"Mine," his friend said, polishing off a stack.

"Okay, I'll be here fighting Yongjoon for pancake supremacy." He gave Maliah a half smile.

At her mildly panicked look, he nearly spoke up, but something stopped him. Cho gently tugged Maliah's hand, leading her out of the room. Walking over to the stove where a large portion of pancakes were being held in a warmer, Seong grabbed himself a portion before going into the refrigerator for milk. He held up the container, looking at his friends who both nodded. Pulling down two glasses, he filled both before walking over to fill their glasses as well. Finally, he walked over with his plate and glasses of milk.

"Why two?" Minjun asked.

"Maliah, when she comes back," he explained, shoving a whole pancake in his mouth. They were chattering when Maliah walked back into the room.

"Yongjoon, your mom is killing me." She sat in the seat next to Seonghun, "She asked if I went to school around here. I told her I went to Brebeuf. She stared at me for a moment, walked off, pulled out an album, then asked me how I felt about Korean baby names. She also told me to tell you that she was willing to bend her rules. What rules? Have you told her about Min?"

"She's basically saying that she'd let you sleep in the same room with me. Yes, Mom is well aware of Minjun, loves him to death, and supports us both, but it's been a while since I brought anyone over that had ovaries. Also, she really wants grandchildren." He drained his glass of milk. "She'll calm down in a little bit once she sees you with Seong."

Maliah nodded. "Okay. Also, your baby butt was cute, Yongie." She hid her smirk behind the glass of milk Seonghun slid her. He choked as Min laughed uproariously.

Yongjoon stood up. "AY MA! YOU CAN'T SHOW MY NAKED BUTT TO EVERY PERSON THAT COMES THROUGH THE DOOR!" He grabbed Minjun's hand, tugging him to help him find his mom.

"Do you want to see my favorite part of Yong's house?" Seong asked. He offered her the last bite of pancake on his plate.

She nodded, chewing the fluffy cake. He stood, cleaning off the table. "Can you grab the plates?"

Maliah did as he asked, following behind. He rinsed everything, before setting them in the dishwasher. Grabbing her hand, he picked up their shoes, leading her out the back door. "Look."

"Oh my god." Maliah walked forward. The backyard looked like a very fancy park. There were topiaries, a large pond, places to sit, and in one corner a hammock. It had started snowing, so everything was coated in a light dusting of white snow. "This is beautiful."

"It's prettier in the summer when everything is green. She planted the tulip bulbs I gave her out here too." He watched her walk around, looking at everything. Seong noticed she only had a sweatshirt on. "Liah, you need a coat."

"I hate coats. Too bulky." She walked over to the pond, peering in.

He reached in his pocket for his hat. "Come here."

She walked over; he put the hat over her head. "Your nose is red." He kissed the tip of her nose. "You really need to wear a coat," he chided.

"I will wear every hat, glove, scarf, boot, earmuff, any winter accessory you can think of. I just really hate winter coats. I feel stuffed into them at best, swallowed by them at worst."

"Talk to Min. He'll find you something you love. He's really good at that actually."

"Seong, he keeps trying to shove me into clothes that show my legs, belly, and boobs. This man will find the first fuzzy halter coat," she deadpanned.

"I think you made your point crystal clear at the mall. He should behave now," Seong said. "Look at it this way, you don't need to be in a dressing room to try on a coat."

"True."

He kissed her mouth this time. They were lost in each other for a moment before Maliah tapped him gently on the leg. "Sorry," he blushed, "didn't mean to get carried away."

"No apologies needed; you weren't the only one." She looked up at him. "Oh my god! I forgot! We need to go to the car." He grabbed her hand and pulled her to the side gate, leading her to the front. When she got to her car she got into the backseat and motioned for him to do the same.

"I thought we were too old for car sex?" He grinned.

"You have a one-track mind lately," she teased him.

"Yeah, you sort of started that in the studio," he admitted. "It's kind of hard focusing when I—" He closed his mouth quickly.

"When you... think of your mouth on me? Or think of mine on you?" She blinked at him innocently.

"Both. Definitely both." He closed his eyes and tried to focus on anything else.

He heard her unzipping something. Opening his eyes, he saw it was the bag she put in the back when Seong picked her up from work. She tossed him a small packet. "Those are the safe photos. I printed everything, so you have copies. These," she waved a green envelope around, "are not safe for work, life, or anywhere else but your own personal hands. Keep 'em secret, keep 'em safe, please."

He nodded. "I'll keep them in the car for now. When we get back to the dorm, I'll lock them up," he promised her.

She slid a bigger envelope out. "I did more edits to the photo before I printed it." She slid out the one he requested for framing.

"Oh my god." He looked down. They looked sleek. She'd emphasized the veins in his arms and the grip he had on her thigh. He was grateful that she didn't start hacking at her body again. "This is beautiful."

"What's beautiful?"

"Why are you two in the backseat of the car? I know Mom said no sleeping together in her house, but she's not going to like you trying to have sex in a car right outside her house."

Their friends climbed in the front seat, turned, looking at the two of them. Seonghun tossed the safe packet of pictures at them. "Liah was just showing me the pictures from the studio," he explained.

He watched as she discreetly pushed the green envelope back in her bag.

"What's the big print?" Minjun asked.

"When I picked her up at the gallery, they had these sensual prints for sale. I bought one," he lied smoothly. He went to put it back in the envelope, but Yongjoon grabbed it. Maliah clutched Seonghun's thigh as if to stop herself from snatching it back.

"That's the kind of art I'd put up in my apartment. It's pretty." Yong handed it to Min.

Minjun stared hard. "Yes. It's very elegant." He handed it back to Seong.

"You guys come back soon. It's cold out here." Yong left, running into the house.

Min watched as he walked in before turning back around.

"It was a good lie you two, but it was a lie. I can see now why you were worried about Casey seeing you in the studio." Minjun looked at both of them.

"What are you talking about?" Maliah looked at him with wide eyes.

"I've known this man longer than you have been born—"

Maliah interrupted Minjun. "I'm only two years younger than you," she pointed out.

"I've known him that long." Minjun grabbed the print, pointing at the finger on his hand. "He broke that finger when we were twelve, the doctor didn't set it right, so it's slightly crooked." He looked at Maliah who was looking more and more horrified. "If that's him, then that's you. He wouldn't touch another woman like that, art or no, while he's dating you."

"Min," Seonghun warned him, "you need to keep this quiet. We already had one scare with Casey."

"It's an art print, it's not bad or wicked or even overtly sexual. Well yeah, it's overtly sexual, but it's an art print. It's not like you were—" He stopped when he saw Seonghun's face blaze purple. "Oh. You were. Well then." Minjun cleared his throat. "Anyway, it's not my place nor my business, but if you were thinking of hanging that up in your room, it's only going to take Yongjoon three or four looks at that print to figure out what I did. Just FYI."

Seong looked at Maliah who looked almost catatonic. "Please calm down. No one here is going to say anything. It's art."

"The other pictures aren't," she whispered softly.

"No one will see those. Only you or me. Okay?"

"I'd like to see the other pictures," Minjun spoke up.

Seonghun and Maliah spoke at the same time. "No you don't."

"You're welcome to see the pictures in the yellow packet. Those are the ones I took of Seong."

Minjun hesitated for a minute. "Can you take pictures that look like this with people partially clothed?"

Maliah thought about it. "The clothing would have to be miniscule; I'd probably still have to finesse the editing."

"If I could convince Yong to pose, would you take our picture?"

Maliah looked at him. "If I shoot you two, present the photos, he'd know that the one he just saw isn't an art print."

"Yes, but he would assume you had on skimpy clothes like we'd have," Minjun pointed out.

Maliah sighed. "Let me think about it and do some research. I'm not typically a portrait taker, I take pictures of things. I think we kind of got lucky with this."

Everyone stepped out of the car. Minjun opened the packet of photos. He stopped walking as he stared at them. "These are really good. How did you get him to look like that?"

"What do you mean? That's how he looks." Maliah looked over at the picture.

"No, he looks like an actual model," Min said.

"Min, that is how he looks every single day. I swear, I did nothing but add lighting and tell him where to stand. I edited shadows, but that's about it." Maliah took the photos from him, flipping through. "I did a little heavier editing on this one, but this is the heaviest I did."

The men stared at the photo. His head was turned away from the camera, his shirt was off, and he was almost glowing. Minjun looked at her.

"Do research. Do all the research. Do you need me to buy you photography books? Because I'll do it. I want you to take our pictures." He took the packet before running into the house, hollering for Yong.

"You're really talented, you know that?" Seong looked at her. "You could be an artist if that was your dream."

"It's just a hobby. I love it, but it isn't where my heart is." Sliding her shoes off, she looked at him. "It makes me happy you like your pictures though. You're beautiful."

He didn't know what to say. "I don't think I'm ugly, but I'm not sure beautiful is the word I would use."

"I would. You're beautiful. You have eyes that crinkle up when you laugh, your smile is genuine. You have this full pouty mouth. You have these long fingers that…" She grinned to herself. "Anyway, you have sort of this nerdy look when you have your glasses on that makes it easier to approach you. You're kind of intimidating with your glasses off."

Seonghun stood there stunned.

"I'm going to do laundry. I'll see you in a bit." He automatically bent so she could kiss his cheek. Liah left him there, contemplating her words.

SEONG WANDERED around the house for a bit, searching for his friends. He finally ran upstairs to Yong's room. Normally he'd just open the door, but things were changing these days, so he knocked. His roommate opened the door, ushering him in. "Just so you know, Mom said you need to change rooms."

Seonghun looked at him. "Why?"

"Because she put Maliah in that feminine purple room. It's right next door to yours. You need to be in the room on the opposite side of mine."

"I'm going to talk to Cho really quick after this. I respect her, but she's being a little chaotic. She told us how she felt. If I was intent on breaking the rules, me being two doors down is no more of a deterrent than being one door down," he huffed.

"What's got you in a twist?" Yong asked.

"Do you think I'm beautiful?" he asked them.

"Seong, I've been telling you how handsome you are since we were like eighteen. You know you're attractive," Minjun said, flipping through a magazine. "You've brushed off the comments for years."

"I know I'm not ugly, but I've never heard anyone use the term beautiful," he said. "She called me beautiful. It isn't the first time."

Yongjoon looked at him. "Why are you so ruffled by this?"

"I don't know. She says these things and it's like she has a grip on my heart. I don't know what to do." He looked at them before shutting the door quietly. "We were talking on the way up here. I mentioned when my dad finally retires, we're trading houses, because their house is more of a home to start a family in. All I can think about is starting a family with her." He looked at his friends. "It is way too soon to even think that. She's the first girl I've ever—" He closed his mouth abruptly.

His friends waited patiently for him to figure out what he was going to say. "It's been a month. One month. I want to fight every single battle for this girl." He felt the pressure building in his chest and his eyes welling. "The way she lays out her thoughts make me want to listen to her speak forever. I want all of her."

Minjun was silent.

Yongjoon spoke up again. "Are you okay?"

He shook his head. "It feels like I've been sucker punched in my chest when I think about this. I want to make her happy. I love how well she interacts with you guys. I want to introduce her to my mom," he blurted.

"Have you talked to her about how you feel?" Min asked.

"I barely understand how I feel. Me talking to her right now would basically consist of me handing her a garbled word ball. I have to figure out what I'm trying to say before I say anything to her."

"That sounds like a good plan," Min said slowly.

"Thanks for listening. I'm going to go talk to your mom, Yong." With that he left the room.

CHAPTER 36

Seonghun went in search of Cho, finding her in the kitchen starting dinner. He rested his head on her shoulder, pouting. "Yongie said you'd try to break me down on the room situation." Cho didn't even bother looking at him, just kept stirring the pot on the stove. "He's tried for way longer than you. No dice."

"It's not even that I want to do anything with her. I like being close to her. We haven't even taken that step yet," he protested.

"And you won't be taking it in my house. She seemed very accepting of the rules," she pointed out.

"If you told Liah she had to sleep in the basement because you didn't want her anywhere near us, she'd comply," he said dryly. "She's a rule follower; you make her nervous."

Cho turned around at that. "What did I do?"

He hesitated before speaking. "Did Yongjoon actually tell you why she stays at the dorms during the holidays?"

"He said that she doesn't get along with her parents."

"That's putting it mildly. Liah hasn't seen her parents in two years. They kicked her out when she was accepted into Silver Leaf. She doesn't really know why; she just knows they didn't want her to go off to college."

Seong looked at her. "There was also a lot of emotional abuse. I suspect some physical abuse as well. Parents make her nervous."

"It explains a lot," Cho pulled out a small spoon to give Seonghun a taste, "she avoids the touch of people she doesn't know."

"Yeah, she'll let us touch her arm, or her side. We have to be careful touching her face or just grabbing her. That has nothing to do with her parents, I don't think. She's been through a lot of shit."

"Language."

"Sorry. Anyway, I understand your rules. But do I really need to switch rooms? What is the difference being two rooms away going to make?"

Cho sighed and looked at the young man. "Do you see how you look at her? You follow her around half the time like a lost puppy. You always have a hand on her. One of you is constantly reaching for the other. I'm trying to prevent disaster as best as I can."

"Disaster isn't going to strike, Cho. We have no intentions of having sex any time soon."

"You can keep the room you always stay in."

"Thank you!" he beamed.

"I mean it, Seonghun, no sneaking into her room tonight. I highly doubt she'll sneak into yours."

"She might if she has a nightmare. She hasn't had one in a while, but we're sleeping in a new place."

"If she has a nightmare, you two need to come downstairs and sleep in the living room."

"We will." He put his spoon in the sink, giving her a quick kiss on the cheek before going to the laundry room. When he walked in, Maliah was bent over the washing machine reading a textbook with earbuds in. Coming up behind her, he gently grabbed her waist. He felt her stiffen for a second but relax almost instantly. Standing up she turned around. "Hey."

"Hi. Are you okay?"

"I'm fine, doing my laundry. I'm almost finished if you need to get in."

"You haven't been down here long; I take it you didn't have much?" he asked.

"Not really, I try not to let my laundry get out of hand. I had two loads."

"You know, you could study in the kitchen with Cho. She'd probably like the company."

"I-I didn't want to bother her." He saw her look longingly up the steps.

"She'd let you cook on the stove if you asked, you know."

She hid a smile. "Is it that obvious?"

He laughed at her, "Yes. What's the big deal?"

"My parents don't own their home. They rent a townhouse; the stove is shitty. Our stove at the dorm is okay but doesn't heat evenly. I like to cook. I get joy out of making things for other people but making cookies in that oven at the dorm is impossible."

A voice that was coming closer called out, "You're welcome to use the kitchen for anything you like. I have no problems sharing." Cho stepped into the doorway.

Liah tried to subtly slide behind Seonghun. He wouldn't let her.

"T-thank you," she said quietly.

"It's not a problem. Would you like to help with dinner?" Cho stared as if she were fascinated by her.

"I-uh." She looked at Seonghun.

"I'll take care of your laundry. Go on." He knew how hard it was for her to be around people she didn't know, but he had a feeling Cho would be good for her.

"O-ok. M-my basket is right th-there. If you just put the dry clothes in there, I'll fold them." He kissed her forehead and pushed her toward the door. As she left, he flipped through her book, wondering about what Cho said. He skimmed a paragraph on the hippocampus. Pulling out his phone he texted Shiwon.

Seong: *I have a question.*

Shiwon: *Whoa, long time no talk, where the hell have you been? Prof told me you were excused until Monday, but he didn't tell me what was going on.*
BTW, we have to make up our lab on Monday. Can you stay after class to work on it?

Seong: *Yeah, that isn't a problem. Sorry about it, I should have been in communication with you. Casey assaulted my best friend. They put a warrant* *out for her arrest, but when they went to get her, they found that she had moved out of her dorm. They aren't sure how long ago.*

Shiwon: *She's in a sorority, I've made out with quite a few girls in that house. I've seen her there.*

Seong: *They booted her after they found out about the lab incident.*

Shiwon: *Craziness. What did you need to ask me?*

Seong: *Do I look weird at Maliah?*

Shiwon: *I don't think so. You look at her like you're half in love with her. If she asked you to jump out a window, you might question it briefly, but you'd still jump.*

Seong: *Gee, thanks.*

Shiwon: *Not a problem. It's not a bad thing. You're always checking for Shorty. Making sure she's comfortable, that sort of thing. She always looks to you as well, so I would assume the half in love feeling is mutual. She thinks my face is cute, but she likes you.*

Seong: *How do you know she thinks your face is cute?*

Shiwon: *Because I'm Pok Shiwon. ;)*

Seong: *Bye Shiwon.*

Snorting he put his phone up. Half in love. *What does it mean to be half in love with someone?* He sat on the dryer, thinking. He barely introduced his ex-girlfriend to his parents. She pushed the issue, wanting to be close to his family. How would he feel introducing Maliah? Taking out his phone again he switched his keyboard and began to type. It was incredibly early, but his dad would have been up already for at least an hour.

Seong: *Papa, if I met someone here, how would you feel about it?*

Papa: *What do you mean?*

Seong: *She isn't Korean or Korean American.*

Papa: *How serious is it? It must be serious because your last girlfriend had to pull teeth to get you to bring her over.*

Seong: *I like her a lot; a friend told me I look at her as if I'm half in love with her. I haven't sorted my feelings out about it yet.*

Papa: *Sort your feelings out. I'm here if you want to talk about it, but you*

need to actually figure out what you want. It may also help to figure out what she wants. What is her name?
Seong: *Maliah (Mah Lee Ya)*
Papa: *Interesting name. You have a picture?*

Seonghun scrolled through his phone and sent his father a picture of Maliah with Minjun on her lap, running her fingers through his hair.

Papa: *You boys are going to fight over her? You've never fought over a girl before.*
Seong: *He's her friend. Min is seeing someone right now.*
Papa: *Well, she is very pretty. You know you'd have to explain some things to her if she came over here, right? The stares she would get, the outright rudeness at times. She'd have to learn to read, write, and speak a whole new language.*
Seong: *I know.*
Papa: *Figure out what's in your heart son. Talk to the girl. Worry about the rest later.*
Seong: *Thank you. Love you.*
Papa: *I love you too. Next time I want a picture of you two together. Text your mother soon. She worries.*

The washer had stopped. Pulling her basket over, he pulled her clothes out of the dryer, throwing the wet ones in the dryer. He threw in a couple of dryer sheets before turning it on. He saw that the majority of the dry ones were her under things. He folded her underwear and bras as best as he could as he thought about her not being around to talk to, or cooking. He thought about watching her study, her dry wit, and the strength in which she got Casey away from him. He thought about how she reacted when he was pushed in the street. She came to him with no other concern but him. How she always sought him out for comfort, even when she was used to doing things by herself. He thought of passing letters, sharing ice cream; her love of lemon. The feeling in his chest wanted to burst.

He also looked realistically at the time they'd been together. Their lives were set on two different courses. He couldn't stay. Even if he wanted to, he couldn't. He also didn't want to stay. He missed his home. He knew he would miss her fiercely though. Would she want to come to Korea if he asked? Could she be a practicing therapist in Korea? Would she need other credentials?

She liked expensive things; he'd seen for himself. She had no problems saving to get the things she wanted. Living on a farm wouldn't give her the opportunity to use that fancy four-thousand-dollar purse if she bought it. Could she be satisfied being a farmer's wife?

Wife? We're just dating. Where did wife come from? He shook his head before leaving the basement with the freshly folded laundry, his head still as confused as before. When he got to the kitchen, Liah was stirring something, but Cho was nowhere to be found. She turned around, relaxing when she saw Seong.

"When Mrs. Pae heard I liked to bake, she ran to the store because she didn't have a lot of things here. I told her that wasn't necessary, but she insisted." She cut the stove, putting the pot on a cooler part of the range.

"Have the others come down?" Seonghun asked.

"No. I haven't seen them."

"They usually stay downstairs. Where are they at?" he wondered.

Liah snorted. "They're in a relationship, have a bed bigger than that tiny twin bed we have at the dorms, and we haven't seen them for over an hour. Where the hell do you think they are?"

"Oh."

"Indeed." She looked at the basket in his hands. "Thank you. You didn't have to fold anything."

"I wanted to, though I may have mangled your bras. I've never actually folded one before." His mind was preoccupied with the thought of the king size bed he usually slept in upstairs.

"It's fine, I can refold if it's too—" She stopped talking as he stalked closer. "What are you doing?"

"We're in a house, alone," he pointed out.

"I'm not disrespecting this woman's house or her rules because your hormones are running wild." She crossed her arms.

"Can I at least kiss you? What's the harm in kissing me?" He looked at her with an entirely too innocent look on his face.

"Sure," she shrugged.

He stalked over, laying claim to her mouth, pulling her roughly against him. Typically, of the two of them, she wasn't as vocal, but he was delighted to hear a low moan escape from her throat. He worked his way over to her ear, down her throat. "Come upstairs with me," he whispered softly.

"God, I can't, we can't," she moaned.

"She really can't. My mom finds out, she will never let you forget."

They jumped apart. Yong walked in the kitchen with just his pants on, opening the refrigerator.

"I—" Liah opened her mouth, closing it quickly. Grabbing her laundry, she raced up the stairs. Both men heard her door shut.

"Did you have to—"

"Yeah, I did." Yongjoon poured two glasses of juice. "I get it. You want her. From the looks of it she wants you as well, but you can't. Not here. Also do you honestly feel like she's ready for sex? Are you ready for sex?"

"No, on both counts."

"There's no reason for you to take it upstairs. Have you realized that every time you two get a moment alone, you both get carried away?" he pointed out.

"Not the last time. We went exactly where we wanted to," Seong protested.

"I'm not telling you or her how to live your lives. You're both adults. But you need to get a grip on your hormones. Figure shit out so you aren't banging for the first time in your friend's mom's house." He arched his brow. "She deserves more than that. So do you."

"Why does everyone assume we're going to have sex the minute we're alone!? NEITHER OF US ARE READY FOR SEX!" Seonghun yelled, frustrated. "I like being with her, I just like laying with her. We've had discussions on this. Neither of us are ready!" He stormed out of the house.

CHAPTER 37

Seonghun didn't know how long he was at the park. It was one of his favorite places to go around Yongjoon's. In the spring it was green; he liked to watch all of the families barbecue. Sometimes Cho would pack him a simple lunch. He'd lay on the grass, reading whatever book he had. Seong had grabbed his coat on the way out, but didn't grab a book, so he was just sitting there lost in his thoughts. All of a sudden, a book waved under his nose. Looking up he saw Maliah looking at him sympathetically. She sat beside him on the hard stone bench.

"You want to talk about it?"

He turned to look at her. There was no judgment in her eyes. He dug his hand into the pocket of her sweatshirt, pulling out his hat. Seong sat it on her head. "It's cold. I don't want you getting sick." He stared out at the swing set. "It feels like everyone thinks I'm just this massive raging ball of hormones that is using every opportunity to try to get into your pants," he finally said. "I care more about you than that. If you told me you didn't want me to touch you anymore, it wouldn't stop me from lo-liking you as much as I do." He stumbled over his words.

"I don't think anyone thinks that. If they do, well, they're dumb. You show me how much you care every single day." Liah wiggled her feet before she spoke again. "Have you ever heard of the love languages?"

He shook his head.

"It's kind of an old book, but it started resurging in popularity a few years ago," she explained. "It explains how you give and receive love. Yours would be physical touch. You like hugs, being held, and... other things. It's how you like to give affection and receive it as well."

He'd never heard of this before. "What are the other languages? What's yours?"

"How about I tell them to you, then you can guess what mine is?" She pulled out her phone, searching for the information. "They are physical touch, words of affirmation, acts of service, receiving gifts, and quality time." She paused, looking at them. "I think you're a combination of physical touch and quality time, which makes sense. I feel like those two go hand in hand."

"I think you are acts of service and words of affirmation," Seong guessed.

"I'm a combo of those, yes, with a small bit of receiving gifts. I don't want random crap given to me as a gift, but a well thought out, intentioned gift warms my heart."

"So me just showing up with a random gift isn't appreciated?" he questioned.

She started to shiver, so he pulled her up from the bench to make their way back to Cho's. "Well, a gift given usually means someone thought enough of me to get me something, so I'll be grateful. It's just I appreciate it more if it's something that shows you really know me."

"I get it," he said.

"Speaking of gifts, Minjun's birthday is next week," she said. "I wanted to show you what I got him."

"He's kind of like you in the fact that he appreciates all gifts," Seonghun said.

"I figured, but he's feeling self-conscious about his bruise, he's in love for the first time—"

"He told you?" Seonghun asked, surprised.

"No. But I'm not dumb. He's in love. The looks he gives Yong..." She gave him a bright smile. "Have you ever seen something that made you so happy it felt like your heart was going to burst?"

He stared directly into her eyes before replying, "Yes."

Her cheeks, already flushed with cold, turned even redder. "Oh. Well, when I see him look at Yongjoon, it feels like that. I'm happy for him."

He stopped walking so she did too. "Is that," he cleared his throat, "is that the only time your heart feels like it's going to burst?"

"No."

He leaned down to kiss her.

"I feel a strange heart pang when Shiwon tosses his hair." She smirked, running down the street cackling madly before he could grab her.

He chased her after a moment, his long legs catching up to her quickly. Wrapping his arms around her, she squealed as he lifted her up. "Shiwon's hair huh? That's it?"

She was giggling. "Put me down really quick."

Setting her back on her feet, she turned around to face him. "When you do your little wiggle after getting Jeopardy answers right, when you have a bite of food that is really good to you." Her eyes looked a little teary. "When you look at me like I'm the only person around. All those things give me the same feeling." She blinked quickly, Seong thought he must have imagined the tears.

He touched her face, gently kissing her. He would have continued to kiss her, but her shivers were getting worse. "Come on." He grabbed her hand, pulling her towards the house. "How did you know where to find me anyway?"

"We're somewhat close to my high school. I just thought of where there would be a huge swath of nature around here within walking distance. The park building has a nature center. I went there on a field trip." The two of them walked companionably back to the house.

Cho was back when they got in. Liah slowly crept into the kitchen to see what she could help with while he went into the living room to find Yong. His roommate was tossing logs into the fireplace while Minjun dozed on the couch.

Seong looked over. "Has he been asleep all day? Is he sick?"

Yongjoon smiled broadly, trying to tone it down. "He's uh fine, just tired." His dimples kept popping out as he went back to focusing on piling the wood. "Where's Maliah?"

"In the kitchen helping Cho," he shifted his feet. "I'm sorry for yelling. But I'm not sorry for what I said. I care about her; apparently my love language is physical touch. So I always want to be around her. It's frustrating because we never really have time alone. When we do, something always happens. Crazy stalkers, you two, put limits on the time we have to spend together."

"So do something about it." Yongjoon started shoving kindling strategically around the logs. "You have income, you have time, she has a car. Figure something out."

"Doesn't it make it seem like I'm putting her in a position to have sex if I get a hotel or something?"

His friend shrugged. "Talk to her. Let her know there are no expectations. That you just want to spend time privately with her."

He was hesitant. Though she said she understood he wasn't gunning for sex, he was worried that it seemed like it was all he wanted. He'd talk to her about it. Leaving his friends, he walked into the kitchen, smiling. Cho was asking Maliah questions as she put something in the oven.

"So they are chocolate chips, caramel, and bacon?" Cho asked disbelievingly.

"I know it s-s-sounds strange, but it's really good. You have to get the bacon really crispy o-o-otherwise the texture feels off. You'll see." She looked up at him. "Do you think if I write to the campus resident life people, they will put these stoves in the dorm rooms?"

He laughed. "You literally have like six months left in the dorms, then you'll be in an apartment in California with a better stove hopefully. You wouldn't be there even if they did."

She sighed. "You're right."

"So you've decided on USC?" Cho asked.

"I-I-I still have three other schools I need to hear from, but I don't see anyone giving me a scholarship package like I got from USC. I'd only have to work one part time job." She sighed wistfully.

"Do you actually need to work both your jobs now?" he asked.

"Honestly? Probably not. But the thought of not having enough money or my account dipping past a certain level sends me into a minor panic attack," Maliah admitted.

"If you don't mind me asking, what's your comfort threshold?" Cho asked.

"I try to keep my account at twelve or above. If it falls below that I freak out a little. Lower than ten, I start pulling double shifts."

"Twelve... hundred?" Seonghun asked, confused.

"Twelve thousand," she corrected. "Remember, I told you I'm responsible for everything in my life. If my car breaks, if I end up sick in the hospital. Any unexpected costs, I don't have a support system." She looked at him. "Summer tuition was included in my scholarship, but money for the classes wasn't. I had to pay out of pocket for that."

"I thought you were in the hospital in the summer?"

"I was for the first summer session. Second summer session I was back." She looked down at her watch.

Seong saw Cho open her mouth to ask; quickly he shook his head. "Later," he mouthed.

"Why don't you show me these bizarre cookies you talked about while we wait for dinner?" Cho asked instead.

"Okay."

She pulled bowls down while Liah began explaining the cookies. He went upstairs, pulling out his laptop to start studying. He sent Shiwon notes on the labs for next week, as well as notes to his professors thanking them for allowing him this time off to deal with everything, before getting down to work on his assignments.

After a while he looked up and saw Maliah at his door. "Hey. What are you doing there?"

"Watching you study. You're cute," she said simply.

"Have you been there long?" he asked.

"No, I came up to tell you dinner is ready; you looked cute, so I just watched." She gave him a half smile.

"Close the door and come here."

"Seong." She had a warning tone in her voice.

"I'm not going to do anything except kiss you. I promise." She arched her brow but complied. Leaning over the bed she kissed him briefly. He pulled her toward him again. "More please."

She kissed him a little deeper. Sliding his laptop off his lap, he tugged her until she was on top of him. He lightly bit her lip before releasing her. "I have something to ask you."

"Okay." She looked cautious.

"How would you feel if I got us a hotel for a weekend?" He saw the stricken look on her face. "Before you flip out on me, I'm not doing it so we could have sex, I'm not ready for that step myself. I don't get to cuddle you or spend time without people staring us down or analyzing what we're doing."

"Or bursting into the dorm early in the morning when they are supposed to be in another city," she pointed out.

"Exactly."

"Can I think about it?" She gently rolled her hips on his lap.

He stilled her instantly. "Don't start what you aren't willing to continue please."

"Sorry." She gave him a quick peck on the cheek, walking to the door. "I'll think about it."

"Thank you. I'll be down in a minute. I'm going to grab a shower. A cold shower." He blushed.

"I barely did anything," she protested.

"Everything reminds me of the photo studio," he said.

She came back to his bedside, kissing his forehead, before kissing him deeply again. He was thoroughly enjoying himself when he felt her hand open the button on his jeans. His eyes popped open. "Liah."

She opened her eyes, looking seriously at him. "Can you keep quiet? You need to keep quiet."

He nodded quickly. Liah pulled his dick from his jeans, pumping him with her hand slightly. Just as she went to lower her mouth on him, there was a knock at the door. "What are you two doing? We're waiting," Yong's voice called out as he began to turn the knob on the door.

Maliah stood straight up, grabbed the laptop, setting it on his lap. She sat at the edge of the bed quickly. When the door opened Yongjoon saw Maliah looking calm on the edge of the bed. Seonghun probably looked a little frustrated, but he had been pretty frustrated lately.

"I let him know, Yong. We were talking for a bit. I'm coming down. He wanted to grab a quick shower."

"Hurry up. The meal is huge." He zoomed out of the room.

Maliah smiled at him sadly. "Raincheck?"

He hit his head on the headboard, whimpering. "I'll be down in a minute." He let out a frustrated strangled scream as she left the room. She must have heard it as he heard her snicker before the door closed.

Everyone finally made it downstairs to overflowing plates. There were fried pork chops, mashed potatoes and gravy, corn, and green beans. Seong had his favorite noodles, little Korean side dishes that everyone explained to Maliah, along with rice. The dinner was chaotic; a mashup of different flavors.

"This tastes kind of like 돈까스," he said as he took a second bite of his pork chop.

"Say it again." Maliah focused on his mouth as he repeated himself slowly. "What's the difference between the two?"

"돈까스 is boneless and the breading is different," he explained. "It's served with a gravy as well though."

She nodded as she continued to eat.

"Mom, this is so good," Yongjoon said as he plowed through fluffy mashed potatoes.

"Thanks, but I didn't make anything except the sides and Seong's noodles." The boys looked at Maliah who shifted uncomfortably.

"You really know how to cook," Minjun said.

"I like all sorts of home stuff. The reason I don't do it at the dorm is because I don't have time and our oven is shitty."

"Language."

"I'm s-s-sorry." She looked apologetically at Cho. "I don't have much in the way of vices. I don't drink, I don't smoke, I don't play video games. I study obsessively hard, roller skate, and cook. That's about it." She shrugged, going back to her plate.

"You've never drank?" Minjun asked.

"No. One, I'm underage for another month. Two, the medications I'm on," she sighed, "they mess with my tolerance, so I don't bother with it at all."

"Wait, your birthday is coming up?" Min asked.

"Yes, in December."

"Did you have plans?"

"My normal stuff. Class, therapy, work. I'll spring for Mexican food though." She went to take a bite when she saw the look on her friend's face. "Min, no. Absolutely the fuck—"

"Language!"

"I'm sorry. Min, no. I don't want any type of party. I don't want any special event. I just want my birthday to go in peace. Please." She stood up abruptly. "Excuse me." She left the room, running upstairs.

Everyone looked at each other. Seong thought back to the letters. She mentioned her birthday, but what did she say? "I'm going to go check on her." He stood up, taking another bite of noodles.

"Take her plate, she barely ate." Cho handed him the plate. "She also made really bizarre but very tasty cookies for you guys." Standing up, she handed him a stack wrapped in a paper towel. "Chocolate chip caramel bacon cookies."

He headed upstairs, knocking on her door.

"Come in."

As Seong opened the door, his heart broke at the sad look on her face. "Do you want to talk about it?" he asked, setting the plate on the bed.

"I just really don't like birthdays." She was tightlipped about it.

"Min sees a birthday as a time to celebrate your life, the life you've lived, the friends you've made, the joys you've seen across that year. That's why he looked so excited. He has another friend to celebrate a birthday with, that's all."

She sat up, cross legged on the bed as he munched on a cookie.

"Oh my god." Seong swallowed. She looked over at him. "What the hell is this and how do I get you to make more?" He quickly shoved another one in his mouth.

A smile ghosted her face. "They are the best cookies I've ever made. I have the recipe written down, but I know it by heart."

There was a pounding of feet running up the stairs. Her door burst open. Yong was standing there with an unhinged look on his face. "I know you have cookies left."

Seonghun slowly slipped another cookie in his mouth, he looked like a squirrel as he chewed as fast as he could. "No cookies left. That was the last one."

"Liar."

"You'd have to take me to figure it out; we both know you can't."

Minjun slid in the door, sitting next to Maliah. She looked at him. "Are they seriously about to fight for cookies?"

"I only got one and a half," Minjun said. "He found out how good they were."

They both looked at Yongjoon who was scooting closer to Seonghun. Seonghun slipped Liah the paper towel that still had two cookies left. "If I die, you can have my lockbox." He gave her a quick kiss before jumping Yongjoon.

The fight didn't last that long. The two men were quickly broken up by their significant others. Yong retired with Min for the night after realizing the cookies had been eaten while they were fighting. While Liah brushed her teeth, Seong took her plate downstairs. She was in her pajamas waiting for him when he returned to say goodnight.

"Where's Mrs. Pae?" she asked quietly.

"She's in bed." Seong sat her clothes on the edge of her bed.

"Minjun made a point while you two were wrestling out there. Close the door please."

He did as she asked. "What point did he make?"

"Loopholes." She stood up, unbuttoning her pajama top. "You see. Mrs. Pae is worried about pregnancy. I don't blame her. I'd feel awful if someone who wasn't supposed to be pregnant got pregnant on my watch." She slid her shirt off her shoulders, staring at him. He was breathing a little harder, focused on her breasts. "But Seonghun, we haven't done anything that would facilitate pregnancy."

"Oh god." He strode over to her and kissed her hard, palming her breasts. Seong quickly replaced his hand with his mouth, sucking on her nipples. Sliding his hand into her pajamas, he began to touch her. "We have a problem." Seong tried stroking her like before, wincing at the feel. "We don't have any lube and you're not— I can't make your coaster drop like this."

"Well how about you think about that for a bit while I cash in your raincheck?" Liah dropped to her knees, unbuckling his pants. "You have got to keep it down, Seonghun."

"I will."

He didn't. He couldn't. In the end he had to cover his mouth with both hands as she took him into her mouth. The effort to keep silent nearly made him cry. Liah swallowed all of him this time, not leaving a trace. She tucked him back in his jeans and buttoned him up, standing up.

"I thought about it," he said looking at her.

"Hmm?" She looked over at him. She looked drowsy.

"You told me to think about getting you off. I thought about it," he repeated.

"I'm surprised you could think of anything with all the yelling you were trying to cover up." She smirked at him.

"Let's see how you handle it." He slid down her pants and panties. "How flexible are you?"

"I don't really know. It's not something I've ever had to contemplate."

He knelt down in front of her. "Can you throw one of your legs over my shoulders and hold on?"

She did as he asked, wobbling slightly. Seong bit the inside of her thigh, smiling when he heard her gasp. Running his nose up her inner thigh, he grabbed her hips and began an assault on her clit. He heard her struggling not to yell.

"I really hate this," he said. "I want to hear you cry out for me." He dove back in.

She gripped his shoulders tighter and clenched her teeth. "I-I-I want…"

"I know, baby, I got you." As he slid his first, then second finger inside, he was surprised, she was only slightly wet. "Is everything okay?"

"Yesss," she moaned. "More please."

"Shhh." He nibbled, and licked and sucked at her, until her hips started to buck. She was finally getting slippery, then…

"Seonghun, stop please." He eased out of her, pulled back to take a look at her face. Liah was fidgeting, not making eye contact.

"Your rollercoaster rolled back, didn't it?"

She nodded.

"It happens, we know this. We can't get lucky every time. But you know what?"

She looked at him as she reached for her pants. "What?"

"You have to work tomorrow; you didn't tell anyone what time. I also have a doctor's appointment. We can spend a little time tomorrow before we come back here, trying to make you drop more than once." He patted her back. "It's nothing to feel bad or embarrassed about, so I hope you don't."

"I researched it, you know?"

He stared at her. "Researched what?"

"My antidepressant's effect on my sex drive. It led me down a hole. One of the options was weed. I'm not comfortable with that though. Another option is switching my antidepressant all together, which I'm going to talk to my doctor about," she said quietly.

"Really?" he said surprised. "You were against lowering your dosage."

"I talked to Dr. Stewart about some of the problems we've been having when we're intimate," she ducked her head bashfully, "she reminded me she wasn't pleased when she found out which antidepressant I was on. There have been better breakthroughs in medicine since fluoxetine. She suspected they put me on it because I wasn't nor had ever been sexually active at that point."

"But you still felt sexual desire. It messed with that too, right?" he asked.

"Yeah, but I didn't really bring it up because it seemed like a small price to pay for mental stability."

Seonghun didn't think so. It seemed like it would cause more grief in the long run. He didn't say anything though. Instead, he observed her for a minute. "Are you tired?"

"A little bit," she said. "Why?"

"Will you have a hot chocolate with me? The fire that Yongjoon started is dying off, but the embers are still there."

"I'd like that very much. Let me get cleaned up; I'll meet you down there." She walked into the bathroom.

Seonghun walked downstairs. He found the hot cocoa mix that was always in the cabinets. Grabbing a saucepan, he pulled the milk out of the refrigerator, pouring enough for two mugs into the pan. Setting it on the stove, he sprinkled cinnamon into the milk as he was taught.

"It gives it a warmth you can't quite place," Cho always said.

He felt two arms wrap around his waist. Turning around, he kissed the top of her head. "It's almost ready. Go sit by the fire. I'll be there in a second."

"Are you sure I can't help?"

"Nah, I got this. Go sit."

She walked into the living room. As the milk began to steam, Seonghun took it off the heat.

"Don't leave it on too long," Cho told him as she taught him to constantly stir, *"It burns quickly."* He worked quickly, dumping spoonfuls of the home-made cocoa mix into the mugs before pouring the milk over it. *"To me it always seemed easier to pour milk over the mix, rather than dumping it into the milk. Less clumping."* He smiled as he remembered listening to Cho explain it. A handful of marshmallows completed the drink. He walked into the living room, pausing to look at Maliah.

She was watching the glowing coals of the fire. When she heard him approaching, she smiled at him. Her smile faded as he kept staring. "What's wrong?"

He swallowed. "Nothing at all." As he handed her the mug, the last words Cho gave him the day she taught him to make this rang in his head.

"Nothing makes a spouse happier than the small things. Jewelry, gifts, things like that are great, but just approaching them with a drink or a listening ear, well. You want to see your wife happy, you'll keep the cocoa recipe in your arsenal. It's one of the things my husband first served me. I knew that day I would marry him." She ruffled Seonghun's hair. *"Go get the other two so they can have a drink."*

Maliah sipped and closed her eyes. "This is really nice. Thank you." He smiled and sat down next to her, wrapping his arm around her as she leaned into his side.

CHAPTER 38

Seonghun woke to clatters in the kitchen. Looking at the time, he winced. It was 7:30. He knew Maliah wanted to be on the road by then. "Baby, wake up." He shook her slightly, surprised she slept through the noise in the kitchen. She was an incredibly light sleeper. "It's 7:30, we have to go."

She rolled over, blinking. Squinting she moved her hand around searching for her glasses. Liah looked at him. "You fell asleep with your glasses on again." She reached out a hand to straighten them on his face.

He rested his forehead on hers for a moment. "We have to go. You're going to be late."

"Okay. Let me get dressed." She stood up, folding the blanket.

"I got this, go get ready." Seong tugged the blanket from her. She ran upstairs as he walked in the kitchen after he folded the blanket.

"I know you two have to go, so I made breakfast sandwiches you can eat in the car." Cho pointed to a couple of aluminum foil wrapped sandwiches on the kitchen table. "You'll be back, right?"

"Yes. We're going cosmic bowling tonight with the other two, then we'll be staying over the rest of the weekend."

"There will be a ton of different 김밥 in the fridge if you need a snack after bowling." She cleaned the stove as she spoke. "Did she like the cocoa?"

"Very much so. Thank you for teaching me how to make it." He rested his chin on her shoulder as he always did.

"Welcome. I like passing on pieces of my husband. I know that way he'll never be lost." She smiled at the young man she regarded as a son. He squeezed her shoulder, following Liah to get dressed. He tapped lightly on Yongjoon's door. After a moment, the door cracked and Yongjoon appeared, looking wild eyed.

"Uh, we're going to go. We'll be back this evening."

"Okay." Abruptly he shut the door in Seong's face. He heard a giggle and turned around.

Maliah was standing there. "I told you, large bed, plus no one to bother them. They're going to be busy when he's not with his mom."

He shook his head. "He had the nerve to talk about my hormones." Seonghun walked into his room with Maliah's snickering behind him. "Do you want to come in? This won't take long." She walked in, sitting on the edge of his bed. He took off his t-shirt before turning to say something. Liah's eyes were riveted to his body. "Liah, we don't have time or privacy."

"I know."

"You're going to be late to work, don't you have a lesson?"

"Yes." She looked up at his face.

He kissed her. "We have to go," he whispered against her mouth.

"I'm fine." She pulled away, biting her lip. "I'm going to go downstairs. I want too much right now." Without another word, she left.

Seonghun put on his clothes, wearing the new white sweater he'd purchased. Rushing down the steps he turned to see her in the living room but she wasn't there. He walked into the kitchen to see Cho teaching Maliah how to roll 김밥.

"You can't have it too full, it will burst." Under Cho's watchful eye she layered egg and vegetables on the rice and seaweed. Both women looked up. "Are you ready?"

"Yeah, am I driving or are you?" he asked.

"It's up to you."

"I don't get to drive often; I'd like to if you don't mind."

Nodding, she walked over to the sink to wash and dry her hands. After she tossed her keys to him, she turned to Cho. "Thank you for teaching me to make... um, kimbop?"

"김밥" Cho corrected.

"Gimbap," Maliah tried again.

"Good job. Both of you have a good day." Cho deftly rolled the one Maliah was working on before slicing it into medallions.

They walked out of the door and to the car. Liah sat in the passenger seat before pulling a sandwich out of her purse. "Mrs. Pae gave us sandwiches." She handed it to him.

He devoured it in four bites. "I can't eat while I'm driving, plus I'm starving," he explained.

"I'm not judging." She set back, peeling the aluminum foil from her sandwich, nibbling as he drove.

"Can I ask you some more about switching your meds?" he asked suddenly.

"Sure. It affects you after all," she replied.

"I guess, what can I expect? What do you need from me, from all of us actually?"

"I'll have to be weaned off my current meds before being put on other ones. I don't know how that is going to happen, If I will be on both meds for a short amount of time, or if I will be off one before jumping onto the other. I can give you an expectation if that happens. My period on steroids."

"I don't understand," he said as he drove.

"A lot of crying, not communicating, trying to isolate myself." She took a bite of the sandwich. "I struggle with eating, and a little ah, eagerness when it comes to pleasuring myself."

"I'm sorry, what?" He wanted to look at her but couldn't while he was navigating onto the highway.

"It's—" She paused as she tried to figure out how to explain it. "I told you my libido was healthy before this. I'm going to have to assume that is going to come back with a vengeance."

"How healthy?"

"You're really focused on this." She laughed quietly. "Okay, so you know how you said you can be ready to go in ten minutes after the first time, but it takes longer each subsequent time?"

"Yes."

"I could get to a point where you couldn't be ready to go for an hour or more."

He laughed. "No way." He glanced at her quickly. She was staring at him, not laughing.

"I've never had a partner, but I have literally run batteries out of vibrators in one session." She shrugged.

"You gave that up? Why?"

"It was distracting anyway. I'd like to be healthier about, well, pleasuring myself while focusing on other tasks. I swear sometimes I was like a fourteen-year-old boy who had just discovered his dick."

He snorted. "We discovered them much earlier than that, sweetheart."

"Whatever. It was distracting."

"You didn't answer the other half of my question."

"I'm sorry, what was it?" She balled up the aluminum foil, sticking it in her purse.

"What do you need from us?" he repeated.

"Honestly, you're going to need to understand that I may just cry for no reason. It doesn't mean you did anything, or that you're hurting me. I just cry a lot, as you have seen. I blame myself for things that I logically know are not my fault, but they still feel like it."

"Like Casey's crazy ass?" he asked quietly.

"If I would have pressed charges—"

He interrupted her. "Were they or were they not pushing you to student court? Didn't they push that as the best option for you?"

"Yes but—"

"You've never had an issue with the police, never had anyone put you in a position where you had to take action like this. The school led you wrong. Casey is a nutcase. You did nothing wrong." They both went silent. After a beat he spoke up again, changing the subject. "If you could go anywhere in the world, where would it be?"

"For like a vacation?"

"Yes."

She tapped her bottom lip as she thought for a while. "One day I'd like to go to one of those places that has villas you can rent, and everything is in soft colors, and you can sleep with the windows open and watch the curtains gently blow around. I'd like the villa to be on or near the beach so I can see it when I wake up." She hid a smile.

"What is it?" He glanced over at her.

"Nothing. What about you? Where would you go?"

"I like your idea of the beach. I'm also curious about you in a swimsuit."

"I just used the swimsuits at school."

"You've never owned a swimsuit?"

"I live in Indiana. Why would I need a swimsuit?"

"To go to the pool in the summer."

"I told you I can't swim."

"That's right, I forgot about that. Do you want to learn? I'd be happy to teach you," he offered.

"Maybe after Yongjoon teaches me to throw a punch. He's pretty much scheduled a lot of my off time. Also, it's cold out. I don't really like being cold."

"You don't like being cold, but you won't wear a coat. Make it make sense." He smirked.

"Oh hush." She pouted as he laughed.

He pulled up to the building she worked at. "What are you going to do today?" she asked.

"I'm going to study, maybe watch some tv or hang out with Shiwon for a bit."

She sat for a moment thinking. "D-do you want to have lunch with me? You could invite Shiwon if you wanted."

"I would like that very much. What time?"

"Around one thirty. I'll meet you at the diner."

"Sounds good. I'll see you this afternoon." He leaned over, giving her a quick kiss.

"Can—" She paused, fidgeting. "Can we try and finish what we started last night?"

"I have no problems with that." He pressed his forehead to hers. "I'll talk to you in a few hours."

"Okay" As she got out of the car, she opened her purse, handing him the photos in the green envelope. "Please make sure you lock these up when you get back to the dorm."

"I will, I promise," he said. She shut the door, waving at him before walking inside the building. He drove toward campus. Once he arrived, he pulled out his phone, asking Shiwon to meet them for lunch. Shiwon agreed. Seong gave him directions to the diner as he climbed the stairs to the suite.

They forgot to leave the heat on when they left so it was freezing. Seong placed their private pictures in his lock box before turning on the heat. He grabbed his second slice of chocolate cheesecake from the fridge. Getting settled, he pulled out his textbooks, studying as he ate.

He worked on his homework and various school tasks for a while when he realized he had her car. He could drive to the greenhouse. Packing up his books, he left the dorm once again. As he started the car, he noticed she had about a fourth of a tank of gas left. He pulled up to the closest gas station to the greenhouse to fill up. Walking into the gas station, he picked up a candy bar. He also saw something called Lemonheads, that he chose for Liah. As he walked back outside, he stopped short. Casey was leaning on the car.

"Get off," he said calmly. He pulled his phone out of his pocket, turning on the camera.

"Gladly, want to help?" she simpered.

"Ew," was all he replied with.

"Haven't seen any of you around. I've missed you. How's your friend?" She grinned.

If looks could kill, she would be dead. "Why don't you just turn yourself in? You need help. You probably wouldn't get much jail time because you are literally nuts." He stopped the camera briefly, sending it to the detective along with a location pin. Turning the camera back on, he looked at her.

"Why are you filming me? Are you going to watch it later?" Her voice lowered. "Are you going to think of me?"

"I honestly never think of you. Why would I? You're a nuisance, a pest. One of the worst people I've ever met." He stared her down.

She met his eyes, seemingly calm. "She's better than me? Do you know, we used to call her chunky monkey behind her back—"

He had never wanted slap the shit out of a human being more in his life. "If you ever talk about her again…"

She grinned at him. "Like I said, we called her chunky monkey. She was so fucking emo all the time. Teaching other sad kids how to be miserable all the time or something. Like how is that even a job? Is that what you like? Sad girls?"

"I like kind people. So that automatically leaves you out." He roughly shoved her away from the car, getting in, quickly locking the doors. He shut the camera off, looking up when he saw Detective Drake's SUV fly into the gas station. Casey saw it too. Narrowing her eyes, she took off running.

He saw the detective run after her. Seong sent her a text, letting her know where he was going before he pulled off. He was working in the greenhouse, planting things for the winter when he heard his name being called. "I'm in the back corner," he called out, distracted.

"This place is beautiful. I didn't even know it existed." Detective Krishna walked toward him looking around.

"It's apparently a well-kept secret. I didn't really understand how much of a secret it was," Seonghun said, looking up at the detective. "Please tell me you caught her?"

The detective shook her head. "As soon as I saw her, I called for backup. I chased her, but she got into a car. I told backup which way she was headed, but they lost her. I really don't understand how she slips away like she does."

He planted some more before speaking quietly. "When she got into the studio, she was flirting with the front desk guy. Is there someone on your backup team that may know her? Maybe they allowed her to get away. She has people helping her. There is no way she could sneak around campus like this, stalk me, and not get caught otherwise."

"I had the same idea you did. I'm looking, but I haven't come across anyone yet. There are a few people I trust. They are looking as well."

He looked at her. "She's cocky. I know she's delusional, but there is something on top of that. Like she knows she'll never get caught. Someone's helping her, I feel it."

Detective Krishna leaned back on the wall. "Talk it through with me. Why do you think someone's helping her?"

"I saw how the guy reacted in the studio. Even when Maliah approached him, asking who he gave the key to, he lied." He put his spade down and looked at her. "Even when she was an absolute asshole to people, she had friends who were loyal. Are they scared to be on the receiving end of her anger? Is that why they stay loyal? I don't know. Maybe she has dirt on people." Seonghun stared off into the distance. "Liah said she couldn't make her a minion. She's an open book with absolutely nothing to hide. There was nothing Casey could do to force her to stay in line."

"What are you in school for again?"

He gestured to the dirt. "Agriculture. I'm a farmer."

"If it doesn't work out for you, maybe police work would." She shifted slightly. "So she's gone on the run, all of her friends aren't helping her, so who would be?"

"Minjun was sleeping with one of her friends for a little bit. When Casey went on this obsessive tirade in front of him, Min said she seemed to get embarrassed. You should talk to her."

"Do you have a name?" she asked.

"Uh—" He walked over to the sink to wash and dry his hands. Pulling out his phone, he called Minjun.

On the fourth ring he picked up. "Hi. When are you two going to be back for bowling?" Minjun asked.

"Later this evening. Min, the girl you were seeing that got embarrassed by Casey's rant, what was her name?"

"Ashley Greaves, why?" Min asked.

"I think I might have figured out how Casey is sneaking around without getting caught," Seonghun said.

"I don't think it's Ashley. She had a lot of distaste for her after the tirade."

"Not her, but she can prove my theory. I'll explain this evening."

"Okay. Hurry back, we miss you two." Minjun hung up the phone.

He looked at the detective. "Ashley Greaves."

Detective Krishna took out her phone, making a note. "If anyone but me approaches you to talk about this case, I didn't send them. I won't send anyone else to any of you. Understood?"

"I take it, you're seeing it now too?" Seonghun asked.

She smiled sadly. "I'll keep you posted." She walked out of the greenhouse, leaving Seong to his work. He spent another hour digging in the dirt before cleaning up to eat lunch with Liah and Shiwon.

CHAPTER 39

When he arrived at the diner, Shiwon and Liah were already seated. She was trying, but he could see her trying to hide behind her hair. Waving to the owner, he walked over, sitting in the booth beside her. "Hey." Seong kissed her briefly. Liah's eyes flashed hot. He smirked before looking over at Shiwon. "I'm sorry again for not keeping you posted. I'm not normally flaky, just a lot has been going on."

"So you said. Are all of you okay?" He flipped his hair out of his face.

Maliah held out her arm, tugging at something on her wrist. Quietly she handed over a black ponytail holder.

"Hey thanks, Shorty." He pulled his hair back.

"You c-c-can keep it," she said. "I h-h-have three on me."

"Nice." He pulled his hair back in a small ponytail at the top of his head.

"Jesus," Maliah muttered.

Seonghun snorted. "To answer your question, we're mostly fine. Minjun has a nasty bruise, but he's healing. She hasn't come near Liah, and I just spent time with Detective Krishna."

"What happened?" she asked. Before he could explain, someone came to take their order.

"Order what you want because we're celebrating. I'm paying," Shiwon stated.

"I'm going to g-g-go all out." Maliah said dryly, ordering her usual BLT with a side salad.

Seonghun ordered a cheeseburger and fries, and at Maliah's stare, he also ordered the vegetable of the day. "What are we celebrating?"

"Graduate school acceptance. I got accepted to sunny, sunny UCLA."

Maliah was mid drink and choked on an ice cube. She hacked it free; it went flying out of her mouth hitting Shiwon directly in the forehead. "I'm s-s-so sorry."

"No worries." He blotted his forehead.

"Maliah got a bunch of acceptances too. Where is UCLA?" Seonghun asked.

Maliah looked at him. "Fifteen minutes from USC."

"You're going to USC?" Shiwon stared at her.

"Unless the other three colleges I'm waiting on give me a better package than they did, yes."

"What exactly is your major?" Shiwon asked.

"Psychology specializing in art and music for children. You?" she said without a stutter.

"Pre-med, Shorty."

Liah cocked her head to the side, staring him down. "You're about to sit here and tell me you want to specialize in OB-GYN, aren't you?"

"Yes, but not for the reason you're thinking. I like babies. Like I'm absolutely crazy about babies."

Both of them were taken aback. "I'm sorry, what?"

"My youngest sister, and coincidentally my favorite, is ten years younger than I am. I was there when she came into the world." He took a sip of his coffee. "I delivered her, I was the first person to hold her. I was greatly upset when I was told that she was not mine."

"Wait. How on earth did you deliver a baby at such a young age?" asked Liah. "Why not go into pediatrics?"

"Mom was early, ignoring her labor signs, which is stupid because she had six kids before this, you'd think she'd have the routine down pat." Shiwon rolled his eyes. "Anyway, labor was a little farther along than she thought. I was the only one home. Called emergency services, but they weren't going to get there in time, so they coached me through it." He squirted ketchup on his hashbrowns. "I like babies, Shorty, not toddlers, not kids. I don't mind them, but babies are awesome. You just want to cuddle them."

As Maliah cut through her sandwich, she looked at Shiwon. "How many vaginas have you gotten to look at based on that story?"

Seonghun choked on a fry.

"Shorty, I have cut a swath through this campus." The tall man grinned as he scooped up eggs. "I'm having fun now. The science stuff is child's play. I'll be a bit more serious when I go through my rotations. Hey! Do you want a roommate?"

"No."

"Absolutely not."

Maliah glanced at Seonghun. He'd dropped his burger onto his plate. "I'm going to be very blunt right now because it seems like you need it." She waited until his eyes met hers. "I have a father. He doesn't give a damn what I do. So, the idea of someone making decisions for me, especially as far as I have come, does not fly. Jealousy doesn't fly either. Especially when there is no reason to be. Get it together please." She ate a forkful of salad.

"Sorry," he mumbled.

She nodded. "Shiwon, this will be the first time I'm financially able to live on my own, so thank you, but no. Also," she glanced at Seonghun, "it makes him nervous because I stare at your hair a l-l-lot."

"Understandable. I'm pumped to live by myself as well. My parents made me stay in the dorms all four years. I won't have much time to hang out or anything, but maybe we can have lunch from time to time?" He looked at her.

"That would b-b-be nice," she said quietly.

Seonghun bit into his burger, feeling awful. When they left, she would be starting over with no friends nearby. He shouldn't begrudge Shiwon reaching out. Why did it gnaw at him so bad?

Shiwon expertly changed the subject to their labs, even drawing Maliah into the conversation. As he talked, Seonghun realized he was jealous. Shiwon talked to Maliah so easily without knowing her. Maliah seemed calm around him. It ate at him. He had to fight for her to trust him enough to speak with him. He focused back on the conversation as Shiwon looked at his watch.

"I have to get going, I have some other work I need to do. Thank you for inviting me. I'll see both of you later. Thanks for the hair tie, Shorty."

"Welcome." Liah was finishing up the other half of her sandwich.

Shiwon slapped Seonghun on the back before going to pay for the bill. Maliah watched as Shiwon left before turning to him. "Do you understand why I'm so comfortable with him?" she asked.

He shook his head.

"Because he is your friend. You know and trust him. He was good to you when you were hurt. If I met him as a stranger on the street, I wouldn't talk to him. I wouldn't acknowledge him. I'd think his hair was nice, but that's about it." She smiled at him. "I'm not lusting over him. Please stop worrying."

"I've never actually been jealous before. It wasn't jealousy when I asked you not to kiss Minjun anymore, I just didn't like it. This is full blown jealousy. He gets to be near you while you go to graduate school."

"There is that. We have time, Seonghun. We'll sort it out." Maliah looked at her watch. "Do you have anything going on?"

"No, I have a doctor's appointment in an hour. What's on your mind?"

"I have about forty-five minutes before I need to go back. Do you want to sit in the car and kiss me for a while?"

Without talking, he grabbed her hand, pulling her out the door as he waved to the owner. Maliah laughed as she was tugged along.

After Liah went back to work, he headed to his appointment. It was very quick. He explained he hadn't been sexually active in a little over four years but wanted to reassure his girlfriend before they jumped into anything serious. A few blood draws, a handful of free condoms in a paper bag, and he was out the door, heading back to the dorm. Walking in, he set the bag of condoms in his drawer. He was mostly done with his work, so he started to read the book on black history he picked up. After reading a chapter he picked up his phone.

Seong: *Have you been discriminated against blatantly?*

Liah: *That is a really random question.*
Seong: *I'm reading a book on Black history and Jim Crow laws.*
Liah: *Nothing is ever blatant. I was on scholarship at a very rich school, so people would make offhand comments about how lucky I must have felt to go there. I earned my place there. They didn't just offer to take a poor child out of the ghetto and drop her in this school out of the goodness of their hearts. I jumped through more hoops than a paying student did. Casey's mom made a comment about my financial aid packet, not knowing I was my school's valedictorian. I make it a point to correct people when they make stupid assumptions about me.*
Seong: *If I hear someone making an incorrect assumption or a rude comment, should I correct it?*
Liah: *Yes. Why?*
Seong: *It's a long story, and I'll explain it on the drive back tonight, but I had an altercation with Casey today. I wanted to hit her.*
Liah: *…That's sort of hot. I want all the details.*

He guffawed and went back to his book. He wavered a bit and began typing again.

Seong: *Have you given any other thought to my hotel idea?*
Liah: *Yes.*
Seong: *Is that the answer or…*

Seong saw the dots indicating she was writing; from the looks of it, she was writing a novel. He didn't know if he should be terrified or not.

Liah: *I know I'm not mentally ready for sex. I don't want to screw this up. I like you. A lot. If I go into a hotel room with you right now, I'm going to have sex with you, I already know because I'm physically ready. It's setting myself up for failure; I don't do that. So I'm going to decline for now.*
Seong: *I'm not surprised. I understand where you're coming from. I will just have to figure out how I can get cuddles with you otherwise.*
Liah: *You're welcome to cuddle with me anytime, people around or not.*
Seong: *I want naked cuddles.*

It was silent for about ten minutes and then...

Liah: *I'm sorry, I dropped my phone, and then couldn't stop laughing. Nude cuddles? Nakey embrace? Clothes-less canoodling?*
Seong: *You're still laughing, aren't you?*
Liah: *Everyone is looking at me because I can't stop! Okay, you can have nakey embraces anytime we aren't at Mrs. Pae's house. Okay?*
Seong: *So, if I asked for them in the bowling alley?*
Liah: *If you're down to take off all your clothes on public furniture while having me sit equally naked in your lap, I feel like I have to reward you for your bravery before we both get carted off to jail for public indecency. Oh, BTW, my evening viewing got canceled, I'll be done by six.*
Seong: *We aren't expected until later. Do you want to come back to the dorm for clothes-less canoodling?*
Liah: *I would love to clothes-less canoodle with you. I'll see you in a little while <3*
Seong: *<3*

Laughing, he returned to his book. He immediately put it back down, picking up his phone again.

Seong: *You know that flameless votive candle you had for the pumpkin? Do you have any more of those?*
Liah: *Yeah, I have a ton. Look in the second drawer of my nightstand. There should be a bag full of them.*
Seong: *Thanks. I'll leave you alone now.*
Liah: *<3*

He stood up from his bed, peeling the comforter off. He also grabbed his spare comforter. Heading out to the living room he went to work.

He picked up Maliah from the art gallery. She walked out dressed in one of her black dresses, with his sweatshirt over it. "Sweetheart, promise me something?" he asked as she got into the car.

"What is it?" She closed the door and looked at him.

"This weekend, at least go with Minjun to look at coats. It is entirely too cold for you to be running around in just my sweatshirt."

She groaned. "Fine. I was hoping you'd forget about that."

"You're going to get sick. I wouldn't forget." He slid his hand across the armrest, clasping hers.

As Seonghun drove, Maliah spoke, "How long do we have before we have to head back to Indianapolis?"

"I texted Minjun earlier. He said if we can make it by nine that would be great. I told him to send me the address of the bowling alley. We'll meet them there."

"It takes about forty-five minutes to get to Indy, so about two hours to ourselves."

"I have a few ideas, mind if we get into the suite before I share them?" He pulled into the parking lot and cut the car.

"Sure. Also, this parking tag is awesome. I guess that's one thing I could thank Casey for. Speaking of, why on earth did you slap her?"

"She said she called you a chunky monkey behind your back." He told her about everything they discussed and how he spoke with Detective Krishna.

"It would make sense if someone with authority is helping her evade capture. I wonder how she's going to figure out-oh!" They walked into the suite to see the votive tea lights he'd scattered across all the surfaces in the common area. Seonghun had moved the couch from the entrance she could see that he'd made a makeshift bed on the floor in front of the tv. He'd pulled out one of the pieces of cheesecake with a fork, setting it on the coffee table.

"This is pretty, thank you," she said quietly.

Seonghun got what he truly wanted. He sat with Maliah as they shared cheesecake. There were kisses in between eating. Eventually there was clothes-less canoodling.

"We need to get ready to go soon." He kissed her on her shoulder.

"Mmm, what if we just stayed?" Liah arched against him, smiling as she heard him gasp at the contact.

"We promised." He had to foresight this time to grab everything they would need. His fingers glistened with lube as he touched her again.

"Seong, how do you expect me to want to go anywhere when you're doing that?" She turned to lay on her back so he got a better angle. He simply smiled at her as he moved his fingers as she liked. She quieted down, trying to focus on her orgasm. He watched as she controlled her breaths. "Faster please," she whispered.

He obliged, swiping his thumb across her clit faster. He saw her breathing pick up as if she was close but then he saw her eyes open, looking at him with disappointment.

"I can't, it's gone." She tried to push his hand away.

"Hold on. Are you sensitive?" He touched her gently to test. She shook her head. "Focus and let me try again, okay?"

"Okay."

He did everything he knew she liked. Starting with gentle pressure, he ramped it up to firmer. As he stroked her, he also touched her all over her body, starting at her neck, rubbing her shoulders, down to her chest. He stopped and focused attention on her breasts, gently squeezing them and pinching her nipples.

She called out when he did that, so he focused a bit more attention, pinching harder, when he felt the slight tremor he was looking for. "There it is. It just took a little more time."

"I really wish it wasn't this complicated." She looked up at the ceiling, sighing.

"The fact that you know your body and what you like makes you ahead of the curve, I think. Could you imagine if you didn't?"

"I think that being horny but not knowing what to do about it is the worst. I remember being like sixteen and not quite understanding what I needed to do. It took some research."

"How do you even research that? Do you search 'how to masturbate'?" he asked.

"That's what I did," she admitted, stretching. "That and I watched masturbating porn."

He looked at her. "You watched porn."

"Yes?" She looked puzzled at his reaction.

"You... watched porn?" His voice went up an octave.

"Yes."

"Did you watch anything other than masturbating porn?" He watched her face closely.

Liah opened her mouth, closed it, looking slightly embarrassed. "It's personal."

"I'm going to take that as a yes. If I guess what kind, would you tell me?"

"No."

"I'd tell you if you asked!" he whined.

She looked him dead in his eye. "You watched girl on girl." Staring at him as he began to blush, she cocked her head to the side. "You watched something else too, but I can't really tell what it was."

"How are you reading me like that?" he asked her, astounded.

"When I spend enough time with someone, I learn their cues, it's a habit that's kept me mostly safe. I'm off sometimes though, which is how Casey was able to get me." She shrugged as she burrowed down in the blankets. "I don't want to leave, Seonghun."

"I know, but a promise is a promise." He slid his hand under the blanket, smacking her ass, making her yelp. "Go clean up, we have to go."

She rolled over on her back instead, pulling him down to her. "Ten more minutes?" She nipped his lip before drawing him into a kiss.

"Mmm, ten more minutes, then we have to go," he agreed as her hand wandered lower.

Thirty minutes later they were running around trying to get everything cleaned up. "I said ten minutes!" Seonghun said desperately as he turned off all the votive candles. "Not thirty. We're going to be late; Min is going to whine."

Liah was busy laughing. "I asked if you wanted to stop fifteen minutes in, did I not?"

"You had my dick in your mouth when you asked!"

"You could have said no."

"I'll never say no when that's going on."

Maliah started giggling again, falling down as she hopped around to put her sock on. This made her laugh harder. Seong glanced over at his girl-friend, who was on her back flailing like a turtle, laughing. Walking over, he grabbed her sock out of her hand, pulling it on her foot. "You're the worst," he said, chuckling at her.

"I'm the best, quit playing."

"I don't know why I put up with such abuse, I give you romance, mood, then I get laughed at." He looked around the room. Spying her boots, he grabbed one as her giggles got worse.

"Why are you putting on my clothes? Shouldn't you be taking them off?" Liah was snorting she was laughing so hard.

"I take your clothes off again, we'll never leave this dorm." As he focused on putting on her shoe, he heard the soft noise of a sweatshirt unzipping. Looking back at her he saw that she was staring directly at him with her sweatshirt opened, her shirt raised slightly. "Liah," he warned.

"I know, I know." She giggled as he tied her shoe. "I'll get the other one. Thank you though." His girlfriend crawled over to her second shoe, putting it on. "Are you going to teach me how to bowl?"

"I'm not great at it, but I can show you the basics. Also, I'll buy you cheese fries. I normally have a beer, but uh—" he paused.

"You can drink, I don't care. Even if I was legally able, I wouldn't. I don't expect you to abstain just because I can't. Thanks for the sentiment though." She grabbed the empty plate that held the cheesecake. Taking it over to the sink she washed it quickly, putting it in the drying rack.

"We'll see. Depending on how the others drink, I may need to be a designated driver." He put the comforters back in his room, before putting the votives where he found them. "These little candle things are handy."

"They are," she agreed. "I'm looking forward to a space where I can light actual candles, however." Liah grabbed her purse as she opened the door.

"It kind of sounds like you have ideas in mind for how you want your space to look. Care to share?"

"Sure, do you have Pinterest?" she asked.

"Do I have what?"

Maliah laughed. Pulling out her phone she chose an app before handing it to him. "Look for the board that says apartment life."

Before he did, Seong poked at the other boards. Liah had vacation ideas, first home ideas, crafts, photography tricks, and art. Seonghun explored the apartment life board. Everything was neutral with pops of soft pink, gold, or rose gold. The bed she had selected was a beautiful white wrought iron frame. The kitchenware was really neat. They came with a removable handle, so the pans could be transformed into serving dishes. There was a listing of candles she wanted as well as plants.

"I obviously won't be getting exactly everything on that list. I won't be able to afford it. My plan is to thrift as well when I get wherever I'm going, but that board shows the aesthetic I want to go for. Light, airy, feminine, a little retro," she explained.

"I think it will suit you nicely. I do hope I get to see it in person at least," he whispered, handing her back her phone.

"We'll make sure you do, Seonghun." She squeezed his arm gently. "Let's go see the others and watch me try not to make an ass of myself."

CHAPTER 40

Though smoking hadn't been allowed in the bowling alley for years, it still smelled like people were chain smoking in it. He saw Liah wrinkling her nose. "Where do we go?" she asked as she looked around. It was chaotically loud and dark, with neon lights flashing everywhere.

"Min said turn left then walk down to the other end. They already got shoes for us," Seonghun screamed over the thumping music. Grabbing her hand, he started walking. He started chuckling as soon as he saw the pair of them.

Minjun was in sunglasses dancing around to the music. Yong was laughing at him with a beer bottle clutched in his hand. He waved when he saw them. "Min is vibing. I'm just letting him go for it." He handed Seonghun a bottle, offering one to Maliah. She easily declined so he rummaged around in the bucket for a can of soda. "I know you aren't legal yet, but they aren't going to card you if we buy."

"No thanks." She took the can of lemon lime soda from him gratefully.

Yongjoon nodded, handing over shoes to both of them.

"How did you know my size?" Maliah asked as she untied her boots.

Yongjoon pointed a thumb at Minjun as he flailed in the corner. "If you go shopping with him, he keeps track of all your sizes for presents. He knows my mom's ring size at this point because they've been jewelry shopping together."

"I guess it's a good thing I kicked him out of Victoria's Secret," she muttered.

Yongjoon snorted. "Yes, he would have noted your sizes there too. He keeps really good records."

Maliah didn't say anything else as she quickly put on the bowling shoes. "What now?"

"We need to find you a ball." Seonghun pulled her toward a rack with bowling balls on it.

"This one is pretty." She went to pick up a hot pink ball.

"Liah, wait, no!" Seonghun tried to stop her.

"Oof!" Maliah went to the ground with the ball. "Why the hell is it so heavy!?" She scrambled up, leaving the ball where it landed.

"That's what I was trying to tell you." Seonghun hefted the ball easily, turning it so she could see the three holes. "There is a number on each of these. That is how much they weigh."

She peered at the sixteen on the ball. "Oh, well, shit."

He chuckled. "Yes." Seong put it back, checking the others before he found a neon green one. "Try this."

She slid her fingers into the ball, pulling it from him. "This is better, but the other one was prettier."

He searched around to find a fifteen-pound ball for himself. "By the end of the night it won't matter, I promise." Carrying both balls, Seong walked them over to the lane, setting them down. Looking over, Minjun had calmed down enough to order food. "Min, three orders of cheese fries, two orders of chicken strips, and a pizza please. Also, probably two more cans of soda."

Min nodded as he ordered.

"Who in the world are you feeding?" Maliah looked at him in disbelief.

"You know I can eat; I always end up eating more while bowling. You'll see." All of a sudden, the computer booted up to enter their names, the room got darker and Maliah jumped as smoke started spraying from the lanes.

"This is intense!" she yelled over the music.

"Yes, but Min loves it. Look." Seonghun pointed. Sure enough, Min was still bouncing to the music, singing along while typing everyone's name in.

"Yongjoon, you're up first," Minjun called as he finished up the names. Yong stepped up, reaching for a bright blue ball.

"His ball is prettier than mine," Maliah pointed out.

Seong rolled his eyes as he took a sip of his beer. Yong threw his ball down the smoke-filled lane, hitting a handful of pins. Maliah watched eagle eyed, as Seonghun explained the game to her.

Finally, she spoke up. "The goal is to hit as many of the pins as possible with one throw, right?"

"Correct." Minjun sat beside her.

"So if I hit all the pins in one shot do I get a second turn?" Maliah asked.

"I doubt you will get all the pins on your first try, but no, you don't," Min replied.

"What do you mean you doubt I'll get all the pins?" Maliah looked at him.

"You've never played, you don't understand bowling techniques." He shrugged.

Seonghun saw her look at Min with her lip poked out. She turned to watch Yongjoon carefully. "You look incredibly deep in thought," he remarked.

"I—" She stared as Yong rolled the second ball. "I tend to focus hard. It alarms people because I can tune out everything around me."

"Is that what you're doing now?" he guessed.

"Yes."

"Why?"

"Because I'm going to kick Minjun's ass for saying I can't do something. I need to learn how to kick his ass."

He chuckled as he walked up to Yong before taking his turn. "Ten dollars says Liah wipes the floor with Minjun on scoring tonight."

"Min is better than I am, and she's never played. Never saw you taking a sucker bet just because you like a pretty face," chortled Yong. "You're on."

Seonghun took his turn, not clearing all the pins, but coming close. As he turned around to step off the lane, he saw that food had arrived. Minjun had set it up so he went last, so Maliah was up next. She walked up and cocked her head to the side looking at the lane.

"Hey, Min?" she called out.

"Yeah?" he replied, eating a piece of pizza while dancing to the music.

"I'm really good at math," she announced.

"That's nice, but what does that have to do with anything?" He stopped dancing to stare at her, confused.

Seong understood where this was going instantly. He crammed a chicken finger in his mouth to keep from laughing out loud.

"Most activities that have to do with math I excel at. Like pool, for example. Pool is just geometry. Bowling is geometry and physics." With that she hefted her ball, stepped to the left before rolling it down the alley.

Liah got a strike.

"Did the person who has never bowled get the first strike of the night?" Yong looked at Seong in disbelief.

In response, he crammed another chicken strip into his mouth.

She looked at the men innocently as they each took their turns.

"Now, things happen to affect geometry, like my arm will get tired, or I angle wrong, or I'll trip over my own feet—" She stepped to the left again to roll, leaving two pins up. "But one thing about me is I will always figure something out." She rolled again, knocking the two pins down, then looked over at Seong who had swallowed the last of his chicken strips. "You promised me cheese fries."

He walked to her, pulling her over to the food.

The night went on. It was the best time Seong had had in a while. In between bowling, Minjun and Maliah danced to the music that was playing loudly while occasionally pulling their partners to dance with them. They discovered a little alcove to the side, where he would pull Liah from time to time to kiss her. She ended up winning the first set of games, which surprised everyone.

"I was just trying to beat Min." She shrugged. "Don't ever doubt me. Proving people wrong fuels me."

"Got it," Minjun said as he sipped his beer.

Maliah eyeballed his drink.

"You're welcome to one if you want one," Seonghun said. "I understand your reasoning on why you don't want to drink; I respect it, but you keep glancing over as if you're curious. If you're concerned, I'll stop drinking now. I can drive us home if something happens. Nothing is going to happen to you with all three of us here."

"Thanks, but I think I'm good. Maybe some other time." She went to grab cheese fries, but they were all gone. "I don't normally eat this much but I want more."

"It's all the bowling. We can call for more food," Yongjoon said, pointing to the phone.

"I'll do it. Do you guys want anything?" Maliah asked.

They gave her a list of things to order. When Seonghun pulled out his credit card, she swatted it away, pulling out her own. After hanging up the phone she sat by Minjun.

"I forgot to tell you I talked to Shiwon today."

"What is he up to?" Minjun asked.

"A couple of things. Apparently, he's pre-med and he loves babies. So he's going to school to learn to deliver babies."

"Did not expect that," Minjun replied.

"Neither did I. He's also going to UCLA for medical school," Maliah said.

"Where is that?"

"Less than thirty minutes from the USC campus," Yong piped up. "You're about to be neighbors with a gorgeous doctor that loves babies?"

"If no one offers me a better deal, then yes. He offered to do lunch occasionally. It will be nice to have someone close to eat with on occasion." She looked at Seonghun who nodded understandingly. "What about you, Yongjoon? Any word from... I don't even know where you applied?"

"Georgetown Law, no, not yet. I have decent grades, but I don't have the grades or extracurriculars to get early acceptance like you do."

"I heard Washington D.C. is pretty in the spring with all the cherry blossom trees," Maliah said.

"I'm looking forward to it, a little change of pace. It's breaking my heart to leave my mom behind though."

"I'm assuming that you're planning to stay in the Washington D.C. area after you graduate?" Maliah asked.

Yongjoon glanced at Minjun. "I haven't decided yet." He stood up to start the next game of bowling.

Maliah looked at the other two. "Did I say something wrong?"

"No, you didn't," Minjun sighed, "we have a bit of a logistical problem, that's all. Same as you."

Maliah nodded. Grabbing his hand, she squeezed. "You'll figure it out." She stood up, pulling Seong to the alcove. He thought she wanted to kiss him, so he leaned in, but she stopped him. "A-a-are we making a mistake not talking about logistics? I know we haven't been together long, but in six months we'll be a literal world away from each other."

"We can discuss it if you like, though there isn't a whole lot we can do. I have to go back to Korea. You have to go to graduate school to have the career you want. We'll make time for each other. I'll visit when I can. I'd like for you to visit me if possible. I want to show you where I live."

"You described it for me once. I'd like to see it," she said, looking at him.

He kissed her quickly. "We'll make sure you do." Seong tugged her arm. "Let's go. You're about to win me money."

"How?" she asked.

He explained the bet with Yong.

"Glad to know you have faith in me." She smiled at him as she grabbed a pile of gooey fries.

"I don't believe there's anything you can't do," he said, grabbing an onion ring.

The group played four games. Seonghun laughed at Minjun's antics to try to get Maliah off track. He'd try to distract her, but quickly learned she was too focused. He stole her bowling shoe, but she bowled a strike on one foot. Eventually he gave up, playing fair.

Maliah won the second group of games, while Minjun won the third. If he could win the fourth, they would be tied. Their partners sat the final game out, watching them from the couch. Min sat cuddled with Yongjoon as Liah took her final turn. She'd gotten a strike the first time and knocked down eight pins the second time. She was unable to get the last two for the final turn. Sitting beside Seonghun, she looked at the scoring screen, asking for his help to comprehend it.

She looked at Minjun who was staring at the scoring board as well. "Good luck."

He nodded as he stood up. Min rolled a strike first. The second shot he knocked down 7 pins, but was unable to get the last three. Liah won the final game. Seong held his hand out to Yong; he slapped a ten-dollar bill into it. Both men laughed as Min nearly shook Liah's arm out of the socket. After returning their shoes, everyone headed back to the house.

CHAPTER 41

rriving home, Seonghun saw Liah's surprise at Cho sitting on the couch, watching TV. "I was just waiting for you guys to get in. I'm going to bed. There's plenty to eat in the fridge if you're hungry." She ruffled Minjun's hair, kissing Yongjoon on her way upstairs.

"Why did she wait until we got in?" Liah looked at the stairs.

"Peace of mind. She was making sure we got back okay," Yong said as he wandered in the kitchen.

She turned to Seonghun, confused.

He saw what the problem was. "It's what a lot of parents do. They make sure their kids get home safely." Maliah shrugged, following Yong.

"The fact that parents looking after their kids is foreign to her, is a little alarming," Min whispered.

"I think she understands that parents clothe, feed their kids, and support them. But she never had the little nuanced things that a parent does, so she doesn't understand," Seong explained. "Her parents never supported her with extracurricular things, they didn't even really feed her properly. So how is she to know?"

Min nodded. They walked into the kitchen to a humorous sight. Their partners were both eating gimbap, but while Yongjoon had normal wooden chopsticks, Maliah had these odd, pink chopsticks with an octopus face on them.

"What on earth are those?" Minjun guffawed.

"Training chopsticks," Yongjoon gestured at her trying to use them, "I handed her regular ones. It didn't go well. We have some around from when I was a kid."

"I don't have dexterity apparently." Her hands were slightly shaky even with the training chopsticks. The boys plowed through three rolls each to Maliah's one. "Min, did you get to use the bath bombs?" she asked.

Minjun turned red. "Uh yeah, I got to use two of them so far, they are very nice. Thanks. The scrubby stuff makes my skin feel really soft as well."

"I'm glad you enjoyed them. Lush always cheers me up a bit when I'm feeling low." She rinsed their plates, placing them in the dishwasher.

"You can't really cheer yourself up in the dorm like that since we only have a shower, so what do you do?" he asked.

"There are these gooey chocolate brownies at the bakery next to The Den. I'll buy one of those, sit under my blanket, and listen to music. I also use the scrub. I can use that in the shower."

"If you ever want someone to sit under the blanket with you, I will," Minjun offered.

"Thanks, but I'm usually very quiet when I'm like that. I'm not good company."

"Well in that case, it wouldn't be about being good company would it? It would be about providing comfort," he pointed out.

She just shrugged.

Yong changed the subject. "Do you have plans before you guys go out tomorrow?"

"I don't have any, I'm pretty far ahead on my work for classes," Liah said.

"I'm all caught up," said Seong.

"Did you guys want to have a movie marathon? We could do all the Marvel movies in order."

"That sounds like fun," Maliah said. "We won't get through all the movies though, before we have to leave."

"We can finish it up on Thanksgiving break. Will you make those cookies and Chex Mix tomorrow?" Yongjoon asked.

"Yeah, that isn't an issue, as long as your mom is okay with me using her stuff." Maliah yawned, leaning against Seonghun.

"She won't care. She liked them a lot too. She likes cooking with you. Only other person that cooks with her is Seonghun, and she has to watch him to make sure he doesn't eat everything before it gets to the table."

Seonghun blushed.

"Mmm." She closed her eyes.

"It's late, let's get to bed before we can't even get up before noon." Yongjoon stood, grabbing Min's hand, leading him upstairs.

Seonghun looked at Maliah who looked like she was thirty seconds from crashing. "Let me walk you to your door," he said sarcastically.

"Don't be like that," she admonished sleepily, "it's nice that I was even welcomed here. Besides, we don't sleep together every night."

"I wouldn't mind it if we slept together every night," he said.

"Really?" She looked at him dubiously. "I seemed to remember getting a letter at some point saying that sometimes you need space. I respect that, I need space at times too."

"Well, this isn't one of those times. I just want to be with you," he explained.

"We'll be watching tv most of the day tomorrow, so we can cuddle. Then after skating I'll put the heating patch anywhere you need it."

Seonghun was confused. "Why would I need a patch after skating?"

"Skating works different muscles that I'm going to assume you don't work out." Maliah stepped inside her room as she stopped speaking. "Goodnight, Seong."

"Goodnight, Liah." He kissed her softly. She quietly shut the door as he trudged back to his room, flopping dramatically on the bed. As he lay there, his phone went off.

Liah: *I can feel you pouting from here. That's intense.*
Seong: *The other two get to go at it like rabbits and I can't even cuddle you. It's not fair.*
Liah: *Life isn't fair, honey bunny. You know that.*

Seong: *Honey bunny?*
Liah: *It's cute, like you. We'll have our turn at going at it like rabbits at some point. I promise.*
Seong: *You don't have to promise that, you know?*
Liah: *I know. But I'm still promising it. G'night. <3*
Seong: *Night <3*

He tossed his phone. *I'll see her in the morning. It's fine.* His final thought before going to sleep was the look on Maliah's face when she threw her first strike. She was so cocky. It was endearing.

When Seonghun woke up in the morning he raced downstairs... to see Liah not there. Everyone else was having what looked like a rather serious discussion.

"Good morning, sleepyhead." Cho smiled at him. "Breakfast is on the stove."

He looked around. "Where's Liah?"

"I'm assuming she's still asleep. She hasn't come down yet," she said.

"I'm going to go get her. She usually doesn't sleep later than me." He took off for the stairs.

Yongjoon looked at Minjun. "When has he ever done anything before eating?"

"Never," Min said.

Seonghun tapped lightly on her door. There was no answer so he peeked in. He could barely see her under the blankets. He left the door open out of respect to Cho and walked in. Maliah had one leg in and one leg out of the blanket. She chose to sleep in shorts and a tank top, something she never really did at the dorm. They were short and the angle she was at, he could see some of the freckles on her inner thighs. He slid under the blanket, wrapping his arms around her for a brief moment. "Liah, wake up."

She shifted, turning in his embrace. "We're going to get in trouble," she mumbled.

"Nah, I just came to get you for breakfast. Nothing else." He watched as she nodded before dozing off again.

He smacked her butt lightly. "Come, eat breakfast, watch movies. You can just wear your pajamas. We all are."

She looked down. "I'll throw on some sweats."

He shrugged. "Whatever makes you comfortable." He kissed her forehead before leaving to give her privacy.

"You don't have to leave. I have to use the bathroom." She ran inside the restroom. As Seong heard the water running, he lay back on the bed, waiting for her.

"Liah," he yelled. "Can I use your phone to send your Pinterest to me? I want to look at your boards."

"I don't care," was the muffled reply from behind the door. He quickly went to the app, sending himself the link. Back on his phone, he clicked the link. He discovered if he selected something on a board it would go through, showing him where to buy it or a webpage that instructed on how to make something. It was a pretty cool site. He counted the boards but something didn't add up. She came out of the bathroom as he looked up.

"There were like thirteen boards, but when I used the link there were only ten."

"That's because three of the boards are private. You can only see them on my account or if I give you access," she explained, as she threw on one of his sweatshirts. "The rest of the boards are public. Anyone can add my collection to their own board." Sliding sweatpants over her shorts, she sat beside him.

"May I ask what's on the hidden ones?" he ventured.

"You know how you can click on the things on those boards then they send you to different pages? The private ones are more collages for my dreams in different aspects of my life. You know most of what they say. Things about my career, me wanting a dog, me wanting a home of my own. That type of stuff." She rested her chin on his shoulder as he scrolled through the photography ideas. Seong closed the site, pocketing his phone before looking at his girlfriend.

"Let's go eat." He took her hand, leading her out of the room.

CHAPTER 42

After breakfast, Maliah made double batches of cookies and Chex Mix. Yongjoon started the first movie in the living room. Seong started a fire while Cho brought out extra blankets and pillows for everyone to spread out. Seonghun angled Liah close to the fire. He saw how enraptured she was with it.

As the movie started, Cho pulled out her laptop as well as a huge basket that she sat down next to her. "Ma, it's movie time, not working time," Yong complained. "Can't you work when I leave on Sunday?"

"I just have to send two emails to home buyers about some houses I found. It won't take long. Besides, aren't you a little preoccupied?" She stared at her son cuddled up with Min.

"I still want you to be part of the experience," Yong said, looking at her.

"Let me send the emails, it won't take long," she reassured her son.

Seonghun observed Liah as she watched them. He wondered what was going on in her mind. He knew bits about her home life, but he didn't understand how her everyday life went. It didn't seem like a great time to ask on the cusp of their first date.

Which brought him to another thought as she shifted in his arms. How in the hell were they only going on their first date? Could their other outings have been seen as dates? Maybe bowling could be seen as a double date with their friends, but it wasn't stated as such.

"What are you thinking about so hard up there?" she murmured sleepily.

"Are you still tired?" he asked, surprised.

"I never stop going, so when I do, I tend to sleep a lot. This is the most downtime I've had in years."

"Years?" He looked down at her.

"I had to work hard to get the scholarship to Brebeuf. I then had to work hard to maintain my grades, take all the college level courses I could, while working to basically support myself. Same thing with college. I bust my ass non-stop. I don't mind it, it's not like I have a lot to do when I'm not working. I take pictures, draw, or I play music. That's about it. I read when I have time." Under the blanket she snuggled him tighter.

"What do you like to read?" Min asked.

She laughed. "Straight trash. I love a good period piece romance novel."

"Oh lord." Yong rolled his eyes as his mom perked up.

"When you say period piece," Cho began.

Maliah looked over. "I want someone's virtue ruined by stepping out of a small alcove with a rake she had no business being with, being forced into a wedding, falling in love with tumultuous sex, but he didn't realize he actually had sex with her on their wedding night because he was so drunk but their bond is so strong that when they do finally have sex again he realizes it was her the first time, gets upset because he felt like he was deceived then goes to cry into the arms of his mistress."

The boys stared at her. Cho looked like she was going to explode. "Come with me." She stood up, running upstairs. Maliah shrugged, following.

Yongjoon started laughing. "She's going to freak out. Mom owns a ton of those bodice ripper books."

"Bodice ripper?" Seonghun asked.

Maliah came back downstairs, dazed with two books in her hands. "She said I could get more when we come back for Thanksgiving."

Seonghun giggled at the front of the books, understanding what Yong meant. A woman was thrown back over the arms of a man with an unbuttoned shirt, about to kiss her. She had on a long elaborate gown that was ripped with the man's hand covering her bare chest.

She sat the books next to her before cuddling back into Seong to watch the movie. Cho came down shortly after, laying on the couch to watch as well. An hour into the movie, Seonghun whispered into Maliah's ear. She nodded, sitting up so he could move. He wandered in the kitchen, coming back with a tray of the cookies and snack mix she'd made along with five glasses of milk.

"The fact that these cookies are so delicious is baffling to me," Cho admitted.

"I know. They're odd, but so good," Maliah agreed. "I learned to mix different ingredients based on what I had around. I wanted something both salty and sweet one day, so why not? I also make a very good brown butter toffee cookie."

Cho looked at her thoughtfully, but didn't say anything. Everyone continued to munch on cookies throughout the movies, talking quietly every once in a while. Eventually, Maliah dozed off in Seonghun's lap.

"She's never relaxed." Cho was staring at Maliah asleep. "All this kid has ever known is work." She looked at Yong. "Spring break."

"What about spring break? We were going to go camping again this year," Yong said.

She scoffed lightly, turning to look at Seonghun. "Were you planning on asking her to go camping?" When he nodded, she continued, "She doesn't seem uptight, and would probably follow you wherever you go, but I don't think she is going to want to camp in a tent while peeing behind trees," said Cho. "Hear me out, I'm owed a favor. I helped a sale go through with some cabins in Gatlinburg, so I was offered a free stay. Two of us could drive, so we would have two cars available at all times just in case you guys want a date night or whatever."

"How many cabins would we be staying in?" Min asked.

"Just one, but the cabins are made for families." She pulled her laptop back to her, typing furiously. "The one we would be staying in sleeps twenty-six. Twelve bedrooms with fourteen bathrooms," she read off.

Seonghun goggled. "We don't need all of that space."

"So we wouldn't use it. We'll just use what we need," Cho said.

Seonghun stared at her. "Would house rules apply there?"

"Yes."

"No."

Cho stared at him. "Excuse me?"

"I'm not going if I cannot sleep in the same bed as my girlfriend. What's the point? I'm not a teenager, I'm an adult. As such, I should be allowed to do so. If we did get pregnant, it's not a huge issue, as we're adults."

Yong looked at Min. "This is about to be good." He grabbed two cookies, passed one to his boyfriend as they watched the showdown.

"Have you not listened to a word out of that girl's mouth? Getting pregnant right now in the middle of how hard she worked would be a massive issue!" Cho whisper shouted at him.

"You're acting as if we're thinking with our glands. Even if we were to do that, which once again, let the record show neither of us are ready yet—"

"Record noted," Yongjoon interrupted.

"Neither of us are stupid. There are ways to prevent pregnancy. We aren't teenagers, Cho. We aren't thinking like teenagers. So either I'm allowed to sleep with my girlfriend on this trip, or I'm not going. We can hang out at the dorm together." Seonghun glanced down to make sure Maliah was still asleep. She was drooling slightly. He smiled gently, using his sleeve to wipe the drool from her mouth. Looking up at Cho he saw her face soften fractionally.

"Look, talk to her, see if she would even want to go. I'll think about it."

Seonghun nodded and went back to the show, rubbing Maliah's back as she lay.

After the second movie Cho excused herself to go make lunch. Maliah was still asleep and the boys were talking. "What would we do in Gatlinburg?" asked Minjun.

"Shop, explore, drive around, eat a bunch. It's kind of a country area. There is an amusement park there as well, Dollywood," Yong said. "I've been before; the cabins are really nice. There is usually a hot tub, cable tv, with decent Wi-Fi. We can also eat out or bring food to cook. We've done a combo of both."

Maliah shifted in Seonghun's lap. "Are you coming back to the land of the living sweetheart?"

"Mmm." She wrapped her arms around his waist. "This is nice." She cracked an eye, squinting at the screen. "How long did I sleep?"

"Through two movies. Your body probably needed it though," Min said.

"I guess." She sat up and stretched before leaning back on Seonghun. "Min, I have been asked to buy a coat for the winter."

"You don't have a coat? Why?" Minjun asked.

"I haven't found a coat that's comfortable. They either swallow me because I'm so short, or it feels too snug," she explained.

"Do you want to go somewhere tomorrow morning?"

"That's fine. We can't stay out long. We have the lunch date thing."

"We'll be quick," Minjun assured her.

"Lunch is ready!" Cho called.

Yongjoon paused the show as they walked into the kitchen. On the table was a large soup tureen. Beside each place setting were small bowls of rice along with an empty bowl. Little side dishes like the previous night were scattered.

Yong stopped short, glancing at Liah.

"What?" She looked at him.

"I'm sure we probably have a porkchop or something left if you aren't interested in lunch," he said.

"Why wouldn't I be interested in lunch?" Maliah looked over at the table confused. "It's soup, rice, and veggies."

"Some people get weird about different foods," Seong said.

They saw the light click on in Maliah's head. "You've had people turn up their nose at Korean food, right?"

The boys nodded, sitting at the table.

"I eat what's put in front of me. It's nice your mom cooked for us. Cooking is a labor of love, I think. Why would I turn it down? Also, it smells really good." When she sat down she saw that the training chopsticks had been set out for her. She looked up at Cho. "Thank you for not treating me differently. What is the soup called?"

"청국장찌개" Cho said.

Maliah blinked. "Um. I can't say that."

They laughed as they sat down to eat. Between bites of the soybean paste stew, Seong tried to teach her how to say the words. She struggled a bit with the chopsticks, but was handling it well. Liah tried everything that was on the table, but seemed to go back to the soup and kimchi.

Seonghun was happy she gave it a try. He remembered Yong speaking of people he'd brought home that turned their nose up at his mother's food. "I don't expect them to devour everything, but at least give it a try. It's my culture, I'm trying to share," he'd complain.

It didn't look like he was going to have that problem with Maliah. She ate like each of them, then helped to clean up after. They all piled into the living room after, taking their places and watching the movies, feeling warm, comfortable, and full of food.

After a few hours, Seong looked at Liah. She was thoroughly enthralled with the fight scene on the screen. Leaning close, he whispered in her ear, "Do you need to start getting ready?"

She looked at her watch. "Are we eating first or skating first?"

"Skating, I figure it would make for a bigger appetite."

"Okay. I'll go get ready. Dress casually, you'll probably fall." She stood up, kissing his forehead before wandering upstairs.

His friends looked at him as they paused the movie. "What are you wearing?" Yong asked.

Seonghun shrugged. "I have the blue sweater for tomorrow. I have jeans, sweatshirts, and t-shirts with me."

Seong watched as the couple looked at each other. "He's taller than both of us," Yong said to the unspoken question.

"We're going to have to at least try, so he doesn't look like a hobo," Minjun said, getting to his feet.

Cho watched on with amusement. "You boys have fun. I'm going to go read for a bit. Yongie, when you and Min get done attacking this poor man, come find me. We can do a puzzle or something."

Yongjoon gave his mother a kiss as Minjun pulled Seonghun up the stairs. "I know you two are very casual dressers. I'm trying hard to respect it, but you can still look put together." Seong rolled his eyes as he sat on Yong's bed, patiently awaiting the direction of his oldest friend.

CHAPTER 43

Downstairs, Seong was pestering Cho over dinner. "Get out of here before you smell like garlic! You look so nice."

"Give me a chestnut then I'll leave." He laid his chin on her shoulder.

She grabbed a small bowl with a chestnut in it. "Go!" she ordered.

He left the kitchen chortling with his treat when he saw Maliah standing there with her skates in her hand. He stared at her as she shifted around. "You look pretty."

The dress was bright blue, leaving one of her shoulders bare. He could see a simple gold heart necklace in the hollow of her throat.

"You look handsome yourself," she said quietly. He'd paired his own jeans to the turtleneck he borrowed from Yong, along with some sneakers. "What's in the bowl?"

"Chestnut, here." He broke it in half, handing her a piece.

Instead of taking it, she wrapped her mouth around the fingers holding it. The feeling of her warm mouth traveled south on him.

She looked in surprise. "It's not sweet. I figured chestnuts would be sweet."

"Uh, no, not for this." He popped the other half of the chestnut in his mouth before putting the bowl back into the kitchen.

"Are you ready?" he asked.

"Yes." She walked to the door to put her shoes on. Seong followed after her.

"Look at our babies, all grown up," Yong called out from the top of the stairs.

"Don't have her out too late," said Min.

"Yes, have her home at a decent hour." Yong nodded.

"No sex!"

"But if you do have sex, wear a condom." Both men dissolved into laughter.

"I don't like either one of you," said Liah.

"You adore us. Have fun." Minjun waved.

They walked out to Liah's car. She got in the driver's seat, immediately adjusting it so she could actually reach the pedals. As Seong sat in the passenger seat, her head popped up.

"What's wrong?" he asked.

"I thought I caught whiffs earlier, but wasn't sure. But when you shut the door, I smelled it again. You smell really good."

"Thank you. Yongjoon has two big spinning racks of cologne. I chose this one." He saw she was still staring. "I know this part usually comes after the actual date, but I think we both could use it." Carefully he leaned over to kiss her, touching her neck to pull her close. He opened his mouth; Seong felt her tongue tease his, while she made a slight whimpering sound.

They stayed like this for about twenty minutes, their pace becoming heated, until they heard a knock at the passenger window. Pulling apart, slightly dazed, Liah turned on the car so Seonghun could roll down the window.

"You have car trouble, Liah?" Minjun smirked.

"Uh, no." Seong saw her eyes widen as she avoided eye contact with their friend.

"Just checking. You two have fun." Minjun walked back to the house, closing the door. They saw two faces peeking out of the window.

Seonghun snorted. "They are such weirdos. Let's go before we're ambushed again." She nodded, pulling off into the evening.

Arriving at the skating rink, Seonghun thought it looked similar to the bowling alley; the main difference being that it didn't smell like smoke. The place was loud, full of thumping bass. After he paid their entry fee, she led him to the rental booth to get his skates.

"Have you ever skated before?" she asked.

"No."

"Skateboard?"

"No."

"Okay, this is going to be interesting."

Seong tied on the skates, standing up. He nearly fell face first into the carpet. Liah quickly pushed him to sitting. "Hold on." She lifted the dress slightly, kneeling at his foot. "You need to tie them tightly, so you have ankle support." He watched her yank the laces, tying the skates tighter than he did before. "Stay seated until I get my skates on," she ordered.

Unclipping her skates from the rainbow suspender, Liah put them on, tying them tightly before looping them into a bow. When she finished, she stood up, holding out her hands to him. He slowly stood up, stretching his arms to grab her hands. However, as soon as he wobbled, he immediately abandoned that tactic, holding onto her waist for dear life. To her credit, she didn't even laugh.

"Hey, it's okay. I got you. Just stand up straight," she whispered reassuringly.

He slowly stood to his full height, loosening his grasp on her waist, putting his hand in hers.

"There you go. Now, we're on the carpet, that's the easiest to skate on. We have to make it to the floor. You're going to push off with your right foot, then your left."

He followed her instructions. Seong was pleased that he did it without falling. She took a couple of turns with him on the carpet. He felt more confident than he did when he stood up.

"Okay, now, I know you're feeling brave, but like I said, this was carpet. We need to go out there." She pointed at the glossy wooden rink. "We're going to skate on the outside so you can grab the wall if you need to, okay?"

"Okay." He nodded.

They skated over to the opening on the rink. People were whizzing past. In a free moment Maliah stepped onto the rink. Holding his hand, she eased him onto it too. They took a few glides; Seonghun nearly toppled. "Oh my god!" he yelled as he went down. She pushed him up against the wall quickly as he held onto her waist.

"It's okay to fall. That's how we learn." She slowly let him go, held his hand as they began their slow turn around the rink.

Seonghun fell multiple times, but she was always there with a patient hand. At one point he pulled her down too. She simply dusted herself off before helping him back up. By the fifth glide around the rink, he was falling a lot less. Maliah turned, so her back was facing the flow of traffic.

"Look at me, don't look at your feet."

He looked into her pretty brown eyes. He saw no amusement, just patience. They skated around the rink like that, with her leading. He looked over to the other side of the rink. There was a little kid celebrating a birthday.

"That's a fun idea," he said.

She looked over. Liah smiled, but it looked a little sad to Seong. "Yeah. I always wanted to have a birthday at a skating rink." She looked behind her to make sure she wasn't going to hit anyone. "It never panned out for me."

He saw people skating and dancing at the same time. Maliah glanced over to see what he was looking at. "There are different types of skating. I think that is called soul skating."

"It looks intimate." The man was basically grinding on the woman while they skated.

"It is. It takes a lot of coordination because you're dancing and skating in time."

"Can you do it?" Seonghun asked.

"Never tried." She swung around, letting go of one of his hands. She skated on the inside just in case he needed to grab the wall.

"How did you get into skating?" he asked.

She was quiet for a while. "When I was seven-years-old a school friend invited me to go skating. I wasn't very good, but I was hooked. They took me every weekend they went, until I was nine. They moved away so I didn't get to go back until I was in high school. When I got my license, I was able to drive myself."

He thought very carefully about what he was going to say. "I don't want to bring the mood down—"

"Then don't please." She avoided his gaze.

"Liah," he said quietly, "we need to talk about it."

"Let me have this. Let me have one night skating with a handsome man like I don't have a care in the world. We can go back to the real world tomorrow." She still wouldn't look at him, but he saw the tear roll down her face.

"Okay." He went to wipe her tear, stumbled, and fell.

She held her hands out to him, helping him up. Once Seong was steady, she dashed the tear with the back of her hand as they continued skating silently.

"So you think I'm handsome?"

"I think you're one of the most handsome men I have ever met."

"When's the last time you had your vision checked?" he said teasingly.

"I see clearly with my glasses. I know you do too. You see what I, along with quite a bit of the female population, do." She swung back around so she could see his face.

Seong shifted uncomfortably, stumbling, but catching himself before he toppled down.

"When we go back Sunday, come to my room. I'll show you what I see." They continued steadily around the circle. All of a sudden, the lights dimmed. Half the people stepped off the rink.

"What's going on?" Seonghun looked up to see a sparkly disco ball descending from the ceiling.

"Couples' skate."

"What?"

"You skate with a partner. Look around."

Seonghun did as she said. Everyone was coupled up. There were two little girls holding hands skating side by side. Obvious couples were wrapped around each other as they skated to slow music.

"You don't have to be in a relationship or anything to skate," she pointed at the little giggling girls, no more than eight or nine, "but you have to have a partner on the floor."

"I wanna skate like that." He pointed at the couple across the rink. The man was basically holding the woman with her back facing his front.

"In order to do that, you'd be leading. You feel comfortable doing that?" She looked at him skating. It was smoother, but he was still stumbling.

"Can we try?" he asked.

She nodded before swinging around easily on her skates. He grabbed her by the waist as they slowly skated. Anytime he would nearly go down, he'd grab her tighter, causing her to gasp quietly.

"Am I hurting you?" Seonghun murmured in her ear. He saw goosebumps break out across her collarbone.

"N-no."

They slowly made their way around the circle, completing just as the song ended. The lights came back on just as the normal loud thumping music began to play. They continued to skate through the evening. All of a sudden Seong heard Maliah's stomach roar. Not rumble; it was a literal roar that he heard over the music. "Are you hungry?" He chuckled because she seemed embarrassed.

"I swear, I've eaten more in the past few days than I normally do in a week. I'm starving," she admitted.

"Let's go eat. I found a place for wings. I was going to take you to Hooters, but that didn't seem like a great idea," he said.

"I don't mind Hooters, they have good wings." She led him to the steps to get to the carpeted section. "Can you turn in your skates? I want to take a couple of turns around the rink."

"Yeah. I'll meet you by the bench that your shoes are under." He watched her roll off. As he walked to the rental booth, he realized she was holding back with him. In the time it took him to do a single lap, she'd done two. She rolled a few more times before she stepped up on the carpet, skating over to their bench.

"You're really good at that."

"I love it. It's good exercise and I like the feeling of flying." Liah unlaced her skates. "I also do my best thinking on the rink. I'll just skate for hours running thoughts through my head. When I started falling for you I came here, ruminating on how starting something was a bad idea."

He was surprised. "You were talking yourself out of dating me?"

"Yes."

"Why?"

"We'll talk about it over dinner." She tied her boots, clipped her skates back together on the suspender before standing up.

He slowly stood as well, kind of hurt. She looked at him, grabbing his arm gently.

"I didn't talk myself out of it. I'm here with you. I'm happy. Okay?"

Seong gave a singular nod. Grabbing her hand, they walked out of the rink. "Can I drive?" he asked.

She handed her keys to him before sitting in the passenger seat. As he got in, Liah studied him for a moment. "Hand me the keys for a moment."

He did as she asked, watching as she slipped her spare car key off the key ring, giving it to him. "All I ask is that you let me know before you take my car please. You're welcome to use it as long as I don't need it."

"Thank you." He attached the spare key to his own key ring. Queuing up navigation on his phone, he drove them to dinner.

When Seong did his research, he was happy to find a family friendly pub that Liah could enter. Once seated, they began to look at the menu. "Do you want to try fried pickles?" he asked, scanning the appetizers.

"I love fried pickles," she said, drinking her water.

He watched her as she flipped through the menu, as focused as she normally was on assignments. Seonghun had already decided on his burger while he waited patiently for her to talk. The waitress came by, took their orders, quickly leaving them in silence.

She sighed quietly before she began to speak. "You've met my therapist, seen the meds I take, along with the issues I have when we try to be intimate. You see how I handle stress and what happens when I fall into a minor depressive cycle." Those big brown eyes focused on him. "The last thing I want to be is a burden on anyone. I've been there. I didn't like how it made me feel. The guilt that you're dragging someone down into your muck."

He opened his mouth to protest, but she held up her hand.

"Please. You wanted an explanation; I'm giving you one." She took another drink of water before she continued. "We're adults. I knew at some point you'd want to have sex. What if I can't get to that point before you become impatient? What if I grew to care for you, but you dumped me? What If I had to dump you because you became pushy? What if this was a joke, an incredibly cruel joke that you actually liked me? All of this was circling in my brain non-fucking-stop."

His heart broke a little at her thinking his feelings were a joke. "What changed your mind?"

She gave him a half smile. "You did. Your relationships with our roommates. The way you asserted when you needed food, how unabashed you are consuming it. You're kind of like Kirby in the video game, you know?" She smiled at him.

He blushed.

"I had to trust in you. You gave me all the reason to doing that with how openly you love and support your friends. Also the fact that you barely blinked an eye at Minjun loving Yongjoon."

At that point, a waitress set fried pickles on the table, along with a beer and an orange soda. She patiently waited for the waitress to leave before she continued. "You're supportive, you're kind, you know how to set boundaries when things are making you uncomfortable. I've never actually seen you get angry, even when you have cause to." She dipped a fried pickle chip in ranch. "As a matter of fact the one time I've heard you get angry it wasn't because something was done to you."

"She's a rude bitch," Seonghun said as he tried a fried pickle. "Oh my god, I want to eat all of these."

Maliah giggled at the look on his face. He quickly shoved another in his mouth. After he chewed, he spoke.

"Despite what's been said or shown to you thus far, you're very easy to care about. You're a good person. Do you remember coming to get me when I was pushed out into the street? You were studying hard. You could have just said that it wasn't your problem, but you showed up with words of encouragement, taking me back to the dorm. You tended to my wounds. It wasn't out of obligation. It was out of the goodness of your heart."

It was quiet between them as they ate their appetizer when Seonghun spoke up. "I have something to ask you." He felt a lurch in his belly. *Too soon, too soon, too soon.*

She looked at him as their meals were delivered. Focusing her attention on her wings, she divided them, giving half to him, while he split his burger, giving her half as well. "I know it's incredibly early to even be talking about this," he continued as she started eating, "but is it out of the realm of possibility for you to maybe come to Korea after you're done with your education?"

"We already talked about me visiting." Maliah bit into a wing.

"Not for a visit," he said, watching her. He saw her face go from confused to understanding to confused again.

"Seonghun, we've been dating for a month. You're asking me to move to another country?" She dropped her wing in disbelief.

"Not now, not in six months," he assured her hurriedly. "I'm asking you to think about the future."

"I don't speak the language. I don't know anything about your culture. Are there Black people there?!"

"Uh." Seonghun stared at her as she proceeded to work herself up.

"And work! Where would I work? What would I do!? I'd have this degree and what!?" She was looking at him wild eyed.

"Liah, calm down. It was just a question."

"A really loaded question." She picked up the dropped wing. "It's way too soon to be moving countries for a relationship. No offense."

"None taken." He meant it. It was out there; he'd planted a seed to get her thinking at least.

"Answer the question though, black people?" She watched his face.

"In my area, there are none. But I live within two hours of Seoul where there is a large expat community. black people live in the city."

"So you live in a town, as opposed to a city, correct?"

He waffled his hand. "More like a village than a town."

She blinked. Pulling out her phone, she began to type.

"What are you doing?" he asked with a mouthful of his hamburger.

"Finding out the difference between a town and a village." Her head bowed as she began her search.

He snorted. "You really do look everything up."

"If I don't know, someone else out there will." She looked up from the phone. "It's smaller than a town." Sticking her phone back in her purse, she went back to eating. "It's still too soon to talk about this."

"I didn't mean to rile you. It's been on my mind lately," he admitted.

"I want you to feel comfortable talking about anything that deals with this relationship, but you also need to be prepared for me to not be able to formulate a well throughout response. Like now." She started on another chicken wing.

"Fair enough. It's been brought up so it can stop running rampant through my head." He bit into a crispy wing.

They spent the rest of the time talking about everything they could think of. Seonghun told her what it was like growing up in a village. Maliah told him what it was like growing up downtown.

He looked at her for a long second, worried about asking the question. He was dying of curiosity though. "Can we drive past where you grew up?"

She shrugged. "I suppose so. It's late enough that no one is going to see us." She finished up the last of her soda before mock fighting him for the last pickle chip.

"I'm a growing boy!" he whined.

"That is your excuse every time there is a bite of food left." She laughed at him.

He paid the bill, going back to her car.

CHAPTER 44

Maliah drove them downtown. "I've been this way before," Seong said looking around, "Yong took us here to go to the mall."

"Yeah, there is a ton to do in this area." She turned off into a side street, parallel parked, before cutting the lights. She pointed to a rickety townhouse. "There, that's my parent's house." It was pale blue that was in desperate need of painting. The lawn was mowed and someone even attempted to put flowers outside. A wreath was on the door; despite its rundown appearance, it gave the house a homey feel. Seonghun said as much.

"My mom liked to decorate. The things she had, she kept tidy, I guess that's where I get it from." All of a sudden an older model car swung into the driveway. A tall man got out of the driver's side, followed by a woman much taller than Liah getting out of the passenger seat. It was dark, Seonghun couldn't make out many of their features. Her father's hair seemed cropped. His shoulders were slumped. Her mother's hair was long with bouncy curls at the end.

"Both your parents are tall. How are you so tiny?" He looked over at her.

"Remember, I look like my dad's mom. She was my height."

They watched as the two people started bickering while her father was unlocking the door. Liah's mother began jabbing her finger in his shoulder.

"No offense, Seonghun, but I lived this, I don't need to see it again in real life. I'm ready to go." She turned on the car, pulling off without another sound.

She started driving back to Yongjoon's house. Seonghun gathered his thoughts before he spoke. "Maliah, did your mom ever hit you?"

"I was spanked as a child, yes." She kept her focus on the road.

"I don't believe in that, but that's not what I meant," he said.

"I know what you meant. She stopped permanently after she broke skin. I fought back, which shocked her." She glanced at him quickly. "I don't talk about it. I've barely broached it in therapy. I know it was wrong. That she was wrong. I don't honestly feel like rehashing it. I've dealt with it." She took the exit that led to Yongjoon's neighborhood, bypassing the turn that headed into his neighborhood.

"You missed the turn for Yongjoon's house."

"I know. I figured you'd want to kiss me goodnight without a bunch of faces pressed up against the window." She turned into the park near Yongjoon's house, finding a dark corner.

"That's smart." He looked at her as she cut the car. "I've had a lot of fun with you tonight. We should go out more."

"I had fun too. I haven't had anyone to skate with before. You're kind of graceful, so you'd actually be really good once you've gone a few times," she said.

They stared at each other for a moment before Maliah got bashful, looking down at her hands.

"Hey." He tilted her chin up. "It's just us. No one else out here." He kissed her softly. They were at an awkward angle because of the armrest. "Can we get in the backseat? The armrest is in the way."

She looked at him sternly. "This is just a kiss, Seong. You aren't going to have me splayed chasing an orgasm in the park."

He smiled at her, his eyes dancing with mirth. "If you can control yourself I can too." They quickly got into the backseat of her small car. "Why does this feel so awkward?" he said aloud.

"Because everything between us has happened organically. From that first picnic, everything just flowed. This was an actual date. There's a rigidness in calling something a date."

"Everything has flowed, hasn't it?" He traced her collarbone gently with his finger, pleased to hear the little hitch in her breath.

"Surprisingly yes, from the first time you sat outside my door," she said quietly. "We've had bumps. We'll probably continue to have them, but we kind of go together nicely." She gasped as his lips replaced the finger he was running along her collarbone. "Seong," she whimpered, grabbing his shoulders.

"Yes?" He worked his way up her neck to her ear. "You always smell so good. It's not just the perfume, it's you too. Your natural scent," he whispered in her ear. Seonghun kissed her, delighted as she responded eagerly. He wrapped his arms around her as she began softly stroking his arms.

She pulled back slightly, looking at him. "I'm about to be splayed in my car chasing my orgasm, aren't I?"

He chuckled. "We can stop now if you like."

"That's the problem. I don't want to stop! I don't ever want to stop, but we get to a point and I feel like something is holding me back. I can't put my finger on it."

"Why am I getting the feeling we're talking about more than kissing or foreplay?" he asked.

She sighed. "I want to have sex. I want to have sex with you. But something doesn't feel right. I go to tell you while we're mid-foreplay but in the back of my brain I hear, 'you'll regret it. He'll never look at you the same'. Then part of me wonders if I want to have sex just to see what it feels like to have someone want me in that way. There is another part of me—"

"Liah, no offense, but you have a lot of parts." He tried not to laugh.

"I know, but hear me out because this is the most important part." She swallowed. "You know how at dinner I said it was too soon?"

He nodded.

"When you and Yongjoon were fighting over the cookies, Minjun asked me if I was in love with you."

He waited for her to continue.

"I told him I didn't know, but if I did, I would tell you first because I've never said it to anyone before."

"No one?" Seong was astounded.

"Who would I have said it to at this point? My mother who hates me? My father who is indifferent? No, I haven't said it to anyone. It feels so soon to feel this way, but sometimes it feels like it is choking me. I'm scared if we have sex, I'll basically be an emotional wreck, even more so than I already am. A lot of it is programming that I need to overcome. I'm working through it in therapy, which is why we've been able to go as far as we have."

Seonghun tried not to focus on the fact that she may love him. If he thought about it, he'd lay her out in this car. He focused on what he could. "Do you want me to go to therapy with you again?"

"Maybe? I don't know. We'll see. Let me talk to Dr. Stewart. You, uh, us, usually take up the last fifteen minutes of my call." She took a breath. "This got really heavy really fast."

"I don't think so." He kissed her neck again and pulled her to him, cuddling her. "You have feelings for me, which is always a nice thing to hear. You're a little scared, which I get. I'm a little scared too." He adjusted so she was sitting between his legs. Seong wrapped one of his long legs around hers.

"What are you scared of?" she asked.

"I care about you a great deal. I was worried about you not returning the affection, but I don't think that's an issue. I worry about Casey hurting you again, about me hurting you. I worry what's going to happen after next semester." He kissed her head. "I worry about physically hurting you when we're messing around."

"You've been nothing but gentle," Maliah said.

"Because I focus on being gentle. During sex, I can't focus as hard as I do during foreplay. I'm worried I'm going to scare you off because I'm a little rough." He scraped his teeth across her collarbone as he heard the memory of his ex's words in his head. *You hurt me, Seong.*

"The next time we're together like that, don't focus as hard. Let go. If it's too much I'm not afraid to speak up."

"Okay."

They were silent for a minute. He absentmindedly slipped his hand up her dress and began to fondle her breasts. He stopped, ghosting his hand over the bra. "This is really lacy."

"Yeah, pretty bras are easier for me to find than underwear. I don't like walking around with a perma-wedgie." She leaned her head back.

"I still owe you underwear. What size do you wear?" he asked. He continued to touch her, lightly pinching her nipples.

"Size seven in panties. You don't have to buy me underwear," she said. "Seong, I really don't want to mess around in the car."

He slid his hand from under her dress, straightening it out. "I think it will be an interesting trip to the store. Can I take the guys?"

She tilted her head to look in his eyes. "Make it very clear to Minjun that friends or not, it is inappropriate in my eyes to present a woman he is not dating underthings."

He grinned. "Noted. I'll make sure he behaves." Seong kissed her collarbone again. "You should show this part more. It's sexy."

"It's my collarbone. What's sexy about a collarbone?" She sighed a little as he continued nipping at it.

"You like the lines of my back, I like your collarbone, deal with it." Placing one final kiss, he patted her thighs. "Let's go before I have you half-undressed in this car."

She crawled to the door, slowly getting out. "Do you want to drive back to the house?"

"Yes, that's fine." As they sat in the front seat, Seong immediately turned on the heat before leaving the park, driving the short distance back to Yong's house. Getting out of the car first, Seonghun took off his coat, walking around to let her out of the car, before quickly draping it around her shivering body.

"Did you talk to Min about a coat?"

Yeah, we'll go in the morning." She stood, waiting for him to open the door.

Opening it they were greeted by Cho, Minjun, and Yongjoon shouting at each other in Korean over a board game. Maliah watched for a moment before looking at Seonghun who was trying not to laugh. "They are accusing Cho of cheating, saying she didn't have that much money during her last turn. They are making her do a full accounting of her money.

"Is the only reason you guys don't speak Korean to each other in the dorms because I can't understand?" Maliah asked.

"Yes and no. We want you to be able to participate in the conversation. Also Yong is a fluent speaker, not native." He continued at her confused stare. "He speaks it very well, and would be fine in Korea, but sometimes he misses nuances. He speaks English natively, while we speak it fluently. It's also good practice for us."

Minjun stopped yelling, staring at him. "He's a goner," he whispered in Korean.

Cho looked up. "So is she." She switched to English as she spoke in a normal voice, "Did you two have a good time?"

They looked at each other. "Yes, we did," Seonghun said. "Skating is hard, but fun."

"Speaking of, I need to probably apply a heat patch to your lower back. You're going to feel it in the morning." Maliah smiled at everyone. "I'm going to change into my pajamas. Knock on my door when you're ready for me to apply the patch. Goodnight, everyone." As Liah went to walk off, Seong grabbed her arm.

"I had a really good time," he said, looking at her.

Their friends all watched intently.

"I did too." She smiled at him.

"Typically at the end of a date, there's a kiss."

"I uh—" she glanced over as everyone was unabashedly watching, "we had this discussion in the car."

"I know, but I feel like it wasn't enough, also I'm going to let you in on a secret." He bent down to whisper in her ear, "I don't really care who's watching." He kissed her. He was a little more showy than he normally was. Seong felt nearly scorched by the heat between them. When he came up for air he looked at her eyes. They were dark, almost predatory looking.

"I-I-I'm g-g-g-gonna go get ready for bed." She looked at the three people gawking at them from the couch. "Knock on my door when you need the patch applied." She waved at everyone else before running up the stairs. The click of her door shutting was deafening.

"Ten dollars says she screamed when she shut the door." Yongjoon looked at Minjun.

"That's a sucker's bet," he replied.

"I'm going to get my pajamas on, get my patch applied and go to bed." He waved goodnight to everyone, running up the stairs.

They all went back to arguing about their board game, demanding an accounting of money.

Seonghun knocked on Maliah's door. His girlfriend yanked him into the room, pressing her mouth to his, shutting the door tight. "Liah, you have to slow down." He unbuttoned her soft top, attacking her breasts with his mouth.

"I don't want to slow down, I want you to touch me." She arched toward him, moaning.

He pushed her toward the bed, climbing between her legs. "This is going against everything we talked about tonight." He slid his hand down her pants. "Jesus you're—"

"I know," she moaned, writhing against his touch, "it happened when you kissed me downstairs. I don't know why."

He focused for a moment on the woman under him, her glasses crooked as usual, desperation in her eyes. He closed his eyes for a moment, gathering every bit of strength he had before looking back down at her. "What do you want?"

"I want you. I honestly want all of you."

"We had this discussion in the car. You need to talk to your therapist. You deserve more than me sleeping with you in our friend's mom's house." She stared at him for a moment. "Also I don't have condoms," he said sheepishly.

Maliah whimpered.

"I'll ease the issue you have going on here, but we aren't sleeping together. We both have some hurdles we need to overcome. He began playing with her when he felt another gush. "How are you so wet?"

"I d-d-don't know. It just happens sometimes. God, more please!" she cried out.

"Baby, shhh." He yanked Liah's pants down, spreading her legs. His girl was basically glistening. "Fuck. Get off the comforter."

"Wha—" Maliah was slightly dazed.

"Cho will wash the bedding when we leave. It will be less noticeable on the sheets than on the comforter." Throwing the comforter off of the bed, Seong immediately dove between her legs. Liah nearly screamed. "Shh, remember, you've got to be quiet," he mumbled.

She tasted so good. He drew her clit into his mouth sucking hard as he slipped his fingers inside her. At the tightening sensation he felt around his fingers, he continued licking. As he looked up, he smirked, seeing how affected she was. Liah covered her face with a pillow as she screamed what sounded like obscenities into it. All of sudden she froze. Her walls clamped down hard on his fingers. It was the hardest orgasm he'd ever felt from her. Gently, he removed his fingers and saw she was watching him. Maintaining eye contact, he stuck his fingers in his mouth, sucking every bit of her off of them. He had no clue where he'd gotten his bravado from. She made him fearless, unafraid to try new things with her.

He helped her put her panties and pajamas back on before pulling her into the bed.

"Seong."

"Hmm?"

"I've never felt that out of control before."

"Are you okay with where we landed?"

"I'm grateful to you for stopping it from going further. I felt almost out of my mind." She bumped his chin gently with her head.

"I want you, but like I said, we both have hurdles and issues we need to deal with. Talk to your therapist. Get the clarity you need." Seong kissed the top of her head.

"I will," she said sleepily, "you still need a patch."

"Yeah."

"After I put it on, will you stay for a bit, just until I fall asleep?" she asked quietly.

"Sure. I'm going to leave the door open so they don't think anything is going on though."

"'Kay."

He looked at her, chuckling. "When we do make love, are you going to go to sleep after the first orgasm?"

"The really hard ones like that make me tired. They are rare as hell though." Liah slipped out of bed, pulling one of the warming patches from her bag.

Seong took off his shirt. "You have no clue what triggered it?"

"No, one minute I was fine, the next I wanted to drag you upstairs." She looked at his back. "Are you feeling any tenderness anywhere?"

"My lower back is a little sore, but nothing like when I pull it." He rubbed it a little.

"Alright, I'll put one there for now. If you need more, let me know. If I'm gone when you wake up, they are in my bag." She gently placed the patch and opened the door as he requested, before sliding back into the bed and covered them both up. He pulled her to his chest, cuddling her tightly before they both dozed off.

"C'mon, Seonghun, into your room."

Seonghun rolled over and blinked slightly, squinting at Yong. "She wanted me to stay until she fell asleep, but I think we crashed at the same time."

"It happens. You guys had a lot of activity tonight."

Though he was groggy, Seonghun blushed slightly.

"Come on, go to bed." The two men left the room, cutting out the light, and shutting her door.

CHAPTER 45

Seonghun woke the next morning with his thighs screaming. Remembering that Maliah was off with Min, he texted Yong.

Seong: *Can you please come here? My legs are in pain. I'm scared I'm going to fall out of this bed if I move.*
Yong: *Maliah had a feeling. Check your bedside table, let me know if you still need me.*

He glanced over. There were two pain pills, a glass of water, a granola bar, and a note. He took the pills immediately. Seong crunched on the granola bar as he settled in to read his note.

S-
I'm up early, looking out the window in this gorgeous room. There's a hammock in the backyard. I want a hammock one day. Laying in a hammock in the sunshine seems like it's fun. Such a silly little thought.
This letter is so beyond late that a lot of information in yours is moot. We both know Minjun is in love; sadly, there was no loud boombox with old school Korean romantic songs. I'm happy for them. They are really sweet to each other. They seem to temper each other really well. I've been looking up poses for

them so I can photograph them. I'm a little squicked out by the whole studio situation, but it was more the thought she had pictures of me in a compromising position.

Will it be lonely returning to your village by yourself? Will you be going straight to your village or will you be helping Min move into his new home? Speaking of him, do his parents know he's bisexual? The relationship is serious, is he going to tell them?

I won't be having Yongjoon's babies. I don't think any of us (me, you, Yongjoon, Minjun) want me to have Yong's babies. Except Mrs. Pae. Both of them would make good dads, I think. I have my first lesson with Yongjoon next week. I really don't like the idea of throwing a punch at anyone. I'm not particularly a violent person. It would be nice to deck Casey though.

I had a lot of fun with you yesterday. Yeah topics got heavy for a bit, but it was still a lot of fun. I also realize I owe you an explanation. I don't really celebrate my birthday because my birthday wasn't really celebrated. I didn't realize birthdays were a thing until I got to elementary school. Parents would bring in treats for their kids' birthdays. Even the kids who have birthdays in the summer, their parents would bring stuff in on their half birthday, so they could share with their classmates. I never did. My birthday was never really mentioned. In the 5th grade a teacher got me a pencil and pen wrapped up for my birthday. It may seem like an odd gift, but I love stationery, so it was perfect for me. It was kind of like she gave me the moon. It was one of those old timey pencils, the lead was individual pieces encased in plastic while the pencil itself smelled of strawberry. I may not be describing it well. The pen was cool because it was erasable ink. Funny the things we remember, you know? Anyway, I don't bother with birthdays. At this age, what's the point? Another year gone.

Seonghun immediately grabbed his phone.

Seong: *Do not let her see this text. We need to plan a birthday party. I have ideas, but I'm going to leave most of it in your hands.*
Min: *Consider it done.*

He went back to the letter.

I can completely understand you not wanting me to bury my feelings and emotions in you, but sometimes I just don't want to feel anything but pleasant things in that moment; I don't know how to achieve that. There is only so much processing of my emotions I can do, you know? I'm working on it. I'm glad I can still come to you for hugs.
Min is knocking. He must be ready to go, so I'll end this here. I left pain pills, water, and a snack for you on the table. I hope you feel okay when you wake up.
Yours
-L

He folded her letter, sticking into his bag. Standing up, Seong took tentative steps. His legs hurt, but it was manageable. Quickly he stripped his bed linens before going to do the same in Liah's room. Gathering all the sheets, he went to laundry room where Yong was dumping his own sheets in the wash. "It can fit yours as well," he said.

Seonghun put their sheets in. "I just remembered we have another date today. I really hope it is nothing strenuous." He rubbed his thighs.

"I think they are taking us to eat." Yongjoon arranged the sheets before closing the lid, pouring detergent into the compartments. "Min said Maliah thought of the place."

"I hope she isn't expecting to pay," Seonghun grumbled.

"They asked us, so I believe they are. We've had this discussion," Yongjoon reminded him.

"You said that about when we hang out in groups, not on dates," Seonghun protested.

"Don't ruin this for her. She's trying to learn how to date, let her," Yongjoon said firmly. "Relationships are give and take. You can't give her everything. It creates a weird imbalance."

"She's never been given anything," Seonghun said quietly. "I want her to know what it feels like to know someone lo-cares about her." He stumbled over his words again.

Yongjoon looked at him for a long time. "You know, it's okay to say what you were going to."

"It is way too soon. A month, Yong. One month."

"About the same amount of time as us; we've said it," Yongjoon pointed out.

"You guys built upon a friendship. We're starting at the ground. Also she's a little freaked out that I basically asked her to move to Korea." Seonghun winced.

Yongjoon looked at him and started laughing. Hard. He was doubled over with tears in his eyes.

Cho came around the corner at all the noise. "What on earth is going on?"

"He won't tell her he loves her, but asked her to move to a foreign country where she doesn't speak the language." He burst into hard laughter again, choking and coughing.

Cho looked at Seonghun who was ready to jump on Yongjoon again. "Yongie, finish the sheets. Seong, come with me." She walked out of the room, not leaving any time for argument.

He followed her into the kitchen where she pulled out saucers with her light fancy china. Putting a kettle on to boil she grabbed a teapot and placed a few bags of tea into it. When the kettle began to whistle she poured the water in the pot.

She pulled down cookies, setting them on a plate. Seonghun looked down. They were the cookies that Maliah made. His heart began to twist.

Cho poured the tea and looked at him. "Talk."

So he told her everything. He told her how they started, how he felt, his fears about Casey. Everything came pouring out of him. Cho listened silently as she drank her tea. When he finished, he sipped his tea quietly and began to eat cookies. Cho got up, pulling a plate of leftover 김밥 out of the fridge, sitting it in front of him.

"So here are my thoughts. You love the girl. That's fine. I know she has strong feelings for you. But I think the issue with the crazy white girl on the loose is making you a little… frantic in your feelings. Slow down, take a deep breath, and please stop asking people you've been dating for a month to move to a new country."

A little calmer, he chuckled. "I didn't actually ask her to move. I asked her to consider it after two years."

"Still, calm down. Also, if she planned the date, she planned on paying. Let her pay. Yongjoon was right about that part. She's learning to be part of something. Let her share in it." She rubbed his shoulder. "She's a good kid; so are you, but you need to slow down. You both have time. Enjoy the buildup of what is looking like a beautiful relationship. Calm down."

He ate a roll of 김밥 as he thought about what she said. He knew she was right, but he wanted to grab hold of everything greedily. He told her as much.

"Only child syndrome. Your parents didn't spoil you, but you're used to getting what you want. You're an adult. You need to act like it. Enjoy getting to points in the relationship, Seong. Don't rush. You can't get the time back."

He nodded. She kissed him on the forehead like his mom would. "Finish your breakfast, then go make nice with my boy." She got up to leave the kitchen.

"Cho?"

She turned around expectantly.

"If I'm an adult, I should be able to sleep with her while I'm here."

"I'm still the bigger adult; my rules go." She winked as she walked out of the kitchen.

He snorted as he finished up the plate of food.

CHAPTER 46

Yongjoon and Seonghun were sitting on the couch shoveling mouthfuls of Chex Mix in their mouth when Maliah and Minjun walked through the door. Maliah was wearing a beautiful pink belted woolen coat. Soft looking cream gloves adorned her hands. Each of the friends had three bags each, one of hers being one of those striped bags that piqued Seonghun's interest before. Min saw where his attention went and smirked. Liah ran upstairs to pack her things, so Seong followed.

He sat on the bed as she showed him her new coat. "I really like it. It's comfortable." She set her bags on the bed as she unpacked them. There were a few shirts, and a couple of new bras.

"Those are pretty." He pointed at the bras.

"Thanks. They aren't what I wanted, but they are nice." She started folding everything, neatly packing it away.

"What is it that you wanted?" he asked.

She looked embarrassed, which intrigued him more. "Liah?"

"I can't explain it because I don't know what it's called. I know about basic girl things, anything past bras, underwear, stockings, things like that, I don't know. I have to do research," she explained.

"Fair enough." He kissed her. "What time do we need to leave?"

She looked at her watch. "Our reservation is at 1:30, so I need to get in the shower now."

He opened his mouth to offer to shower with her when Cho's voice rang in his head. *Slow down. Enjoy the journey.* "Okay. I'll do the same. We'll go home from the date, so make sure your stuff is packed."

"I pretty much have everything packed, except what I'm wearing today." She walked over and closed the door.

He arched an eyebrow.

"No, I'm not trying to do that." She smiled. "I wanted to show you something." She dug in her bag, searching around until she found a small box. "I wanted to show you the other day, but I got distracted. This is what I got Min for his birthday."

He took the box from her, opening it. Inside were two cufflinks nestled on a bed of cotton. They were silver with a blue gem embedded in them. At first glance they looked like stud earrings. "He'll love these. They are simple, so he can put them on any shirt." He handed the box back.

"That's what I was going for, thank you. A lot of them were obnoxious. I thought about showing up with the roaring tiger ones simply because they made me laugh." She placed them carefully back in the bag. "I have wrapping paper back at the dorm."

He gave her one more kiss as he headed to the door. "I'll meet you downstairs."

She turned to undress as he shut the door. Walking back into his room, he pulled out the outfit he was to wear. The sweater that he'd picked out with Yongjoon, with a plain white t-shirt underneath. Dark blue jeans with his brown dress boots. He shaved, brushing his teeth before hopping into the shower. As he secured the towel around his waist, he heard a knock at his door.

"Seonghun?" Minjun's voice called out.

"Hold on." He walked out of the bathroom. Minjun was sitting on his bed with a brush, hair spray and a blow dryer.

"Min," he groaned. "Please? No?"

"Normally I'd leave you be, but not today. Get comfortable." Minjun plugged in the blow dryer.

Seonghun's hair normally flopped in his eyes slightly. He kept it on the longer side in the front and shorter in the back. Minjun parted it, giving him more of a coiffed look, by slightly stacking his bangs on one side. He used the barrel brush to make sure his hair was straight. It looked sleek.

"See? Painless. We're all done." Minjun unplugged the hairdryer, leaving him to his devices.

Seonghun checked his hair out in the mirror; had to admit, it looked really nice. He squirted on cologne before getting dressed. Grabbing his things, he did a once over in the room to make sure he had everything before heading downstairs.

His friends were already downstairs, dressed similarly to him. Minjun had on a sweater vest over a long sleeved button down shirt, while Yongjoon had on a white turtleneck cable knit sweater, similar to what Seonghun had purchased the other day. Cho looked at them and smiled. "You boys look handsome. Where is Liah?"

"I'm coming." Seong turned around at her voice.

"Holy crap, she didn't put a shirt on under the sweater," whispered Min.

Maliah had on a long sleeved dark gray sweater dress that came to a v in the front. Her breasts were slightly exposed. It was nothing indecent, but it was a lot more than she ever showed. The dress was simple with ribbed edging. Completing the look was black tights. Her makeup was a bit heavier, making her eyes look even bigger behind her glasses. She had the heart necklace that Minjun had gotten her, with her new coat over her arm. Her hair was down, with a black beret covering her head.

"You look—" Seong walked up to her, unable to finish his statement.

"You do too," she said, staring at him.

He couldn't help it, he kissed her, and didn't stop. Yongjoon hid his laugh behind a cough. Minjun shook his head while Cho rolled her eyes.

Eventually Maliah tapped his shoulder. "That's a lot in front of other people."

"Yeah," all three people said behind them.

Seonghun blushed. "Sorry."

Maliah walked over to Cho. "Thank you for having me."

"It was my pleasure. Come with me though." Cho left the room with Maliah following after her.

Seonghun looked at Yongjoon. "It's personal. If she wants to tell you, she will."

Liah came back, fidgeting slightly.

"I'll see all of you next month. Bring your appetites." She hugged the boys, squeezing her son tightly. "Safe drive home and be mindful of the crazy lady."

"We will," Minjun promised.

"Seonghun," she looked at him, "remember our conversation."

"I will, I promise." With a final wave, everyone left the house.

CHAPTER 47

Maliah drove the two of them toward downtown. The other couple were in Yong's car with Min driving. "Can I ask you what Cho said?" Seonghun asked.

"She said I live with a lot of testosterone, that it may be hard on me. I might want a woman to talk to. She gave me her number."

"That was nice of her," Seonghun said.

"It was," she agreed, "what did you two talk about?"

Seonghun blushed. "Enjoying the ride, while not running full tilt."

"I don't understand."

"It's complicated," he said.

Liah nodded as she pulled into a parking garage. Cutting the engine, she moved to get out when grabbed her arm. She looked at him, seeing the intent in his eyes. "Just one time, Seong. The others are waiting for us." She leaned over to kiss him.

Seong tried to take the kiss deeper, but was blocked. Liah pulled away. "Every time we get too deep into it, someone shows up."

There was a tap at the window. She arched her brow at him as she opened the car door. "Are you two going to go at it, or can we go in?" Yong looked at them.

"I'm ready," Maliah looked at Seonghun. "He is too." Seong grabbed her hand; together they followed their friends.

"What is this place?" Seong looked around.

Yongjoon started chuckling. "You're taking us to Fogo? Nice." He opened the door to usher everyone in.

She turned to Seonghun who still looked puzzled. "Think of it as an all you can eat meat buffet," she said.

He couldn't imagine what his face looked like right now, but judging from Maliah's laugh, he probably looked like he'd just touched heaven. They were quickly seated. The concept was explained to them. They each had a coaster by their plate. If it was flipped on the green side, the meat carvers would come with more meat. If it was flipped red they wouldn't stop by. There was also a small salad bar with side dishes. The waiter took their drink order, recommending the caipirinha cocktail. Everyone but Maliah got it.

Seonghun immediately flipped his card over to green. He watched Maliah get up and wander over to the salad bar. Minjun flipped his card to green as they watched Yong follow Maliah.

"Did you know about this place?" Seonghun asked.

"No, Maliah showed me the website. I figured you'd be excited. Also it sounded like fun, so I wanted to go too."

All of a sudden men with meat on skewers began walking around. They walked up to the table, told the men what was on the skewer before carving off a slice of the meat for each of them. This happened several times. Soon the two friends had a pile of meat on their plate. Flipping their cards to red, they began eating.

"We're over here, sweetheart," Yongjoon called out loudly.

Seong looked over. Maliah was looking highly uncomfortable, Yongjoon had a hand around her waist as he led her to their table. Behind them an older man was leering at Maliah's ass.

"What is going on?" Seonghun asked.

"Dude accosted her, cornered her by the cheese." Yongjoon set his plate down. "I wasn't paying attention, otherwise I would have stopped it sooner."

"It's one of the reasons I dress like I normally do," she explained quietly. "This has been happening since I was thirteen. It happens a lot less when I'm in jeans, sweatshirts, or baggy t-shirts."

Minjun looked guilty. "I didn't know."

"You shouldn't have to know to understand I'm uncomfortable showing off my body. I'm very aware of what my body looks like to people. Even if I'm chubby—"

"Which you aren't," Seonghun said, pointing at her with his fork.

"I tend to get older men who lose their faculties when they see my bottom half." Maliah ignored him as she cut into her salad.

Minjun and Seonghun looked confused.

"Men tend to get stupid over her ass," Yongjoon clarified.

A waiter came over, placing a drink in front of Liah. "A gentleman sent this over to you."

Maliah sighed as she stared at it. "I'm underage. Please tell said gentleman I'm not interested." She glared at the offending drink until it was taken away.

She looked slightly morose so Seonghun quickly changed the subject. "Thank you for bringing me here. It's really cool." He flipped his card back over to green.

She flipped hers too. "I figured you could make a dent in a lunch buffet." She slid him a piece of bacon from the salad bar.

The skewers of meat made another round to the table. The men, kept their card green while Maliah turned hers red. They chattered over the food, taking multiple trips to the salad bar. Anytime Maliah went, one of the men went with her, whether they needed food or not.

Eventually, even Seonghun's bottomless pit was filled. As they waited for the bill, a man walked up to their table. Maliah grabbed Seonghun's hand, taking deep breaths. "I'm sorry my drink wasn't to your liking. Was there something else you're interested in?" The man smiled at her.

Seonghun looked at her face. She was pissed. Without stuttering, Liah spoke up, "I explained to you I wasn't interested at the salad bar. I sent your drink back as I'm not of legal age. What the hell would I possibly want from you? Also, hitting on me in front of my significant other is very poor form." She glared at the man.

"At least take my card, I could help you out. Pretty girls like you always could use a helping hand." He held out a card.

Seonghun had enough. Sitting down, you couldn't really see, so he stood to his entire 6'4 height, towering over the man. "I believe the woman said no. You need to leave, now."

The guy finally slumped off. Seong sat back down.

Maliah slowly turned her head. "Min."

He saw the look on her face. He suppressed a smile. "Yes, Liah?"

"We'll be late to the cake shop. I'll meet you there."

"Don't get arrested for public indecency," he warned.

"I won't." The bills came. Seong reached for one until he saw Maliah's glare. He quickly retracted his hand. Grabbing the bill she looked at it. "I need to balance my account when we get home." She handed her card over to the waiter.

After the bill was settled, they walked out of the restaurant. Seong watched his friends get into their car, pulling off. Maliah turned to him with a dark look. "Get in the backseat."

Seong was a little frightened at the look on her face. "Thought you weren't chasing your roller coaster drop in a car?" He smiled nervously.

"We aren't chasing mine," she declared.

"Oh."

Seonghun and Maliah arrived at the cake shop twenty minutes after their friends. The two men observed them walking in. Seonghun's hair was a mess; he looked frantic. Maliah was smirking, her beret was lopsided while the barrette that was holding it in place was gone. "When the time comes, she is going to fuck his whole world up," Yong said.

Both men burst out laughing. Seonghun slid into the booth. "What's so funny?"

"Your hair is all over the place," Minjun pointed out.

"Liah, where is the cute little barrette you had in your hair?" Yongjoon asked. Both of them reached for their hair looking at each other.

"Uh—" began Maliah.

"I—" Seonghun said.

This made their friends laugh even harder.

"Shut up. Some of us weren't afforded privacy this weekend," Seonghun shot.

"Fair enough," Yongjoon conceded, handing them the menu.

They poured over the menu and decided on a pot of earl gray tea and a slice of chocolate fudge cake. Seonghun looked around the restaurant. It was very feminine with crystal chandeliers, soft rose gold tables, and seating. Fake topiaries and vines with white and pink flowers dangled from the ceiling.

Maliah looked at Min. "Min, what's your favorite cake flavor?"

"Fruit cakes."

She looked confused. "Like the holiday stuff with the candied orange peels?"

"No, cakes with fruit in them. My favorite candy is chocolate covered cherries," he explained.

She got a faraway look on her face. "How do you feel about coconut?"

"Love the stuff." A waiter came over, setting a giant piece of cheesecake between Yongjoon and Minjun along with a pot of tea.

"I have something to talk to you about," said Minjun, looking at Maliah.

"Yes?"

"I need a copy of your class schedule."

"Why?"

"You'll have someone walking you to class from now on." Minjun scooped a bit of cheesecake in his mouth. "I called on some contacts—"

"By contacts, he means the girls he's slept with that he's on good terms with," Yongjoon said dryly.

"Yes." Minjun nodded. "Anyway, they'll show up and walk with you to class. They're all nice. I promise."

"Oh. Well, thank you." She pulled out her phone and sent him her schedule.

"I don't honestly know what we're going to do about your work schedule. You typically work while we're in class," said Yongjoon as he sipped his tea.

"I'll be fine. She can't get to me at the doctor's office when I'm giving lessons and Mr. Mays is aware of the situation. He'd hit her with his cane." She snorted.

The server dropped off their cake and tea. Seonghun went straight for the cake as she poured herself some tea. "What about you three? She hurt both Min and Seonghun."

"As I've said before, she's the least of my concerns as far as physically harming me." At her puzzled look, he explained further. "I used to box in high school. I don't anymore, but I still train like I do. That's why I volunteered to teach you how to throw a punch. In the summer I volunteer with the local Y, giving self-defense courses to women. I like doing it plus it gave me something to put on my college applications." He pulled out his phone, flipped through it and handed it to her.

Seonghun leaned down to see, though he had seen some of the pictures before. It was Yongjoon with a group of women, helping them with their follow through on punching. There were pictures of him smiling with groups of women.

"They look like they are having a good time," said Maliah as she handed the phone back.

"We have a good time, but there's also meltdowns. We'd pretend to attack so they would have to force their way out. I had to have sensitivity training. Some of these women came from really bad situations." He pocketed his phone before looking at Maliah. "I'm not going to lie, I'm difficult to work with. I'm mean and I don't accept excuses. I'll also push your buttons to get the result I want, so you need to be prepared for that."

"Push my buttons, how?" she questioned.

"I know what scares you. I know what makes you freeze. I'll attempt to use it constantly so you don't freeze. I won't be malicious with it; I'm not trying to traumatize you," he explained. "But I want you to get out of your head."

She nodded slowly.

"I'm not going to go full out the first day and have you in extra therapy sessions, but it may bring up a few things. Just be prepared for that as well. Let your therapist know, give her my name. I'll give you the information from the Y. Like I said, I've been fully trained, so I'm not just working on wild misinformation." He looked at her without a trace of humor in his eyes.

"You're scaring me," admitted Maliah.

"I don't mean to, I just need you to understand what you've signed up for. By the time we're done, you'll probably be able to beat Seonghun's ass."

"Why would I—"

"Not saying you should," he interrupted, "but you could."

Looking over she noticed Seong had demolished over half the cake. She took a small bite. "This is dry as hell."

"It's still good." He slid the plate closer to him to polish it off.

Minjun changed the subject. "We actually wanted to talk to you two." They looked at him.

"We were wondering if you were up for a room switch? Seonghun actually."

"This doesn't affect me if you two switch," Maliah said.

"It actually does. The walls are thick, but noises do float through," Minjun paused before delicately continuing, "there are things that you may not want him to hear."

Maliah looked horrified. "Have you—"

"No, I haven't heard anything I shouldn't, I don't think anyway, but sometimes music floats over, or I can hear you cry," Yong said quietly.

Seonghun spoke up, "Is there a particular reason you want to switch?"

"There is a reason why the rooms in the house are soundproofed. I'm the lightest sleeper. I can't help it. I frequently have earplugs in when I sleep. I want to switch before we get to a point where I have to approach you about strange noises at night," Yongjoon said unabashedly.

Seonghun blushed. "I'm fine with it. If it's okay with Maliah, we can switch out on Tuesday."

Maliah nodded. "Have at it."

After a bit of back and forth, Seong watched as Liah paid the bill again. "We'll see you two at the dorm," said Maliah as she stood up.

"Are you headed straight back?" asked Yong.

"We may make a stop at the store, but that's about it. Did you need me to pick up something?" Maliah looked over at him.

"Nah, we'll see you in a bit. Thank you for the double date idea. It was nice."

She smiled. "Anytime. I had fun planning it with Min."

Seonghun grabbed her hand as they left the shop.

CHAPTER 48

In the weeks that followed, their lives evolved. Seong traded rooms with Min, but started spending more nights sleeping in Maliah's room.

Liah was working through some of the intimacy issues she was having. She even had Seonghun in on a few of her therapy sessions. It made him feel like they had a solid foundation for their relationship.

His blood test came back negative for everything. He gave the papers to Liah.

Minjun's female friends had a rotation. They would come to the dorm, introduce themselves, say hi to Minjun, before walking with Liah to class. They were all quite nice as Minjun said, but a touch vapid. When it came to women, Seong noticed he had a type.

Yongjoon had been working with Maliah in the gym. At first Seonghun attended. He quickly realized he was going to be a hindrance. Whenever Yongjoon restrained Maliah, Seong jumped to separate them. The worst day was the day Maliah froze and couldn't even say her safe word.

The two of them had landed on 'onion' as a safe word. She wasn't a big fan of them. If things got too intense or he was actually hurting her, she'd call out; he'd immediately let go, but she had to call out. A lot of the things they were doing were forward facing. One day, Yongjoon grabbed her from the back by her neck, she needed to fight him off. She was working at it until he stroked her face.

Yongjoon wasn't facing her, but Seonghun saw her face when she completely shut down. "Yong, she's not there, let her go," he called out.

"She needs to talk to me or fight. Liah, say something," he said in her ear.

She started shaking. "I-I-I-"

"You're better than this. I've seen you. Fight through it please, or call out your word."

Seong saw tears plop on Yongjoon's arm.

He must have felt it because he spoke again, "Don't hold back, fight through it."

"LET HER GO, YONG!" Seonghun was on his feet, coming to separate them.

"Don't let him fight your battles, sweetheart. You can do this," Yongjoon told her.

All of a sudden an animalistic roar came from Maliah. Seong froze as she broke the hold, punching Yongjoon in his eye before collapsing in a sobbing heap.

Seonghun dropped down to his knees in front of her. "Hey, you're safe. You're here with us. No one is going to hurt you."

Maliah wildly grabbed for him, sobbing.

Yong was holding his eye as he walked over. He squat in front of her so she could see. "It's okay to get scared, it's even okay to freeze in an instant, but you need to use that adrenaline to save yourself, like you did today. I know that was hard, I'm proud of you." He smiled at her gently. "I'm going to have a shiner."

She was calming down slowly. "M-m-m-my hand h-h-h-hurts. I'm s-s-s-sorry." She sniffled.

"Let Seonghun take you home and put some ice on it. I'm going to get some food. I'll be back at the dorm later. You have nothing to be sorry about. You did what I asked." He kissed the top of her head before leaving them in the private room.

"I want ice cream."

"I can make that happen. Ice cream or milkshake?"

After a brief pause she spoke again. "Milkshake. Strawberry please."

"Let's go get you taken care of." He stood up, helping her to her feet.

After that, Seonghun stopped attending the practice. It was hard not to come to her aid when Yongjoon swung at her; Seong knew he was hindering her progress. There were times where she would come back to the dorm sobbing in his arms, but Yongjoon assured him it was normal.

They celebrated Minjun's birthday. Maliah asked Yong to let her take care of the cake. She left early Saturday morning, the day they were going to celebrate, coming back in the afternoon with a chocolate cherry cake covered in a fudge icing with toasted coconut flakes. Minjun was in heaven. He practically bounced around the house at the cufflinks, along with a note that Maliah left in the box, offering to take the pictures he wanted. Seonghun got him a few clothing items he knew he'd been looking at for a while, as well as a shirt that would look nice with the new cufflinks Maliah bought him. It was a small celebration between all of them, and Min was over the moon.

Minjun and Seonghun had been working on a surprise party for Maliah's birthday as well. Liah had taken Seong to the skating rink she frequented in West Lafayette. From there a deposit was paid. On a day that he knew Maliah had class, Seong drove to her job. He spoke with Diane, inviting her. He also asked her to invite anyone else that Maliah was friendly with, letting him know the final count.

"You have any older brothers? An uncle? A single father?" Diane looked at him.

Seonghun laughed. "I'm an only child. I have an uncle, but he's happily married."

"Pity. You're a good kid. I'll send you a text of how many people are coming."

He nodded, thanking her before walking out of the building to do the same thing at the art gallery.

There hadn't been any instances of Casey lately, but Detective Krishna had visited their room and informed them that Seonghun was right. A lot of the 'friends' that Casey had, she had blackmail information on them. It was one of the reasons Casey tried to get Maliah to drink all the time. She thought she would spill her guts if she did. When Casey went underground, everyone deserted her because she no longer had the ability to hold their secrets over their heads.

Minjun was in the room while the detective talked about everything. "What did she have on Ashley?"

Detective Krishna looked at Minjun. "This does not leave this room, understand? She's not really concerned about it now, but still."

Minjun nodded.

"She was sleeping with three out of four of her teachers last semester." The detective looked at Minjun who turned pale. "If you were sleeping with her, may I suggest an STD test?"

"I've had one since. I'm clean," said Minjun.

"Very good. So following your line of thinking Seonghun, we found out she'd been sleeping with someone in the department."

"What?" Maliah said in disbelief.

"Yeah, he's married, with two kids. He'd been messing around with her for a while. He's the sole reason she's gotten to student court so many times."

Maliah looked stricken.

"He's working with us; we should have her hopefully by the end of this week." Detective Krishna stood up. "You three," she pointed at Minjun, Maliah, and Seonghun, "will probably be asked to testify."

The three of them nodded.

The detective left shortly after. Everyone tried to ignore the feeling of dread in the room by turning on a movie.

The semester was flying by. It was finally fall break. Everyone was packed to go to Cho's house again. Maliah had a gift bag with wads of tissue paper in it. "What's that?" Yongjoon asked.

"I made it for your mom as a thank you. I was in the process of making it before we went down the first time, as I wasn't expecting to stay any sooner, but it's a thank you gift for welcoming me."

"She loves a good homemade present. Ask her about my macaroni art."

Maliah snickered.

Seonghun pulled her to the side. "Can we go back to the meat buffet place while we're down there?"

"Yeah, sure," she agreed, "just not the Friday after Thanksgiving. I've been coerced—"

"Asked," interrupted Minjun.

"Coerced," Maliah said louder, "to go Black Friday shopping at like four in the morning, with Cho and Min."

"It's fun, we'll bring snacks," Minjun soothed.

"Snacks that I've probably made," she shot back.

"Yes, but I will bring them." He smiled brightly at her.

She rolled her eyes.

"Are you guys ready?" Yong asked, grabbing his bag.

"Yes, we'll see you there," Seong said.

The couple cleared out of the dorm. Seonghun looked at his girlfriend who was checking her bags. "Do you realize this is the first time in roughly a month we've had time to ourselves?"

"We've had dates, you sleep in my room all of the time now," she pointed out.

He started walking closer to her. "We're really limited on what we can do in that tiny bed."

She smirked. "Seong, they haven't even left the building yet. There's a chance someone is going to come back because they forgot something."

Seonghun whipped out his phone.

Seong: *Do you have everything?*
Min: *What do you mean? Yes, I have all my stuff.*
Seong: *I need you two not to come back upstairs, at all. If you forgot something, send me a text. I'll grab it.*
Min: *...WE'RE GOING TO BE IN A PLACE WITH BIGGER BEDS IN AN HOUR!*
Seong: *We aren't allowed to sleep together, remember?*
Min: *Oh yeah. Sorry. Enjoy. Will see you in an hour or so. <3*

He put his phone back in his pocket. "No one is coming back up. It's just me," he kissed her, "you," he grazed his teeth on the side of her neck, "and the floor."

"I actually wanted to, uh, right there," she moaned quietly, "talk to you about something."

"Let me go get the blanket and the condom, then we can talk," he said as he walked into his room. The condom was something Dr. Stewart suggested. They noted that they tended to take things further sometimes than they meant to. Because of that Dr. Stewart suggested that when they mess around there was a condom at eye level for both of them, so if it got to that point, it was readily available. They followed her advice.

He spread the blanket out before pulling her onto his lap. "What's on your mind?"

"Us." She craned her neck so she could see his face. "I'm ready when you are."

He realized instantly what she was saying. Seong bumped his forehead to hers. "I'm touched." He kissed her slowly. "That isn't going to happen right now though, you know? I want to be able to take our time while not on the floor." He chuckled softly. "Besides, we have sex now, and I can't hold you or sleep with you or anything until we get back. It's not how I imagined it going."

"You make good points. I also didn't mean for it to be right now, but I wanted to let you know that when you're ready." She kissed him softly.

"Got it." He laid her down on the blanket. "We don't have much time left. Cho is going to be holding dinner for us." He lifted her shirt and nipped at her navel.

"I can work fast, can you?" She smiled at him.

"A lot faster than before, that's for sure," he replied.

When they'd come back from the long weekend at Cho's, Maliah had her annual physical. The doctor worked with her therapist to put her on a medication more suited to her. At first it was awful. Balancing everything out caused her to have emotional meltdowns. She tried to have them in private, but Seonghun wouldn't let her. He made her talk about her feelings while feeding her right after. As a result she'd gained ten pounds, which set her off again. Working with Yongjoon, she'd taken it off, but he always made her talk about whatever was upsetting her. The medication was almost at the level it needed to be now. She was mostly back to normal.

One of the immediate benefits was her sex drive. She actually got aroused. There were times where they still needed to use lube, or he wasn't able to make her roller coaster drop, but it was a lot less than before. They loved foreplay while just enjoy one another, but they were on a time crunch. He had his mouth on her while she was making those little cries that he loved, when both their phones began to ring. "Ignore it, god please ignore it," she called out. The ringing stopped for a second but started right back up. She opened her eyes. "I'm really close, please don't."

"What if it's an accident? I'll answer mine. Just be quiet." He continued to move his fingers inside of her. Both his hands were slick with her juices, but he managed to answer. "I swear to god this better be an emergency," he called out.

"Uh, no, we were just wondering how far away you are? Mom's holding dinner," Yongjoon said.

"Oh god," Liah cried in the background.

"Seonghun, have you two even left yet?"

"How are you there already?" Seong asked, surprised.

"Look at the time, Seong," Yongjoon said patiently.

"It's been an hour!?" he cried out. "Jeez, okay, give me ten—"

"Fifteen! Oh god, fifteen," Liah called out.

"Fifteen minutes," Seonghun corrected. "We'll get on the road. Don't hold dinner." He quickly hung up the phone, focusing on Liah.

CHAPTER 49

Arriving at Yong's home, the two of them were subjected to a bit of ribbing. Afterwards, Cho pulled Maliah and Seonghun aside. "I'm realizing that you two are adults; I have no right to separate you. It's hypocritical of me, especially since Yongie and Min stay together."

Seonghun felt the hope blooming in his chest as Cho spoke.

"I have no objections to you sharing a room. Just keep it safe you two, understood?" Cho looked at both of them.

They both nodded. Seonghun wanted to take her upstairs immediately but thought that was a little too obvious. Maliah didn't look interested anyway, She was taking a seat by Minjun to play Monopoly. Sighing, he sat down to join them.

"How do you have Park Place and Boardwalk and hotels on both already!?" Yongjoon screeched at Maliah.

"You saw me when I bought them both, Pay up!" She held out her hand.

Yongjoon, counting out his bills let out a huge sigh. "I don't have enough."

"You know what to do." Maliah smirked.

Yong sold most of his property to be able to pay her astronomical bill. "This is bullshit."

"Language."

"Sorry, Mom. She owns everything!"

"She plays the game well," Cho said, patting Maliah's shoulder as she dropped a plate of cookies beside Seonghun.

Without looking, Seonghun took a bite of a cookie, chewing once before staring at the dessert baffled. "What on earth is this?"

Liah glanced over from counting her fake money. "Trash can cookie."

Yongjoon and Minjun grabbed one as well. "There are like fifteen different textures in this cookie," Minjun said as he nibbled.

Yongjoon, who normally didn't rival Seonghun in eating, grabbed the entire plate before taking off at a run, shoving cookies in his mouth. Seonghun gave chase; pretty soon they were rolling on the ground, once again fighting over cookies.

Liah looked over at Minjun while standing up. Walking over to the cabinet, she pulled down the cookie jar, handing him two cookies, while taking one for herself. "Thank you, Cho, for a good dinner. I'm going to go to bed. Those two can clean up the game." She brushed a kiss on Minjun's forehead. "Night."

"Good night, sweet dreams. I'll see you in the morning." He squeezed her hand as he watched her leave.

Minjun gave Cho a squeeze as well. "Make them put it up, they messed up the game with their greediness."

"They will, don't worry. Go get some sleep." Cho brushed his hair out of his eyes. After he went upstairs, Cho calmly pulled a wooden spoon out of the kitchen drawer, silently walking over to where the men were rolling around in the back room.

THWACK!

"Ma!" Yongjoon stopped tussling immediately as he rubbed his head.

"You cannot grab everything she cooks then fight about it. There is always plenty of food around here," Cho admonished.

"She never cooks like this in the dorms. She makes some basic things, but never desserts," Yongjoon complained as he stood up. He grabbed a cookie from the plate as he pouted.

"The stove in the dorm doesn't work well for her. I hope her apartment stove allows her to cook all she wants."

Seonghun felt a pang at not being there to try out her new stove.

Cho saw the look on his face. "Go to her. You have time. Don't rush it away." He went to go upstairs, but Cho grabbed his arm. "After you two clean up the game. The other two who behaved themselves left it for the both of you."

The men made quick work of cleaning up before heading upstairs. Seong nodded at Yongjoon as they split off. Tapping on Liah's door, he opened it, staring at his pretty girlfriend. As their relationship developed, Maliah's sleep clothes had started to evolve. Silky short sets usually greeted him in various colors. Occasionally she slept in her flannel pants if she was cold, but it was a shock when he saw the pale lavender nightgown with a dark purple butterfly embroidered in the corner. The material looked silky. It had thin spaghetti straps, showing more of her body than she was normally comfortable with.

"Nice to see you two broke it up." She arched an eyebrow as she sat at the vanity to apply lotion.

Seong didn't say anything at first. Instead, he reached over her shoulder to grab a little of the thick lotion she used on her body. A while back Seonghun realized it wasn't just her perfume that made her smell like that. His girlfriend always had a layer of lotion that smelled like cocoa butter. He slid the straps down her shoulders in order to moisturize them.

Seonghun delighted in living with her and loved finding out little bits about her. Liah was indeed messy, but worked hard to keep up with her space. Her belongings would be scattered all over her room, but within fifteen minutes everything would be in its place. To both of their surprise she was a cuddle bug. If he was in the bed, she was glued to his side. He'd started to wear the cologne Yongjoon had given him; occasionally during cuddle sessions, he'd catch her sniffing him.

Because of the issues she'd had with Casey, he was respectful of her space, asking before he delved into anything. Seong went through his girlfriend's photos often, looking at pictures of her when she was in high school, along with the few she had of her home life. He'd finally given her a picture of himself when he was a child; it was the only framed photo she had in her room.

"When do you take pictures of our friends?" He began rubbing her back as she continued moisturizing the rest of her body.

"The day after we get back. I hope I can do them justice. The clothed photos are fine, it's the half-naked ones I'm a little concerned about."

Minjun had found scraps of clothing to preserve both their modesty as well as Liah's sanity. She wasn't really keen on seeing her friends naked, but she kept telling Seonghun that if she thought about it as just art, she was fine.

"Do you want me there?" he asked her.

"While I would love to have you there, I don't think it's fair to them. We didn't have anyone around when we did it; it was less inhibited that way." She slid her straps back up as she stood up to walk toward the bed.

"I understand." He removed his clothes, leaving his underwear on before climbing into the bed. She got in on the other side, immediately putting her feet onto his legs. "Why are your feet always so cold!?"

"It's a talent," she said dryly. They snuggled together, with Seonghun's arms wrapped tightly around her. "Seong?" Her voice was drowsy, he could tell she was close to falling asleep.

"Yeah, sweetheart?"

"Now that we're allowed to sleep together at Cho's house, are we going to have sex here?"

He knew that question was coming. "Do you want to?"

"I'm concerned about Yong or Minjun busting in, thinking they're joking," she admitted.

"I don't think they would do that. Min's been respectful ever since the trip to the mall."

It was true, Minjun took to heart the fact that even though she was his friend, she was still a girl. He couldn't do everything with her that he'd do with the guys.

"True," she said.

"We don't have to think about this right now, or even this whole vacation. I'm in no real rush to take any large steps. I like where we are." He buried his nose in her neck. "I have no complaints about our intimate moments."

"Me either." She was silent after that.

Seong heard her deep breaths indicating she was asleep. As he listened to her soft snores, he realized something was holding him back on moving forward. He didn't know if it was Cho's advice or what. All he truly wanted during this break was to be able to cuddle with his girlfriend. Seong was telling Cho the truth on that. Liah was lovable; he enjoyed being around her. Eventually listening to her breathing made him sleepy, so he closed his own eyes.

The next morning when Seonghun woke up, Maliah was gone. On his bedside table, near his glasses was a note. Perching his glasses on his face, quickly scanning the note.

S-
With Cho cooking breakfast.

CHAPTER 50

She included a cartoon drawing of herself making pancakes. Ever since their talks before, along with the subsequent ten-pound weight gain and loss, Maliah had been working on how she viewed herself; as a result, the cartoon was accurate to her actual proportions, curvy wide hips, and all.

She also made Seonghun stand in front of a mirror and she proceeded to outline everything she liked about him. It wasn't just his abs or his muscular arms that she pointed out. She mentioned his kindness and patience, how he gave the best hugs along with how he made her feel safe. They both worked on not deprecating themselves. Seong realized that he left his bag in his old room. Grabbing it, he ran back to Maliah's room to shower.

When he stepped in the kitchen, he saw she was sitting next to Yongjoon eating. She looked up, hearing his footsteps. "Good morning." She smiled at him.

"Morning." Sitting on her other side, he quickly stole a sausage from her. Calmly she stole one from Yongjoon.

"Hey!" Yongjoon exclaimed.

"Blame him. He took mine."

"Mom! Maliah stole my food!"

"SHARE!" they heard Cho screech from the other room.

Maliah looked smug as she ate the sausage.

Yongjoon stole her last bite of eggs.

"CHO! Yongjoon STOLE MY EGGS!"

"Do I need to come in there!? IF I COME IN THERE EVERYONE IS IN TROUBLE!" Cho shrieked.

Both of them slunk in their seats as Seonghun giggled. Standing up to fill his plate, he looked around the kitchen. "Where's Min?"

"He finished breakfast, so he's helping Cho put the extra leaf in the table," Maliah said.

"What are we doing today?" Yongjoon asked.

"I don't know about you three, but I'm starting the baking for Thanksgiving." Maliah stole a sausage link from Seonghun, giving it to Yong.

"What are you baking?" Seonghun spoke over a mouthful of pancakes.

"Peach pie, bourbon pecan pie, caramel cake, cornbread for dressing, and rolls." Maliah ticked off each one on her fingers.

"No pumpkin pie?" Yongjoon asked.

"I'm black. I typically don't do pumpkin pie. I can make a sweet potato pie if you like."

"Please. What's the difference?"

"One's a tuber, the other is a gourd," Maliah deadpanned.

"Smartass." Yongjoon shoved her before popping the last piece of sausage in his mouth. He took his plate to the sink, rinsed it, and shoved it in the dishwasher. "I may get a head start on my Christmas shopping." He glanced at Seonghun. "You coming?"

Seonghun shook his head. "I want to watch her cook."

"You want to eat," snorted Yongjoon. "It's alright, let me know if you need me to pick up anything."

Seonghun nodded as he finished eating. Maliah also got up. Seong watched as she cleaned her plate, then ran upstairs. He knew that Maliah had been spending time with Cho. Though it cut into the time they had together, he couldn't begrudge her that. She adored Cho, delighting in cooking with her. It was something Liah never had before. The difference between how she navigated the house the last time they were there to now was night and day. His girl didn't hover on the peripherals of the room, she walked right in with no fear.

She came back downstairs with the gift bag. Yongjoon was on her heels, curious as to what was in it. Finding Cho in her dining room, Liah handed it over. "Thank you for having me for Thanksgiving."

Cho pulled out the tissue paper and gasped.

"Well this blows macaroni art out of the water," Yongjoon said.

It was a purple vase with gold lines in a geometric pattern on one side. Liah had painted it so the vase had an ombre effect; the top was a deep dark purple while the base was a pale lavender. The gold lines stood in bright contrast. It was large, somewhat wide, but flat.

"You made this?" Cho looked at her.

"I had help," Maliah explained. "I can sculpt by hand, but I have a hard time working the pottery wheel. I'm not coordinated enough. Someone in the art department helped me with it."

"This is lovely. You have a talent for art, you know that right? You could sell your artwork as a side hustle so you wouldn't have to actually work anymore," Cho pointed out. She placed the vase in the center of the table amidst the fancy china before looking at Seonghun. "You're responsible for flowers."

Seong glanced at Yong. "Looks like I'm going with you."

"I never really thought about selling my art." Maliah stared at the vase. "I don't really make it for public consumption. I just do things I enjoy."

"Well I enjoy this," Cho said, gesturing at the vase. "I'm sure other people would enjoy your stuff as well."

Maliah stared at the vase again before retreating back into the kitchen. Seonghun watched as pulled a giant box of peaches from the counter.

He wandered over to her, absentmindedly pulling the bowl from the top shelf that she was trying to reach. "Do you need anything while I'm out?"

She stared at him for a minute before lowering her voice. "Did you bring—" Maliah took a deep breath, trying again. "Did you bring condoms with you?"

"No. There was no point."

"We always have one when we mess around," she pointed out.

"Fair enough, I'll take care of it." He gave her a quick kiss. "Anything else?"

"A candy bar please."

"Got it. I'll see you in a bit." He squeezed her shoulder before walking over to Yong.

THE MEN DECIDED to save the flower buying for last. They wandered the mall, with no real destination in mind. "What are you getting Maliah for Christmas?" Yong asked as he flipped through a rack of shirts.

"I'm struggling. Her birthday is so close to Christmas; I don't want to overwhelm her." He picked up a long sleeved t-shirt to look at. Yong promptly took it out of hands, handing him a button down striped shirt.

"You need more date clothes," Yongjoon admonished. "After her birthday she's going to have a few more pieces of jewelry. Why not get something to house it all in?"

"Like a jewelry box?"

"Yeah, does she have one?"

"No, she keeps her fancy jewelry in the box it came in, storing the box in a plastic bag with her other jewelry." You could tell she'd had the bag for a while, Seong giggled when he saw it.

"You love wooden boxes. Find her a nice jewelry box, chuck a small piece of jewelry into it. Nothing too expensive," Yongjoon said quickly as Seong opened his mouth to protest, "I don't think she'll wear the bracelet you're giving her all the time. Pearls scratch easily. Get her something she could wear all the time." He picked through the rack, holding up a shirt for himself.

Seonghun looked down at the shirt he held, thinking. He really liked the idea of a jewelry box. "You're getting her a necklace for her birthday, so that's out. Rings have a weird connotation; I don't want her to misunderstand. Maybe another bracelet?"

"Let's walk over to the jewelry stores in the mall. Maybe you'll see something you like."

They both checked out at the clothing store, Seonghun accidentally buying the shirt Yongjoon had given him. "You put any thought into where she's wearing that dress?" Yong asked.

"Yeah." Seonghun pulled up a flyer on his phone, handing it to his friend. "It's formal dress, with dinner and dancing. If we pay a little more, we're guaranteed a hotel room on premises for the night. Are you interested?"

"Yes." They stopped by a kiosk, picked up a pretzel, and talked about plans as they entered the jewelry store.

Seonghun was silent as he peered in a jewelry case. It happened to be rings. "Look at that." He pointed to a ring. The band was a silver metal, encrusted in tiny diamonds all the way around. On the front there were thin silver lines, intersecting in almost a wave-like pattern.

"You talk about not wanting her to misunderstand stuff, that looks like a wedding band," Yongjoon said.

"Some people use them as promise rings." A sales clerk walked over to them.

"What's a promise ring?" Yongjoon asked.

The sales clerk paused for a moment, as if to figure out how to explain, "It can honestly be a promise for anything. You could be asking them to promise to move in together at some point, but a lot of people use it to promise engagement down the line. It's a way to show commitment, I guess. It used to be really popular with high schoolers, but I'm seeing more young adults use them, especially college students. For a lot of undergrads, their bachelor's degree is just the beginning. Relationships end up being long distance as the couple goes to pursue their dreams. it's a way to show you're still committed to working on the relationship." The sales clerk looked at them. "I'm sorry, am I rambling?"

"No, you make perfect sense." Seonghun looked at the ring one more time before looking back at the clerk. "I'm looking for something a little less meaning laden. Just a simple Christmas present."

The sales clerk nodded before asking questions, trying to figure out what Seong could not. She was an absolute godsend, steering them to earrings. "Every girl can always use a sensible pair of hoop earrings. They never go out of style. Are her ears pierced?"

"Yes," Seonghun said, peering in the case. "She always wears a pair of small gold hoops."

The clerk pulled out silver, white gold, and rose gold hoops, "If she has gold already, you don't want to get her a repeat, I don't think."

Seonghun looked at the hoops, before staring back at the ring. Glancing over, he saw the clerk's face soften in understanding. "I'll give you two some time to talk about it. My name is Beth, just call me if you need me." Beth walked to another counter to wait on someone else.

Yongjoon spoke up. "Seong, no. I know you care about her, but no."

"I know that, but my heart—" Seonghun sighed.

"You can always save up for it, because I saw the tag; it's a rather large chunk of money to be handing over for a two month relationship. Consider it an exercise in patience. Save the money for now. Purchase it later if that's what you want."

"I just want her," Seonghun said.

"You have her. She doesn't need a ring to declare that. You don't need one either."

"You're right, but I like the idea of it." Seong continued looking at the hoops. "I like the rose gold ones, because I know she likes pink, but the white gold or silver will match her necklace, her watch, and the metal surrounding the jewel on the pearl bracelet."

The two men then began looking at the silver colored metals. "These," Seonghun said finally. "They are simple, no design, and slightly bigger than her gold ones." He held a pair of white gold hoops in his hands, "They are also reasonably priced." He waved Beth over, handing her the earrings.

When Beth rang them up, Seong was surprised to see that the total was a bit less than on the tag. When he asked, she spoke in a lowered voice. "I'm going to give the both of you a little piece of advice. They expect you to haggle slightly when buying jewelry here. I gave you the biggest discount I could without getting management involved. I love when people come in to buy jewelry for people they care about." She smiled at both of them. "It's why I like this job so much. It gives me warm fuzzies." Taking his credit card, she stuck it in the machine before handing each of them a business card. "If you ever need anything else, feel free to stop by and ask for me. I'm happy to help."

They both thanked her. Beth handed Seong his card with the small bag. They continued to walk around the mall, with Yongjoon trying to do his Christmas shopping. "I'd like to get Min something more meaningful than clothes. I know he'd like them, but—"

"I get it, you don't have to explain. But I don't think you're going to find something special at the mall," Seonghun said.

"True," admitted Yongjoon. "Anything else you need?"

"Yes, but I need to stop by a drug store or something. Maliah wants a candy bar." He hadn't forgotten about her second request, but Yong didn't really need to know about that. After picking up what was needed at the drugstore, they grabbed flowers before going home.

CHAPTER 51

Back at the house, they walked in and saw Minjun peeling sweet potatoes, Maliah mixing something in the mixer, and Cho at the stove. They were all laughing at something. "Care to let us in on the joke?" Seonghun asked.

Maliah turned around looking flushed in her face. Whether it was from the question or the heat in the kitchen he didn't know. "No, I don't think we will." She smirked.

"Fair enough." He searched around in his bag, pulling out a candy bar.

"CHOCOLATE! Gimmie!" She reached for it with outstretched hands. As she tore open the wrapper, Liah started to devour the chocolate.

Seong stared at her for a moment. "Are you okay?" he asked.

"I'm fine, why?" she asked through a mouthful of chocolate.

He eyeballed her stomach. She was in baggy sweats, covered by an apron so he couldn't really tell. "You aren't normally as enthused about chocolate as this."

She stopped eating for a moment, immediately pulling out her phone. Seong watched her bring up a black calendar with different marks on it. On tomorrow's date there were red stripes that went on for about six or seven days. "Shit."

"Language!" Cho said, not even turning from the stove.

"Sorry. Can you guys watch the cornbread? I have to make a trip to the store." She untied the apron from around her waist.

"I can go, I know what you use. I've seen it before," said Seong. He quickly tied her apron back on.

"Are you sure? You just got in."

Minjun watched them go back and forth, confused.

"It's fine. Put these in the fridge until I get back." He handed her five different bouquets of flowers.

"Why so many?" Maliah sniffed at one of the bouquets.

"I can break them down, creating prettier arrangements than what I saw at the store," he explained.

"You know how to arrange flowers?"

His ears turned red. "I went to a lecture on it for extra credit last semester."

"That's cute." She smiled at him. "Hurry back." He kissed her before leaving the house again. Back at the drugstore, Seonghun found the brand of pads she used quickly before walking around the store. He picked up random bags of chocolate, as well as her favorite salty treat, Doritos. The nacho cheese ones though, never the blue bag. "I had a class project with a guy in high school that smelled like spit and Cool Ranch Doritos. I can't eat them," she said to him one day when he offered her a chip. He shuddered at the thought before slowly putting the bag down.

As he walked to the front, an idea hit. Seong redirected toward the bath aisle, hitting the jackpot almost immediately. Strawberries and cream bubble bath with matching scented lotion and bath bombs. Quickly adding those to his basket, he checked out before driving back to Cho's. Instead of handing over the bag, he ran upstairs to their room (it was so odd thinking of it as theirs), setting it on her dresser. Seonghun was going to head back downstairs when he saw his book laying on the night-stand. He picked it up fully intending to read only page or two, however, exhaustion overtook him almost instantly, making him doze off mid-sentence.

Coming back from sleep, Seong smelled cinnamon, sugar, along some-thing fruity. Opening his eyes, he realized Liah was curled up beside him, reading a book. "You smell good." His voice came out raspy.

"You always say that," she replied, not looking up from her book. "I've been making pastries though, so I probably smell like that."

"Did Min help you guys?" Seonghun asked.

"He peeled fruit for me and squeezed lemons when I needed him to. He did little things that were helpful."

"That's nice. He likes to feel included."

"Doesn't everyone?" Maliah stretched her arms over her head. "I like to be included in activities too."

"I bought your things." He pointed to the bag on the dresser.

"It looks like you bought enough pads for an army." She got up to look through the bag. "You got me bath bombs? And Doritos?"

"I know it isn't from the fancy place, but I thought you would OOF—" He was abruptly silenced by her mouth on his.

"Thank you very much." She pulled away, staring at him. She must have seen what he was thinking. "I promised Yong we'd go downstairs to watch movies when you got up."

"They don't know I'm up," Seonghun protested.

"You left the door open, so yes, we do." Yongjoon walked in with Minjun following after him. They both laid at the edge of the bed.

"What are you two doing up here?" Maliah asked.

"Checking on you, seeing if you guys are ready for dinner," replied Yongjoon. "Since Thanksgiving is tomorrow, we're having pizza for dinner. Mom isn't cooking tonight. We're also going to start the movies back up."

"Sounds like a plan. I'll be downstairs after I go to the bathroom." Maliah grabbed the bag from the vanity before going into the restroom.

Minjun smacked Seonghun's leg. "Let's head downstairs, she'll meet us down there."

The men rolled off the bed. Cho, knowing Seong's appetite, ordered him two large pizzas of his own. She also purchased chicken wings, breadsticks, along with two salads. Everyone wasted no time in filling their plates. Maliah showed up a short while later. After getting her food, she took a seat beside Seonghun, who managed to sit near the fireplace again.

"Do you always sit here?" she asked him.

He shook his head. "I'm normally on the couch with Minjun, but I noticed how much you like to be near the fireplace."

"It's pretty," she replied.

"Whenever I'm home, we try to keep a fire going the whole time," said Yongjoon, looping a string of cheese on his tongue.

Maliah picked at her pizza, mostly eating the breadsticks and salad. They watched the movie while making jabs at the characters. "So who's your favorite superhero? Black Panther, Captain America? Bucky?" Seonghun asked her.

"Carol Danvers. She's just sick of everyone's shit. I also like how she says, 'Hello, Peter Parker.' It's cute." Maliah handed over her slice of pizza to him.

"Are you okay? You've barely eaten anything." He consumed half the slice in one bite.

"My stomach is upset. Besides, I'll eat a lot tomorrow." They all stayed awake chatting until the fire burned down to embers. Cho left earlier citing a busy day tomorrow, leaving everyone else downstairs. "Is Cho making a turkey?" Maliah asked. "I didn't see one in the refrigerator."

"She's making a few traditional 추석 dishes. We'll be frying a turkey. There is a fridge out in the garage, it's out there," Yong said.

"That will be interesting. I've never had fried turkey before."

Yongjoon began talking about marinades and why he preferred it being fried. Seong watched her listen with the intensity of someone who was going to be quizzed later. Eventually conversations petered out. Everyone started yawning.

"Let's get to bed. We all have a busy day tomorrow," Seonghun suggested.

Maliah stood up, watching as Yong poked the last of the embers out before retiring.

SEONGHUN WOKE the next morning to the sounds of retching. Rolling over, he saw the bathroom door was shut. "Liah," he said cautiously. "Sweetheart, are you okay?"

"I'm fine," she moaned. "My period just started. This happens sometimes. Can you grab the pain meds?"

"Give me five minutes; I'll do you a little better." Seong stood up, throwing on clothes. Maliah didn't respond; there was just more gagging.

Seonghun ran downstairs to the kitchen. Cho was by herself cleaning meat. "Where's Liah? I thought she would beat me down here."

"Cho she's ah— She's sick. Do you have any type of tea for nausea?"

Cho glared at him. Seong stared back confused until it dawned on him. "She isn't pregnant, she's on her cycle. She doesn't do well the first couple days."

She calmed down. "I'll make her some chamomile tea. You make her some toast with a little butter. Make sure she eats it. She barely ate last night. Is that why you left again so quickly yesterday?"

He nodded while placing two crusty pieces of sourdough bread in the toaster. "She doesn't really eat a whole lot of chocolate unless it's around that time. All she wants is chocolate, and to cry. A lot."

"Poor thing. We'll get her fixed up. Get her some food, let her know she can come down when she's ready, I can handle it without her if needed." Cho gave him a tray with a teapot, two tea cups, and a small container of honey on it. He buttered the toast, putting it on a plate. Seong went to pick the tray up, but stopped, staring at it.

"What's wrong?" Cho asked.

"Do you have a small vase or jar?" Seonghun asked her.

Opening the cabinet below the sink, she pulled out a small bud vase. Opening the fridge, he pulled a carnation from one of the bouquets he brought home. Trimming it to size, Seong stuck it in the vase. "She'll like that," he mumbled to himself. "Thanks Cho!" He took the tray upstairs, missing the smile on his friend's face.

Upstairs, he slipped into the bedroom, shutting the door behind him. Maliah was lying face down on the bed. "How is your stomach?" Seonghun asked her.

"A little less queasy, but my back hurts," she said. Her voice was muffled by the pillow.

Setting the tray down, he looked in her bag. She'd put patches in there. Seong grabbed the box along with her pain pills. "Why don't I put the patch on you, we share a bit of breakfast, then see how you feel?"

"Alright." Liah lifted her shirt so that her lower back was exposed.

He pressed a kiss to her back before putting on the patch. Smoothing it on, he patted her gently. "Come on." Getting settled with the tray over his lap, he poured her a cup of tea. "Cho said if you don't feel well she can handle the rest of Thanksgiving."

"I really want to help. I like cooking with her." Maliah's voice wobbled but she tried to rein it in.

"Well let's get you stable so you're able to cook." Seong handed his girlfriend the plate with the toast, taking a slice for himself. Liah slowly drank her tea as she nibbled on the toast.

"Thank you for taking care of me. I appreciate it. I'm normally more aware of when my period is coming, I just forgot to pay attention."

"We've had a lot on our plate lately. Stalkers, schoolwork, dates, working. Speaking of, did you bring your skates? Minjun wants to do a double date skating."

"I brought them. Is he thinking about Saturday? I should be fine by then." She drank the last dregs of her tea, setting half the toast down. "That's all I can do for now. I think I'll be fine by the afternoon."

He brushed a kiss on her forehead, eating the rest of the toast. Pouring the last of the tea in her cup, Seong stood up, grabbing the tray. "Are you coming down, or are you going to sleep?"

Maliah stared at the bed longingly. "I'm drained, but I want to help cook."

Seonghun hesitated but prodded gently. "Do you want to cook because you feel like you need to, or you want to?"

"I really like cooking; I especially like cooking with Cho. She doesn't mind messes at all." Liah stretched as she stood up. "Besides, I don't miss classes when I have my period, I just get through it. I should be fine. I can take breaks if it gets bad."

"Promise me you'll sit when you need to." He opened the door to the room.

"I will. I'll be fine, I promise." Maliah began fiddling with her phone. "I've set alarms so I'm on top of my pain pills."

He nodded as they walked downstairs.

CHAPTER 52

Yongjoon had always taken them home for the holidays, but Seong didn't remember having this much fun. They always had a good time, but it seemed as if there was more laughter this time around. Yong was shooed out of the kitchen after the third time of him trying to see what they were making. Giving up, he motioned to the two men to help him grab the frying gear.

Seonghun carried the turkey, which had been injected with everything his friend could think of, out to the backyard. Minjun carried the oil and the contraption for frying the turkey, while Yongjoon had the fuel and the lighter in his back pocket.

"We have this, it's fine," Seong said out loud.

Min nodded as he helped Yong set the fryer up. Carefully he tipped the giant carton of oil into the containment unit of the fryer. The three of them waited silently as the oil came up to temperature.

"Seong look," said Yong, glancing at the window.

He turned; Liah and Cho were pressed up against the window staring at them.

"What are they doing?"

"Your girl was curious about the turkey; she's probably just interested." Yong pulled out a thermometer, to gauge the temperature. "We're ready." He stared at the other two sternly. "Are we going to have problems?"

"We're fine, let's do it," Seonghun brushed away his concerns. As carefully as he did when they lifted weights, he basically spotted Yong, just in case something went wrong. However, at the first pops of the oil, Min screamed, which caused him to scream. Both of them took off running as Yong yelled at them.

"GET BACK OVER HERE YOU BIG BABIES!" he shouted in Korean. As they walked back over, he swore he heard laughter coming from the house.

THE TURKEY WAS FRYING NICELY when they heard Cho call. Yong went to the door, to see what she needed. When he came back, he asked Seong to go help his mother.

"What do you need me to do?" he asked as he walked inside.

"You need to arrange the flowers, put them in the vase, then start setting food out in the dining room," said Cho as she started plating food with Liah.

He washed his hands to begin on the flowers. He saw Maliah watching him so he motioned her over. "Because the table is so big, I picked taller blooms, because the table can handle it, if that makes sense."

She nodded.

He began stripping leaves from flowers, explaining how he was putting it together. Eventually he had two bundles of flowers. One he stuck in the vase that Maliah had brought. The other went into another vase in the living room. Trimming the stem of a blue flower, Seong stuck it behind Maliah's ear.

"I don't get to leave you flowers as much, as we don't pass notes back and forth hardly anymore, except to let the other know where we're at."

"I miss it sometimes. I keep them in a folder in my room," Maliah admitted.

"I keep mine in a box," he replied. He washed his hands again before helping to put food on the table. Liah elbowed him slightly as he shoved an entire dinner roll into his mouth. "I'm a growing boy! All I had today was toast," he protested, his mouth full of bread.

"It is almost time to eat, you can wait," she admonished. They set the food on the table before going back for more.

It took them three trips to get everything on the table. On their last trip, Yong came in with the turkey, setting it in its place. When everyone was seated, they all looked around, appreciating the table. Cho had a ton of place settings. As a realtor she had access to people who staged houses. They frequently refreshed their supply, selling the old items at a bargain. Cho had easily coordinated the table around the colors of the vase. Everything was lavender and gold. Everyone had a pair of lavender or gold chopsticks by their setting, Maliah included.

"You've been doing better with the training ones, I thought you may want to try using regular ones for a change," Cho said.

"They are really pretty." Maliah picked up the purple set closest to her.

Yong began to slice the turkey as everyone else started passing around the other dishes. Cho uncorked wine and a bottle of sparkling apple juice for Maliah. "Just because she doesn't drink alcohol doesn't mean she doesn't get a fancy drink too," Cho told Seong when he saw it in the fridge.

Everyone got their plates filled. Seonghun's plate was basically mounded. Maliah stared at it, giggling. "You can always go back for seconds, you know this right?"

"I know. I'm starving." He began to strategically eat from the mountain so that it didn't fall over.

"What is this?" Minjun asked, holding up a small bowl of what looked like shredded carrots.

"Carrot salad," Maliah replied, "carrots, raisins, a little mayo, pineapple."

Minjun scooped some on his plate.

"Where did you learn how to cook?" Cho asked. "You've explained that you had to cook for yourself a lot, but kids your age usually go for convenience. I wasn't expecting you to know how to cook a holiday meal."

Maliah was quiet as she ate her soup. "My mom hated my dad's mom.

She wasn't a fan of her parents either as they all basically forced the marriage."

Seonghun paused while eating to listen to the story.

"When they got married, one of the gifts that my dad's mom gave to my mother was a small box with all these neat recipes in it. It mostly stayed on a shelf collecting dust. Someone worked really hard on it. They stamped each card, then printed the recipe neatly on the lines. My mom never used it, never opened it; she seemed to resent it a lot. Around the time I was twelve, my mom tossed it out when she was cleaning. I crept behind her, stealing the cards. If she would have noticed the box was missing, there would have been hell to pay." Liah went back to her soup.

"You didn't pull out a recipe card to cook with," Cho pointed out.

Maliah smiled. "It's going to sound weird, but reading those recipes as a kid was a comfort to me. Someone cared about my mom enough to do this for her even though she's mean as shit."

"Language."

"Sorry. Anyway, I loved reading them, so I would read them all the time. Most of them I have memorized at this point. I still have the cards though. They're upstairs in case I need a reference."

"Can I see them after dinner?" Cho asked nonchalantly.

No one noticed the tone in her voice except for Seong. As Maliah nodded, he looked at Cho, who had a gleam in her eye. She was up to something.

Everyone continued eating, asking questions about the different foods on the table. Maliah contributed most of the American fare, cornbread dressing, mashed potatoes, fried cabbage, macaroni and cheese, and jambalaya. Seonghun nearly ate the entire plate of jambalaya himself.

Halfway through the meal, Maliah's alarm went off. Discreetly she took a pain pill. "How are you feeling?" Seonghun's voice lowered.

"Not queasy, a little emotional, but that was going to happen period or no, the holidays are rough for me." She used chopsticks to wrestle a piece of short rib. "I wonder if my family even cares that I'm not there. But I know the answer to that because they would've reached out. I try not to let it bother me."

"Have you made progress on your letter to them?" he asked.

Maliah shook her head. "I would like an apology. I'd like to know why I was treated so badly, but I need to figure out how to ask them to come but not bombard them with all of my emotions."

"They deserve to be bombarded with your emotions to be honest," Seonghun said.

"I agree, but if you agreed to come to a mediated event with someone vomiting everything you ever did wrong to them on you, how long would you stay? I have to think about this rationally, even if I don't want to. I can rage afterward."

"That's a mature outlook," Yong said, overhearing.

"It took a while to get to this point. I'm still not all the way there if I can't write the stupid letter." She aggressively stabbed her chopstick at the soft rice cake on her plate.

When everyone was mostly finished, the three men rose to clear away plates. Maliah stood up to help when Seonghun grabbed the plate from her. "You cooked. You're crampy and I know your back hurts. Sit down, we have this," he said as he walked into the kitchen with the plates. Min walked out with two pies and a plate of lemon bars. Yong came back with a cake.

"This was my first time making that cake. It is super finicky. I hope it came out okay," Maliah said.

Seong sat back down with plates, setting a cup of tea in front of her.

"Thank you so much." He heard her voice wobble.

Minjun cut a slice of the cake, took a bite, then looked down mid-chew. "What in the world is this?"

"Caramel cake, did the icing not set right?" Maliah asked.

Instead of responding, he gave a bite to Yongjoon who had a slice of peach pie on his plate. After one bite he sliced a massive hunk of the cake adding it to his plate as well.

"This is really good. It's better than the cake at that fancy cake shop," said Yongjoon in between massive bites.

"Oh good, I'm glad you guys like it." She went back to nibbling at a lemon bar.

Cho had a massive slice of the peach pie. "For someone who doesn't have the resources to cook all the time, you're amazing at it."

Maliah didn't say anything as she ducked her head slightly.

"What are some things you struggle with?" Seonghun asked curiously. "You seem like you can master anything you do."

"Sadly, this is not true. I'm awful with video games because I don't have great hand eye coordination. I struggle with learning foreign languages. Math and art are my strongest points."

"Yeah, her hand eye coordination is hilarious. I wondered if the prescription in her glasses was off, she punched weird," Yongjoon chortled.

"I still got you though," Maliah pouted.

"That you did." He patted her on the shoulder.

"Why don't you go lay down? Aren't you going to be up at like 4 a.m.?" Seonghun asked.

"Ugh. Yes. Why are we doing this again?" She looked at Cho.

"THE THRILL OF THE SALE!" Minjun and Cho screamed together.

"Fine. I'm gonna go lay down. Min, feel free to wake me in the morning. Thank you for letting me help cook, Cho."

"No need to thank me, you're welcome to cook anytime, dear." Cho smiled at her.

Maliah nodded as she walked out of the room.

Cho sat at the table and drank her wine, watching the boys clean up. Seong was still sneaking mouthfuls of food as he put everything away. Minjun and Yongjoon worked together to stack the dishes in the dishwasher. After everything was put back together, Yongjoon walked over and gave his mom a smacking kiss on the cheek. "It was good, Mom. Seonghun can't stop eating."

"That boy is going to burst," Cho said as she stood up. "I'm going to go to bed as well. Min, I'll be downstairs waiting for you in the morning."

"I'll be down as soon as I drag Maliah out of bed," he replied.

She bid the boys good night. The three of them sat in front of the TV, turning on a replay of a game from earlier.

"It feels like it's been a while since it's just been us," Seong said.

"Things are changing. You spend most if not all of your free time with Liah," Min replied.

"Does it bother you that we don't hang out as much anymore?" Seonghun looked at his best friend.

"Of course not. I'm happy you've found someone and that she isn't mean," Minjun said.

"Mean? There isn't a mean bone in her body, what are you talking about?" Seong looked at him confused. Minjun began to squirm uncomfortably.

Yongjoon stood up, kissing his boyfriend. "I'm going to bed. You two need to actually talk about this. It's been a secret for a while; Min needs to come clean. Have a good night." With that, he went upstairs.

Seonghun watched him go up the stairs and then turned to his friend. "What happened?" He switched over to Korean.

Minjun hemmed and hawed for a bit before finally coming clean. "Your ex? She hated me, our friendship, thought I was going to take you away from her." It came out in a rush.

He was astounded. "What?"

"We weren't alone often. Never on purpose either, but you would get up to go get something, or go to the restroom then she would start. She'd say that she noticed me looking at you; I may be able to fool everyone else, but I wasn't fooling her."

"Min."

"You asked, let me finish." Minjun cleared his throat. "No matter how many times I said I wasn't attracted to men, she wouldn't let up, she was relentless. Only when you weren't around though."

"Min, why didn't you ever say anything? I would have dumped her."

He shrugged. "I thought you were happy. You seemed happy. But now that I've seen you with Liah, I know it wasn't happiness. I don't know what that was."

"It was a young man having sex with someone he tolerated for the first time," Seonghun said dryly. "Min, you're my best friend. You would have come before her, end of story."

"Could you say the same for Maliah?" Minjun asked.

"No, but she'd never intentionally hurt you, or if she had a jealousy issue, she'd talk to both of us," Seonghun pointed out.

Min smiled. "I'm glad you see her for what she is, not for what you want her to be. That's how you saw Jia. You saw what you wanted her to be, until she showed you she wasn't."

The friends were silent for a while. "Min, you have to tell me when things like this happen, so I can fix it."

"She wasn't saying anything anyone else in that village hadn't thought."

Seonghun looked at his friend. Min had been hiding so much from him. "I see."

"What do you see?"

"Why you spent so much time at my house, why you were loath to go home sometimes, why we ate more at my house than at yours. Why you found this opportunity to come to the US. You were trying to get away. All this time. Min, I'm so sorry, I never knew." He had a lump in his throat as he reached over to hug his friend.

"It's okay. It really is. I didn't talk about it because I knew it would hurt you in the long run. Look at it this way. I won't be going back to the village. I'll be living in Seoul and hopefully Washington DC part time. Things turned out okay."

"I wish there was a way I could make the past up to you."

"Live your life, be happy, make her happy. That's all I want. That's all I've ever wanted." He stood up. "I have an early day tomorrow. Don't dwell on it, Seong. I would have kept it to myself but Yongjoon insisted we should probably talk. It just sort of came up now." He ran his fingers through Seong's hair before heading upstairs.

Seonghun was troubled. Immediately he went to the room he shared with his girlfriend. Opening the door, he saw her tossing and turning on the bed. "Sweetheart," he whispered. "Are you asleep?"

"My back hurts. I'm trying to get comfortable," she said.

He quickly stripped down to his underwear before sitting beside her on the bed. "Lay on your stomach," he said. When she did as he asked, he used this thumbs to apply pressure to her lower back. Liah tensed up slightly before letting out a low moan. Knowing what she needed, he continued the kneading motion. The room was quite except for her soft grunts. All of a sudden he spoke up. "Do you think I'm a nice person?"

"You're one of the nicest people I know," she replied. "Why do you ask?"

He proceeded to tell her the conversation that he had with Minjun. "Stop. Lay down," she ordered. Doing as she asked, he laid on his side, facing her. She scooted closer, resting her arm on his waist, snuggling as close as she could.

"You're a very kind man. The fact that you're so troubled about this proves it. I think sometimes it's hard to relate to other people's experiences. Min sounds like he was a very closeted bisexual man."

"Closeted?" Seonghun asked.

"No one knew," she explained, lightly scratching his side. "No one knew except you. You knew what he was, immediately accepting it, moving on with life. It never occurred to you that anyone would treat him badly because Min is Min. He's a sweet guy with a good heart, who would hurt him? That being said, it goes back to being mindful. There were probably hints that things were going on between him and— What's her name?"

"Jia," he supplied.

"Huh, you've never actually said her name, just referred to her as your ex," Maliah pointed out.

"She isn't important," he said.

"Everyone's important, Seong," she said quietly. "Even though she pissed you off, everyone in your life teaches you something. She taught you that you can't always take everyone at face value."

He looked down at her, snuggled into his chest half asleep. "Is that how you cope?"

"Mmm," she continued, trailing her hands down his side slowly. "I've had a lot of painful lessons in my life. But it's taught me to be kind to the people I interact with as best as I can, because you don't know what they're going through. It also taught me to keep my guard up around people."

"That doesn't seem like the greatest lesson, Liah."

"I think so. People can be too trusting, then they get taken advantage of. That's not an issue I have anymore." She kissed him. "I need to get some sleep, baby. We can talk more about this tomorrow if you want."

"Goodnight. Sorry for keeping you up."

"Anytime you need to talk I'm here." Her hand slowly stopped moving as she dozed off. He watched her sleep, stroking her hair as she began to snore softly.

He wondered what he taught her. He wondered why he was scared to ask.

CHAPTER 53

When Liah returned from Black Friday shopping, she looked as if she were going to pass out from exhaustion on the spot. Not really thinking anything of it, Seong picked her up in a fireman's carry, hauling her up the steps. She got excited about him picking her up and wanted to show her appreciation. She basically swallowed him completely as he tried to muffle his cries. He went to reciprocate but was firmly blocked by her hand. "Period," she reminded him.

"I could—"

"I'm not comfortable with you touching me like this. No offense."

"None taken. Get some sleep." He was amazed as she dozed off instantly. After catching his breath, Seong got under the covers with her. Pulling her close he sighed. He didn't talk about it with Yong, just telling him he had to run an errand earlier today. He met with Beth the jeweler again, asking to see the promise ring she showed him earlier.

Seong held it in the palm of his hand as looked down at it. It felt... Right. It felt like her. To be fair however, he sat it aside to look at a few others. Nothing else felt the same. When he told Beth his concerns about it being too soon but not wanting to lose out on the ring, she called her manager over. The manager set him up with a payment plan. It was reasonable; no interest, plus he would be able to pay it off by the middle of

April. Just enough time before they said goodbye. Though his bank account was looking a little shaky lately, he plunked down the first payment. His stipend would be in his account at the beginning of December. Honestly, he'd blasted through a large chunk of his savings in the past few months. Maliah always fought with him to help pay for things, but he wanted her to understand that this was how he treated someone when he—

That was another issue. He loved her. But he'd never said it before in a non-platonic, non-parental way. He understood how Minjun felt when he said he wanted to make it special. But there was her voice in his head. *Not everything has to be a big event, Seong.*

But wasn't it okay for it to be special? To want to write her name in the sky with a plane? He didn't know what to do or even what to say to her. He remembered what Minjun said to him when he told Seong how he told Yong. *"It wasn't how I wanted it. I wanted to scream my words from every corner of the world, I wanted everyone to know that I love this man. But in the end the person who needed to hear the words and feel the sentiment I had behind them got them. That's all that really mattered, Seong."*

"It's hard to sleep when you're thinking so hard over there." Her voice was slurred.

"Am I moving too much?" He thought he was laying pretty still.

"It's going to sound odd, but whenever you have something heavy on your mind, I feel you. Like I feel a shift in you." She turned over, snuggling into his chest. "It's hard to explain. I don't know if it is a good or bad thought, I just know that you're thinking extremely hard about something."

He didn't really know what to say to that.

"Do I need to slow your brain down?" She rolled on top of him. Liah nipped his full lower lip before going in for a kiss. They stayed like that for a while, kissing, teasing tongues when Maliah's hand started to go lower again.

He broke the kiss. "Does it bother you that I can't touch you right now?"

"You act as if I don't get pleasure from this," she said. "I enjoy being with you. It's never bothered me. I just like being with you in any way I can. You know this. So sit back," she slid his boxers down, "relax, and enjoy."

His eyes rolled in the back of his head as he felt her mouth on him again.

Shortly after his second blowjob of the day, they both crashed. Maliah was truly worn out from the day's events while Seong was in a post sexual coma. There was a light tap at the door that made his eyes open. Everything was blurry but he saw Min cracking the door, observing Liah asleep on his chest. Min didn't notice he was awake when he walked to her side of the bed and tapped her shoulder. "Hey, Cuttlefish."

Maliah stirred. "Is that my name now?"

"It fits." He smiled at her. "We're getting ready to start decorating. Get up. You need to eat too."

"Alright. We'll be down in a second." She fluttered her hand at him.

Taking the hint, Min left the room.

"Seong." She tapped his arm.

"Yeah?" He squinted at her.

"It's time to get up and decorate the tree." She tried to wriggle out of his grasp.

"But you're warm, and soft, and you smell nice." He snuggled her tighter, feeling her shake slightly as she chuckled at him.

"As are you, but I've never decorated a Christmas tree with people. I really want to," she said.

"Never?"

"No. The tree was usually up when I got home from school. Mom put it up herself," explained Maliah. "She wanted ornaments just so."

Seong let her go so he could get dressed. "Write your letter, Maliah. You need closure."

"I will. I want to get it done by the end of February, so that I can hopefully have a meeting before I leave the state."

"Have you decided what you want from this?" he asked as he pulled on a shirt.

"I want peace. How that peace is given is up to them." She walked into the bathroom.

Seong headed downstairs, immediately walking into the kitchen. In the fridge, he saw there was still a lot of pizza left. Walking back into the living room with a pile of slices on his plate, he saw his friends staring at him. "What?"

"Haven't you been eating all day?" Minjun asked.

"I'm a growing boy!" he exclaimed.

"You're pretty much out of time to use that excuse," pointed out Cho. "Puberty stopped for you a long ago."

"I'm hungry. All the time. Maliah doesn't mind." He bit into one of the slices.

"I'm gonna check the mail while we wait on Liah." Yong walked out of the door.

Minjun was untangling garland so Seong sat beside him to help. All of a sudden the front door flew open. "LIAH, GET DOWNSTAIRS NOW! COLLEGE PAPERS!" Yong hollered as he ran into the living room. He sat by Minjun, setting the envelope in his lap.

Maliah flew down the stairs. "Are you going to open it?" She sat by the fireplace, waiting patiently.

"Yeah." But he just sat there with the envelope in his lap, staring at it.

"Let me." Minjun gently took the envelope. "Dear Mr. Chin, We are pleased to welcome you to Georgetown Law…" Minjun smiled. "Congratulations!"

Maliah hooted while Seong started shaking Cho.

Yong stared at the paper, disbelieving. "Mom?" His voice cracked.

Cho walked over to her son who was trying very hard to keep it together. "He would have been so proud, Yongie," she said softly.

"I'm gonna be a lawyer, Mom." Two tears fell, plopping on the acceptance letter Minjun handed him.

"A great one, I have no doubt about that." She ruffled her son's hair.

Seong scooped up Maliah, sitting her on his lap. "I'm so happy for him," she whispered.

"It's all he's ever wanted. We talked about it when we went camping last year." He kissed her cheek. "We were going to go camping this year, but Cho offered us an alternative that I wanted to talk to you about. How do you feel about Gatlinburg?"

"I have no feelings for or against Gatlinburg; unless you're asking me to move there to become a country music star. The answer is no," she said.

He chuckled. "No, spring break. We'd stay in a cabin for free. Yongjoon said something about an amusement park called Dollywood."

"I usually work through spring break, so let me talk to my bosses." She gave him a quick kiss before standing up. Reaching in her pocket she pulled out a small pack of tissues, handing it to Yongjoon. "Congratulations."

He pulled her into a hug. Seong saw her stiffen at first but relaxed in his embrace. They weren't particularly affectionate with each other, so the hug took Maliah by surprise. Seong went into the kitchen to make her a plate. By the time he got back she was crying and Yongjoon was handing her the tissues back.

"What happened? I was gone for like two minutes getting her some food." Seong looked on helplessly as she wept into Cho's shoulder.

"Mom, we forgot a tote outside, we're gonna go grab it." Without waiting for a response, Yongjoon pulled the two men out to the garage. He got in his car, motioning for the other two to get in as well. As he backed out, he looked in his rearview mirror at Seong. "Do you remember how to get to Maliah's parents' house?"

"If I thought about it hard enough. It was dark though, and there were a lot of side streets. Why?"

"Because I want fucking answers."

Seong looked at Yongjoon. He rarely cursed because of his mother, so when he did, something was seriously wrong. He started driving.

"She was confused, Seong. She's never had a stocking. Minjun told her that's what families do. He reminded her he was looking at stocking stuffers earlier. She thought he just meant little presents. I asked her if Santa ever filled her stocking when she was a kid." He turned a corner a little too sharp, jerking the car. If Seong didn't have his seatbelt on, he would have gone flying. "She stopped getting presents at seven-years-old. There was never an explanation. She assumed she was a bad girl until she figured out the whole deal with Santa at nine. Two years, Seong. TWO YEARS! She thought she was bad until she figured out that her parents were shit."

He pulled into the park that Seong usually went to. "No wonder Casey got to her. She wanted a friend; she got a nightmare. Jesus Christ!" He hit the steering wheel.

Seong thought quickly about how to approach this. Yong was fairly mild-mannered, but when his temper was triggered, he was a wildcard. He wasn't close with a lot of people, but the people he let in his circle were his. He would literally kill if they were harmed, to say nothing of his mother.

"Yongjoon. Even if I was completely sure about where her parents lived, I would not take you there, not in this state. You just got accepted into law school. I don't know the rules, but I'm pretty sure they can take that away if you go to jail. Not to mention how Maliah would feel that you confronted her parents before she had a chance to. I know it is upsetting, but you have to let it go." Seong looked at Minjun who was rubbing Yongjoon's arm.

"Who denies a little kid a stocking, or presents? I get it if you're poor, I know shit like that happens, but to not tell them!? It feels like you're torturing them!"

"There are so many pieces to her story that make no sense. We won't get the answers until she gets them," Seong said patiently.

"How are you so calm about this? You love her! How can you live with this?" Yongjoon demanded.

"Because I've talked to her about it instead of storming out of the house looking to pick a fight," he pointed out quietly, "I've laid with her, listening to her cry, worried if there was something actually wrong with her that made them not like her. She wonders if she's just not remembering correctly that she actually has done something wrong. I know, Yong. I want to rage too, but someone has to be there to listen with a rational head. She's already carrying so much, she doesn't need to carry my emotions too."

It was silent in the car as Yongjoon stared out of his windshield, gripping his wheel tightly. "I get it now. I get why you always want to treat her, why you're always fighting about who pays, I understand now." He checked his phone. "Mom said they're making hot cocoa. We need to bring home some candy canes or something so Liah isn't worried she scared us off." He drove toward the nearest store. "So, am I wrong in wanting to overdo her Christmas?"

"Don't," Seong warned. "She wants to be equal. If she comes downstairs to a mass pile of presents, it's going to make her feel bad as she can't do the same. She's working really hard to find nice gifts for everyone. She's so excited that she's able to give something to someone. Just get her the singular thing you had in mind for her."

"I won't go overboard, but she's going to be spoiled. If not by me, then by Ma. Mom loves her to death."

"I think she bought her that expensive pot we saw today," Minjun chimed in.

"What expensive pot?" Yong asked.

"I don't know what it's called, but it was on sale for two hundred and fifty dollars. She saw Liah basically petting it."

"Maliah likes really fancy things. She takes really good care of her expensive things, because she worked so hard to secure them. She never writes or highlights in the textbooks she had to buy brand new so she can sell them back at the best price. She is very particular," Seong said.

"How is that working for you two? I know you like to poke through belongings," Min said as they got out of the car.

"I'm not careless," he said as they walked into the grocery store. "I ask before I touch anything. She doesn't really care because she knows I'm not going to destroy her stuff, I'm just going to look at it. I like seeing what is special to people," explained Seong, "I like going through her pictures, or flipping through her art, stuff like that."

"Did you learn anything new?" Yongjoon glanced at him as he threw three boxes of candy canes in the basket.

"The type of porn she likes," Seong blurted.

His friends snapped their heads to him. "What?!" Minjun yelled.

"I-I shouldn't be talking about this." Seong sped ahead, picking up other flavors of candy canes. His face was the color of a strawberry.

"You can't bring that up and not elaborate. That isn't fair!" Minjun shrieked.

"Wait a minute," Yongjoon said. "You don't have to tell us what she likes, that's her business. But how did this all come about?"

"Well," Seong swallowed, "you know how if she doesn't know something, she researches it?"

His friends nodded.

"Well, that's how she learned how to... take care of herself. I've known that for a while. When I asked her if she watched any other types, she wouldn't answer." He scratched his head. "She knows of this really cool site where she can tour museums virtually. One day I asked her for the link. She told me to just grab it out of her bookmarks. Since I was in there, I clicked on the other bookmarks. I've never actually seen her get that red. I didn't know she could get that red."

"What happened?" Min asked.

Yong was hiding his laughter behind his hand.

"She snatched her laptop from me, asking me to keep it to myself." He shrugged. "It isn't my cup of tea, but I told her I'd watch it with her if she wanted. She asked me never to speak on it again."

"I really want to know. What do girls watch?" Minjun wondered.

"There's a whole 'for women' category on most of those sites," Yongjoon said. "She probably goes there."

Seong wisely said nothing. The men paid for the candy, leaving the store. At the house, they saw Maliah in front of the fireplace beside Cho. They both had cups of hot chocolate. Her hair was pulled back, as she saw them, Liah wiped self-consciously at her whipped cream mustache. "Hi."

"Hi, sweetheart, we got candy canes." Seong held up a bag.

"That's cool. I didn't mean to scare you off."

"You didn't. Yongjoon wanted to give you some space. Also, candy canes were needed."

"Let's get started," said Cho standing up, "Your hot chocolate is in the kitchen."

Though Cho would have loved a real tree, she lived in absolute fear of them. "My mom used to tell me they could catch on fire randomly. I don't know if it's true, but I'm not risking it," she often told the boys. Instead, she purchased the most realistic fake tree she could find. As Yongjoon and Minjun were putting it together, Maliah and Seong looped lighted garland around the stairwell banister. Cho hung wreaths on the doors throughout the house. Each wreath had a color theme. Yongjoon's room was ocean blue. The room formerly occupied by Minjun was green. Seong's former room's wreath was red, and Maliah's room was pink. Cho's own room's wreath was dark purple. The main door to the house was a normal wreath with silver balls looped with red ribbon.

Maliah opened a tote gasping as she looked inside.

"What is it?"

"It's a Christmas village!" she exclaimed. She pulled out the pieces and studied them. "I would see these in my classmate's homes. One of the parents said that some of the pieces had been passed down from her mom." Liah looked under one to find a switch. Flipping it, a light in the little cottage came on.

Cho walked over. "When I first started getting successful with home selling, a lot of vendors I would recommend to people sent me these. I always thought they were cute. Pretty soon, I had a whole town." She pulled out the bell tower, flipping the switch on it. A light came on as the bell chimed lightly. "Come on, I'll show you where this goes."

Seong carried the tote to the back dining room for them, before leaving them to set up. He continued hanging up garland and lights throughout the house, until they were finished with the village. Yong hung the stockings on the fireplace mantle. Seong saw Liah hold back tears at the sight of her stocking. At last, everyone came together to work on the tree. Before starting, Cho silently handed out a box to each of them, and Yongjoon handed one to his mom.

"What's this?" Maliah asked.

"Your ornament," said Seong. He opened his box to see an enameled bowl of noodles hanging from a ribbon. "Thanks, Cho." He laughed.

Minjun opened his box to find an enameled heart with his and Yongjoon's name on it in Hangul.

Maliah looked over. Slowly she reached out to trace the characters. "What does it say?" she asked.

Minjun took her finger, tracing as he pronounced them for her.

"Loosely translated it has Yongjoon and mine's name, the date, then first Christmas." His voice cracked slightly.

Maliah rubbed his back as he looked at his ornament.

Yongjoon opened his. "This would have been bad had I gotten a rejection, Ma." It was an enameled diploma from Georgetown.

"I had faith in you. I'll always have faith in you, Yongie," Cho said as she opened hers. Yongjoon had framed one of the very few pictures there were of both his parents and him around Christmas. Cho was looking at Yongjoon while his dad was looking at her. It was in a tiny gold frame with a red heart dangling from the base and a red ribbon to hang it on the tree.

"Where on earth did you find this?" Cho asked.

"I have a handful of photos I don't think you know I have," he explained.

Everyone watched Cho trace the frame as Maliah quietly opened her box.

Nestled in the soft cotton was an enamel ornament like everyone else's. A paintbrush lay across a canvas. A summer scene was half painted. On the other half of the canvas it looked as if words were scrawled using the paintbrush. *Be the change you want to see in the world.* "This is pretty, thank you, Cho."

"You're welcome. Let's get them up." Cho stood up, dragging a tote closer. Maliah peered in, seeing all of the ornaments. Smiling, she reached in, pulling out a reindeer made of clothespins.

"I made that when I was four," Yongjoon said as he knelt next to her, pulling out ornaments. They had typical balls and garland, but most of their ornaments had a story behind them.

"This is when Yongie was obsessed with Tonka trucks."

"Mom had just gotten into sewing, so I saved my money for a sewing ornament."

"This is Seong's from last year, it's an apple tree."

"Look at the little boxing gloves!"

Slowly the tree came together. Seong was the tallest, so he put the star on. Liah was the shortest, so she put the tree skirt at the bottom. Cho took a few pictures, before turning off the lights in the living room so only the tree and the fireplace were lit.

Seong looked down at Maliah who looked like she had stars in her eyes as she looked at the tree. She reached out to touch a branch but pulled her hand back. He grabbed her hand, placing it on the branch she was aiming for. "Christmas trees are made for touching. No one is going to yell at you for touching it," he whispered.

She quietly trailed her fingers through the tree, touching the ornaments. "I didn't see this one in the box." She held a tiny patchwork quilt in her hands. "I love the colors."

"It's scraps from some of Yongie's baby clothes," Cho explained. "I had a really hard time giving up the idea of having more than one baby, so I wanted to preserve a lot of what I had of his, to remember what he was like at that age. There's pieces of his clothes in a lot of stuff around the house. Quilts, stuffed animals, things like that."

"Why did you give up the idea of having another baby?" Maliah asked.

Cho snorted. "Honey, I'm missing a few pieces to be able to have another baby."

Maliah blushed. "But there are other options, adoption, IVF, stuff like that."

"I should have been clearer. I wanted another baby with my husband. It wouldn't have been the same without him," said Cho. "I couldn't ask for a better kid anyway." She squeezed Yongjoon's arm before wandering around the tree to make sure it was evenly lit.

Maliah looked at Yong. "Do you get sad that you don't have siblings?"

Yongjoon looked over at Seong who was sneaking into the kitchen to eat again. "What do you think your boyfriend is? He couldn't get much more brotherly unless we were blood related." She went to wander over to the tree when Yongjoon grabbed her arm, pulling her back. "That is also how I feel about you as well. You're one of the best things to happen to each of us, my mom included." He kissed his hand, smacking her forehead with it.

Maliah snorted at the display of affection. "Same to all of you." She looked around at Min sitting while drinking his cocoa, while Seong entered the living room with a slice of pie. "It's weird to think of sitting in the dorm room with my meal for one, trying to keep myself busy during this time."

"You know you'll never have to do that again, right? Even if you can't make it to see Seong, my door, our door will always be open." He looked down at her. "You understand that? You're part of us, part of this." He gestured around. "I don't let go of my friends easily."

"You're gonna make me cry again," she sniffled.

"Let's avoid that and get some pie," He shifted, pushing her into the kitchen, "Are we all still going skating tomorrow?"

"Yeah in the evening. I'm going to do a cookie blitz with your mom during the day."

Yongjoon looked at her. "Would you be making trash can cookies?"

She nodded. "Along with a few others you haven't tried."

He smiled happily as he cut slices of sweet potato pie. "This isn't half bad. I really like the crust."

"Thanks. Frozen butter makes it flaky," she said as she took her plate.

"Who knew?" Yongjoon ate his slice. "Are you going to stick around downstairs?"

"I'm actually still tired. I think I'm going to bed."

"We need to get a lesson in tomorrow. I have equipment here; we can work out in the backyard."

"That's fine. When are we going back to school?" She scraped the rest of her plate before standing up to wash it. He took it from her rinsing them both before putting them in the dishwasher.

"We'll probably leave Sunday evening." They walked out of the kitchen; Liah walked directly to Seong.

"I'm sleepy. I'm headed to bed." She gave him a kiss. "Goodnight."

"I'll be up in a minute," he said, squeezing her hip. She said goodnight to everyone else before leaving.

"Cho, do you still do a lot of antiquing?" Seong asked as soon as Liah was out of sight.

"Not really. Why? What's up?" She sat on the couch next to Minjun, drinking cocoa.

"I want to get her a jewelry box for Christmas, but I have some exact things I want. I looked online but I'm not having luck. I want it to be her style. But everything I find when I put in keywords like girly, feminine, or ornate, I get boxes that look old fashioned with garish details. I also want it to have a lock. Like an old school lock with a skeleton key."

"I can ask around, I'll let you know."

With that, Seong bid everyone goodnight following his girlfriend upstairs. When he opened the door, Maliah was lying in bed. She wasn't asleep, but she seemed to be daydreaming, playing with her fingers. Quickly shedding his clothes, he cut the light, climbing into bed with her.

"Do you want to talk about it?" he asked quietly.

"It's hard to explain."

"Give it a try. We can sort it out together."

"Okay." She shifted closer to him. "All my life I've worked toward my goals. I've had a singular focus. Go to school, get good grades to get a scholarship to college. Go to college, get good grades to get a scholarship to grad school. Do well at grad school, get a job, and help people."

"Those are all very good goals," he said.

"But I never had any personal goals," she pointed out, "I knew I wanted to live in a nice apartment, but that's it."

"Okay?" She was right, this was hard to explain. He was confused.

"I want... this. I want a family. I want traditions with Christmas villages. I want memories and pictures, fireplaces, and cocoa. I want people I love to share it with." She looked at him teary-eyed. "I don't mean to cry like this all the damn time. I'm not sad, I'm happy. I've never actually had a decent holiday before, this was just wonderful."

He wiped the errant tear falling from her eye. "It's honestly too soon for me to be making this promise to you, but I'm going to make it anyway, okay?"

She nodded.

"As long as we're together, you'll have a good holiday. We'll make traditions, we'll laugh until we cry, we'll eat until we're miserable—"

She chuckled at that, though it sounded a little wet from her tears.

"You're not alone anymore, Liah. I won't let you be alone anymore." He kissed her softly before gathering her against his chest. "You have people that care for you very much. I don't think any of us are going to let you go."

Just tell her. Just say it. You're nearly there. Open your mouth and say it! Seong wanted to tell her badly how much he loved her. But something was stopping him. Part of it he realized was that two months was such a short time to feel as strongly as he did. Another very tiny part of him was scared she didn't feel the same way. He knew she cared about him. But to what extent, he had no clue. *We'll sort it out eventually. None of us are going anywhere.* It was his last thought before sleep overcame him.

CHAPTER 54

Cho and Seong were eating cookies while chatting when Maliah came downstairs to the kitchen.

"Are you and Yong okay?" Seonghun asked. Liah had been practicing her self-defense with Yong earlier; things got woefully out of hand, causing the two to be separated.

"Yeah, we're fine. He pushed my buttons, harder than either of us expected, to be honest." Seong watched her cast an embarrassed glance toward Cho. "I'm sorry for fighting in your house."

Cho dusted her hands of cookie crumbs. "Stay right here." She went around the corner near the formal dining room.

Maliah looked at Seong, but he only shrugged. He had no idea where she was going.

Cho came back shortly with an old leather album. "I'm the middle kid of three." She patted the chair next to her so Liah sat down. "Our fights were epic." She opened the album to a page that had them laughing. All three kids had dimples. A male teenager was holding onto a girl by her waist. The girl had her hands in the air trying to swing on the other who had his hands in her long hair.

"What was going on here?" Maliah asked.

"My eldest brother was babysitting us, and my younger brother had aggravated me for the final time. My parents came home to this mess, quickly taking a picture before breaking us up." She flipped through the album; sure enough there were tons of pictures of two of them fighting, or all three.

Seong laughed at one particular picture where Cho's face was covered in cake while she was screaming.

"My point," she interrupted the two giggling, "is that siblings fight. He wasn't swinging, he was blocking, because if he'd actually hit you it would hurt. Yong loves you; he wouldn't want to hurt you if he could help it. You've never had a sibling, so you don't get it. He's been fighting the boys for years now, so I know he gets it. You two sort it out?"

Maliah nodded.

"That's all I care about," Cho said, closing the book.

"Where are your siblings now, Cho? Were you the only one who moved away?" Seong asked.

"No. My eldest brother is in Germany, the younger, that punk, is in Canada. He comes through on occasion. He's a bit much though."

"A bit much, how?" Maliah stole the cookie on Seong's plate.

He pouted, but went to grab another.

"He flirts with everything in a skirt. He thinks he's charming. I think he's creepy. He'll probably be down for Christmas since he hasn't been here in a few years. You'll meet him then. He'll take Seong's old room."

She stood up to return the photo album and Maliah glanced over at Seong. "I owe you an apology too."

"You owe me nothing of the sort. You were angry. Not a great way to resolve your anger, but I get it. You trusted him with something. It's a hard thing to deal with, especially when it's from someone you love."

"You know I love him?"

"I don't think you would have shared that piece of yourself with him nor be as mad as you were if you didn't love him," Seong pointed out. "When people we love break promises, it hurts more acutely."

She looked at him as Cho walked back in the room. "How'd you get so smart?"

He smiled at her. "I'm nothing but a simple farmer. I just hang out with therapists and lawyers, it makes me sound smarter than I am."

Liah kissed him. "I don't believe that at all. If anything, the simple farmer has it figured out more than the rest of us do."

Seong was beginning to believe she might be right. *I promise to be worthy of you every day, to not let ego get between us.* He watched her talk to Cho and felt her small hand slip into his. She squeezed as if she knew what he was thinking. Maybe she did, it seemed as if she knew every part of him.

"I want you to meet my parents," he blurted out mid conversation.

The women looked at him. Maliah looked confused, Cho looked alarmed.

"I can't really afford to travel to Korea right now, Seong, I'm sorry." To her credit, Maliah took his random blurting in stride.

"I can't either, I was thinking of maybe setting up a video call? Next weekend?" he asked.

"I mean that's fine. I'll check my work schedule." Maliah took a bite out of her cookie.

He swallowed and nodded, avoiding Cho's gaze.

"Sweetheart, can you do me a favor? I put a load of towels in the washing machine. Will you transfer them to the dryer for me?" Cho gave Maliah a faint smile.

"Yeah, sure." She headed downstairs to the laundry room.

Cho snapped her head at Seong, immediately switching languages. "I know you haven't been here that long, but I know you know that meeting the parents here is different than meeting the parents at home," she whispered.

"My dad knows about her," Seong said quietly.

"Your mom?" Cho asked.

Seong shook his head. "Not out of any real concern, I just haven't talked to her recently."

"You need to let them know everything. You also need to explain to her the cultural difference of taking your girlfriend home to your parents. It's time, Seong. If you're going to be with her, and plan to make this permanent, she's going to need to know the culture." Cho patted him on his shoulder before following Liah downstairs.

After dinner, Cho turned on the tv with a basket of crocheting materials in front of her. Seong watched as Liah looked longingly at the couch next to Cho. Their friend chuckled, shooing her away. "Go be with your friends. I'll teach you to crochet another time," she said as she turned on a food show.

He headed to their room, pulling off his shirt as soon as he entered. He could feel Liah's eyes on his back, admiring him.

"It makes me laugh how I feel you stare at my back." He could always tell.

"You're beautiful," she said simply, wrapping her arms around him.

"As are you." He gripped her arms tightly. "Is your period over?"

"I'm at the end of it, so it's light, why?"

He picked her up. "I haven't been able to touch you all break. I want you."

"So take me." She grinned at him.

They didn't have a whole lot of time, as they were going skating with their friends, so he wasn't able to explore her body as he liked. "I promise, I'll have a little more finesse this evening," he said as he raked his teeth across her neck.

"Oh god!" Liah cried out. "You're doing just fine, finesse or no." Her hips bucked against him. He worked quickly, removing her pants before plunging his fingers inside of her. He realized he was still holding her mid-air so he quickly moved to the bed, unceremoniously dumping her, before following. He began to move his fingers as she cried out. Quickly lifting her shirt, he covered her left breast with his mouth, tugging lightly at her nipple.

"Close, I'm close," she panted.

He stroked her clit rapidly with his thumb when he felt her walls bear down. Seong heard her faintly call his name as she came. Seong ran to the bathroom as she calmed down. He wanted to get out of her way, because he knew she was going to want a quick shower. When he exited the bathroom, she went in. He finished dressing, applying a light layer of the cologne she liked. Sitting on the bed, he waited on her. Seong smiled as she walked out of the bathroom. She had on skinny jeans, a tank top with an open flannel on top. Her requisite mismatched socks were on her feet. Liah looked adorable; he let her know.

"Thank you, you do as well." He had on a forest green henley shirt that he had no idea where it came from with a pair of jeans. "Are you ready to go?" she asked.

"Yeah, let's head downstairs." He opened the bedroom door for her, swatting her butt as they walked out.

AT THE SKATING RINK, Maliah gave the other couple the same talk she gave to Seonghun the first time they came. They both were extremely confident on the carpet. Min went down like a rock on the actual rink floor. He went too fast for Maliah to catch him. She helped him up, placing his hand into Yong's. "Help each other out. If one of you falls, both of you will."

She grabbed Seonghun's hand as they slowly skated behind them. "When I fell, you didn't," he pointed out.

"That's because one of us knows how to skate. Neither one of them do, so they are bound to topple-oops, there they go." In front of them Yong went down, dragging Min with him. She looked at Seonghun.

He nodded. "I'll be right here."

She skated in front of them, helping them up. As she did with Seonghun she took their hands while skating backwards, forcing them to look at her. They made a steady lap around the rink before she connected their hands again. When she skated back over to him, Seong spoke up. "I actually need to talk to you."

She looked at him. "You aren't asking me to move to Korea again, are you?"

"Ah, no. It's about meeting my parents."

"Okay." She waited patiently for him to continue.

"Meeting parents in Korea, means something different than meeting parents here. It's more serious." Seonghun swallowed.

"You weren't serious about your ex; she met your parents," Liah pointed out.

"Good call out. It was different because my parents knew of her, we grew up in the same village so it wasn't 'hey, Mom, Dad, this is the girl I intend on marrying' it was more 'me and the neighbor girl are getting to know each other, not sure if this is serious yet'."

For the first time since they started skating together, Maliah was the one that fell. She stumbled over her feet, tumbling down, pulling Seonghun with her. She abruptly stood up. "Marry?!"

He'd freaked her out, he could tell. "Can we sit for a minute? I'm explaining this horribly and you look like you're about to take flight."

They skated over to the carpeted area, finding an empty bench. "Marriage is a strong term," he started out. "What I'm trying to say is that this meeting indicates to my parents that you're important to me, that you're going to be around for a while. My father knows of you; he's seen a picture." He snorted. "It was one of the ones where you're playing in Minjun's hair, so he asked if I was stealing his girlfriend."

Liah laughed at that.

"I haven't told my mom yet because I haven't talked to her recently. I'll talk to her sometime this week."

"Seonghun, did—" She paused for a second to collect her thoughts. "Cho never made it seem like a big deal; Yong is Korean American so it's nothing to him, but is it going to be an issue to your parents that I'm black?"

He knew this was coming. His dad even warned him to talk to her about it, but he wanted to avoid it as long as possible. "Not my parents, no?" Seong's voice got high at the end.

Liah arched a brow, waiting patiently.

"Can we go on a walk tomorrow before we leave? I want to get my thoughts in order before I explain."

"Sure, I can live with that." She stood up, grabbing his hand before heading toward the rink again. Min and Yong shuffled by slowly. The two of them skated behind their friends.

"Are you guys doing okay?" Maliah asked.

"My thighs are burning," Yong whined.

"You can go take a break. We just took one." She pointed at the benches scattered around.

He kissed Minjun before stumbling off. Seonghun looked after him.

"Go with him, I'll stay with Min."

Seonghun kissed her forehead and skated away. As he skated away, he heard murmurs of their conversation, something about the studio pictures she was planning on taking.

By the end of the night everyone was exhausted and hungry. "This was so much fun! I want to do this more often," Minjun exclaimed.

"We try to go once a week or at least every other week," Maliah said, "you two are always welcome to come along." As they pulled into the driveway, there was a man getting into his car.

He nodded tightly before backing out.

"Who is that?" Maliah asked.

"That's who my mom calls when she wants company sometimes. They were both married but their spouses died," Yong said.

"Yong." She was struggling to keep a straight face. "Did we just roll up on your mom's booty call?"

Yongjoon heaved a sigh, glaring at Maliah. "Does Seong have a picture of him going down on you hung in his bedroom?" With talks of the photos Liah was taking for the couple, Yong realized that the couple in the 'art print' Seong had purchased was actually them.

"I understand your point, I'll drop it." The car was silent except for slight snorts from her.

"Liah," Yong warned.

"I'm trying! I swear I'm trying!"

Seonghun looked over at her, practically shaking trying to hold in her laughter.

Yongjoon rolled his eyes. "Get it over, let it out, and I never want to talk about it again."

She burst into loud peals of laughter. "WE COCK BLOCKED YOUR MOM!" she wailed. Liah was laughing so hard she fell face first into Seonghun's crotch, snorting loudly.

"She's a mess." Minjun looked at her.

She sat up, straightening her glasses. "One question though, it's a serious one, I'm not making fun or anything, I promise."

"Go for it," he said.

"Why—" she paused, "why would she hide it from you? She's very open about all of your relationships."

"I've never actually asked, but I have a theory." He cut the car off. "Sometimes I think she's worried about replacing my dad and how it would make me feel. I don't have a problem with her dating; I think she and Mr. Gwan are cute. Sometimes he brings over board games, they'll have a drink and play together. He does puzzles with her, they go out to eat, things like that. Anytime I ask she adamantly says that he's just a friend. But I have never known a woman to spend an hour getting ready for just a friend."

"Maybe you should talk to her. Let her know that you're okay with it," Maliah said.

"You're probably right. I'd never begrudge her happiness, I figured she'd know that." They hopped out of the car. When they got inside, Cho was sitting on the couch where they left her, still crocheting. She had made a lot of progress on the soft rose and cream colored Afghan she was making. It had a thin stripe of fawn colored yarn going through it horizontally. The rose yarn had a soft shimmer to it.

"This is so pretty. I love the colors." Maliah touched the blanket gently.

Cho merely smiled. "You guys have fun?"

They chattered at her about skating. Seonghun went into the kitchen, coming out as they were talking with a plate full of turkey sandwiches for everyone. "Cho, we've about cleared your leftovers out," he said around a mouthful of turkey and carrot salad. "Also I want carrot salad on every sandwich now."

Maliah smiled. "I never really thought about putting it on a sandwich, but it has all the elements that would be good on one."

They continued talking. Minjun and Yongjoon were the first to head upstairs, bidding everyone good night. Maliah looked at Seonghun. "I'll be up in a second."

He nodded, kissing her cheek before trailing after the other two. He was a little sweaty from skating, so he decided to take a quick shower. When he finished, Liah still wasn't in the room, so he laid down to wait for her. As soon as Seong's head hit the pillow, he was out like a light.

SEONG THOUGHT he was dreaming when he felt waves of pleasure across his own body. He jerked awake to see Liah on top of him, shirtless, flicking his nipples with her tongue. "Babe," he choked out, "feels good."

She continued what she was doing, gently rocking her hips over his morning erection.

"Don't stop," he moaned, as he reached up to caress her breasts.

"Do you want to have sex?" she asked quietly. Liah raised her arms above her head, reaching under her pillow, pulling out a foil wrapped packet and handing it to him.

He froze. "I thought you didn't want to have sex on your period?"

She smiled lazily. "It's done."

"Oh." He glanced down at the packet before looking at her. The smile was quickly fading from her face.

"What's wrong, Seong?"

"Nothing," he said quickly.

"Seonghun."

"Do you know how, you always tell me things don't have to be an event? That they can just happen?"

Maliah nodded. "Yeah, things can happen organically with no fanfare."

"I lost my virginity in a barn. It was quick, unassuming, no real passion behind it. It was like a box checked," he said.

"Do you regret it?" she asked.

"Every damn day I spend with you," he admitted. "I don't want to make love to you for the first time with our friends down the hall. I don't want it to be rushed, just checking boxes to make sure you get yours, I get mine. I want to be able to take our time, I want to count your freckles."

Maliah smiled.

"I want more, you deserve more, I just haven't figured out how to give that to you yet."

"Ok."

"Ok?"

"Why don't you figure it out? Let me know when you have it sorted."

"Thanks for understanding."

"I'll always try to understand your feelings. I—" She paused abruptly.

He went still, looking up at her. "You what?" *Say it please, Liah, please.* He hoped she was going to tell him she loved him.

"Nothing, it's nothing." She pulled him to her, kissing him.

He suspected she was trying to distract him. Knowing that she wasn't ready to say whatever was on her mind, he let her.

AFTER BREAKFAST, Seonghun bundled up with Maliah before going on a walk. It was cold out so he was happy to see that she had her new coat on. Though they had no real route in mind, they both knew they were going to end up at the park. Seonghun began to speak about halfway through their trek. "You know how on campus, it's sort of a mixing pot? Students are all different races, coming from all over the place?"

Maliah nodded.

"America is like that too. Your neighbor may be Sikh, or black, or Haitian." Seonghun stopped walking to look at her. "Korea isn't like that. In the city there is more of a mix of people, but the further you get from Seoul, everyone is Korean. Everyone has similar features, so when someone shows up that is different—"

"It's noticed," Maliah finished.

"Right. When you come to visit, you'll get stares, Liah. No one is going to harm you, or be rude, I don't think, but people may try to touch you, touch your hair, that sort of thing."

Maliah was silent but watching his face as he explained.

"My parents are older, but my dad didn't really say anything about your race when I showed him your picture. He was mainly concerned that I was fighting Minjun for you. I still need to talk to my mom, which I will probably do tomorrow."

"Why not today?" she asked. They continued walking to the park. Liah found a bench, so they sat down.

"We're fourteen hours apart. They're asleep. I try to catch them late at night for us. My dad is usually up early to tend to crops, so I talk to him before my mom. She wakes up a bit later because she works around the house."

"Seonghun, does your mom have a job?"

"I mean, being a housewife is a job, so yes. But if you mean traditional outside the home, then no." He wrapped his arm around her, reveling in the fact she immediately snuggled into him. "She helps some with animals, but Dad has hired hands to do the heavy lifting in that area though. It's kind of a full time job keeping Dad fed."

Maliah looked at him confused.

"I come by my appetite honestly, my dad eats like I do."

Her eyes widened. "Your mom has to feed two of you?! How much does she cook?"

He chuckled before explaining his mom's cooking process. "She always makes something extra that she can roll over to the next meal. She'll cook extra protein, to use in the next meal. On Friday's she'll do breakfast, lunch, and a snack, but we're responsible for dinner. We usually grab something to bring home."

Maliah nodded and was silent for a while. Finally she spoke up. "Did your mom— did she ever tell you what kind of woman she hoped you would end up with?"

He looked down at her and saw the worry and anxiety in her eyes. "She hoped I would end up with someone kind, and patient, because sometimes I'm slow to realize things or react to them. She said she hoped I would find someone who knew how to cook that could at least attempt to keep me fed."

She laughed at that.

He looked at a little boy being pushed on a swing by his father. "She hopes that I will give her grandkids someday, but not too soon. But most importantly she hopes that whoever I choose makes me happy. It's all they've ever wanted for me, was happiness."

"What happens if they don't like me, or don't want you with someone of a different race?" She finally asked the question that he knew was bothering her.

He looked her in her eyes. "I love my parents. Unequivocally, without restraint. But that doesn't mean they get to choose who I— care about. Who I'm going to be with. Do you understand?"

She nodded, tears in her eyes.

"If they don't like you, it's coming from a place of not understanding you. Because I know you. I don't understand how anyone couldn't like you. So we'll try; if it doesn't work, I'll deal with my parents."

Maliah looked at him for a moment. "Please teach me how to say hi to your parents in Korean."

SEONGHUN REALIZED Liah wasn't kidding when she said she was awful at foreign languages. He was trying to teach her as they walked back to the house. "How is your pronunciation this off?"

"I kind of liken it to someone being tone deaf. I struggle with nuance. Minjun laughs at me about chew sock."

" 추석 "

"Chew sock."

" 추석! "

"That's what I'm saying! Chew sock!"

"Oh my god!" Seonghun laughed. "It's nice to know you aren't super human."

"I've never claimed to be."

"Yeah, but you're good at everything. Except speaking other languages apparently." He opened the door for her.

"I'll get it eventually. Can you write down the pronunciation?" she asked.

He wrote the Hangul for hello and how to pronounce it syllable by syllable as best as he could. They wandered into the kitchen to a pile of Gimbap. Immediately they raced out of the room to wash their hands. Returning to the kitchen, Seonghun piled some on a plate, handed it to Maliah before serving himself. He grabbed them both a pair of chopsticks as they sat at the table.

Cho came from upstairs. "Whatever you don't eat, you'll take back to the dorm. I've also bagged most of the turkey and carrot salad so you can make sandwiches for a few days." He beamed happily. "There's a few groceries in bags in the fridge, make sure you guys take those with you as well." She ruffled Seonghun's hair as he ate. "Did you two get your laundry done?"

"Yes. We also washed the sheets and put them back on the bed," Maliah said.

"Good stuff."

"Where's Yong and Min?" Maliah asked.

"Upstairs trying to figure out a clothing situation." Cho grabbed a slice of Gimbap off Seonghun's plate, popping it into her mouth. "Did you two have a good vacation? Fistfight notwithstanding."

Maliah looked at her. "This was one of the nicest breaks I've ever had. Thank you so much for having me. I would have spent the entire time studying or working."

"You're welcome here anytime, you know that." She looked at the young woman carefully using chopsticks. "You're expected here during Christmas as well. Come meet my douchebag brother."

Seonghun choked. Their friends came thundering down the stairs, grabbing food as they talked about Christmas and what they wanted to do since they had a longer break.

"Don't forget your uncle will be here," Cho reminded Yong.

Yongjoon didn't say anything but his lips thinned as he looked at Seonghun. When Seonghun looked back at him he glanced at Maliah before looking at Seonghun again.

Great, Seonghun thought. *I'm going to have to fight Yongjoon's uncle trying to bother Liah.*

Everyone finished their food and double checked they had everything packed. "Seong, can you come help me in the dining room?" Cho called out.

"I'll grab your bags," Maliah said as she gave him a quick kiss.

He wandered over to the dining room to see Cho flipping through her phone. She handed the phone over to him. It was exactly what he asked for. A simple wooden box that came with a skeleton key attached. The box was light colored wood polished to a high shine. The top of the box was inlaid with a soft pink quartz heart. Flipping to other pictures, the inside was pink velvet with spaces for earrings, rings, even bracelets. She would have a small amount of room for coiling up necklaces.

"It's gorgeous." He touched the screen. "How much?"

She looked at him sympathetically. "It's five hundred dollars. I got him to drop it to about three hundred. Can you swing it?"

"Normally yes. But her birthday party, birthday present, Christmas present, and dates have eaten a hole in my savings." He left out the payment plan he had on the ring.

"We can fix this," Cho said. "How much is the birthday party so far?" He pulled out his phone, showing the total amount of the rink rental, the cake, and supplies. "Why on earth is the party place so expensive!? It shouldn't be this cost prohibitive to have a birthday party at the skating rink." Cho looked at everything.

Seonghun blushed. Looking over his shoulder, making sure no one was around, he explained, "Cho, she's never had an actual birthday party. No one has ever greeted her with a cake. No presents, nothing. So I wanted to make it special. I rented out the entire rink for the evening."

"Honey," Cho put her hand to his face, "I know you want to fix every problem she's ever had, but you can't keep trying to make up for her childhood, okay? Just celebrate things normally going forward. This is incredibly sweet, however."

Seonghun looked at her. "I looked up Le Creuset pots to see if maybe I could get her one for Christmas to add to what you got her. Who's making up for bad childhoods?"

Cho blushed. "You hush. Here is what we're going to do." Her plan was simple. They would split the cost of the party. "Have you paid for the cake already?"

"No, I just found a bakery that makes a really good lemon cake," he replied. "I was going to talk to them this week."

"Don't worry about it, I'll make the cake. Where are you keeping the party supplies?"

"Yong's room. She rarely goes in there; if she does, she's definitely not going in his closet."

"What do you have so far?" Seonghun listed the hats, streamers, and the small flag banner he had for her. "Give me your colors, I'll take care of everything else. What's her favorite food?"

"Mexican."

"Follow me." Cho went upstairs to her room with Seonghun following behind her. She pulled her purse out, writing him a check for half the cost of the rink.

He used his phone to send her the money for the jewelry box. "If you have it sent to my house, I'll have it wrapped for you," she said.

"Okay. Could you put a flower sprig of some sort in the wrapping? Her favorite flowers are daisies and lavender."

"I'll see what I can do."

He hugged her. "Thanks, Cho."

"I'll see her at your party. I'll be in touch." Seong automatically bent down so she could kiss his forehead and ruffled his hair one more time before he dashed out of her room to meet Maliah in the car.

"Do you have everything?" he asked her as he sat in the driver's seat.

"Yes. I don't want to leave. This was the nicest time I've ever had," she admitted. She looked at Cho's house sadly.

"We'll be back soon; you can visit any time you want." He backed the car out headed toward the highway, slipping his hand in hers.

"I know. But it isn't the same."

"I get it." He kissed her hand as they headed back to the school.

CHAPTER 55

Pulling into the parking spot next to Yongjoon, Seong got out of the car. "Go ahead and go upstairs, sweetheart. You packed all the bags in here, I'll bring them up," Seonghun said.

"Are you sure?" she asked, still trying to pick up bags.

He swatted her butt. "Go upstairs, relax, I got this."

She still grabbed the bags housing her new comforters and took off toward the door laughing before he could swat her again.

He started pulling all of the stuff out of the car. Together with Yongjoon and Minjun, they made the trek to the dorm and up the stairs. The hallway had a few people milling about, welcoming their friends back from holiday break, Seonghun nodded to a few people but stopped short.

"What's wrong? Why did you stop moving?" Minjun asked.

He looked down and saw the bag with the comforters and Maliah's purse pushed to the side of the wall about ten feet away from their suite. The suite door was open. Seonghun felt the noise of the dorm fade, becoming a slight echoing buzz in his ear. "Shit. Yongjoon, do you have Detective Krishna's number?"

"Yeah, I put it in my phone," Yongjoon said.

"Call her now, Minjun, come with me." Seonghun dropped the bags close to where Maliah had left hers and walked to the room. He pushed open the door and turned on the light. He heard a crunch under his feet. Looking down there were shards of glass everywhere. It looked like their drinking glasses had been thrown at the door. He looked up and nearly had a heart attack at what he saw.

Over by the tv was Casey. She looked filthy, her hair in knots. She had Maliah in a headlock and had a gun pressed to her temple.

Just as Seonghun righted himself from the whirlwind of connecting with his love, girlfriend, future…his Maliah; he thinks it's safe to relax and settle into their undefined relationship.
As their connection grows deeper, they are testing their limits with themselves and each other. In the midst of all of this, Seonghun's lab partner, Shiwon has started taking more than a passing interest in Liah.
Is Shiwon going to be the thing that shatters what he is building with Maliah? Everything and everyone he holds dear is in danger, this time from the actions of a heartless person.
Will Seong have the courage to tell Liah how he really feels before the winter's snow freezes their relationship before it can bloom?

Coming May 2023 – Preorder Now

About the Author

Lisette Blythe is a brand new author with big dreams. As a child she grew up writing, but hastily closed the door on that in favor of a career in IT. Now at her big age, she is embracing everything she loves unabashedly. That includes writing, K-Pop music, and acting as she so chooses, no matter who it embarrasses.

Her writing is a love letter to herself, as well as to the women who look like her and may not be as neurotypical as they play in their day to day lives.

To sign up for her newsletter where she talks about writing and even shares samples of her work, go to https://www.lisetteblythe.com/news-letter-sign-up/

Lisette is on Twitter, Tiktok, and Goodreads as LisetteBlythe. You can also join her motley crew of people in Discord. There, they talk theories, share fan art, and share everything from music to photos of animals and plant babies. That can be found right here: https://discord.gg/qYWVqt2ajc

www.ingramcontent.com/pod-product-compliance
Lightning Source LLC
Chambersburg PA
CBHW070229200726
48293CB00005B/1535